# THE GREAT EDGE

## REVIEWS OF GEORGE GUNN'S PREVIOUS WORKS

*'Gunn does what every fine writer must do: he reminds us we are a part of this frail, cold, vicious, beautiful world.'*

John Glenday, *Northwords Now*

*'George Gunn has never shied away from risk. His way with words lives somewhere between Dylan Thomas and the Viking Sagas... rooted in his own native Caithness background, but sails out into many landfalls, some real, others mythic, always sustaining a radical questioning outlook ... traversing history, current international conflicts and the state of Scotland.'*

Aonghas Macneacail, *The Herald*

*'Spare, lean language honed on brittle, sometimes brutal, stalks of feeling... There is a salty, windswept goodness at this collections "conflicting heart". George Gunn is a poet of energy and lyricism. Fearless.'*

Anne Macleod, *Scotland On Sunday*

*THE PROVINCE OF THE CAT, ISLANDS BOOK TRUST, 2015*

*'The Province of the Cat' has a richly interwoven texture that illuminates in its parts and in the whole. Gunn has produced an outstanding work which no-one who wants to understand Caithness, or Scotland, should ignore.*

Donald Smith, *The Journal of Scottish Affairs*

# THE GREAT EDGE

George GUNN

GRACE NOTE PUBLICATIONS

*The Great Edge*
Published 2017 by
Grace Note Publications C.I.C.
Grange of Locherlour,
Ochtertyre, PH7 4JS,
Scotland

books@gracenotereading.co.uk
www.gracenotepublications.co.uk

ISBN 978-1-907676-94-9



The Great Edge is a work of narrative fiction, set in the physical reality of Caithness. Names, characters, businesses, places, events and incidents are either the products of the author's imagination or are used in a fictitious manner. Any resemblance to actual persons, living or dead, or actual events in locations referred to, is purely coincidental.



A catalogue record for this book is available
from the British Library

*In Memoriam:*

*John "Boxcar" Murray*
*(1965 – 2017)*

# PRELUDE

### *1. The Ice retreats and Jörð, the Earth, rises up.*

Out of the Mighty Gap came the Frost Giants. In the north they built their white fortresses and settled their legions. Their new home of ice they called Ginnungagap. Jörð, the Earth, was pushed downwards by this invasion. For two and half million years Jörð lay trapped beneath the glaciers, a prisoner in Ginnungagap. Then from Muspell in the South came Surt with an arc of fire and attacked the Frost Giants and drove them back. Soon, Jörð stirred.

### *2. Three Irish priests – Grillaan, Eoghan and Caornan – approach the headland during an Autumn storm.*

It was a sunny morning in September when the three monks sailed out of Loch Swilly. The tide was on the ebb and a fair West wind was blowing in off the Atlantic. Their small ship was a good one for its time – some fifteen feet long and five wide, expensively tanned and tarred cowhides stretched over a sturdy frame of alder wood. It was because of Grillaan's promise to his brother the Abbot that they were undertaking this journey into the unknown. Safe in an oak box with an iron lock was housed the holy clarsach of Colm.

### *3. Kylie Swanson and Colin Harper on site at Dounreay.*

From his office window he watched the yellow snake of the day-shift move out through the security gates. Some twenty buses would take them to Atomic City and to Wick and to all places in between and beyond. He noticed the lambs in the field next to the site jumping for joy in the afternoon sunshine. So that is what happiness looks like, he thought. The door behind him opened and a young woman came in and dumped a thick file onto his desk. "These are the ones the Yanks want rid of," she said in her best English.

### *4. Mags, the archaeologist, meets Fracher the fisherman, and they arrange to go to the Cave of Gold.*

The Comm Bar was packed. It was Friday night. The process workers from the nuclear plant, who were always early, were joined by fishermen and bored call centre escapees. Mags had parked her car in Campbell Street as instructed. As she pushed open the pub door the reek of alcohol and the rough music of humanity relaxing washed over her. She struggled to the bar and found him in a corner beneath the TV.

"Weel," said Fracher, "Ye must be thon, thon..."

"Archaeologist."

"Aye, thon lassie wantan a boat."

### *5. Maighdeann Mhara watches the beach and enchants Manson, a local crofter's son.*

The Maighdeann Mhara lay on a rock and watched the beach. The tide was coming in and the wind was blowing steadily off the bay so the surf was high. It thundered, crashed and curved for three miles from Dunnet to Olrig. The salty spray drizzled over the marram grass on the dunes and out over the farmland beyond. Manson crossed the Burniman Sands heading north towards the village. Even though he was far away the Maighdeann Mhara could see him up close. He was young and alone. She decided to take him to the cave.

# 1

# BRAGARMÁL

Before the many winters, as Bragi Boddason the skald has written, was the Mighty Gap. Then was formed Ginnungagap, which was cold with ice-wind until Surt met this with the fire-wind of Muspell. From this result a man was formed – Ymir, the father of giants. The sons of Bor, the sons of stones who roamed Ginnungagap, killed Ymir for they were jealous of his beauty and strength. Some of these sons of Bor drowned in his blood, which became the Sea. Ymir's flesh became the Earth. Rocks were formed from his bones and teeth. Ymir's skull became the sky, his brain the clouds. From his wounds flowed all the rivers of the world. As the remaining sons of Bor walked along the northern shore they came across two storm-washed logs. From them they made people: a man called Ask and a woman called Embla, or Answer. On the stone of the blood-sea, as Bragi has told us, they built a city. Troy. All the while, Jörð, the earth, was rising, stretching, moving, growing. Soon, from deep in Ginnungagap, rose up Storegga, Ymir's lost child. She was angry. She moved to where her father used to be. He was not there. Storegga sees the flesh, bones, blood of her father turned into the world. On this northern shore she meets Jörð and she falls in love, for Storegga also is made from the earth. Bragi Boddason, the skald, tells us that so great was their passion that Storegga fell into the sea and as a result a great wave swept across the oceans and lands of the north.

# 2

The sea is rolling into the bay from the north West. The little craft, with Eoghan at the helm, its sail full of purpose, steers a course through the gathering gloom. Sometimes it disappears from sight beneath an Atlantic roller. At other times it is in danger of being flicked from the sea like a fly from a stone by the wind. Beneath the huge red sandstone headland the boat looks tiny, the men aboard insignificant brown shapes. It's impossible to believe they know where they are going or that, even if they do, their vessel can deliver them to where they want to go. The cliffs are hundreds of feet high and the sea crashes savagely against them. There is something about these voyagers, a strangeness that implies they might believe in miracles, even that they *expect* them and are used to the miraculous.

And so it proves. They land on the little beach east of the Head of Man. They have found the only landing-place on the headland. They have survived. They have a map, a rough one. Grillaan can pick out a cave, *Uamh an Oir*, the Cave of Gold; a jagged inlet, the Geo of the Dead; and a loch, Loch Bushta. It is getting dark as they wash up on the little beach. Two ravens sit on the headland and watch the unfolding drama of the three men and the boat. The ravens are no friends of the miraculous. Eventually the three men manage to haul their boat out of the breakers, struggling against the pull of the surf. The cliffs are much lower here than anywhere else on this massive headland, and Grillaan has guessed they are on the South side. The Prior shelters the map from the rain and spray as best he can.

"It's not much of a map, Holy Father!" exclaimed Eoghan, hauling on a rope.

"No, but this is quite a place," replied Grillaan, almost to himself, his eyes scanning the cliff tops. The ravens look back. "We'll know better where we are, God willing, in the morning."

Eoghan and young Caornan struggle with the boat, heavy with the weight of the sea.

"There seems to be a rough set of steps up the cliff." Grillaan reassures them, for it is his role in this adventure to be reassuring. "We might be able to get off this beach."

"Well, we'd better had or we'll be drowned, surely." Eoghan was shouting over the thrash of the surf.

The three men work together to fasten the boat and off-load their meagre cargo, the centre-piece of which is the clarsach in the oak kist. Once everything else is secure and their boat as fast as they can make it, Eoghan straps the kist to his back, and carefully the Prior leads the way up the slippery flagstone steps to the relative safety of the cliff top. The rain pours down the stone face and over their brogue-clad feet, like a small river.

"It'll be a miracle if she sees the morning," said Eoghan, looking down on their frail boat and the surf crashing onto the beach.

"Well, the good girl has taken us here from Ireland," replied Grillaan. "God will have her path chosen."

"I don't doubt it," agreed Eoghan. "Her lightness may be her saviour."

Grillaan looks at the map again. His eyes are not as good as they used to be and the light has almost gone.

"We go this way, I think." He pointed along a path and set off confidently. Eoghan and Caornan, the warrior and the scribe, follow Grillaan, Prior of Saint Martins of Ceann Cashlagh, along a rough wet heather-banked track. Soon they come to a ruckle of stones between two small hills beside a loch.

"This must be Loch Bushta," said Grillaan, checking his map.

They set about erecting a rough shelter under which they would bed down for the night. They had come a long way, the three of them. They had been at sea for many weeks. Now they were here. Grillaan closed his eyes. *We have come all this way. Mercy be to God.*

*God knows where we are*, thought Eoghan, *and that ould map is as much a guide as a wet hen.*

*This must be Tir Nan Og*, Caornan convinced himself, remembering the stories of his uncle Connell the bard, but soon sleep overcame him. When he awoke in the morning it had stopped raining. As he crawled out from beneath his covering he saw that miraculously Eoghan had made a fire.

"Where's the Holy Father?" Caornan asked, forsaking his morning prayers. Eoghan pointed to a hill in the distance. Caornan could make out the distinctive stocky figure of Grillaan walking slowly down the side of the hill towards them, map in hand. Quickly Caornan said his prayers.

"There's a group of large islands to the north across a firth," Grillaan informed them presently, sitting down beside the welcome fire. "They must be the Orcades."

"The whale islands?" asked Eoghan.

"I imagine so."

"Then by the mercy of God we are indeed on the edge of the world."

Caornan looked out over the bay towards a much larger sandy beach a mile or so to the east of them. To the south and the west stretched two chains of mountains. To the far west and to the north there was nothing but the endless sea. He looked back at the flat land in front of the mountains. *It looks as if it has just risen out of the sea*, he thought.

"There's a fort at the top of the headland," said Grillaan, warming himself.

"Picts?" asked Eoghan nervously.

"Who else? But don't worry. They may not know their maker but in other respects they will be civilised enough. We'll have to get on with them, whatever else." Grillaan had met Picts before, in Ulster in the house of the O'Neill. He remembered them as tall, proud people.

Eoghan stared up the hill Grillaan had just come down. He looked across to the loch and at the stream which ran off it and over the cliff.

"There's water here a-plenty but not so much as a guillemot on the cliffs with it being so late in the season. God alone knows what we are supposed to eat."

"He does that. Don't worry, Eoghan, the people here will be of the Cattach, I believe." Grillaan smiled. *There I go again, always trying to reassure.* "Some of Ninian's monks came on a mission here some fifty years ago. They will be used to seeing Irish holy men."

"Did the heathens not embrace the love of Christ, Holy Father?" asked Caornan.

"In some the pagan belief is still strong, so we must be understanding. Time and a gentle ministry will bring enlightenment eventually," said Grillaan.

"They probably just laughed at the eejits. God alone knows what language they speak," said Eoghan.

"It will be a Gaullish tongue," replied Grillaan. "We will learn it soon enough."

Eoghan went over to Caornan who seemed distressed, and threw his arm around the young scribe.

"How d'ye think you'll get on with the Picts, eh Caornan?" He was genuinely fond of the young man and admired the bravery which lay behind the innocence.

"Will they kill us?"

"Ach no, boy, they'll probably put you out to herd the goats," laughed Eoghan giving the nervous boy a good-natured push.

"Pay no heed to brother Eoghan, Caornan," advised Grillaan. "There's still too much of the warrior in him."

"Aye, well, it was your brother Colm wanted me here," retorted Eoghan. "He was my friend, my master as well as your Abbot. Now I'm with you. It was his wish."

Grillaan tried to keep his smile. "Yes, that is so. Come now, let us give thanks to God and have something to eat. The Sun is coming up and we have much to do."

Eoghan laughed. "Once we've had some of God's mercies – for surely even maggoty oatmeal is a mercy – I'll away down and see if we still have a boat."

They said grace. Grillaan was always thankful for Eoghan's practical attitude. Without Eoghan they would not have made it to this strange land. Was there reassurance in that?

"Looks like a good gravelly beach," he said. "There's bound to be fish-friendly reefs further out. Maybe there is cod to be had?"

"I was thinking more of a whale myself," joked Eoghan, and he set off down the heather path towards the little beach beneath them.

Grillaan watched him go – his brother Colm's loyal friend. It was Colm's clarsach they had brought here. *Take my music to sing in the furthest reaches of Alba,* Colm had said. *They need the dove of Christ and his blessing, which is music.* It was Colm who had given him the map. Colm, who had become Abbot before he died, and would more than likely be made a saint. *How strange is this world*, thought Grillaan, *and what we have been tasked to do, such is the will of the Lord.* The Prior looked at Caornan, who was looking across the bay at the mountains to the West. *There is another dreamer*, thought Grillaan. *How many dreamers can the church absorb? Still, there's plenty of room for dreamers here.* Grillaan followed Caornan's gaze, and for the first time since they had sailed out of Loch Swilly he felt reassured himself.

# 3

The big blue ship with the white bridge and the two red cranes sat out in the bay. Its bow was flat with a square door which could be raised to give access to the trucks and their high tensile casks. The ship could be moored at the old roll-on roll-off ferry pier. The trucks could easily drive on, have their casks removed by the cranes and then drive off, but as yet not so much as a lorry cab had arrived at the harbour, so the ship lay a quarter of a mile off with her engines throbbing at the ready. Colin sat in his grey unmarked bullet-proof Authority car and waited. It was the early hours of the morning. *All this vigilance to thwart the ever-present threat of terrorism.* He drummed his fingers on the steering wheel. *That's what they keep telling us. But here? Hardly. This is the endgame, the decommissioning: the long goodbye.*

He remembered their conversation over a rushed breakfast. "It's all so negative," he had said to her, "all that '*Dismantled, Down, Demolished*' malarkey. Yer giving people the wrong impression. Can't you put something more uplifting on your posters?"

"It's not up to me," countered Kylie. "Anyway, it's the truth, even if it is bad poetry."

"It's not that it's bad, it's just ugly." This made her laugh. Colin? Discussing the idea of beauty!

"The Authority thinks it's modern. Manly even."

"It's like welcoming people to the end of the world," he said, putting on his jacket.

"Well maybe we are," she pushed him out of the way of the mirror. There was something up with him but she had no idea what it was. Getting three words out of him in a conversation she had learned to measure as success. But now, all these questions – it was like a stream of consciousness. From the mirror she watched him, fiddling with some buttons.

How, he thought, did she manage to look like that first thing in the morning – and without even a dab of make-up? Not that she ever used all that much. She didn't have to. Skin like satin, hair naturally the colour of the sand on Dunnet Beach, and her eyes, well, like the blue stones he used to find at the bottom of the rock pool at the Peedie Sannie when he was a peedie bouyag. *Why couldn't they just put her bloody face on the posters? Why all this D stuff... this Deconstruction?*

A fishing boat passed the pier head. *What the bloody hell are they doing? I left strict instructions*. He picked up his radio. The voice on the other end was apologising. Fishermen. What could you do? The harbour master, the voice said, was a useless bastard.

"Well there better be no more. See to it. This is a major shipment."

Whose voice was that he was using? Or was the voice using him? What language did he actually speak at work? Suddenly the night seemed to get darker. His phone beeped at him. That was the signal. The voice in the radio confirmed it.

Down the brae road from the town poured four sets of headlights, their orange beams like knives cutting through the night towards the harbour. The ship was approaching the old ferry pier. Her bulk, suddenly, almost too much to believe in. Suddenly, also, the pier-head was floodlit. The world had expanded like heated gas. Men in yellow fluorescent jackets moved this way and that. He got out of the car.

He was supposed to be in charge, but he had realised some time ago that no-one was in charge. He was just there to be held to account if something went wrong. The Authority liked to plan ahead. He wasn't really one of them. He was a fitter turner, for

Christ sake! He had worked his way up, or in, but whatever it was here he was with the four artic's hissing and whining as they applied and released their brakes. He spoke to this man, he nodded at that man. Soon the huge bow door of the ship swung open. One by one the trucks reversed on. Gently the crane boom swung into action. He was expendable, that was the truth. If anything went wrong he would be slaughtered, binned without thought or fuss. That was the way with Gabfan Nuclear, the new operator, now his employer. The Authority, ever magisterial, never sacrificed one of their own. If an Authority man fucked up he was promoted. That was the way. He understood that. With Gabfan it was film star wages and a butterfly's life.

# 4

Mags had been driving for hours and her shoulders, neck and eyes were sore. The Highlands were new to her, as she had never been north of Perth. The drive through Birnam and up the Drumochter Pass had excited her. It was early October and the hills were a dreamy blue from the late heather bloom, turning russet as the light faded further to the west. In patches they were white, as the first snow of the season claimed the summits. All was strange and gigantic. Her first sight of the Cairngorm had almost made her come off the road. She stopped and got out of the car. It was cold. There was a deep green colour under the ice. Shivering, she breathed it all in. It was as if the mountain glowed. For it seemed to Mags that it was all one mountain. Wherever she looked everything was massive. *It's rising up*, she thought. *That's not a mountain, it's an animal. It'll swallow me.* Mags got back into her car and continued north.  London was a long way away.

By the time she got to Inverness it was raining. The Moray Firth was grey and disappeared into the liquid east. She pressed on over the Kessock Bridge, then over two more bridges, the road rolling on and on. The rain now was intermittent, concealing then revealing the landscape. Is there no end to it? she asked herself. As she crossed the Dornoch Firth Bridge the rain had stopped and the Sun was out again, but low, so that everything seemed velvet or gold. She wasn't hungry although she should have been.  The sandwiches she had made still lay untouched in the bag in the back seat, but she was conscious of thirst

Remembering the flask she pulled into a lay-by, got out of the car for a stretch, and poured herself a still-hot cup of tea. Mags was on the Ord of Caithness. To the east was spread out the North Sea, with the Beatrice Field oil platforms, their flare-off booms adding to the orange glow of the light. The day was almost done. There was not a single car on the road. To the north of her the land pushed in from the sea-cliffs in a plateau-line of stubble-cut barley fields with rising and falling horizons. She had no idea what time it was and she didn't care. Suddenly, from some distance inland, she heard short brutish grunts followed by a long desperate bellowing. The noise seemed to come from beneath the ground. It rose up and hung in the Autumn air, then dissolved out over the sea. On a ridge, high up to the north west she could just make out dark shapes moving against the horizon, antlers rising and falling in the last of the day's light. Deer in full rut. Just as she realised what she was hearing a huge articulated lorry bearing the legend "Steven's Fish" roared past, almost forcing the cup from her hand. *I'd better get to Thurso before it gets dark.*

For a moment before she drives off Mags thinks of all this new country she has just seen for the first time. Some of it looks untouched by man but she knows that there is not one square yard of Scotland where man, at some time, has not set his foot, laid his hand and made his mark. As the Sun lowered red sails behind the far horizon to the west, she knew that whatever is worth knowing in the world, like the sound of those deer, has come from out of the ground. Almost for the first time, she realised why she was an archaeologist.

# 5

Every time he walked up the Westside road his spirits sank. But this, Manson decided, would be a different day. So he climbed the hill-path from The Niss, sat on top of Dwarick Head and looked down on the village, glinting and dumb astride its crossroads. He could see the old croft parks stretched out in every direction, sprouting houses now instead of potatoes, hay and barley. It was as if over the last thirty years the entire place had slid off the edge of history, taking all the real people with it. For he felt that the people in the ranchero houses below him were not real. For Manson, for things to be real, they had to be part of his memory and these people, with their ridiculous houses, were not. All the real people were dead and buried in the kirkyard. They had fallen out of memory and history into Heritage, which was the ultimate theft of their lives. He had wandered around the various museums which purported – and failed – to honour their memory and portray their lives. But the people's lived reality was translated, manufactured and re-presented as a series of sepia episodes drained of colour, blood and knowledge.

He looked down at the bay and the breakers rolling in and crashing on the beach. *Histories – real events – are like waves*, he thought. He spat on the heather in front of him and watched the sticky, dripping saliva catch the gold of the afternoon light.

Scattered amongst the Thatcherite property boom of ugly concrete, kit houses and kitsch of the retired Dounreay managers – all L-shapes and the glass vacuousness of loveless architecture

– were nestled the old croft houses of the Dunnet peasants, unchanged in form and function since the time of the sagas. The newly painted and heritage-trust-maintained red tin roof of the ceilidh shed of Mary Ann's cottage beat out like a corrugated heart. None of the trustees knew it as the ceilidh shed. Nor did they know, or care much – so he assumed – what happened in there over decades, several lifetimes, a century and more. There would have been a dwelling on the site since before Pictish times. The ancientness of the landscape was there for anyone who had eyes to see.

Manson saw it plainly as he looked down from his raven's nest on the headland. He followed the line of the old crofts from the head of the Dwarick brae to the old harbour at The Niss. Most of them had been bought up by middle-class 'Atomicers' from Thurso, Atomic City; yet still they held their traditional long-house shape, hidden like a story, despite the best efforts of modernisation and extension. Mary Ann's had been preserved in aspic, the croft house and its contents, open at certain hours for study by folklorists and camera-toting tourists who would have considered Mary Ann and her man Willie exotic Hottentots, much as anthropologists observe and study bonobos: related but alien. He remembered them both. His mother had nursed Mary Ann in her later years, and his father had cut peats and hay with Willie, and eventually for him as time took its toll. Both lived til their early nineties. Their de-crofted parks still retained their definition but were home now to the horses and ponies so beloved by the new settlers. Their original function, like the stories and songs told and sung in the ceilidh shed, had been forgotten.

He had come up to the headland to rid his memory of last night's dream, which had stayed with him all day like a bad smell. The dream was about his own house, (except it wasn't his house), with his family in it, (save that they weren't his family) and his wife featured heavily (though in reality he did not have a wife). Water had poured from the walls and the ceiling of the house, flowing like streams from cupboards and under doors and the floor. He had been terrified, but his wife – whom he did not recognise because he did not have one – was very calm. She told him not to worry and that everything would be alright. When he could bear it no longer and thought he was going to drown, and the house collapse about him, he woke up. His house was still there.

He could see it now, from the headland, one square in a quadrant beside the manse, the kirk and the hotel. It was an old house, one of the oldest in the village. It had been a school once. People said it was full of ghosts but Manson paid no heed to what people said. People would say anything they fancied and most of it was rubbish. In all the years he had lived there he had never seen a ghost. The garden, unusually for Caithness, was full of trees – apple trees no less – and was surrounded by a wall. He and his brothers had played happily there as children. Now he was alone. His parents and one brother were dead. His other brother lived in Edinburgh – an oilman, rich and distant.

The dream had shaken him. He was not much of a dreamer and those dreams he did have he forgot easily, gladly. But this dream of the house with water flowing out of the walls was different. It meant something, he convinced himself, but he had no idea what. From the top of Dwarick Head, looking down on everything he knew, the horror of the dream dulled, like an echo distanced from the noise of trouble, and he was sure it would eventually fade to nothing. Like the people of the crofting community he'd known as a child, he told himself, it would pass into silence as they had done, leaving nothing behind them but the outline of fields.

# 6

The Maighdeann Mhara had a bag full of Time. She kept it in *Uamh an Oir*, the Cave of Gold, on Dunnet Head. In this bag matter was infinitely dense but had no volume. When people like Manson looked into it they saw nothing, unaware that – even at the moment of their looking – they were already inside it. Despite this, anyone ignoring the Maighdeann Mhara's bag was in her power. Now – then – they were in *her* time, and from that there was no escape. In her bag energy came from nothing; formed into something; and then returned to nothing. There was no point explaining it to people: that time is a hunter; that solidity is illusion; and that the only reality is empty space. No, that was not the thing to do at all. Her sorrow she kept to herself.

For a few people, the world is a huge question to which there is no answer. Some accept it, are content that they will never know, and they at least die serene. But unanswered questions make others extremely unhappy, and they assert they have the right to know. These people are discontented until they die. For most the world is just a floor upon which they walk. They live their lives hungry for something, and mistake that for money or possessions. They may look into the Maighdeann Mhara's bag but they do not know see what is there. Manson was such a person. He would never admit it, but that was his delusion. His talent he ignored. That was his tragedy. Wiser people may never know what the world is nor what it's for, but they are happy to spend their lives looking. These are the searchers. Mags was one of them. As yet – she did not know it. The Maighdeann Mhara was from the sea. She was beyond specificity just as she was from beyond the horizon of human events. No-one could see her unless she willed it. When she wanted to be seen she manufactured the necessary light. What she wanted to see was her own son. She looked into everyone to find him. Her desire was to free the four lost children. She looked into everyone, searching to find a way to undo the past. So it was the day she saw Manson walking across the Burniman Sands.

She saw a young, handsome man with not a thought worth a name in his head. Was he her son? No, he was not. But she had become lonely. She had powers, yes, but what use are they when the collapse of reason is infinite and everything shrinks to nothing? What Manson saw, sitting on a rock, was a beautiful young woman with hair like sea tangle, wearing a long coat of similar colours. She was the most beautiful woman he had ever seen and at once he fell in love with her. Soon he would be beyond Time.

# 7

Some say that music comes from the sea. Others that it is brought to us by the wind, or begins in the fire beneath the sea. Fracher believed all these things to be true. He looked out of the window of his small cottage high on the headland, past the lighthouse. In truth, music will die on the stone deck of the ship of the Earth, where we all die. Then everything will be washed away in the flood. How could it be any other way? So said Bragi Boddason.

Fracher watched the sea sparkling in the sunlight. A flock of gannets was gathering. He had just come in after checking his creels. It was an exceptionally low tide. The Moon was big. He had put six black lobsters in his holding box. Cushie, the collie, had even nabbed a coanie on the way home. It had been a good day. Now the afternoon sun caught the red sandstone of Dunnet Head, turning it bright orange, the colour of the flames which leaped in his fireplace, a peat fire which never went out, ever. The dog lay asleep in front of it. He could see the Chapel Geo and the dark open mouth of *Uamh an Oir*, the Cave of Gold. Why on earth did that lassie want to go there? Beyond all that he could see the Flotta flare burning like a torch above the oil depot across the Firth. He sipped his tea and pushed the plate across the table. Two tatties for the night. He could maybe get a fry later on off Coachie Wares once he'd landed, if he could be bothered to go down to the harbour. He sat back in his chair. He was getting old, like his cottage and his boat. The cottage, or an early version of it, had been standing on this site for two hundred years.

It had always been in his family, built by an ancestor when they had been cleared out of the West. The house had been smart, pretty even, when his wife was alive, but cancer had taken her from him. Now, like himself, it was falling into neglect. Folk complained about the state of the place. His nearest neighbour, Dempster the farmer, had told him just last week it would be a good idea if he tidied up all the scraps of nets, creels, fish boxes and other stuff. One day he would bring that old Fergie back to life again, Fracher promised himself. Dempster was a snob. He didn't even work his own land. A gentleman farmer, born into money. Fracher used to grow potatoes on his three acres but he couldn't be bothered any more when he could as easily go the Co-op, although they never tasted the same. Ami Sinclair kept her three horses on it and paid him rum-money in rent. It kept his old car going too. Cushie was easy to keep, preferring to hunt rather than eat from a tin. You'd think they'd leave a man alone up here, but oh no. Seems he's lowering the tone of the scenic area. What a joke. Dundas, another toff farmer, had recently put up twenty-five huge wind turbines just five miles away. And what about that pair of clowns down in the harbour? The ones who had built that stupid great pier? Surely these were the jokers who were ruining the place.

The pier. Now that was beyond a joke. A complete disaster from the beginning. He'd told them, as all the fishermen had told them, that there was bedrock down there, that their pilings would split, but they wouldn't listen, certainly not to him. He was just a drunken fisherman, an old fool. Well, they know now, some two hundred million later. The decommissioning of Dounreay meant the government and enterprise agency had thrown money at any daft scheme to replace the two thousand "lost" jobs. In truth nothing was being done except to make things a whole lot worse.

He rose from his chair, went over to the old dresser and poured himself a small rum. The collie lifted his head but Fracher did not go to the door. He sipped the rum's rich caramel. He'd been up since five. Maybe he'd have a kip. He went back to the chair, finished his rum and pushed the glass over beside the plate. A hundred and fifty quid just to take her to the Chapel Geo. That would keep him in rum for two months – three, four. He sat back in his chair.

Fracher was 70. In 1988 he'd been 45 – twenty-five years to the day. He never worked off-shore again. How could he? Some went back on the rigs – not him. The following year Kirstag died. From diagnosis to death was three months. Leukaemia is quick, at least. He never thought of himself as an old man, only other people did that. Typical assumptions: folk either aged you, made you younger than you were, or got you plain wrong altogether.

He thought of the girl Mags. But there you go! She's not a 'girl', she's a young woman. To Fracher, she was more like one of the small yellow butterflies that flittered and fluttered in to drink from the purple chive flowers which grew year after year in the planticru Kirstag had created. Every May Kirstag reappeared with the chives and the delicate flowers on the thyme bush, and in August she was the mauve and scarlet poppies which, unlike Kirstag, were indestructible.

He knew nothing about the lassie. Mags, she called herself on the phone, asking to go to *Uamh an Oir* and the Chapel Geo. The Cave of Gold was *Uamh an Oir* on the map which hung in the pub, a hand-drawn ink map, so pretty he would stare at it for hours. When he looked out of his window to the north-east he saw the headland as solid stone. The pub's map of the headland reflected it in a different way: in the poetry of names and human stories. The headland held the poetry of sandstone and of time itself.

He'd met her in the pub and liked her, despite himself. She seemed to be interested in the stories but, more importantly, she understood that Time was bound up in the stone. Some people were interested in one, some in the other, but mostly people were contemptuous of both. "It's just a headland," they'd say. "A lump of rock". In Fracher's view, most people most of the time didn't concern themselves about anything.

He loved *Uamh an Oir*. He loved its Gaelic name. And he loved the fact *Uamh an Oir* still kept its story. Something to do with a mermaid. The Gaelic language was still alive in him, through his mother's people especially. She'd told him *Uamh an Oir* was also an old pipe tune composed by Donald Mor MacCrimmon dating back to 1610. He used to be able to play a version of it on the fiddle. Gaelic was an ancient tongue and it suited his mood. He had been 70 for six months and today of all days he felt that nothing else, much, was left alive in him. Mags was a new tune alive in him somehow. A tune he wanted to learn.

He would take her out in The Searcher. He would take her across the broad bay to Dunnet Head. He would show her the Chapel Geo where Irish priests were supposed to have converted the Picts. He would show her *Uamh an Oir*. He would do all of that, he thought, and not just for a hundred and fifty quid. She was young. He was old. He had been old for too long. He'd been old since the 6th of July, 1988 – the day the Flotta flare went out. It was time he had a future. There was plenty time in Dunnet Head. Maybe the headland, if he helped this lassie, this girl, this young woman, maybe the headland would give him some time back?

He looked up at the fiddle hanging on the wall. It had belonged to his grandfather. Sometimes he played it to himself. Now his fingers struggled with '*A Hens March Across the Midden*', '*The Four Poster Bed*' and '*Da Full Rigged Ship*'. Good solid tunes. *A bit like boats*, thought Fracher. Through the window he watched gannets diving for fish. It was the season for mackerel right enough and they would be in close by. There would be orcas soon, no doubt. He remembered his brother Donald telling him how, when he was in Cape Breton, the people called the pilot whales "black fish". Last year, about this time, a great pod of minkes rounded Holborn Head. The other night, just off the harbour, the bay was full of dolphins. They too would be after the mackerel. His father wouldn't touch mackerel. "A dirty fish," he used to say. Fracher tasted the memory of boiled cod, savouring the salt and the butter.

These were the patterns of his thoughts these days. Like music they welled up in his head and then faded away. Tonight he would fall asleep listening to the sea, in his house high up on Holborn Head: the last man in Scotland.

# 8

Bragi Boddason was the first poet in the world.

In fact the way he told it, at tables as long as Time in halls as big as the Earth, he was the god of poetry. "Everything you know is because of me," he would say. Bragi loved talking to Ægir, the ocean. Bragi spoke in **Bragarmál**, what we'd call poetic speech. Everything to him was **Bragarbot**, a poem's improvement. The world to Bragi was **Skaldskaparmal**, the language of poetry. That is what you are reading now, according to Bragi.

Ægir asked Bragi many questions. As the ocean, he felt it necessary to know everything, especially about poetry. Ægir suspected that poetry contained the entire world's knowledge. Bragi was very willing to supply the answers.

"What is this stuff called poetry that you hold in such high regard?" asked Ægir.

To answer his friend Bragi told the story of Odin, Loki and Hænir's journey across mountains where food was difficult to come by. In time they reached a strath with a herd of black cattle. They killed one of the cattle and made an earth oven, but no matter how long they left it the meat would not cook. Up in a tree looking down was an eagle.

"If you grant me my fill of that beast then the oven will cook it," said the eagle.

Odin, Loki and Hænir agreed, and the beast cooked. At once the eagle flew down and devoured both back legs and the two front legs. Loki was furious. He snatched up a fallen log and swung at the eagle. The eagle was quick but not quick enough, and the end of the log penetrated its body. Up flew the eagle, skewered by the log, Loki still holding on to it. Loki screamed at the eagle to let him down. The eagle said he would, if Loki agreed to persuade Idunn to leave Asgard and to bring him her apples of eternal youth. His arms almost out of their sockets, Loki had no choice but to agree, and the eagle set him down to return home with Odin and Hænir. Sure enough, Loki lured Idunn into a remote forest, telling her he'd found some very interesting apples there, and could she bring her apples in order that she may compare them? Idunn agreed. No sooner had she set foot in the forest than the eagle swooped down – it was the giant Thiassi in an eagle shape – clasped Idunn in his talons, and flew off to Thrymheim.

The gods of Asgard were badly affected by the abduction of Idunn. Whenever they began to grow old they bit into her apples and were restored to youth. Now that there were no apples of immortality they aged and their hair turned grey. They held a meeting of the Asgard Althingi, their parliament, to see what could be done. As a result Loki was arrested. He was ordered to go and find Idunn and bring her back with her apples. So Loki took the shape of a falcon and flew off to Thrymheim, the home of thunder and of the giant Thiassi. When Loki arrived Thiassi was out at sea in a boat and Idunn was alone. Loki turned her into a nut, and clutching her in his claws he flew back to Asgard. When Thiassi got back to his thunder-house and saw Idunn was gone he took the shape of an eagle once more and flew after Loki.

When the Æsir, the gods of Asgard, saw the falcon flying towards them with a nut in its claws they gathered a huge mound of wood-shavings. Once Loki had flown over them and was safely back in Asgard, they lit the wood-shavings which set fire to the eagle's feathers. That was the end of Thiassi. But his daughter, Skadi, vowed revenge on the death of her father. She dressed herself for war and went to Asgard. With Idunn and her immortal apples safely returned, the Æsir offered Skadi compensation. She agreed, with two conditions. First, that she could choose a husband from amongst the gods. The Æsir agreed, but she must make her choice from sight of their feet alone. Amongst the line of feet offered, one pair was exceptionally beautiful. Skadi was sure they must belong to the beautiful Balder, god of love and light, but her choice was revealed to be Niord, whose domain was the sea. So Skadi married Niord and both were unhappy. Skadi's second condition was for the Æsir to do something that she thought impossible, which was to make her laugh. Up steps Loki. He ties one end of a cord around the beard of a nanny goat and the other end around his own testicles, so that when each pulled against the other both parties roared and squealed loudly. As Loki dropped into Skadi's lap the giantess burst out laughing. So the compensation was paid in full. But," added Bragi, "taking pity because of her miserable marriage to Niord, Odin took Thiassi's eyes and threw them up into the heavens where they became two stars, so that each night the daughter might see something of her father."

"That is a good story," said Ægir, "but what has it to do with poetry?"

"Well,"answered Bragi, "it is Skaldskaparmal, which is the language of poetry."

"So what is the significance of the giant Thiassi? What does he mean in relation to your Bragarmál?" asked Ægir.

"Good question," replied Bragi. "Just as Skadi was the daughter of a giant so was Thiassi the son of a giant. He had two brothers, and all were rich in gold. When they came to divide it out they each took a mouthful, so it is that we say that gold is the mouth-story of these giants and we call poetry the talk of these giants."

Ægir looked around the great hall of Asgard. On the walls were immaculately beautiful panels hung with magnificent shields, and all the Æsir were dressed in fine colourful clothes. He realised he must choose his words carefully.

"How did this golden craft of poetry originate?" asked Ægir.

"The gods of Asgard were in conflict with the gods of Vanir," replied Bragi, "Eventually there was a truce, and to mark the peace conference both sides spat in a vat. The gods kept this symbol of peace and so that it would not be wasted they made it into a man called Kvasir. Now Kvasir was so wise that no one could ask him a question for which he did not have an answer. Unfortunately he was killed by two dwarfs who poured his blood into two vats called Bodn and Son, which is where I get my name," said Bragi Boddason. "The dwarfs mixed honey with the blood which turned into mead and whosoever drinks from it becomes a poet and a scholar. The evil dwarfs told the Æsir that Kvasir had suffocated in his own intelligence because there was no one educated enough to be able to ask him questions."

"Did the gods believe such an obscure lie?" asked Ægir.

"No, they did not," said Bragi. "Odin killed the dwarfs, drank up all the precious mead, turned himself into an eagle and flew back to Asgard. The rest of the dwarfs (there is never a shortage of dwarfs) grew angry and summoned the giant Suttung, a noted shape-shifter, to pursue Odin. Suttung also changed himself into an eagle and flew as hard as he could in pursuit. When the Æsir saw Odin circling overhead they put containers on the ground beneath him. With Suttung close behind, Odin spat out most of the mead, which the gods caught. As Suttung closed further Odin shat out the rest. This the Æsir disregarded, because," conceded Bragi, "it is a well known fact that along with the mead of poetry comes a lot of shit."

"Yes," agreed Ægir. "I have learned that."

"In this way," concluded Bragi, "the ocean learned of poetry."

Thanking Bragi for his wisdom, Ægir rose and walked thoughtfully to the door of Brimir's Hall, the great hall of Asgard. Bragi watched his friend leave.

*There is much I have not told you,* thought Bragi. *In time these stories will change. Young poets will have to learn of Troy and King Priam instead of Asgard and Odin. Instead of Ragnarok they will speak of the Trojan war. Thor will become Hector, Loki these poets will call Odysseus, and the Midgard Serpent will be known as Achilles. The creature that killed Odin at Ragnarok was Fenriswolf but it will be Pyrrhus who kills Priam, and Surt's fire will be translated as when Troy burns. So things change. But young poets must not discard what major poets have been happy to use. The gods, it may be told, came out of Asia or the north, or from men's minds but either way all need Skaldskaparmal, the language of poetry, to fashion meaning from ancient kennings.*

Bragi raised a glass and toasted himself, for everything is, as he said, Bragarbot, the poem's improvement.

# 9

Three hot days in a row. *In Caithness this is what we call a Summer*, thought Kylie, as she looked from the bedroom window across the bay to the headland. Tomorrow, the day after, later this afternoon, eventually, the fog would come rolling in from the north Sea if the wind was from the east; or a low front would blow in from the Atlantic to the West bringing cloud and hazy, smooring rain leaving everything tasting of sea-salt.

Yesterday she had been down on Thurso beach speaking to the radiation monitoring crew. She had a press release to write on the benefits of the new improved radiation monitoring technology – the "new machine" as everyone called it.

"The benefit," Morris Mowat, the crew charge-hand and head monitor, told her "is that we find more radioactive particles." This was true. Kylie's job was to tell the world why this was a good thing.

On her way to the beach she had passed the carcass of a dead whale which had washed up on the high tide. A crowd of people were gathered around it; some taking pictures, others just to see what a whale looked like close up. At first she had thought it must be a school picnic or some sports thing, but it was far too early in the day and the schools had closed for the holidays two weeks ago. Then the smell hit her. Not the rotting reek of decomposition, but rather sweetly iodine scented, like ozone or Japanese fish vinegar.

There were a couple of SSPCA officials with long green PVC aprons over their coveralls, clipboards in their hands, writing things down. Their van was parked beside the Salvation Army Mission right next to the monitor vehicles and trailers. A third SSPCA official, a tall man with a ginger beard, was busy pulling sticky blue gloves from his hands. He smiled at her. Before she could even ask the question, in an English accent he said, "It's a minke. An adult female. We don't know what happened to it. We think it drowned."

Kylie was on the promenade looking down on the scene. People getting bored or disgusted began drifting away. The two SSPCA officials pulled a blue tarpaulin over the whale's body, which was about twenty feet long, so that only its tail showed at one end and the head at the other. Its lower jaw was extended and falling away, the fibrous baleen hanging silent and useless like a macabre venetian blind, sifting not plankton, but the rancid air of death. The whale looked as though it was smiling.

"Wae'll hev til wait til they shift id," Morris Mowat told her when she reached the monitoring crew.

"How long will that be?"

He laughed. "Ah'm no sure. How long dis id take til shift a deid whale?"

It was a question for which nothing in her Oxford University degree in English Literature had prepared her. She laughed. The drowned whale laughed back. Morris sucked on his roll-up and inhaled deeply.

"Id'll be ay Cooncil anyrods," Morris added, "so id could be a whilee."

Kylie decided meantime it would be enough to take a photo on her smart phone of the lads at work, so she asked Morris if that was alright. She would come back.

"Please yersel. But Cooncil time's no real time, mind," he said.

She climbed the steps from the beach to the promenade. *Dounreay time isn't real time either,* she thought. When she first came home she had told herself it would be good experience to work in industry, as opposed to the BBC like a lot of her contemporaries. She'd thought the media wouldn't be *real*, too much of a bubble. She quickly learned that the nuclear industry, or at least Dounreay, wasn't real either and was more of a bubble than anything she could have imagined. She laughed when she remembered one of her lecturers telling her that Shakespeare had invented the word "bubble". The "bubble" he was talking about was his life in academia. She'd had to fight off his wandering hands.

The smell from the whale was thicker now, though not unpleasant, yet. She trailed her fingers along the railings. It was around here one Summer afternoon some twenty years ago where her mother took her and her two elder sisters, all dressed in similar polka-dot frocks, to play on the beach. The three of them, ice-cream cones in hand, had been walking along the sea-wall which then was much thicker and shorter, the railings no more than old cast-iron spikes. Her mother signalled for the three sisters to come down off the wall, which they all did, one after the other. Except as Kylie jumped her frock remained attached to the iron spike which had caught her hem as she jumped. Her mother looked on horrified and her two sisters burst out in hysterical laughter as she stood there in her vest and pants wondering what had happened. A couple out walking their dog looked at her in comic amazement, the man trying not to laugh, the woman more sensitive to the humiliation: "Och, the poor wee thing."

In so many ways that was her continuing nightmare – the one which pursued her through High School, Wadham College and then journalism school in Cardiff: standing exposed in public. It stayed with her now, like the tragic smell of the dead whale: a memory of ice-cream, seaweed and tears.

She moved back from the window when she heard Colin come into the room.

Despite the fact that he had his suit on – bare feet mind you – he lay down on the bed. Kylie was fully dressed. She sat lightly, like a pigeon, on the end of the bed.

"This is really the only time we see each other these days," she said.

"Aye, busy busy." It was as if he were speaking to his feet. She realised he was waiting on something. Coffee? Well, he could wait.

"Where ye goin?" he asked as she got up.

"Where d'ye think?" she snapped. "Work. Same as you."

"I'm no goin til work," yawned Colin, "I'm goin til Dounreay."

"I'm sure they would appreciate it if you put in an appearance." She picked up her jacket and bag and had a last quick look in the mirror.

"Ah hev til see iss fuckan stupid Yank," he said, yawning.

She turned around impatiently. "Oh aye, and what Yank's this now?"

"Darcy Nagelstein or whatever the fuck hay calls himsel."

Now she was impatient *and* annoyed. "What are you going to see him aboot?"

"Iss fuckan chob. Ah've telt ye."

"No ye hevna. What job?" Now she was interested.

"Ah hev no idea and Ah can tell ye, neither dis he. I'll tell ye, Kylie, that's the thing aboot Dounreay: nobody knows anything."

"Will it be more money?" she heard herself asking. It was her mother's voice. What was happening to her?

"Oh fuck aye. More money, more hassle."

"Well, tell me about it the night – and good luck." She kissed the side of his head, then she was through the door, out of the house and into her car, driving out into the bright July morning.

As she left Atomic City heading west she saw that the farmers were taking advantage of the good weather to start on their sileage. It was Monday so they had been going at it the whole weekend. The different patterns and colours of green of the fields pleased her. Some still purple-grassy green and as yet uncut, some stripy ones highlighting the contours of the fields where the hay was yet to be baled. Then there were the black dotted ones where the swiss roll bales sat glinting in the sunlight, and the lime green of fields which radiated their emptiness where the bales had been gathered in and stacked on trailers – to be pulled by tractors just like the one she was now stuck behind doing precisely twenty miles per hour. Her meeting with the Baw Bag wasn't til ten so she had plenty of time. He was only going to tell her a lot of stuff about the storage facility anyway. All she had to do was to listen and then read the documents he gave her, make up yet another press release about how wonderfully it all was going, and that was that. She also had the excuse to leave, to go back to the beach and take a decent photo of the monitors.

She had discovered that Shakespeare did not make up the word "bubble". It was a mixture of Latin and Old Norse. Like everything else she had learned at Oxford it was bullshit. She did, however, sometimes recall a quote from Byron about a bubble, which more or less summed up her life:

*What a strange thing is the propagation of life! A bubble of seed which may be spilt in a whore's lap, or in the orgasm of a voluptuous dream, might (for aught we know) have formed a Caesar or a Buonaparte*

Good old Geordie Gordon. For him it was all premature ejaculation and a wet dream. Why that bit of Byron had stayed with her she had no idea. She had studied English Literature for a year because she got bored with economics. Then she got bored with economics and went back to literature. All the writers she liked were either Scottish or Irish or sometimes American. Her tutor – he of the roving hands – disapproved of all of them, which was strange because Angus was Scottish. If he'd come into tutorials wearing a jimmy-wig he couldn't have been more Scottish. He certainly came in plenty times smelling of vodka and lime pickle. His attitude to Scotland was as enlightening as his loyalty to Oxford and the English literary canon was reactionary.

"Scotland suffers from Aporia and Aphasia," he had declared one afternoon which was rather more vodka than pickle. She had asked him to explain. "Aporia is a state of impasse, almost a state of paralysis."

"And Aphasia?"

"Aphasia, my pretty Pict, is a loss of speech, perhaps as a result of cerebral affliction, perhaps from having Aporia? Whatever the cause the result is speechlessness."

"But professor Cheyne, by your own admission, you haven't been back to Scotland in twenty years," she countered him, not fully understanding his point.

"My dear Gollach, I have not been back to Scotland for over two hundred years!"

He was, she later learned, talking about the novels of Sir Walter Scott.

None of this, she decided, was useful. It would not help her get past this tractor-load of hay bales. She had been home for almost exactly a year and had been driving out this road each morning since. What exactly was a Personal Assistant to the Head of Communications at fucking Dounreay anyway? The Head of Communications had no idea, that was for sure. Maybe Colin was right: nobody knows anything. Also, just maybe – and even more hell and hallelujah – Professor Angus Vodka-and-Pickle Cheyne was right as well: maybe Scotland *was* in a state of impasse, of speechlessness. She didn't know much about Scotland and that was the truth. If Scotland was Dounreay then Colin, damn him, was right: nobody knows anything. But Dounreay isn't Scotland: it's Caithness; and as far as Caithness is concerned then old Angus in Oxford was right, his diagnosis fits it like a glove. Tears, the same tears of exposure, embarrassment and rage that had come the day her frock was impaled on that railing, flowed down her cheeks as she overtook the tractor and trailer, the young buck in the tractor cab oblivious to everything beneath his I-pod headphones. As she drove on, the sea to her right appeared infinite. The pale blue dome of the DFR raised its brow ahead of her, like some hellish metal priest rising from prayer to meet her tears. These were the tears of Aporia.

Somehow, Kylie always appeared most beautiful after she had left him. So Colin thought as he struggled to find clean socks. Her form, the beauty of her memory, her beauty itself, the smell of her, it filled him with light. As soon as he heard her close the front door, she was there, behind his eyes, showing him where to go. He found his socks. Put them on. Is this what they sing about in all them bog awful songs? This love thing? Just what the hell was he doing? He looked at his shoes as a man would look at the map of a foreign country. Suddenly realising the time he slid them on. Portuguese. Bought the last time he'd been in Edinburgh: black, soft leather; by far the best pair of shoes in Caithness. Of that he was convinced.

They were both young, successful, so why did he feel they were having a crisis? They could just take off somewhere and do something else. He would be game to throw everything up, to make a new start somewhere different. Not Kylie. He couldn't see her giving up £45k a year.

Who was she, really, the power-dressing ambitious monster he had let into his house, his life? What happened to the simple Caithness lassie he loved? She was still there but she showed herself rarely, only came out to play now and again. Was he also actually willing, in the cold light of day, to give up his job, his lifestyle? Hadn't he smugly reminded her just the other day that he made more than she did. But was that all it came down to – money, competition? If he was honest he would have to admit that was a big part of it. Now that decommissioning was full on, the culture of the plant, demanded it. In the old UKAEA days you could dander on with your own version of unadulterated materialism. But now things, possessions, holidays – that was no longer enough. Now you had to be able to shaft your best friend and think nothing of it. These days you were expected to keep your eye firmly on the money. Nothing else mattered.

He had trained as a fitter-turner, to work with his hands, to make machine parts, *useful* things. "I'm a skilled man, I'll hev ye know," he would tell her. He only vaguely understood why Kylie had laughed when he bought a milling machine and installed it in the spare room.

"You never touch it," she would say.

"I do sot. When yer no here."

She snorted at that. She snorted at a lot of things. Everybody who worked for Gabfan Nuclear snorted, especially the Yanks. None of these bloody Yanks who were running the decommissioning show out on site – (the site he was manager of – another thing he delighted to remind her) – had a clue where they were, geographically or culturally. They even snorted when he tried to enlighten them. Especially then. They didn't give a damn where they were. None of them had wives or children, as far as he knew. They were here to make money, and to do that the job had to be done as quickly as possible. "Don't you just feel that bonus, Colin, baby?" one of them had asked him. No, he did not "feel that bonus", and he'd fooled himself into thinking he was nobody's "baby". Little did he know the waves to come.

If he wanted to become like those company men he would have to learn how to suppress the man he was now. Colin would have to kill Colin in order to become Colin. The prospect made him shudder. Was that what he was going to say to Darcy Nagelstein at nine o'clock? No! I'm not your baby! I'm not gonna sacrifice myself for you!!

Despite this inner scream, as he grabbed his keys and closed the door behind him it dawned on him that was exactly what he was going to do. At Gabfan everybody was everybody else's baby.

# 10

Her first trip in October had been less rewarding than she had hoped. She'd had barely a week and no one would help her. The Highland Council didn't respond to her calls or emails, and nobody would meet her. The curator of the local museum, a stern, nervous, rat-like woman, was extremely unhelpful, even hostile. Mags had formed the impression that she actually despised the local culture.

"Not my area of expertise. I'm an Egyptologist myself, but I don't think you'll find anything of importance."

"Surely Caithness prehistory could rival Orkney?" reasoned Mags. "Those LiDAR surveys I've read about are turning up amazing images of unexcavated long cairns and burial – "

"Nothing in them," snorted the curator. "Nothing significant anyway. Compared to a pyramid it's all very... dull."

"Mmm. Not a lot of pyramids in Caithness, for sure," agreed Mags.

End of interview. The rodent woman knew nothing of and cared less about "the anchorite cell" on Dunnet Head and having made that plain she more or less pushed Mags out through the office door. Disappointed, Mags wandered thoughtfully down the old staircase of the building which, a display board told her, had once been the Town Hall. "Caithness Time" was a new museum, full of high-tech gizmos and applications. *What is the point*, wondered Mags, *of construction, design and flair if the building is staffed by people with no depth of interest, knowledge, training or vision?* There may be beautiful maps and poems on the walls and fascinating objects in cases but what Mags had hoped for was pride and passion in a local story. That this woman did not give a damn was obvious. Tea towels, pots of jam and books about Orkney in the museum shop told her everything about the museum, nothing about the past in Caithness.

*Why are they keeping Caithness a secret?* The question seemed worth finding an answer to. She drifted thoughtfully through a display of Pictish and Norse stone exhibits before heading back through the automatic doors and out into the street. It was raining and blowing a gale as it had been all day. *Equinoctial storm*, her landlady had pronounced at breakfast. *Could last a week,* she added with grim satisfaction, plonking her famous Caithness fry down in front of Mags. The plate heaved with thick bacon, orange-yolked eggs and fat aromatic wads of black pudding. Mags ate hungrily.

That was day one. Day two had been slightly better. She had studied maps and local history books in the library. All the while it rained. She went down to the bay and sheltered in the lee of the Salvation Army building. She watched the sea throw itself against what she now knew to be Holborn Head, spray from the breakers whipping over the top of the cliffs. Out in the bay the waves seemed unnaturally huge, more like surf than the waves she was used to. Dunnet Head was a grey shape to the north east. Orkney was invisible. The Pentland Firth looked to be boiling.

That night she met Fracher. Her landlady directed her to the Comm Bar: *Ye're in luck – There's always music on a Wednesday night.* When she got there the place was packed. But the music stopped her in her tracks. She had heard Scottish folk music before – Who hadn't? But this was different. She could *feel* it. Fluent, strange yet familiar, the music wrapped itself around her like a shawl. It demanded to be listened to, but at the same time allowed her in, drew her close, and gave her space to be comfortable. About a dozen musicians were gathered round a table – fiddlers, guitarists, a mandolin player, a bodhran player, a piper and two singers. Tune after tune, song after song. Then the piper stood up and the whole bar fell silent. He was a tall, burly man who looked as if he might have spent the night on the bar-room floor, but his pipes were immaculate. Tucking the instrument roughly under his arm he squeezed the bellows aggressively with his elbow. The most beautiful and hypnotic tune took slow flight. The music oozed from the pipes like dark water, and hovered like birds in the hot air of the bar; then it reeled away, replaced by more haunting, heart-breaking phrases, over and over until it was done. The piper sat down. After a moment of pure silence the entire drinking company burst into long and loud applause. Mesmerized, Mags relaxed.

She got talking to two rather drunken postmen. In straightforward Caithness fashion they asked who she was, where she came from and what she was up to. She told them. Billag, the less Guinnessed of the pair, was first to understand.

"Ach, id's Fracher ye'll be wantan."

"Fracher?" Was this a person or a product?

"Aye, Fracher – hay's got a boat." The other postman was laughing.

"Aye," agreed Billag. "Hay'll take e oot. Nobody kens ay firth better'n Fracher."

"Where will I find him?"

"Through ay hoose in ay public bar." Billag pointed over her shoulder.

The second postman chipped in. "Iss is ay posh bit. Fracher'll be sittan in ay coarner under ay TV. Choost tell him Beelag ay Post sent e. Hae'll hev a black doug wae a white heid wae him."

She thanked them and pushed her way through the crowd which, after the dream-like pipe interlude, was back to the serious business of shouting to make themselves heard. There he was, just as described: under the TV, a dog at his feet, sat a man like a sack of potatoes. As she got closer she could see that it was just the layers of clothes he had on – two shirts, two jumpers and a jacket. Before him sat a half pint, hardly touched, and a glass of rum, which she soon came to learn was emptied and filled at regular intervals. He looked friendly enough.

That was how she met Fracher. That was when it really started.

But we must leave them there for a bit and take Mags back to the day before. After breakfast she had driven up to the House of the Northern Gate on Dwarick Head and parked her car at the foot of the track. It was pouring with rain. She looked at the Ordnance Survey map. She could see Chapel Geo marked but nothing much else. She walked down to the Head of Man and passed the Peedie Sannie (she didn't yet know it as that yet), curled tantalizingly at the foot of the cliff. The rain forced her to press on along the cliff path, past the Loch of Bushta and on to the knee-high ruin of the Chapel. It wasn't much to look at, just a stone outline, but at least she had physically set eyes on it.

It was her friend Helen who had told her about the chapel. She had been in Caithness on holiday the previous Summer and had come across it on a walk around Dunnet Head, which her guidebook boasted as '*the most northerly point on the British mainland*'. She knew it was the sort of thing which would interest Mags. A rudimentary search of available sources had only scratched the surface, so she had come north to find out for herself. This was her reconnaissance to see what Helen had been so excited about. She had gone on and on about '*unexplored wilderness*', until even Mags' jaded interest was caught. She had also been intrigued about a Cave of Gold at the bottom of the headland cliff, visible only from the sea. When Helen told her the story that day in the pub in Islington it had seemed like a magic world or some lost civilization, and she was hooked. She needed a project now that she had graduated and this was it. For months it had been a vaguely seductive dream. Now here she was, her feet on the ground, the exact place Mags liked them to be – even if the rain water was running down the back of her neck. There was the Chapel, and there was the Chapel Geo leading down to the sea, half screened behind mist with the sea breaking over the rocks at its foot. On the top of the cliff, on the beach side of the geo, two ravens perched and looked at her.

A headland rose in a steep incline behind the Chapel. The ancient Irish priests who built this place had chosen their spot well: the hill would protect you from the worst of the north wind; the hill on the far side of Loch Bushta would do the same from the even more biting north easterlies; the loch itself would provide water; and there was a small burn which flowed from it, then threw itself suicidally over the three hundred foot cliff. As Mags watched it the burn-water was blown high into the air like liquid hair. Mags looked around her at this stark dramatic landscape. She wondered what the priests had made it of it fifteen hundred years ago. It was beautiful, but unforgiving. It won't always be like this she, told herself. In Summer it will be different.

She walked back to her car, took off her wet jacket and dried herself as best she could, and drove back into Thurso. She parked her car in the Co-op car park and walked down to the river. It was late morning by now and it had stopped raining, but the wind was still howling in off the sea. She followed the river down to the old harbour. The pier pointed north out into the bay at the river mouth like a stone finger. Sheltering behind a sea wall Mags looked out over the bay. Holborn Head was to the west, sea-spray still whiplashing over the top. The island of Hoy was a grey lump some twenty miles to the north. To the right sat Dunnet Head, not unlike a giant pier itself. She could see the purpose of this old Viking town. This was what it was: a natural, if dangerous, harbour on the western side of the great nautical highway of the Pentland Firth. She turned and looked at the town with new found admiration. There it was, like some great filleted stone fish split either side of the river, dark peaty water flowing out into the bay like earthen blood. *Thurso has been here for several thousand years,* she thought, *and I have been here for just two minutes.*

How could she do this? She would have to go back to London, go and see Professor Benison, her old supervisor, make her case for a research grant and hope that he lived up to his name. She could just see him looking her up and down the way he always did. But he had a soft spot for her, didn't he?

*Money is tight*, he would say.

*Money is always tight. But the university has a track record in researching early Christianity,* she would counter, *and this is untouched – It could be a revelation.* Then she would look at him that way she always did when she wanted something. She would say it was a gut feeling, but then mention the lottery. *The lottery is the last chance saloon for any academic research project*, he would remind her – and on it would go like this for an hour or so and her dream would either live or die in that room. If she was passionate and had a plan, how could he refuse? Easily. He refused bright-eyed postgraduate students funding for their mad schemes every day. In fact, it was what the university paid him for. *But this is different,* she would plead. *It's always different,* he would insist, *everyone is always different, everyone is always "the one" and everyone is always the same.* Yet here she was in Caithness where she could feel the past, which was her future, calling to her from beneath the ground.

She walked up through the old Fisherbiggins which surrounded the late 12th century kirk of St Peter's. The gates were locked. A rusty padlock joined a length of even rustier chain. *Why on earth is the place locked,* she wondered, *do they not want people to see this fantastic place?* She laughed at the absurdity of it all. With her hands shaking the cast iron gate it started to rain again, so she walked hurriedly back into the centre of the town and nipped into a coffee shop to get warm. A chunky waitress with ginger hair set the latte on the table. "Ayr e go, Caithness coffee at London prices."

Mags looked at her not understanding what she had said. The waitress looked straight back at her.

"E wantan a bap wae aat?"

Again, not understanding, Mags just said "No, no thanks."

"Suit yersel." The waitress sloped off, the tray tucked under her arm.

Mags sipped her coffee and smiled to herself. *Welcome to Thurso,* she thought.

The small town began to fascinate her. She had been to no other place like it. Thurso, she thought, was like one of those ornaments her grandmother had that, when you picked them up and shook them, a snow scene settled over a little landscape. Only this was a big landscape even if the town, compared to London, was tiny. In the short time Mags had spent in it she could see that it was at least four quite different and distinctive places. There was the old Viking town huddled like chickens around St Peters. What wonders lay beneath your feet as you walked along the Fisherbiggins, she thought? Then there was the medieval town which spread from the river up to the set of lights which organized the traffic across from where she sat. It delighted her that the main street was called Rotterdam Street. It connected the place to the rest of Europe in a way that those who lived in the South could not have imagined. What fleets, what ships must have called in here over all these years? What cargoes did they off-load and take on? From where Traill Street and Olrig Street joined Rotterdam Street the New Town of the late eighteenth century, running up Ormlie Hill along the spine of Princes Street, was all solid merchants' houses and walls, parallels and quadrangles; a mini Manhattan in the far north of Scotland. In the rain the sandstone buildings smelled of sea-salt; flagstone pavements turned the colour of seaweed or tanned leather. The soles of your feet slid along them like liquorice.

Then there was the 'Atomics' – the regimented kit-house estate thrown up in the nineteen fifties where the first workers who came to work at Dounreay were housed. Their families still lived there; washed up on the radiation shore of history. If not quite refugees, they had all the cultural signifiers of a lost tribe. Mags thought the Atomics would make a good subject of study for her friend Helen who had graduated as an anthropologist at the same time as she entered the world with her BSc (Hons) in archaeology. Four years is a long time to acquire an acronym. I will do this, she said to herself.

Beside the Atomics were the council estates where the natives lived, spreading over the river and into the surrounding farmland like a human crop. They seemed, to Mags, both severe and human, as if in their construction both extremes of harshness and tenderness were striven for at once. *Maybe that explains the nature of the people here,* she thought.

But she did not think that then, not yet on that day in October in the rain, drinking Caithness coffee at London prices, with the equinoctial storm blowing itself to pieces out in the Pentland Firth. She did not know any of this then. Insight – if that was what it was – came later, the following Summer, when she learned the true meaning of history and how people leave their mark upon it. How history really is a wave which washes over us all.

# 11

For millions of years Jörð had been pushed down by the Frost Giants, the Ice oppressors. Pushed down deep into Ginnungagap. At long last, Surt rose up from Muspell in the South, attacking the Frost Giants with fire and driving them north. Now Jörð found herself beneath the sky – free. Her delight filled the sea, shaping the islands and the fjords of the north. On the shore of one of these she met Storegga, lost daughter of the giant Ymir from whose body the world was made. Jörð was lonely from her time in Ginnungagap, the Mighty Gap where nothing is and nothing grows. When she saw Storegga she knew that she was not alone. Storegga had been saddened by the murder of her father. No matter that the world was all of him, it was not until she met Jörð the Earth that she knew happiness was possible. So it was that Jörð and Storegga lay down in the sea-fields of the ocean and joined themselves to each other.

Then Jörð began to heal from the ravages of the Frost Giants. What was old was made new. What was submerged rose up. By the tenderness of time, Jörð and Storegga shaped the north so that the gods of Asgard could find a home in the world. They called it Midgard. This world, as Bragi Boddason has told us, was created by love out of nothing, because out of nothing comes love, and out of love comes the world. So Ginnungagap, the Mighty Gap where nothing was, where the Earth did not exist, nor the sea, nor the sky, and where nothing grew, was filled up by Jörð and Storegga.

Now, in the north the sea is deep, but the Earth is deeper. From these extremes come the beginning and end of our story.

It was into the deep that Storegga, heavy from love, sank back the morning after that first long night with Jörð. Her children, born beneath the sea, spread out in a wave. These were miracles. Twice this happened. Their marks are Earth-runes in the coast running from Iceland to the Firth of Forth – these were hungry expansive offspring.

Now for a third time Jörð rises up to seek Storegga in her bed off the West of Norway. Every ten thousand years they love. Soon, perhaps, we will see the crest of the fruit of their union pass over headland, island, town. The ocean braids her salted hair to harness their motion.

These miracles are not metaphors as we generally understand them. These images, these rune-stories, these fables depict the reality of this narrative, of all narratives. The formation of the world, the fall of Troy – *all* stories are contained within the wave. The gods of Asgard, as Bragi Boddason has described them, are also the heroes of Troy: a future rune-carver had to translate Odin and Loki for Christian eyes. So one orthodoxy became another orthodoxy. And yet narratives still need heroes and distance, even when we discover – if we keep reading to the end – that there are no heroes. How disappointing is that? Fatal to any story. But not this one. So Thor becomes Hector and Loki is Odysseus; Asgard is Troy, and Ragnarok the fall of Troy; and all the gods of Midgard come from Asia where Troy was to be found. In these equivalents the transfer of images is complete, and we can believe in the story once again, even if we do not believe in Christianity or Odin. We believe in Bragi Boddason. He depends upon us for we are his imagination. So when he tells us of the Frost Giants, of Ymir and Storegga, of Jörð and the Ginnungagap (the Mighty Gap), of Odin and Loki we believe him, because without these images we cannot know ourselves; because they are stronger than reality, and any other idea we can construct. Ideas are dangerous to our narrative because they cause wars and result in untold deaths, whereas these images move smoothly through time. They turn us, like wheels.

In the love between Jörð and Storegga is the beginning of our history, which comes out of the ground and passes over us in waves. The stones we arrange will be what are left of us when our history is over. They will be our image on the Earth, and in that way our narrative will continue without us. In big cities and small towns, in farms and in fields, people live and die, some thinking they are in control of history, others certain they are not. It's all the same to history, which in the end is just a series of images. If the skald Bragi Boddason does not carve them into a set of runes then it will all be washed away into silence. It will return to the Mighty Gap, Ginnungagap, where nothing is or has been. So it is that we depend upon these images, and these images depend upon us.

Jörð loved Storegga truly and deeply, so much so that she dropped into the sea – we can see the effects on the coastlines of the north. How these marks got there: that is our story. It is the story of how we translate reality into meaning, of how Asgard becomes Troy, of how waves create us as well as destroy us.

# 12

The Maighdeann Mhara sat on a rock. Above all other places she loved the Peedie Sannie. It was quiet. Dunnet Beach, even in Winter, had too many people, and people were her problem. From where she sat in front of the waterfall, she could see them coming, from the car park at The House of The Northern Gate or down the path from Dwarick Head. But no one could see her. If anyone came from the sea, she could soon disappear – her cave was just round the coast at the Chapel Geo. Her otter Muirgen was playing in the surf. He would alert her if a boat approached. Muirgen was her dearest friend. Most people, if they saw him at all – and he made it his business not to be seen – thought he was a seal. A big dog otter, jet black and a swift swimmer, it was only his tail that gave him away as he dived beneath the water.

It was good to be out of the cave. The Sun was shining and the sea was blue. She loved watching Muirgen enjoy himself in the waves. There were plenty of small green crabs for him to chase and eat if he was hungry. He was always hungry. After a long spell on his own, when he came back he would tell her what he had been doing. She loved his stories about all the creatures he met. His otter-speak was limited but when he wanted to expand into detail he spoke Gaelic. They could chatter for hours, the pair of them, in her cave with all the pigeons cooing and chuckling to themselves on the ledges above their heads. She loved Muirgen, which was her name for him, and means '*Sea Born*'. He liked the name, but his own name for himself was Dòbhran. *'S mise Dobhran*, he would insist. Dòbhran called her Fand, '*Pearl of Beauty*'. She laughed from embarrassment whenever she thought of it. She had no name for herself. Her name was lost with her past.

Local people used to call her Maighdeann Mhara, maiden of the sea, but since people on the West Side of Dunnet did not speak Gaelic anymore, she had no idea what they called her. She could speak English if she had to but she did not like it much. She preferred the Old Norse sound of the Caithness dialect. In fact she could speak any language if she put her mind to it. But with Muirgen it was all otter and Gaelic.

She had just bathed in the waterfall. She relished the taste and feel of fresh water, so luxurious, smelling of flowers and peat and of the sky. It tasted of apples, which she loved. She hardly ever had them. Once, short ago, some apples in a box had washed up on the Peedie Sannie. Muirgen wouldn't touch them. *Air partan*, he snorted, and swam away. Red, with a ring of nobbly bumps at the bottom, most were rotten but about a dozen were still good. ***RED DELICIOUS, CANADA*** was stamped on the box. She made them last for two weeks. Each time she took a bite she wondered where Canada was. A man Calder from the village had gone to Canada, she had heard. He'd not *meant* to, but the ship he was piloting through the Pentland Firth would not – or could not – stop, so he ended up in Quebec (in his slippers). It took him a while to get back. He had left in the Voar and made it home in time for the Hairst. All those people had gone now and she wasn't sure about the new ones. She avoided them.

Beside her on a rock was some dulce, drying in the Sun. Other than the odd apple this was her favourite food. Dry and crispy, it melted in your mouth and tasted of the sea. This she found reassuring. The sea had become her home. It wasn't always so. Sometimes she'd recall herself as Time had once seen her, a little girl living peacefully in a house with her parents. The house flooded spectacularly one year as a spring burst beneath it. Her parents both drowned, swept into what is now Loch Bushta. Somehow – she never knew why – she was born to swim. Muirgen told her it was the work of the gods. That it was her destiny. He was a great believer in destiny, her otter. She waved to him. Immediately Muirgen bounded from the waves, scrambled over the rocks and nestled his head in her lap. She stroked his head and admired his fine moustache. He was very proud of his moustache was Muirgen. The flood: that was one version of her life. In truth her life was a river of sorrow and regret.

She saw him come down the path from Dwarick Head, and had watched him as he sat on a rock with his back to her and looked back down at the village. He was a strange one, she could tell, not like the others somehow. She had seen him before. He had come down to the beach here quite often of late. She had known his mother and what had happened to her. She had watched them when they were bairns, him and his brother; how his mother had brought them down here after the peat cutting; how they would play in the water; how she would wash her little boys in the waterfall, just as she washed herself. She had spoken to the mother only once. A good woman, but sad and lonely just as Maighdeann Mhara was herself. The mother wore her story in her eyes – you could tell everything about a human by their eyes. Otters were a bit trickier. Muirgen got fed up being petted and scampered back to the sea. He also had seen the man.

She had almost spoken to him last year when he had come down and stepped out to the finger of rock separating the two small beaches. He had hurled bottles of pills far into the sea. Then he had been weeping, broken. His sorrow attracted her, for sorrow was in her blood: she was a child of tragedy. In every man's eyes she looked for him: her saviour, forgiver of her guilt, companion, lover, the father of her child. So far, she had not found him. Was he the one? She doubted it, but she had not looked yet into his eyes. Would she dare? Who, in reality upon this earth, had the power to forgive her for her one true crime, when it had been committed in another world?

Manson stood up. *This is where my ashes will be scattered.* He told himself this every time he climbed Dwarick Head. He turned and crossed the brow of the headland. Beneath the cliffs nestled two white sand crescents – the Peedie Sannie. He thought about eating one of the apples he had in his pocket but decided to save them for later. The Sun was high in the sky, the water was Mediterranean blue and clear. A couple of seals swam lazily some yards from the shore. What was that – a dog, he wondered – splashing in the waves? He couldn't be sure. Thankfully he couldn't see any people. He had absolutely no desire to see anyone.

His brother had been on the phone again last night. Both of them were drunk. They could only talk to each other when they were pissed. It was the same old story: *When was he going to sell the house? He didn't need such a big place. He couldn't look after it properly. The place would deteriorate. He needed* – his brother – *some money to put down a mortgage on this house he'd seen in Leith. He* – Manson – *was just being romantic, stupid and selfish. Could he not think of others instead of himself for a change? He had a wife. Didn't he understand that? She was pregnant. They needed a home.* "You're just standing in our way!" he had shouted down the line. "Think of the future. Both our futures." His brother hung up. Manson wasn't sure who the "both" in this "futures" business was. He didn't want to think about anything. Jeezus, his brother wasn't the only one who needed money. Manson was sick to the back teeth of being broke. Some days he would even cadge a lift into Thurso and walk the streets looking for coins people had dropped. He always hoped he might find a wallet dropped by a tourist. He had no scruples about this. If there was money he would take it and throw the wallet in the river. Once he found a purse on the floor at a wedding dance. Twenty pounds. That got him drunk. The purse disappeared into the sea. After school lunch breaks was the best time on the streets. He might find enough change to go to the Comm for a pint, speak to people he knew. Usually they would buy him a pint or two. But in the end he would have to find his way home to Dunnet. To lentils, or tatties, or corn beef – or nothing. He hated poverty. He was not used to it and was not designed for it, neither habitually nor emotionally.

He had somehow spiralled down into it. No journalism any more. No teaching either. No holiday pay. No pension. Sometimes there was the odd story Aberdeen wanted. Sometimes there was the odd art night class to teach at the college. But nothing that gave him much money. He had sold the land. That was one of the battles his brother had won. Seven acres of de-crofted land, plus the out-buildings. That had kept him going for a few years. Kept him in whisky and lentils at least. He wanted to be a painter but he lacked the dedication. His water colours and drawings were very good – folk who saw them said so – but they didn't get any better, so he did fewer and fewer, then stopped altogether. He still carried a sketch pad. He had carried it around for three years and all it contained was a sketch of his own head, one of a boor tree, and another of a willow. Not so much as a scratch for over eighteen months. Nothing beyond the continuous grinding anxiety about money.

The house was paid for many years ago so he had no worries there. But drinking was all he seemed to do: sessions in the village pub or in Thurso, or drinking in the house. He had lost the lecturing job through drink if truth be told but the drinking was just the surface symptom of a deeper unhappiness. He hated the college. But without the Scottish educational establishment to rile against what was there? The peasant in him grew tatties, cabbages, carrots and sometimes even courgettes and other stuff in the ramshackle greenhouse his father had built, which leaned against the high wall separating his garden from the manse. But he wanted more. That was his problem: he wanted to know what too much was, but he despaired that he never would.

The Summer breeze blew all this from Manson's mind as he climbed down the rough stone path to the Peedie Sannie. He spotted the long tail of what he now recognised as a dog-otter disappear beneath the surface of the water. He was down on the sand by the time he saw her. She didn't seem to notice him. Poised on a rock, just staring out at the waves. She had to be the most beautiful woman he had ever seen. Nervously he scanned the beach for photographers or the camera crew he half expected must be filming her. But there was no-one else on the beach; just himself and this divine creature, her long mane of naturally-streaked blonde hair tumbling over a flowing multi-coloured robe or coat of some sort. His heart pounded.

Then he realised the power of her eyes. They were of the deepest blue. *Like iodine*, he thought as they looked at him. He felt them reach through to the back of his head, like a laser beam.

"I'm sorry," he said. "I didn't mean to..." Stare, he meant.

"You're not. Please, sit down."

He did, on a sandstone ledge. All the while his eyes feasted on her. Her hair seemed to swim from the top of her head to the beach of her shoulders, the honeyed yellow of a hillside in Autumn. Manson had never seen anything like it. Pouring from her shoulders, the mellow streaks in her thick wavy hair blended and became indistinguishable from her long dress, more of a coat, which responded to her movement with the liquid quality of silk. Sunlight seemed to be absorbed into the material and then flare back out, radiantly colouring the air around her. She looked very young, yet there was a look of authority about her, of confidence. She was totally in control of her own space.

"Are you on holiday?" He struggled to speak, his mind a blank. There was a deep need in him to engage with her. Atheist though he was, this piece of heaven could only be an angel.

"No more or less than you are yourself." She smiled.

In the pub the previous night a tourist from the campsite on the links had asked him that very question. That was typical of how others perceived him, and symptomatic of how he saw himself. Although born and raised in the village, he had come back after many years away, and the villagers thought of him as an outsider. Leave to "better" yourself then they might respect you for your ambition, but they'll despise you for your desertion. If you come back they're admiring if you've achieved something, but they'll hate you because you've changed – *And who do you think you are*? This cloud clung to Manson like weather to the headland. He didn't belong even though he did. A campsite tourist, recognizing a fellow stranger, had asked if he was on holiday.

"Hae's aalweys on holiday," slurred Chocky Sutherland.

Manson, who'd had too much to drink, went for him. He almost got himself barred and resolved the situation this morning only by a lot of apologising and grovelling. Now here he was asking this beautiful, mysterious vision the very same stupid question.

"I live here," he said, trying to validate himself.

"I know. So do I."

"I've never seen you before." He allowed himself to looked at her closely. Was it a trick of the sunlight – Fluid shades of colour highlighting her cheekbones, her nose and her lips?

"You have seen me," she said, "often. You just haven't recognised me, that's all." She laughed.

"I would recognise you," he said. "I think I would remember you."

"You might think so, but you don't know," she said, raising her hand briefly to her cheek. "People pass by things they should recognise all the time. People see what they want to see. They remember what they need to remember."

"Is that the same thing as seeing what you want to see?"

"In your case, yes." She laughed again. Muirgen emerged from the sea, clambered onto a rock next to her, and proceeded to consume a small green crab. Manson stared at the otter in disbelief. "This is Muirgen," said the Maighdeann Mhara, seeing Manson's uneasiness. "He's my friend. Are you going to be my friend, Manson?" And she looked at him.

Manson's skin prickled. "How do you know my name?" Something unsettling and uncomfortable was stirring him, and it had nothing to do with his hangover.

"Oh, you are very well known." Before he could formulate his next question she answered it for him. "My name is Fand. So now we all know each other. Isn't that lovely?"

Having dispatched the crab, the otter leapt from the rock and put his head in her lap. Manson was suddenly violently jealous. "*Ah, ceart, ceart. Mo leannan, mo Mhuirgen.*" She stroked the smooth fur on the back of his head. "He likes the sound of Gaelic," she said.

"So do I," said Manson. "My grandparents used to speak it on the croft."

"I know," she said sadly. "History is not a happy place."

At that moment, in his mind, he saw his grandmother on a three-legged stool milking a cow in the byre, and heard again how the rhythm of the song she sang matched the rhythm of the milk hitting the bucket. The memory filled him with a warm creamy goodness, a connectedness, his grandmother's Gaelic air embracing him into a security he would never know again and would spend his whole life searching for, trying to recreate. He realised his entire life, up to this point, was that pursuit. All those milky feelings of archaic continuity, of safety, came pouring back into him now as he listened to the rhythm of the sea, and the Maighdeann Mhara's voice.

True to habit, he panicked. What if he never saw this woman again? Maybe he should take a photo of her on his mobile phone? But that would be a violation. A violation of what? This moment, this sacred, beautiful moment. Maybe he could sketch her? But he would never be able to do her justice. The colour scheme alone would have defeated Matisse.

"Your history surrounds you like the sea around Stroma."

"My history?"

"People are all islands, surrounded by their own particular stretch of ocean which defines them. Most people when they see an island assume it has always been so, as if the island is responsible for its own shape. But islands are shaped by the sea. You, Manson, are no different."

The otter, clearly bored by this conversation in English, raised his head from her lap, twitched his magnificent moustache, and in a couple of bounds was on the rocks and into the sea. He disappeared beneath the water.

"He is always hungry," she said affectionately.

Manson remembered the two apples in his jacket pocket and dug them out – one green, the other red.

"Would you like an apple?" he asked innocently, offering her the red one. "They're off my mother's trees."

The Maighdeann Mhara had been watching the otter. As she turned and saw the apple in Manson's outstretched hand, he would have sworn at that moment he saw the colour of her eyes shift through deep blue to green to amber, then back to blue.

"She planted them when we first moved into the house. That must be over thirty years ago now." His voice seemed not his own, coming back at him from far away.

Slowly she reached out her hand and took the apple from him without touching his fingers. She held the fruit up to the Sun and looked at it longingly. She said something he did not understand, and pushed the apple deep into a pocket of her dress. Manson's grip on himself was wavering. He tensed his leg muscles against the rock he was sitting on. He needed to feel its solid reality. *Am I going mad?*

"Such a beautiful gift requires an offering of equal weight." She fixed her gaze on him.

His voice seemed to come from deep inside himself, as if he was shouting from the back of a cave.

"It's only an apple."

"Apples are the taste of life." Her voice was musical, like an instrument he could not name. "Even when they have been grown near death." Her voice drifted around him and up with the fulmars nesting in the cliff ledges above.

"Our trees are across the wall, well away from the kirkyard, actually." He spoke before he could stop himself, a nervous schoolboy scoring petty points to make himself feel stronger. *Jeezus – She's intense!*

"Some say apples are the food of the dead. What do you think, Manson?"

He had no idea what he thought about anything. Right now he was playing in the rock pool a hundred yards away, while his mother swam in the sea, then got out to sit on a rock staring out over the bay. He could hear the waterfall splashing onto the rocks behind them. He remembered the shock of the cold fresh water on his shoulders as his mother scrubbed him and his brother from head to foot.

"I have a way of storing them in boxes in a shed," he said. "It keeps them amazingly well."

Why was he telling her this? Why couldn't he just tell her he'd got them from Lidl's with the rest of his shopping before he went to the pub? He looked out to sea hoping to find an answer. Muirgen, the otter, was swimming on his back, holding a mussel in his front paws and prising open the shell with his teeth.

"If you come back here at the same time tomorrow I will have a gift for you in return."

"Please. Like I said, it was only an apple." He tried to curb the excitement her offer provoked.

"The greatest gift is giving itself." She stood up as she spoke, taller and more slender than he'd expected.

"Muirgen is calling to me. Tomorrow then?"

"Y-yes. T-tomorrow." His stammer gave away his lack of control.

"Remember, my name is Fand."

She moved to the water's edge, then she was swimming, and then she was gone. *She's bound to surface in a minute.* He stood for fully ten minutes, looking out onto the water. Neither sight nor sound of the woman or the otter.

Eventually he roused himself to climb the path back up to the cliff top, and began the walk back up to Dwarick Head. *I never did see her feet. I mean, she's bound to have feet? Right?*

# 13

It took a year but they built their chapel. Grillaan, the prior, dedicated it to Colm. He wasn't Saint Colm yet but Grillaan knew it would only be a matter of time and time is what they had plenty of. In the long term (or so they thought). In the short term, after they had landed, time was of the essence. They had to prepare for the coming Winter and they had, precisely, nothing. So, the first thing Grillaan did was to go and call on the Picts in the fort on the hill at the top of the headland.

The Chief of the Cattachs, Dungal, was polite and hospitable as was their custom, although he was naturally cautious and somewhat sceptical about their undertaking.

"We can see that you are holy men."

Dungal sat with Grillaan by the fire in the great hall.

"You can deposit your relic in *Uamh an Oir*. You can dedicate it to your brother Colm. You can even build your temple – I will give you one of our best masons to help you. But your religion will not sit so easily with my people, I think. Oh, don't be alarmed, they will not harm you, they won't interfere with you at all. We have had other holy men here before and like you they wanted little and spoke of the dove and the fish. They either died or went on their way. The power of our own priests goes deep into the people and we are, as I'm sure you realise, and as you were once yourselves in Ireland, a deeply religious people."

Grillaan had to smile at this. Dungal was a sophisticated, influential man and that he was extremely civilized there could be no doubt – his hall was decked in splendidly patterned tapestries and from the walls hung fine ornamental shields embossed with colourful symbols – but that he considered Christianity a trifle – doves and fish – hardly a religion at all, tickled Grillaan. The Picts had lived in these northern fastnesses for many centuries. Their culture and skill in carving, weaving, ships and building was renowned all over Europe. Grillaan decided, as he drank the ale that was offered to him and ate the venison which was put in front of him, to go easy on the converting for a time.

Dungal was courteous, generous and respectful but Grillaan knew the Pictish priests, the Druids of the ash and the oak groves, would be hostile – dangerous even. This was their land. He was a mere refugee, literally washed up on their shore. Yet even in the few days he had been on Dunnet Head Grillaan had felt at home. The landscape, he told himself, was not dissimilar to Donegal. The people here were Picts, yes, and their language and customs and religion were different but he and Dungal were both Celts. Dungal had Gaelic and Grillaan a smattering of Brythonic picked up from Welsh traders, so that they could communicate well enough at first. But after a while Grillaan's words ran out. Dungal laughed: "Good Prior, I have enough of the Irish in me to speak it plain. The language of the Cruthin is difficult for you Ulstermen. So, tell me, how are things in Ulster these days?"

"Oh, much the same as they are in the rest of Ireland. Each clan is at the other's throat. Every Chief wants to be the High King and to sit in power at Tara." Grillaan was glad in many ways to be out of the raiding.

"You will find things quieter here," said Dungal. "Since the Romans left the South we have no need for war, although the Norse are beginning to want more than trade. I believe they too have wars in Norway. But there is plenty room in the Province of the Cat." Dungal indicated the broad wooden door, entrance to the long hall. "*People* are welcome. Divisive cults who confuse our people, and warring raiders who will rob us blind we do not tolerate."

Dungal's warning was considered, and Grillaan was left in no doubt of its sincerity. As he left, Dungal accompanied him to the door of the hall. From there they could see north across the firth to the whale islands, *Arcaibh* Dungal called them, vast oceans stretching out on either side. Dungal raised his arms in supplication:

"From the mountains of Naver in the West to the Ord and Morven in the South, these coastlands, this plateau: these are the ancient clan lands of the Cruithne of which we are the Cattach. Six more provinces lie South of us and in such a way is Alba known. You are welcome here, Grillaan, and we will see to it that you do not starve or go without shelter for we, the Cattach, would never allow that. You will be free to worship your own god and to practice your religion. As I have said, we have our own. And as you can also see, because it is a fair day turned, there is light, space and ground enough for all the pathways of the heart."

As Dungal spoke Grillaan looked out over the magnificent scene arrayed below him. He was impressed by how Dungal had named it and given it human form. Below the fort, at the foot of the headland in the cradle of the beach, Grillaan could see smoke from the home-fires of the village; beyond that were fields recently harvested, and cattle, sheep and horses grazing. As Grillaan thanked Dungal for his kindness and walked down from the fort back to Bushta where they had landed there were tears in his eyes. Eoghan claimed that they had come to the '*edge of the world*', implying that this was where everything stops. But Grillaan felt in his gut that they had come in fact to the top of the world, where everything begins.

That was October. Now it was July. And they were, all three of them, very much alive. They had dug a vegetable patch out of the heathery grass. Kale was growing and they had even planted some oats, as Dungal had sent them a sack of seed. He also had given them oatmeal to see them through the Winter, and a man came to show them where the best fishing was to be had. He was as good as his word, the Chief of the Cattach: they would not starve. They had built stone huts for themselves. The founds of the chapel had also been dug: the nave, chancel and altar. The three brown priests from Loch Swilly were beginning to make their mark on the Province of the Cat. The clarsach sat tight in its oak casket, waiting.

The day after Grillaan went to see Dungal, Chief of the Picts, the rain had stopped. After prayers of thanks and a breakfast of oatmeal, Grillaan lifted Colm's clarsach gently from its casket and carried it to the top of the cliff above the geo. He had wrapped it in a cloth and when he had got to the spot he had chosen he set it carefully on the heather. He knelt down and cupped rainwater from a puddle into his hands, then slowly washed his face. Then he unwrapped the instrument from the cloth and held it above his head so that the wind blew through the gut strings. The air sounded a soft melancholy as the clarsach translated wind into music. As this music drifted over the sea towards the beach Grillaan closed his eyes and spoke:

*Thanks to you, God*
*who brought us from Ireland*
*to our beginning in Alba*
*to earn for our souls*
*everlasting joy*
*we three*
*with good intent*
*and for every gift of peace*
*you bestow on us*
*our thoughts and our words*
*our deeds and desires*
*I dedicate this music*
*from my brother Colm's clarsach*
*and this chapel that we will build*
*and dedicate in his name*
*to you*
*I offer you this in supplication*
*I beseech you*
*to keep us from offence*
*and to shield us always*

*for the sake of your wounds*
*with your offering of grace*
*we offer this up to you*
*this endeavour*
*the chapel of Saint Colm*
*if it be your will*
*we offer this music*
*this clarsach*
*so, dear God*
*bless the world and all that is therein*
*Amen*

Grillaan lowered the clarsach. The offering of its music drifted into silence. He sat down on a heathery tussock and cradled the clarsach in his lap. He felt the north-west wind blow over his tonsured head. If they had ever thought of it, there was no going back now.

# 14

A man and a woman go down to the shore at Brims Ness just below the small chapel and graveyard and begin to pick wilks. Each has a black plastic bucket, and as they bend over the rock pools the fog from the Pentland Firth blows over them like blue-grey smoke. Sometimes, as Kylie watched them, they disappeared altogether, reappearing as the east wind blew the fog before it. It could be a scene from the Middle Ages, or from one of the stark 1930's Danish films she'd developed a taste for.

In the field above the shore a herd of dairy cattle munched the thick July grass, their black coats shimmering in the sunshine. Oyster catchers whistled nervously amongst the seaweed. The sea was a constant lapping presence at the edge of the foggy rocks. Beyond that was the mighty Atlantic, the centre and the edge of everything. Kylie couldn't decide whether it was thunder she was hearing in the distance or the fog booming through the blades of the six wind turbines at Forss, just west along the coast. There they stood, constantly bowling invisible balls of dubious promise. The old United States Navy Base had been turned into an "enterprise park". Military occupation and the Cold War. Who knows what nascent business they might kick start in Caithness?

It was 5.30 pm and Kylie had just left the site. As she drove out of Dounreay she had realised she just could not face going straight back into Atomic City. She came to Brims often to watch the Atlantic surf roll in. This afternoon there was no surf to see, just the graveyard, the cows, the oyster catchers, the wilk pickers, the fog and the hidden sea. Above the fog the Sun shone brightly and the sky was blue. It was an atmospheric afternoon and a beautiful end to a long, pointless day. It was also, although she didn't know it yet, the beginning of a difficult evening. Kylie looked west over Ushat Head and the beautiful ruin of Crosskirk. The sky was darkening to an alarming black over Strathy Point. Little blue-white feather flickers of lightning which occasionally savaged the air at the bottom of the clouds told Kyle it was indeed thunder she had been hearing. It grew louder, closer and heavier. The wind picked up and the yellow and white heads of the sand daisies bobbed more regularly. Off Strathy the clouds had turned themselves into upside-down tornado islands, the wind curving their fine cone peaks to the east while their bloated grey bases floated like mythical beasts just above the horizon. The couple picking wilks also looked up at the sky. Cutting their losses, they ran with their buckets back to their car. Headlights on full beam, they drove off up the road past the old castle and the Port of Brims, through the farm and onto the road into town.

The blackness moved slowly east. The wind dropped and then came a strange, airless silence, interrupted occasionally by the sucking timpani of the thunder. The Sun, which had been a pale-yellow ball hanging in the south-western sky, disappeared. The clouds, huge now, some jet black, some virginal white, began to ripple and twist into fantastic mountainous shapes. Kylie felt fat warm rain drops fall on her face. They tasted of salt and flagstone. They were heavy and irregular as if some huge eye, some god, were weeping. Kylie got into her car. The rain rapped onto the roof and splattered onto the windscreen. Everything blurred into the face of Neville Daimler, Head of Communications and her implacable enemy.

How childish was it all? Quite simply he hated her because she was more intelligent and better educated than he was. She was a threat. Kylie turned on the windscreen wipers and Daimler's face melted into an arc of liquid. Today it was all about equipment. Tomorrow it would be something else. She'd written her story about particle detection on local beaches, but it had caused trouble. Her good news story had been that the new improved radioactive particle detection equipment finds more particles, therefore people can feel secure that their interests and welfare are being protected. The trouble was that the old monitoring vehicles hadn't detect all the particles, just those with a high enough radioactive level. So in the past people had felt *more* secure, because results told them there were fewer particles! Now that the monitoring equipment was better many more radioactive particles were being discovered. Surely this was good? No, this was bad. People were now claiming they had been misinformed or just plain lied to. The local paper ran stories, week after week, about leukaemia and other cancer clusters.

She had pointed this out to him earlier in the afternoon. That was a mistake. What she had done, although she did not realise it until she had walked out of his office, was to disarm him. By expressing the moral bind the absurdity of the monitors placed them in, she had challenged and offended his authority as her line manager, implying that she did not trust him. She had as good as told him that she had no confidence in him, and that he was a coward to deny the problem. The result was he hated her. He hated her already but this only gave him proof for his theory that she was a smart-arsed Oxford-educated bitch.

He had this habit of sharpening pencils when he was anxious. Daimler was anxious a lot. A big mug full of spear-pointed pencils sat quiver-like on his desk.

"Aye, well, that was then but this is now," he had said as he looked at her copy. "We'll run it but we have to have our disclaimers in from the start. We're not to be held to account by the decisions of previous managements." That was the standard line when the truth started to get hot. It's not our fault, it's the fault of some people twenty years ago for which we have no responsibility. It was a pathetic defence and everyone knew it. Everyone except Daimler, that is. He loved it.

He was a pathetic little man, really. That he was forceful she couldn't deny. That he was effective in "communicating"

Dounreay's mission she had to admit, although with Daimler it was always the image rather than the reality which concerned him. No, he was not just "concerned" with it: he was *obsessed* by the image of Dounreay. It was his ideology, or rather his imagology. Other than that, she reasoned, there was nothing to him – intellectually, politically, psychologically – nothing at all. She had never seen him actually *do* anything. He never wrote anything down, not that she had observed anyway. He never made coffee or tea – his secretary did all that for him. He never answered an email or returned a call. She had never met anyone like him before. Despite this, she recognised him in a way that had nothing to do with emotion, inheritance or history. This was what made him so dangerous. It was not that he cast no shadow; it was more that he had no presence, no *matter* if you like. When she walked into a room heads turned to look at her. When Daimler walked into a room he disappeared. But he did have an effect: like anti-matter, the dark matter in the universe scientists can't explain or measure; they just know it is there.

Daimler used to work for the local press, freelance at first then as a reporter on The Groat. She had heard that for years he'd had the reputation of being a thorn in the side of the UKAEA, constantly exposing them for their ineptitude and secrecy. Then one day the UKAEA recruited him. They gave him a job as Public Relations Officer, then promoted him so that now he had his own department. Small, admittedly – but it was his domain. During this time Daimler lost two stones in weight, his hair fell out, and his wife left him.

Kylie drove down Scrabster Brae into Atomic City. As she passed Lidl's it had stopped raining and the Sun was shining again. Hoy sat like a huge stone ship on the northern shore of the firth. Her reluctance to return to Atomic City wasn't all due to Daimler and his black leather fetish world of deceiving the deceivers. She had arranged to have dinner with her aunt Patreen and that was always an ordeal. Her aunt brought out the worst in her.

Patreen was her mother's younger sister, her surviving sister. As Kylie parked the car in Campbell Street behind the Pentland

Hotel the usual nervous fizz filled her stomach. Her aunt Patreen had a gift unequalled by any other living human being (including Daimler and Colin) for loading her with guilt. And it wasn't just because she had missed her mother's funeral. Patreen's antipathy was deeper than that – it was cultural conflict; sometimes just pure animal hostility.

From the polished heritage of its nineteenth-century revolving front door, Kylie spun into the foyer of the hotel. She looked around her, then guiltily down at her watch. Well dressed people sat at low tables drinking coffee. A full half-hour early! Timekeeping was not her strength, and she had to make doubly sure that she turned up on time for meetings. She had learned the hard way, once she left university, that turning up late was not "fashionable" it was just unprofessional. But she was never, *ever* early. She went through to the bar and ordered a large glass of white wine.

The place was getting busy. She sat at a table in a corner so she could see across the bar to the entrance and through a window out onto the street. Trying to calm down she concentrated on the other folk in the bar. Decommissioning contractors sat at tables and fiddled with their computer tablets and smart phones, pints of lager half drunk in front of them. A couple of families were laying siege to plates of fish and chips and bowls of ice cream. Couples were dotted around staring blankly into each others' eyes or out of the window. Occasionally someone laughed nervously. Had they just discovered the comic pointlessness of existence? Or that one of them (both of them?) was having an affair? Perhaps they laughed because the end of the story had been revealed to them, and they wanted to block the horror? A good-looking waiter with an Aberdeenshire accent brought over her drink. She sipped the cool fruity vanilla of France or Chile. No sign yet of Patreen with her dutiful attempts to mother her. Just what is the difference between adults and children anyway? Halfway down her glass of wine Kylie decided there was no difference at all. As the handsome waiter – from Fraserburgh, as it turned out – brought her a second large white wine Kylie had resolved that all people, both children and adults – and especially her aunt Patreen – were just individual egos, crazy in search of love. It was good wine.

By the time Patreen sat down beside her she was drunk. Her aunt was two years older now than her mother was when she died. The cause of her mother's death – leukaemia – was not uncommon in Atomic City. Across West Caithness, it was rife. Kylie knew of one family where two brothers had both lost their wives to leukaemia, and one of their sons had recently buried his young wife, another victim of the same cancer. This, of course, the Authority had explained away as they would do a prolonged period of bad weather. The gathering together in one place of many people from various and different origins – That was their current favourite hypothesis, with the qualification that "no one can be certain". Or it was an act of God – a strange formulation for a scientific establishment to come up with, better left to the witless minister who had blethered nonsense as each of the poor women was lowered into the ground. Either way the Authority was covered. The image was maintained. The nuclear imagologists were very thorough: they worked hard to change everything, while making it appear that everything stayed the same.

Through a Chardonnay haze Kylie looked at her aunt. Patreen and women like her – even her own mother – hadn't changed since the nineteen fifties. The imagology was perfect. In black and white photographs in the Authority museum she saw them walk the streets of the town, staring at the wonders in Lipton's shop window, or buying their brave new sons brand new school uniforms from Fred Shearer's clothes shop for the new term at the shining new school on the hill. No-one in the town had progressed into any kind of forward development.. Instead these people had moved from side to side both in time and dress code. It was as though they tried to fulfil the demands of history by avoiding reality. *But history has stopped here*, thought Kylie grimly. *No one is going to fight to free these people and get them to think – All they do here is dance from the back of the queue to the front and then to the back again.*

"Hello, auntie Patreen."

"You look terrible." Direct and unforgiving as always, Patreen sat down.

The (increasingly) attractive Fraserburgh waiter returned to ask Patreen whether she would like a drink. She hesitated before ordering a glass of water, but Kylie took the opportunity to arm herself with another glass of white. It seemed to Kylie that her aunt had landed firmly on her soul.

"It's been a long day, but it's good of you to point it out," she responded, gaily. "I mean, I haven't been insulted so thoroughly for oh, at least a month. Oh, I know – it was the last time I saw you."

"Oh Kylie, yer so vain." Patreen picked up the menu. "Can ye no understand concern when it's shown til e?"

"Oh, that's was what it was?"

The waiter brought the wine. Kylie watched him move back to the bar counter. *Probably a surfer in his spare time.* She sipped her wine.

"Morris said he'd been speakin til e the ither day."

"Uncle Morris? Oh, yes! I was on the beach with them briefly. They've got new equipment. I was told to write something for the paper."

Patreen raised her eyes from the menu, scanning her niece's face like a searchlight across a cliff. She hoped to pick out some clue to validate Kylie's existence. When she found none to her liking, she clicked off the searchlight.

"Aye. Morris says yer fairly gettan on."

"I do my best," said Kylie. *God, I can't even convince myself.*

"Are ye enchoyan yer chob?"

"It's the sort of occupation which could break your heart," said Kylie.

"Oh my." Patreen wasn't listening. The waiter came back to take their food order. "Aat canna be good fur e. I'll hev ay battered haddock. No chips. Choost salad."

Kylie ordered. Her eyes followed the waiter as hunger follows an American.

"Ay money'll be good, and aat's ay main thing," said Patreen, rearranging the cutlery. Kylie sipped her wine. It could have been mercury. *It'll go this way until it's ended.*

"I've been til ay doctor."

"Oh?"

"Aye. Inverness."

"Inverness? Raigmore?"

"Aye."

"Is there something..."

"Leukaemia. Choost lek Chrissie. Yer mither."

Kylie began to get a hangover. She stared at her aunt. *Oh you are so beautiful and ugly*, she thought. *Beautiful like my mother. Ugly like this place.*

"Oh Patreen. I'm sorry..."

"Och, id's common enough in Thirsa, as e know."

"But... but this is terrible!"

"Please, Kylie, keep yer voice doon. Folk are lookan." She reached across and pressed her niece's hands. They sat like that until the waiter brought the food. Kylie stared into her pasta, then looked up into her aunt's deep blue eyes. This time the searchlight was Kylie's. *She's terrified. No matter what she says she's terrified.*

"Ah've hed a good life. Ah canna complain. Ah believe in God an I've got Morris an mah two lassies an Ah thank him for aat."

"But you're too young, Patreen... I mean..."

"I'm fifty-seven." Patreen looked as if she had just realised it.

"Fifty-seven. Oh, auntie Patreen."

"It's only three years since yer mother was taken. Poor Chrissie. It's fittan, d'ye no think, aat wur goan ay same way?"

In many ways this came as a relief. For a moment Kylie had feared Patreen would launch into the usual tirade: what a bad daughter she was; that she hadn't even turned up for her own mother's funeral. Pointless to say she had spoken to her mother just days before her death; that she had been in the middle of her finals; that the day of her mother's funeral she had got so drunk and stoned that she almost drowned in the River Isis.

Instead, Kylie looked at her aunt and said nothing. Perchink morality and small-town evangelical anger left Patreen exposed, naked somehow like the branches of a winter tree suddenly abandoned by a crowd of chattering starlings. On the street outside people came and went. The last of the shift workers and contractors had gone home or to their digs or to the pub. The restaurant area was nearly full now. The Sun still burned down on Princes Street. A Stagecoach service bus with nobody on it raced purposefully by the window and off to Wick. The two women sat in silence.

"*I am become death, the destroyer of worlds*," said Kylie.

"I beg yer pardon?" said Patreen, startled.

"Robert Oppenheimer," Kylie replied dreamily.

"Dis he work at Dounreay?"

"Oh yes," smiled Kylie. "One of the first."

"They're all different oot ayr now," agreed Patreen.

"So, you've not come to remind me what a bad daughter I've been, a worse niece and a generally hopeless human being..."

Kylie stopped mid-flow, horrified at her habitual callousness.

"I'm so sorry, Patreen. I'm really sorry. Forgive me."

Patreen snorted.

"Aat's aal right, Kylie. Ee've aalweys been self-obsessed. Anyway, id's no ay leukaemia I wanted til talk til ye aboot. Weel, no entirely."

The restaurant was now very busy. The more Patreen tried to lower her voice so that she could not be overheard the more she had to raise it so that she could be heard at all.

"Id's aboot ay Nuclear Archive," she said, almost shouting. She pushed her plate away. She had hardly eaten a thing.

"What about it?"

"Ye've got something til do wae id, aye?"

"Well, I've got to try and sell it to the people of Caithness." Kylie stared at her pasta.

"Who generally dinna want id," said Patreen, trying to push the conversation forward.

"Well, they're not exactly dancing for joy at the prospect. They think the NDA, the government, is selling them a pig in a poke. That the whole thing is tokenism instead of real jobs, that it doesn't mean anything. And I can't really argue against that." Kylie tried to fork fusilli into her mouth but the wine and Patreen had killed off any trace of appetite.

"Weel," said Patreen, suddenly coming alive. "I think I can help ye there."

Kylie looked sceptically at her aunt. Red hair unceremoniously piled on top of her head, faint traces of make-up around her eyes and lips, Patreen looked exotic yet fragile, a fading image in a fresco on the wall of some small Italian chapel.

"You can help me? Really? How's that now?" The idea sounded ridiculous.

"Weel." Patreen sat forward doggedly. She had obviously been steeling herself for this.

"As ye know ay learnan centre I manage is... weel, ay building hes seen better days. Ay Cooncil is reluctant til bring id back up til standard. I've telt thum for years hids a new building wae need, boot they choost wave thur hands in ay air: *Wur far too small an ay cuts are far too beeg*. Ye know the story."

Kylie did know. She also knew she was too drunk for this conversation but she could see that Patreen was sincere, terrier-like, and not about to stop. She fought a sudden urge to kill her aunt, and concentrated.

"Aat's all I get: *Id's ay cuts.*" Patreen scrunched up her napkin.

"Don't you know there's a war on!" Kylie had aimed for solidarity but hit flippancy. Patreen could not disguise her disgust, but carried on.

"Ay Highland Cooncil blames Edinburgh an Edinburgh blames London and London blames Brussels."

"And who does Brussels blame?"

"The good Lord knows." Patreen sipped at her water.

"Well, I'll bet they don't blame the banks, the City of London or Wall Street, do they?" Kylie was authoritative. "Your education centre is part of the price we have to pay for all that fraud in 2008."

"Weel," said Patreen, "id seems til me that if e want til sell ay Nuclear Archive then e could include my learning centre intil yer plan. It wid be great PR for e, would it no? I mean, I thocht public relations wis supposed til be yer thing?"

"It's my *job*, Patreen. I wouldn't say it's my '*thing*'!"

"Weel, what do ye say?" Patreen was leaning forward again, her eyes like lasers.

"It's a brilliant idea!" Kylie was genuinely surprised. "I'll put it to the NDA at our next monthly meeting."

"Really?" Patreen was cautious, distrusting this uncharacteristic enthusiasm. "E'll do aat?"

"Of course. It makes perfect sense. As you say it'll help to sell the new archive to both central and local government. They'd willingly spend well over the odds for a partnership, even though it would be cheaper to do it themselves. Maybe it'll help with the folk round here but I have my doubts." Kylie gestured to the people in the restaurant. "All you need to do is to put a proposal together. One side of A4 only and get it to me as soon as you can."

Patreen said nothing, but nodded. Again the conversation fell silent. The waiter came and took the plates away. Kylie's glass was empty. She thought it would be better if it stayed that way.

"Id wid mean a lot til me, Kylie, if thur wis a brand-new learning centre in Caithness. A place where aal ay fowk could access educational opportunities." She fiddled with her purse. "Even if I'm no aroond till see id."

Instinctively, Kylie reached across the table and took her aunt's hands in her own.

"Don't worry, auntie Patreen. I'll do my best to make sure it happens. The costs can be absorbed easily in the Archive. The NDA are throwing money at this one."

Patreen was caught off-guard.

"Morris hes worked at Dounreay aal his life. Wae canna complain. Wae hev a good hoose, an wur twa lassies both went til university lek yersel. Thur off Sooth workan. Clair's a lawyer and Fiona's trainan til be a teacher lek mahsel. Morris wis determined they widna end up at Dounreay. Thirty years that man hes put in there. Aye, hae's got a pension – but ye never ken iss days whut wae banks, as ye said, bein what they are. Thirty years, Kylie, thirty years!"

Kylie felt her aunt's hands stiffen.

"Thirty years an id's aal bein buried in a hol in ay ground. Aal aat work – gone. An me... as good as gone."

Patreen withdrew her hands. Nothing in her life had prepared Kylie for this moment.

"Two sisters oot oh wan femly seems a high price til pay for an experiment, d'ye no think?" But she wasn't asking Kylie. Her question was for the invisible shades of history who follow each of us wherever we go and for those other occult beings who venture out in front of us, those silvery, wispy angels of fate who lead us irresistibly forward to our destiny yet who always insist that we are the unknowing, involuntary vehicles of their greater desire.

Then, as if her angels had deserted her, Patreen stood up.

"I better be going." She reached for her purse. Kylie put her hand back on her aunt's hand.

"No, auntie Patreen. Dinna ye dare!"

Patreen seemed to crumple slightly as she looked her niece in the eye.

"Ay doctor says I've got anither six months, mibbe a year."

Kylie bit her lip. Her sister used to tease her about the habit when they were girls. She'd done the same when she left her frock hanging on the railings on the beach promenade.

"Just give me your proposal and we'll get it done."

Patreen leaned over and kissed her niece on the cheek. Then she was gone, waving once as she disappeared onto Princes Street. Kylie sat down heavily; the waiter came over. He didn't look so attractive any more. Her world had shifted on its axis. Death had come closer.

"You OK?"

She paid the bill and left. She left her car in Campbell Street and walked back to the flat. Oh, that bloody stupid flat. It was in one of those pre-2008 schemes which littered Atomic City like an abandoned game of Monopoly cloned with giant's Lego. The block of flats was built into the back of an old flagstone quarry. Most of the flats were empty. The majority had never been occupied as they had never been sold. Most of the Dounreay contractors lived in the hotels or guest houses so somebody somewhere had made yet another miscalculation concerning decommissioning. Mr bloody smug-guts Harper might be right: "Nobody knows anything."

As she was about to step into the building she noticed some swifts, flying over the roof, in and out of the branches of the few sycamore trees which hung over the high wall separating the quarry development from the nearby merchant house gardens of the New Town. The birds were hunting insects, continuously manoeuvring in figure-eight swoops. Swifts spend more time in flight than any other bird and can even sleep on the wing. Somehow she knew that. Once the chicks hatch and fledge they can spend as much as three years in constant flight. These birds would be feeding up their young. Soon, as the Summer came to an end, they would fly to central and Southern Africa.

When he was younger, Colin had played for the Swifts, his local football team. Would they ever fly, the pair of them? Like these birds? To Africa – or anywhere? Did they have enough faith and courage? Or would they be forever earth-bound, plodding on the shore, picking wilks on the rocks? The two people who were Kylie Swanson climbed unsteadily upstairs, fumbled with her keys, and stumbled into her flat. That was the night she dreamed of the wave.

# 15

Across the sea Storegga and Jörð 's children, their love-wave, kept coming.

# 16

Fracher looked at Mags and sipped the rum she had bought him. Cushie sniffed about her legs. She patted the white head and marvelled at his deep dark eyes.

"Hae's cried Cushie. Collies are usually daft, boot hae's young yet and hae's good company."

"Cushie. That's a strange name."

"Aye, Ah spose id is," mused Fracher. "Id's Gaelic for fairy doug."

Music pouring in from the front bar mixed with the hubbub of human chatter and the tinny noise of the football commentary peppering out of the TV above Fracher's head. The dog took up his usual position at Fracher's feet.

"So e've been till the chapel, then?"

"Yes, I hope to excavate it after I've made a plan," said Mags.

"A plan is always a good thing," agreed Fracher. "Hev e spoken til Minker?"

"Minker? Who's he?"

"He owns ay land. Most oh ay heidland, in fact. E'll need til get permission from him afore ye do anything." Fracher downed the rest of his rum. Another one appeared on the counter in front of him. He reached for another bar stool and Mags sat down.

"Hevna been up ayr for many's a year. What's ay attraction?"

"The chapel's an unexplored site. I'm an archaeologist."

"So e want til make yer name, eh?" laughed Fracher. Mags blinked a little.

"Well...maybe. My friend Helen came across it last year when she was on holiday up here."

"Up here?" snorted Fracher. "If ye wis fae Faroe e'd be doon here. There's a load oh Faroese in Screbster. Up, doon. Id all depends on where yer standin."

The TV crackled a bit louder. There was a roar from a group of men behind them. A team had scored.

"Ay Huns aye make a lot oh bliddy noise aboot nuhain," grumbled Fracher.

"Sorry?"

"Rangers FC. Ay great unloved. How long e plannan til stay?"

"Well, I've got funding for three months, but I'm not sure, it depends," she stuttered.

"So what d'ye need me for exactly?" asked Fracher, fully focusing his dark brown eyes on her.

"I'm told you have a boat and that you know the sea, the firth, I mean."

"It's a tricky place, the Pentland Firth. I work creels, an god kens, e learn somethin new every day."

"The Irish priests would have come by sea, so I want to see what they saw first. Then there's the cave."

Fracher narrowed his eyes. Then a smile caught the corners of his mouth. "Oh aye, *Uamh an Oir*, the Cave of Gold." He drank some more rum.

"Exactly. What do you know of it?" asked Mags, encouraged by his sympathetic tone.

"No more than most folk."

"But what's that? Look, Mr Fracher, I'm from London, remember? I know nothing." She laughed nervously.

"Wae all ken nuhain, lassie. Boot anyway, there's a story oh a mermaid who loved this young loon and took him intil a cave til cure him oh his greed for money. Inside ay cave wis all ay riches an treasure from all ay ships ever wrecked in ay Pentland Firth. The mermaid chained him up til a rock so as he could enjoy ay wealth forever. Good story aat, d'ye no think?" Fracher laughed out loud for the first time since she had met him. Mags relaxed.

"So that's why it's called the Cave of Gold." Questions ran around inside her head like a herd of wild horses.

"Aye, id's a good story – Wan oh ay best. Money, sex an power – whit more d'ye want from a story? He's still in there, they say."

"Will we find him, d'you think?" She tried to match his light-heartedness.

"No for ay next twa days or so. Thurs a Sou-Easterly turnan til ay north. Id'll blow right from Duncansby til Dinnad Heid."

"Ah, the weather," said Mags.

"Wae live an die by id here." Fracher looked to the bar door. "If ay wind blows ay door oh ay Comm open Ah dinna go til my creels. Simple as aat."

Mags wanted to ask him more about the cave but something told her to save it for another time.

"Hev ye got somewhere til stay?"

"Not exactly. I've booked a B & B for three nights. After that I don't know. I thought I'd wait and see how I got on."

"Ye could stop wae me, boot id's mebbe a bittie roch for yer taste. That's anither good reason for speakan til Minker. He's got anys amount of cottages and chalets an what no."

Fracher scratched his head so that his bonnet slipped forward slightly. Mags could see he was getting fed up with the conversation.

"Where does he live?" she asked.

"Minker? Oh, he's ay fool on ay hill. The House of the Northern Gate." Fracher laughed, aping the RP pomposity of the fool on the hill, from Kent. "He lives in ay beeg white hoose on the top oh Dwarick Heid. Ay Hoose oh ay Northern Gate. E'll hev seen id if e've been up that way. Ay locals call id Ay Hoose oh ay Northern Git. When he first came here he thocht he wis ay rich man in his castle and ay poor – ay fowk oh Dinnad – were at his gate. Boot hae underestimated the common grazins committee.

When he tried til stop them cuttan peat or keepan their sheep on ay hill hae soon fun oot that ay crofters kent ay law. He didna."

"How long ago was that?" asked Mags. Dunnet had seemed to her quite suburban.

"Oh, ower twenty year ago, Ah'd say. Aat's when there wis crofters in Dinnad. Damned few oh thum now. No school, shop or post office. Nuhain. No, id's Dounreay Commutersville oot ayr now. Boot Minker still sits in splendid isolation in his beeg hoose on ay hill. Aye, mebbes wae are staggeran til ay new republic efter all."

The TV above their heads crackled out more information and the men behind them roared and shouted some more. The collie sat up straight but Fracher's familiar hand reassured the animal and it relaxed to the floor.

"Game ower. Rangers lost. Good end til Wednesday," said Fracher.

"I don't know..." Mags mumbled as she looked about her. This was a strange world. Maybe this was all a mistake. Fracher must have sensed her discomfort.

"Look, give me yer phone number on a bittie oh paper," he said. "I'll ring ye sometime ay morn an tell e when I can take e oot. Mind on, id's aal weather-dependent."

She wrote her name and number on a page of her notebook, ripped it out and handed it to him. He stuffed it into a pocket of his jacket.

"Mind an go an see Minker ay morn. His number's in ay phonebook. Hae's an erse boot hae's comparatively hermless these days."

Mags realised she was exhausted. She wanted to ask him about the Cave of Gold, about the Pentland Firth, about all sorts of things, but all she could think about was sleep.

"You're very kind, Mr Fracher. I..."

"Look, ay name's Fracher. Aat's id. Everybody kens me an e ken where til find me. If I'm no here I'm doon at ay herbour. I hev ay croft on ay top oh Holborn Heid choost above ay lichthoose.

Yer welcome til come an hev a blether any time e lek. If I can help e, I will."

"Thank you," was all she could muster. They shook hands, which tickled Fracher and made him laugh again. Cushie rose up and forced his head into her hands. Mags patted the dog's head automatically.

"My my, yer a formal sort oh craiter," he said. "But ay doug leks e."

Mags gathered up her bag and pushed her way through the crowd which, like herself, was leaving. Outside she relished the tangy salt air of Olrig Street and the soft cooling rain.

That night she slept between Mrs Calder's functional sheets and dreamed of mermaids, priests and shipwrecks, all to the sound of the pipe tune she had heard in The Comm. When she awoke it was as if she had emerged from a cave: not golden perhaps, but shining with the strange light of a new world, a world that had been destroyed but had somehow been rebuilt. When she looked out of the bedroom window Atomic City was covered by a thick fog. *Where*, she thought, *is Fracher's Sou-Westerly?*

After yet another Caithness fry to "build her up" – as Mrs Calder was fond of saying – Mags drove out of town towards Dunnet. As time and distance progressed and the Sun grew higher in the eastern sky, the landscape revealed itself in shades of flagstone. Past Dunnet Links which stretched out behind the dunes the fog lifted revealing the sandstone hulk of Dunnet Head and behind it a long yellow strip of light. She rolled down the windows and listened intently to the surf breaking onto the beach, the crashing orchestra of it filling her ears and the salt taste of it on her tongue.

She turned off the main village road and headed up the lighthouse road, then veered off and up to the Westside. She could see the unmistakeable House of the Northern Gate: white, squat and Gothic on its redoubt on the summit of Dwarick Head. The retreating mist swirled above its blue slate roof, casting shadows like twisted figures onto the heather hill, then bouncing back up into the misty cloud again. But the lengthening light of the morning was winning and the world grew happier.

She parked her car in the same place she had yesterday at the end of the road and at the foot of the driveway. She climbed over the locked gate and walked up to the impressive white house. When she had phoned Minker earlier there was no answer, not even an answering machine message which she thought was odd. That was before she'd had breakfast. She tried again as she had got into her car. Still no answer, but she had decided to go out and to try and see him anyway. Now, as she walked closer to the house she could see a green four-by-four parked outside a double garage. A sizeable but neglected garden of shrubs and small terraces folded itself into the side of the hill. Below her, as the mist burned off, she could see the washed steeple of the village kirk signalling white to the yellow sand of the long curving beach. Up a track beyond the village a tractor was approaching a field of hay.

A set of six steps led up to the large blue double-door. When Mags pulled on the large brass bell-pull handle she was reminded of playing a huge pinball machine or one-armed bandit. The chain of the bell-pull extended to almost a foot. She heard nothing, no bell or buzzer, just the sound of the distant surf and the lonely cry of a curlew. After a full two minutes she tried again. One half of the door opened.

Humphrey Thaddeus Minker, all five feet five of him, looked out from the inner mirk of his domain and from beneath a green, floppy canvas hat which bore the legend "Fishbones".

"Ah, Miss Beaton, I was wondering when you would call. Please, do come in." He pulled the door wide, stood to one side and ushered her in.

Shyly, Mags stepped into a well-lit high hallway of potted plants and wall-mounted antlers. Glass cases with stuffed birds of prey occupied shelves in an alcove. A broad stairwell swept upwards from the back of the hall. To the right an open door led into a sitting room.

"Mr Minker, I hope I'm not disturbing you?" she began.

"Not at all. As I say I've been half expecting you. Come through, do." He showed her through the open door into the large sitting-room. A broad window looked out over the bay and down to the village. A large flat-screen TV with the volume turned down flickered anachronistically on an antique table in a corner.

"Terrible thing television, is it not, Miss Beaton? But I'm afraid I'm addicted to Jeremy Kyle. Do you follow him?" He switched off the TV.

"Well, not..."

"No," said Minker, looking at her with interest. "I suppose anthropologists and psychiatrists would be more interested in the zoo old Jeremy is the keeper of, eh? An archaeologist like yourself, now that's an altogether different kettle of fish, is it not? Do sit down, if you can find a seat. The old place is a bit untidy since the old woman Oag passed on. Can't get anybody to do for me locally. Damned nuisance. If they're not dead they're retired nuclear physicists – No use for hoovering. A drink?"

"No, no thanks," said Mags, clearing space on a chaise-longue strewn with yachting magazines. "It's a bit early."

"Is it?" Minker sounded genuinely surprised. "Take my advice. Avoid the Jeremy Kyle Show – brings on a terrible craving for gin. Don't mind if I have a snifter, do you? I've been up since five so this is practically lunchtime." He pulled down the lid of a mahogany cabinet and poured himself a gin and tonic with ice from an ice bucket, clearly not the first gin and tonic of the morning. Scooping up a huge grey cat which lay curled on a battered old armchair, he deposited it gently onto a cushion on the floor and sat down amidst the cat hair.

"Poor old Dennis is not what he once was." Minker sat back and crossed his legs, turned expectantly to Mags and raised his glass.

"How do you know my name, Mr Minker?"

Minker laughed.

"Miss Beaton, the whole *parish* knows who you are, where you came from and what you propose to do."

"But how? I've only just arrived."

Minker swallowed some of his gin.

"The question is 'how could they possibly *not*?' People come up here thinking they can get away from it all, become anonymous, indulge a secret passion. It's very comical. Within a day here, everything that is to be known is known by everyone. Strangers don't blend in here. They stick out like a sore thumb. But I must say I am intrigued about your project. Do tell me more. Don't be shy."

*Who was he to press these questions*? Mags felt annoyed. For a moment she saw Fracher's "Git", the Fool-on-the-Hill, King-of-All-He-Surveyed; relaxed, arrogant, and pissed by ten in the morning.

"I have a small research grant for three months from the London School of Economics. My plan is to do an archaeological survey of the chapel on the headland. Maybe next year we can undertake a dig there."

Minker remained strangely quiet. Was he surprised – maybe she'd contradicted what he'd heard on the Caithness jungle drums? Or was it that he couldn't care less? Either way she suspected he was filtering her information, separating what was superfluous from what might benefit him. Recalling Fracher's description, Mags realised the kind of person she was dealing with. This was a monster.

"And to do this, to get access to the site, you need my permission, as I am the landowner? Correct?"

"Correct." Mags smiled. Minker smiled back at her.

"Interesting name, Beaton. Scottish, is it not?" It struck Mags that he might just be very lonely. He was enjoying this conversation because it gave him some power, and he was relishing that.

"My father's Scottish. Mother's English. From London. Like me."

"Are they archaeologists as well?"

"They're both doctors."

"How fascinating. Of course, you know about the Beaton's, don't you?"

"Not much. Dad didn't do family history. I know he's from Glasgow and that he has a sister there, my aunt Mary. Other than that we don't have any relations left. None that I know of."

"I was thinking more of Skye, actually." Minker got up and walked over to the cabinet. "Sure I can't tempt you?" He raised his empty glass.

"No, no thanks." The very idea of gin after Mrs Calder's fry-up made her nauseous. Minker poured himself a generous measure, mixed in his tonic and ice. He crossed the room and looked out of the window.

"Yes, the Beatons..." He continued as if he were addressing a meeting. "They were hereditary physicians to the Chiefs of the Clan MacDonald. In Islay originally, and then later in Skye – Sleat to be precise. They were herbalists. More alchemists than what we would recognise as medical."

"Do you study Scottish history?" Mags asked. No answer. She looked around the room. Some books, but not many. Newspapers piled amongst the yachting magazines – the *Daily Telegraph* mostly. Some white Greek figurines sat lonely on dark shelves.

"I'm fascinated by everything," Minker turned at last from the window to focus his gaze on his young guest. "History, Scottish or otherwise, is just part of the great wave."

"The great wave?"

"The wave that washes over all of us, over everything, constantly, eternally. It brings us here. It washes us away."

Mags was confused. *The Git was no fool. Was he just playing games? She shouldn't be so quick to judge. He looks quite sad.* She was still considering how to respond to this profundity, when a shrill voice in the hallway spared her.

"Ta-aa-day!"

Minker stiffened. He snatched off the *Fishbones* hat and threw it behind a chair. His hair was thin with a ginger echo highlighted in the light from the window, which also illuminated his moustache. He became alert, like a large cat.

"Ta-aa-day! Where the hell are you? Thaddeus!" the voice cried out.

"My wife," warned Minker confessionally, with an air of resignation.

A tall, slender woman in a yellow tweed suit burst through the door. She looked younger than her husband by maybe ten years.

"Oh there you are! I've just been talking to Sanders about re-stocking the loch. You really must pay more attention, Taddy, or the whole place will go to the dogs. That man is so fond of whisky – I had to drink four large drams with him before he made any sense."

Mrs Minker slumped onto another chaise-longue by the door. Mags could not take her eyes off this apparition. The well-worn beautifully cut yellow suit hinted at faded glamour, for this was still a beautiful woman, but it also made her look like an overgrown budgie. She lay back on the chaise-longue and rested her head.

"My god, I'm pissed!" She seemed to have just realised the state she was in.

"Babs, darling, we have company," said Minker, trying to take control of the situation. His wife raised her head slightly.

"Really," she said sleepily. "Who on earth comes to see one at this time of night?"

"It's almost mid-day, old girl. You've been too busy in the bothy with the ghillie."

"I was attending to our bloody business, actually," she reminded him. "Oh, Taddy, you're such a clot when it comes to anything practical."

"My dear, our guest is sitting directly across from you." He leaned over and whispered something.

"A what?" she exclaimed.

"An archaeologist."

"My god!"

This information obviously upset her in some way, and so profoundly that she rolled right off the chaise-longue and fell with a dull thud onto the dusty wooden floor. The impact seemed to revive her. She got to her knees and adjusted her hair, which she wore perched on her head. She propped her elbows on the chaise longue and peered short sightedly across the room towards Mags. Instinctively, and to make herself bigger, Mags stood up.

"Darling, this is Mags Beaton. She's up from London, from the LSE, no less. Mags, this is my wife, Lady Barbara Minker."

Minker relaxed into his habitual courtesy. Lady Barbara pulled a pair of battered glasses from her pocket – the fold-up type sold at airports and supermarkets – and fiddled to unfold them as she got to her feet. Moving round the chaise-longue, glasses now skewed on her nose, she focused on Mags. Mags stepped towards the bright yellow figure and put out her hand. Lady Barbara shook it firmly.

"Pleased to meet you, my dear. I'm sorry I'm a bit pissed. Occupational hazard with gamekeepers."

Mags smiled. "Pleased to meet you, Lady Barbara."

"Oh for god's sake, call me Babs. Thaddeus here is very keen on titles, as only those who do not possess them are. My daddy owned swatches of Yorkshire. All coal mines and dark satanic mills. Only there are no mills nor mines left. Land rich, cash poor. Poor old Taddy. He backed the wrong filly when he married me. Good job he did all right at the used car business, eh Taddy? He doesn't like to talk about that. Is this your first time in Caithness?"

All of this with hardly a pause. Taddy looked as if someone had just shot his dog. Or Dennis the cat.

"No, I was up in October." Then, because they both were staring at her, "Just for a recce."

"How long do you plan to stay?" asked Lady Barbara. Mags was disconcerted by the Minkers' compulsion to control the conversation.

"Oh, some weeks. I'm not sure," she mumbled.

"She has a three months research grant," piped up Minker, like a little boy.

"Clever girl," smiled Lady Barbara. "And where are you staying? Forgive all the questions – It's just a delight for us to have such a bright and oh so pretty English girl with us here. The natives are so sullen and unco-operative. Full of grievances and introspection. They resent everything you do. You know they even have their own laws up here. It's quite preposterous! That pseudo parliament in Edinburgh that pretends to govern, sitting on their fat derrières, it only encourages them. It's a disgrace! Why we indulged them with that the Lord only knows. We just can't go about our business properly because of it. Oh but my dear, do forgive me. Here am I rabbiting on and we were discussing where you are going to live, were we not?"

"Were we?" Mags asked, quite overwhelmed and ready to make her excuses.

"Yes, of course we were!" insisted Lady Barbara. "I imagine you are staying in some quite dreadful dingy B & B in Thurso with some frigid fat old crone feeding you dripping instead of marmalade. God, they'll bleed you through the eyes in that nuclear slum, I can assure you. No, no, we cannot be having that." She turned to her husband. "Why don't we put her in the salmon bothy, Taddy? It's not occupied at the moment." She turned back to Mags before he had a chance to answer. "It's a bit Spartan for tourists, not that we go out of our way to encourage that sort of thing."

"No, no really... I... I couldn't..." stuttered Mags. This was like being swallowed by wet sand.

"It has running water and electricity. There's an open fire where you can burn driftwood of an evening. We can let you have some peats. Bloody cold at nights, I can assure you. It's right by the shore. It's perfect for you. It will be good for us to have someone decent staying in the place for a bit. We'll only charge you a fraction of what you're paying now. Leave your number and I'll get Sanders to telephone you tomorrow. What could be better than that?" asked Lady Barbara in firm conclusion.

Mags searched for just one of a hundred ways to decline politely this unexpected and kind but patronising offer. Lady Barbara was not used to rejection.

"You're very kind. I think..."

Lady Barbara sensed her reluctance. "Don't worry. Nobody will bother you, we will make sure of that. I think you can even get a phone signal down there, can't you Taddy?"

"I do believe you can," said Minker, brightening again, "Would you like to stay for lunch? It's only cold cuts I'm afraid but it is supposed to be Summer. Even in Caithness they have a Summer."

"No, really, thank you. I have an appointment in Thurso at one o'clock," lied Mags. It didn't sound convincing even to herself. "At the college."

"Busy girl." Lady Barbara sat back down on her chaise longue.

"I still haven't explained why I came," said Mags. "It's about permission to access the chapel site."

"Well, you have permission. No problem about that, is there darling?" said Minker looking across at his wife.

"Not at all."

"The thing is, and believe me I'm very grateful," said Mags, "but the LSE needs it in writing. It's one of the protocols they insist on."

"That's perfectly understandable," said Minker being perfectly understandable. "A mere formality. I'll have a letter for you tomorrow. Sanders will give it to you when you come to look at the salmon bothy."

"What is there to look at?" Lady Barbara lay back at ease on the chaise-longue. "It is the perfect place for a creature like her. God knows, if I were a poet or something, that's where I would like to be: alone down there by the sea."

"Yes, quite." Minker snorted softly as Lady Barbara fell into a gentle dwam. "The old girl's quite right. The salmon bothy will be the perfect place for you. It's out of the town and close to the chapel. The hotel's just up the road. Perfect. And don't worry about the rent. As long as you keep the place tidy that will be enough for now. We can come to some other arrangement later if necessary."

Mags thanked him, genuinely relieved to have sorted two of her immediate problems. She was about to say as much to Lady Barbara, but her night-long encounter with the ghillie had taken its toll and she was now sleeping peacefully.

Minker escorted her through the hall and to the door. The day was now bright and sunny as they stepped out into it. The bright blue of the sea in the bay contrasted with the white sand on the beach, leaving a large smile stretching to the eastern horizon and a patchwork of fields. Mags stood still for a moment to drink it all in.

Minker watched her, aware of the impact of the panorama.

"The locals don't appreciate the beauty you are seeing. And the incomers don't give a damn about it one way or the other. The only thing that concerns them is the price of their houses. That's why they are all so vehemently against wind turbines. Then there are the ones who want another nuclear reactor, God help us. But the truth is they're all trapped here in Dunnet. The financial collapse has made them prisoners."

"Does it not affect you in the same way?"

"Oh, most certainly. It affects everyone. But we are quite literally above it all up here. We have the big house, the loch, the heather moors and the headland. We came here a long time before the crash and we're not going anywhere until the Grim Reaper calls. Isn't that obvious?"

Mags could see it *was* obvious. Minker and Lady Barbara had come to the place where Scotland stopped and could go no further. They had run out of solid land as much as they had run out of both time and purpose. They had come to a place that was beyond money.

Minker kissed her theatrically on the cheek before she set off up the gravel driveway back to her car. His breath wafted distilled Juniper and death.

As she drove down through Dunnet, the steeple of the old kirk beat out in the sunlight with the white pulse of life.

# 17

The jeweller held the ring up to the light which poured in through the window. Manson could hear the noise of the Edinburgh traffic intensify in the street outside as the morning wore on. Even the sunlight seemed to grow lighter. He realised he was sweating and his mouth was dry. The jeweller took a short lens out of a drawer, put it to his eye and examined the pearl. After a moment he spoke softly, under his breath.

"This is quite incredible."

He set the ring and the lens carefully on the counter. Abruptly he stood up, crossed the shop to lock the door, and pulled down the small window blind. The new gloom suited Manson's mood. The jeweller came back to the counter, pulled down a lamp and switched it on. He picked up the ring and the lens. He looked at it again, more closely, as if his eye was about to consume the object. After a time he took the lens from his eye.

"This item should be in a museum."

"Should it really?"

Ignoring Manson's flippant tone, the jeweller held up the ring up so that light sparkled around it.

"The pearl I can't be sure about at the moment but the silver ring, the patterning, the quality of the smith-work – this must be at least, oh, twelve hundred years old. Very early medieval. Irish maybe. God, it could even be Pictish. Where the hell did you get it?"

"It's been in the family. I inherited it," lied Manson.

The jeweller sat down, placing the ring gently back on the

counter. He turned to a computer on his left and tapped into it for several minutes, scanning the screen and humming to himself. Then he looked up at Manson.

"This piece is not recorded."

"Recorded? What do you mean?" asked Manson, beginning to panic.

"Here, look." The jeweller swivelled the screen around so that Manson could see it.

Photographs of silver brooches, chains and other stuff Manson wasn't sure of.

"See this." The jeweller clicked on an image of a brooch. "This was found on St Ninian's Isle in Shetland. It dates from around 800 AD. See the markings on the side? Well, your ring is much the same except the torque has been pushed together to form a ring. The mounting has been added and reworked to hold the pearl. I reckon its late seventeenth century but I'm not an expert."

"What about the pearl?" Manson was feeling extremely nauseous.

"The pearl? I dunno. It's probably not fresh water. Probably not even European. By the size and colour I would say it's from the Pacific. But that's just an educated guess."

"How much do you think its worth?" Manson knew his voice was nervous, impatient. The jeweller leaned back in his chair. He looked witheringly at Manson, as if he were a piece of rhinestone not worth his time.

"Well, it's priceless. Like I say, it should be in a museum. Do you have proof of ownership?"

Manson said again that it had been in his family for years.

"Don't bother. Nobody has a piece like this in their family, not even the Queen. Where did you get it?"

Manson had a strong urge to punch the man. Instead he banged his fist on the counter.

"A mermaid gave it to me! What the hell does it matter! Are you going to buy it or not?!"

The jeweller hadn't flinched, just laughed softly.

"Well, the thing is old son, I'd better. Because you won't be able to sell it. There are laws of Treasure Trove in Scotland, you know."

"No, I don't know." Manson was still shouting. "And I don't care!"

"I'm not a pawnbroker!" The jeweller was getting angry himself.

"Look." Manson tried to calm down, "I was told you were a man I could do business with, that you buy stuff."

"Oh I am, and I do," agreed the jeweller. "But I've never seen anything quite like this, not in my hand anyway. This ring is ancient. That's all I'm saying."

"You think I'm a crook?" sneered Manson.

The jeweller got up, moved to the window, and glanced under the blind out into the street.

"If I thought that I would have phoned the police myself. No, you're not a criminal." He turned to face Manson. "No, my friend, what you *are* is desperate, and desperate men make me uneasy. In my honest opinion you are dangerous wherever you go, whoever you deal with."

Manson was chilled by the jeweller's words.

"I'm not dangerous," he said flatly, and slumped onto the jeweller's chair. He stared at the picture of the brooch from St Ninian's Isle. The jeweller, a tall man whose ginger moustache which was greying at the edges, moved back to the counter, joining Manson companionably beside the screen.

"They are some of the most beautiful silver objects in the world," he said lovingly.

"Yes," sighed Manson. "How much?"

"I'll give you twenty-five thousand." Ginger was alert again.

"Forty!" snapped Manson.

"Thirty!" snapped back the jeweller. "And that's as far as I'm going."

"I can go somewhere else."

"You're welcome to try. Nobody will buy it."

"You can sell it on," insisted Manson. The jeweller said nothing. Manson sensed he was growing impatient and wanted him out of his shop.

"Cash."

"I can do cash..." said the jeweller slowly, glancing at a grandfather clock which stood guard in a corner. "...but that will take me a couple of hours."

"I can wait."

"Maybe you can. But you don't like it." The jeweller, his gaze fixed on the grandfather clock, warmed to his theme. "I suspect waiting kills you. Like all opportunists you're tired of time. You'll rush around in a blind fog until you're dead."

"I don't care what you think." Manson stood up.

"No, you don't and that is a fact." The jeweller turned to face Manson. "Meet me in Rutherford's in Drummond Street at three o'clock."

"A pub? Is that the best place? I'd rather –"

"Believe me," interrupted the jeweller, "it's by far the best place. No one will disturb us there and I don't want you back in this shop. Ever!"

The jeweller's tone brooked no argument. Manson looked at him closely for the first time. Late fifties. Distinguished-looking. Someone he could like given different circumstances. Manson was fascinated by his skin. Same colour as old newspaper. He thought he could see the jeweller age right before his eyes.

"What if I have more items?"

"Keep them. I know who sent you. Look, friend, just go." He moved to the door, unlocked and opened it.

Manson picked up the ring and put it in his pocket.

Outside in the bright light of July on the Southside of Edinburgh. Lunchtime. Nicolson Street was busy. Buses droned back and forth in columns; black taxis darted among the commercial traffic and cars. People poured in and out of the many fast food shops. Students, Muslims and mixed-race shoppers sat together at plastic tables in the Mosque kitchen in Nicolson Square eating cheap curries and talking into mobile phones. Nicolson Street snaked off south-east in the direction of Dalkeith.

A strange place, the Southside, thought Manson. No factories like in Gorgie, no financial centre like in the West End, just loads of little shops and an economy dominated by the University. Outside one of the many Asian shops which were a bright highlight of the area he marvelled at the purple of a pile of aubergines stacked high amongst exotic vegetables and fruit. He walked amongst the people and felt like skeollag in the barley.

He walked down to the edge of the square where another shop with a similar pile of aubergines graced the corner. He thought about the Maighdeann Mhara. When she had given him the ring she had not said what he was supposed to do with it. *This is for the apples*, she had said. She looked so beautiful that day. Then there was the next day. And the day after. Many, many days – until she filled him like light. But in the end he had looked at the ring one afternoon and knew exactly to do with it.

He took it into Thurso. At Sinclair the jeweller the woman behind the counter had handed it back to him. *The pearl might be worth something.* She'd been non-committal. Home in Dunnet that night he'd been mesmerised by the Moon as he'd lain in bed, gazing through the bare window, up into the South-East sky. Like a fat luminescent Chinaman. A cosmic Alfred Hitchcock. He'd always loved the Moon. It was stunning and beautiful and unexpected. But now it made him afraid. Because it was all of that and because he was weak, and the Moon reminded him of just how weak he was. How impossible his life was. He had stared at the pearl glowing white and silver on his bedside table. Another Moon, with a beautiful but eerie light of its own. In that moment, as he plunged under the covers desperate for sleep, he'd hated the ring, hated and the Moon, and most of all he'd hated himself.

Now here he was in Edinburgh, foolish and poor and killing himself. He felt crushed by beauty, by its memory and possibility. He thought he saw the Moon in an aubergine. The Moon was a memory in his hair.

"How much?"

Gilbert Henderson looked at the ring dangling from his pinkie and shrugged. "Four hundred pounds? I dunno. Maybe more. It depends."

He had gone to see Gilbert at the Groat Office. Just about the only person Manson liked unreservedly, Gilbert owed him. He had helped Gilbert once with a story. Gilbert needed confirmation. No one would supply. Manson supplied. It had been with a lie. But hey! Sometimes lies are beautiful.

"Lend me four hundred quid, Gilbert."

Gilbert didn't even ask what it was for. He scrutinised the ring.

"Nice silver. Steal it, did you?"

"No."

"Pity. I have an idea for a novel I might write," said Gilbert, "It's about a man in prison. A man who isn't me."

"We're all in prison," said Manson, gloomily.

"Yeah, yeah, yeah. Ok. We'll go to the cash machine and then you'll buy me a pint."

And that was it. Later that day Manson had bought his train ticket. And here he was, staring at aubergines, contemplating the biggest mistake of his life. But he wasn't to know that then. How could he? Mistakes grow gradually, like weeds and everything else. They weave into a mass so that one error, an individual action, becomes indistinguishable from the collective wrongness. There he was on the street in Edinburgh and all he could see was Caithness.

Suddenly and without warning the sky darkened. It started to rain. Little globules of water which formed on the aubergines reminded Manson of the pearl he had in his pocket. An elderly man in a turban came out with lengths of brown paper to protect the fruit and vegetables.

"You going to buy, sir?"

"No." Manson had made up his mind. "I'm going to sell."

He moved away and walked down to Drummond Street. There was Rutherford's, just across from the sex shop and the barber's. He went in. There were a few people gathered round the island bar. Manson bought a pint and sat down. He looked around him. Strange how the earth blows everything in and out. The people in the bar, just ordinary people, workers maybe, a few tourists, they reminded him of the rocks at the Peedie Sannie. The way the water ran on and off the stones, again and again. He took a long drink from his pint. A man came in carrying a small case.

"So," said the jeweller sitting down. "Do you still want to do this?"

Manson nodded. The jeweller set the small case on the table in front of them. Manson reached into his pocket, fingering the ring. For a split second the noise in the bar was gone – drowned out by a roar, the surge of sea water. Unnerved, his hand shook, but he handed over the ring. The jeweller drew a tiny wooden box from his jacket pocket, matter of factly deposited the ring, and shoved the box deep into another pocket. They sat like that for a moment. A waitress, without any instruction that Mason saw, brought over a large glass of red wine and set it on the table in front of the jeweller. Her cheap scent hung on the air. The jeweller picked up the glass and supped.

"I have a boat on the water of Leith," he said. "You're more than welcome, anytime. There's more to life than all of this."

He flicked open the small case and waved his hand dismissively over ten bundles of twenty-pound notes in one hundred and fifty measures. If he hadn't before, Manson now hated his life. He forced himself to speak.

"Is that it?"

"To the last twenty,"

The door opened and a blaze of sunlight brightened the dingy bar. As the door slammed shut again, Summer seemed to go with it.

"... on my boat. The trip's next week if you're interested." The jeweller had started speaking again, but Manson had lost concentration, thrown by this new chill. He felt abandoned by light and warmth.

"You said you didn't want anything to do with me. That I hadn't to come back into your shop."

The jeweller's icy hand touched his. Manson stood up, knocked over his drink, grabbed the case and ran. He was half-way across the Meadows before he stopped and laughed out loud. Pedestrians and cyclists made a detour to avoid him. *That's what happens when you meet Death and discover you're not ready to go. So he wasn't ready yet after all to cross that particular river.* He ran.

At the whalebone arch he stopped running. "*Welcome to Shetland, 1886.*" What was he doing? Could you call this a nervous breakdown? He turned and ran back into Middle Meadow Walk. The ghost of the Spring blossom swayed behind him as he ran. When he reached the old Royal Infirmary he ran out of breath. He watched tourists go hither and thither before wandering slowly up to the traffic lights.

He went into the first pub he saw, ordered a pint, sat down and drank it in two gulps. So he wasn't dead! He started to laugh again. Hysteria wasn't far off when he remembered the small case, now on a chair beside him. What the hell was he going to do? Moreover, just what the hell had he done? For two seconds he panicked. Then he let go. Then panicked again. Relief and stress flushed through him in alternate waves. *Ok, he wasn't dead. But his running days were over, and he didn't have stamina for this.* He bought another pint. *What about going home? But home had changed.* He peeked at the money. *Everything had changed. At home he was poor. Right now he was in Edinburgh with £30k in used notes. Maybe I won't go home.* The tug-of-war went on until finally, exhausted, his mind and body colluded to achieve something revolutionary: Manson relaxed.

It was obvious. He wasn't that cheap. He *had to* go home. He had to get his landscape back. He had to see her again. There was a wave breaking in him and he had to make sure he was on the right shore when it did. The pub seemed to fill with the sound and the smell of the sea. For one heart-stopping moment he convinced himself he could see her. He shot out of his seat, but she wasn't there amid the throng of students and tourists who were listening to folk musicians in a corner.

"Are you a musician?" The American accent was insistent, and a couple pushing past to reach the exit prevented him from reaching his seat in time to ignore it.

"No," he said, as rudely as possible. "I'm a Presbyterian."

"Really?" squealed the voice. "Where I come from they're all black."

"Well, I'm *not* a musician." *God, what next?*

"It's just, I saw the case and I thought it might be a violin."

Manson looked at the case. The voice was right – it *could* hold a violin – or a ukulele, maybe. He sighed.

"Well, no ... But right now I wish it *was* a bloody fiddle."

He was about to ask the girl who owned the voice to piss off, when she waved at a tall blond man who'd just strode into the bar.

"Pardon me." She flashed a smile as she turned to join her friend. "Have a great evening."

Manson was flying through the air. He was sitting in a pub in Thurso. He was still in the pub in Edinburgh. Reality spun into a sequence of broken images, an asteroid belt rather than a planet. An ugly man in a short-sleeved shirt was talking into a mobile phone. Voices hectored each other about football, pop music, jobs, holidays, sex. They all flew past him like bits of hot exploding metal.

"You're all radiation roustabouts!" He was shouting. "You're all slaves! Fools! You're all going to die!"

But no one heard him. Lights flashed and colours flooded the space around him. The folk music stopped as the musicians turned to stare at him. The crowd at the bar parted like the Red Sea and a young hipster Moses emerged through the gap.

"You all right, pal?"

Manson spoke but made no sense.

Moses persisted. "Are you drunk?"

An older woman bustled forward, intent on taking charge.

"He looks too well-dressed to be a drunk."

Manson looked down at his trousers but all he saw was flesh.

Next thing he was lying on the floor of his B&B near the King's Theatre, and a matronly Edinburgh voice was shouting up the stairs: "Last call for breakfast!" He was fully-clothed and every bone in his body ached. There was a bottle of whisky on the table beside the bed, along with the small case and his travelling bag. He shoved the case under the bed amongst the fluff and dust. So much for Visit Scotland. He didn't know where else to hide the cash. He washed his face. Drank some whisky from a cup. Went out into the Edinburgh morning. He walked about the streets. He went to the Meadows. Sat on a bench. Got up and walked about. Sat down some more. The deep restlessness of the sea was inside him. It surged back and forth. Broke on a memory of the red rocks of the steep cliffs he knew would claim him. In the light flickering through the leaves of the trees above his head he saw her hair in the seaweed, and the crashing waves.

Hours passed. He found himself on Forest Road. He turned into a pub called Sandy Bell's, bought a drink and sat down. Two mouthfuls into his pint he realised he was in exactly the same place – the same seat he'd been in yesterday. The same mix of people milled around him: students, tourists; and the same folk musicians playing the same music in the corner. The American girl appeared out of the crowd.

"How's the Presbyterian?"

Manson looked at her blankly. "I mean, are you feeling better? You're still white if that is any consolation."

He had no idea what she was talking about. As he looked into her eyes he saw the jeweller looking back. A tall blond Norwegian strode into the bar. Manson's stomach churned. To prove to himself that he had not altogether lost his sanity he spoke up. "Would you like a drink?"

"Scotch. Thanks."

He bought two whiskies, gave her one, and sat down. *That's it*, he thought. *Everything's going to be fine.* They had another whisky. The young American girl sat closer to him. The tall blond Norwegian walked out.

"Your friend is upset," said Manson.

"He thinks he owns me. Nobody owns me." Then, after a pause, "Does anybody own you?"

"Not yet."

"That sounds ominous."

"It's inevitable." Manson shrugged and gulped his whisky. It went on like that all afternoon. Manson grew happy. It felt like he was being shredded. The young American was bold.

"You seem to have plenty of cash. Are you into stocks and bonds?"

He looked at her through his malt fug.

"Not yet."

Afternoon turned into the evening. Manson and his new friend found themselves in an Italian restaurant eating pasta and drinking red wine. Then it was cognac. Then another bar. Then a hotel, and bed, and at last darkness dropped on Manson like a January night on Dwarick Head. When he woke up he heard the waterfall and the Maighdeann Mhara bathing. All long black hair and young flesh, the American girl stepped out of the shower, reaching for a towel.

"Boy, were you loaded last night."

"Where are we?" He didn't recognise anything. Without waiting for an answer he got up and looked out of the window. The Castle, on its small mountain. He checked his pockets. *Well, at least she didn't rob me.* "What's your name?" he asked aloud.

"Pearl." She kissed him. He looked into her eyes. A deep, sea blue. The jeweller had gone.

"Do you wear contact lenses?"

She laughed, drying her long black hair. "Let's get some breakfast."

Later that day he went back to the guest house, retrieved his bags, paid the Edinburgh matron, and returned to the hotel. Pearl was asleep on the bed. He sat down and watched her. *Lucky kid. Wish I was that out of it.* He took a bundle from the case, slipped it in a sanitary bag from the bathroom, and shoved it into his jacket pocket. He took the case downstairs and asked the hotel receptionist to deposit it in the hotel safe.

"Valuables, sir?" asked the girl.

"Just some papers."

Back up in the room Pearl was awake.

"Do you like apples?" he asked

"Sure. I love apples. I'm from Wisconsin." She laughed. Nakedly she slid across the bed. "You wanna make out?"

They did.

The next day it was shopping. Suits, shirts, shoes. Jumpers, trousers, jackets. Back in the hotel he threw the bags on the bed, where they lay in a deflated pile some two-foot high. He sat back in an armchair chair and drank whisky. *I am in a cave. The cave of my own death*. Pearl lay asleep on the floor, naked. To Manson in that moment, her nakedness was more than that – she looked unnatural – hairless. He leapt up. In a frenzy he tore the new clothes out of their bags and threw them around the room. When he had finished they lay like dead moths over lamps, the flat-screen TV, the bed, chairs, and on the floor. A jumper was tangled in the light fitting, dangling from the ceiling like a noose. He lay down beside Pearl, covered her in a brand-new suit, and fell into a deep sleep.

When he woke she was gone. She had taken nothing but her taxi fare. She had dressed and tried to wake him but he would not stir. He was just too hopeless. She wanted to *live*. She didn't leave a note. Her absence wrote itself in a purposeful script amid the chaos of discarded consumerism. Behind her, littered across the room, on the floor and on the bedside table, were many apple cores.

Manson looked at his watch. Time meant nothing to him. It was July so it was always daylight. He went to Sandy Bell's. Pearl wasn't there. He stayed amongst the voices, the bodies and the music until everything blurred. The next day he caught a train for Caithness.

# 18

That Summer was a good one in The Province of the Cat. At Bushta on Dunnet Head, under the protection, patronage and helping hand of Dungal, Chief of the Cattach, the three Irish priests saw their first crop of oats grow tall and green, and ripen. They dug a vegetable garden and grew kale and cabbages which fattened and established themselves in satisfying rows. Their three rough stone beehive huts had flowers growing around their doors. The chapel walls stood a proud six feet tall and all it needed, for the miracle to be complete, was a roof. Grillaan had decreed that the beams and couplings must be of oak as was the tradition but oak was rare in the far north. Dungal had sent to Naver for the wood and it was only a matter of the timber being delivered. Piles of ready-cut flagstone slate sat in organized readiness like a stone world library in the lee of the eastern gable. All this caused ripples of both interest and displeasure in the society of the Cattach, most notably with the native priests.

It was late August. The once frenzied ledges of the headland cliffs were empty of sound and seabirds now. The silence was interrupted only by the constant booming of the sea, crashing in waves at the foot of the precipice.

"Sure, the ould boy has a soft spot for you lot, right enough," said Ythan the mason. "That he goes to all this trouble to ensure your happiness. This place of yours'll be almost as grand as his own tower. No turf roof for you boys, oh no."

"And why shouldn't he favour us?" asked Eoghan. "Are we not the most exciting thing to happen here since Julius Caesar himself gave you all a doing?" He rubbed his hands which had roughened from working with stone.

"So you think," laughed Ythan, "but that's just what the filidh call history. Fables, if you like. We never saw a sniff of the big man or his iron tortoises here. Sure, mebbe a sail or six passed West of Arcaibh."

"God's tears, my hands are in ribbons," lamented Eoghan as he contemplated his upturned palms.

"Ach, you priests have the hands of girls," snorted Ythan. "Did you not use that ointment I gave you?"

"Ointment!" exclaimed Eoghan. "That stuff smelled worse than fish guts!"

"It *was* fish guts," laughed Ythan. "Fermented fish guts anyway. It protects the skin by keeping it moist. Your hands'll harden to it. Believe me, it works."

"It stinks, you mean."

"Man, man," said Ythan solemnly. "Have you no sense in Ireland at all?" He bent to pick a slate from the pile, checking it for defects. "It'll be a bonny wee thing when it's finished. Perfect for drying fish, or for smoking them even."

Eoghan laughed. He looked at the sturdy man with his broad shoulders and stocky build, his hair the colour of hazel leaves in October. Working with him had been both an education and a joy and the weeks had passed mostly in humour. They learned each other's languages easily enough.

"His holiness the Prior would have kittens if he heard you say such a thing," said Eoghan. "You're a good man, Ythan, but you're a Godless heathen nonetheless."

"What d'ye mean godless? We've hunners of gods."

"Aye, no doubt. But this is to be a place of worship, a holy place. Well, it will be once we get the roof on and the Prior consecrates the ground."

Carefully Ythan placed the slate back with the others. "Ach, well, you sky-divers are all the same. Our lot at least have the good sense to operate in the open air. They hee and haw to each other in the yew trees down by the Dinnad loch. Out of harm's way at least."

"You don't seem to have much time for the Druids, Ythan?" Ythan looked out towards the geo which led down to the sea.

"Och, they're powerful and no mistake. They can have you garrotted and thrown in a bog if you cross them. But I prefer solid material to work with. Good limestone, sandstone – granite if I can get it. Stone is the fruit of the good ground, Eoghan. There are no spells or incantations that come with it. Just the shape of a wall, or the pattern of a well-worked gable."

"You're a mason, Ythan, and I was a warrior," reflected Eoghan. "Now I'm supposed to be a priest. In truth my part of this enterprise is to make sure the Prior and the boy don't get killed. Colm was more like myself than his brother Grillaan, if truth be told. None of us can conceal our true natures."

Ythan traced his fingers across the chapel wall. "Neither can stone," he said. "But unlike men it never lies." He moved around the building. Eoghan followed him. "Builders like me enclose space, but we can never trap time. But the stones do. See, Eoghan, you poor bog-trotting Irish that you are, in here is stored millions of years of time gone by. You've made a peedie chapel out of the petrified ghost of some ancient desert."

Eoghan smiled as he listened to the Pictish builder. He both admired and was jealous of his absolute belief in his medium of stone. Other than God, he believed in nothing. He caught up with Ythan and put his hand on his shoulder. "You're a rare man, Ythan. You sure you don't have Irish blood?"

There was a pause as Eoghan waited for the mason to respond. He didn't. He just looked lovingly at the wall.

"Aye," said Eoghan, tracing his swollen fingers over the sandstone wall. "It is a beautiful thing."

"Still through the sharp whin bush blows the cold wind," said Ythan, "but it won't drive through this wall. And no rain will fall on you either, once we get the oak beams from the West."

Instinctively Eoghan's eyes looked out across the bay to the mountains stretching out across the western horizon.

"I want to talk to you about building a small harbour wall at the foot of the geo there," he said.

"Do you now?"

"We need somewhere to put our boat that's close by and relatively safe. The beach is just too far away and the people here tell me it's haunted. We need somewhere we can haul her up when the weather picks up. She's sturdy enough but she's light. Winter's coming." Eoghan looked towards the geo and to the sea at its base.

"It's the equinoctial storms that do for a lot of things around here. It's not called the Coast of Widows for nothing." Ythan picked up his tool bag. "Come on then. I'll have a look."

"You'll be needing more stone, then?" Realizing the effort his request involved, a wave of gratitude rose up inside Eoghan.

"Ach, I'll just use what's there," said Ythan matter-of-factly, walking over to the mouth of the geo. Eoghan followed him. The mason stopped and peered into the fracture which ran sloping in a tooth slide down the cliff into the sea.

To Eoghan's eyes it looked an impossible task. "Forget it, Ythan. It's too much. I shouldn't have asked."

Ythan wasn't listening. "Aye, aye," he said. "Just above the high tide mark there should do you."

"You're a marvel, Ythan," said the old warrior, relieved.

"No," replied Ythan. "I'm a stonemason."

Ythan looked along the cliff top to the sloping hill of Bushta which protected the chapel from the nor-westerlies, and along the high ridge which ran behind the loch and protected them from the nor-easterlies. A grassy meadow stretched from the chapel to the burn and then over to Loch Bushta itself. All manner of songbirds flew in an out of the several boor trees which grew in self-protecting clumps along the banks of the burn.

"Well, Eoghan, you've chosen yourselves a bonny piece and no mistake."

"Grillaan likes to be close to heaven," said Eoghan. "It's the way of him."

They edged down the boulder-strewn geo until they reached the bottom and could stand easily on the flat sandstone rock, the sea washing over the ridges some ten yards in front of them. They both turned and looked back up the geo where the sky caught in the rock mouth some three hundred feet above. The two sides of the geo were almost vertical and dripped water so that the rocks were stained with the brown reddening rust of the bog. To Eoghan the scene depicted the differences between himself and this Pictish builder, so full of guile and knowing: they were opposite sides of a common formation under the same sky, soon to be linked by a breakwater wall.

"Tell me about walls?" said Eoghan, surprising himself by his interest. "How d'ye go about building such a thing down here?"

"The secret," replied Ythan, "is to have the last stone in your mind's eye before you lay the first. You have to see the end of the wall."

Eoghan looked where Ythan was looking but all he saw was a pile of stones.

"Well, I see another, special wall," he said.

"Oh do you now?" laughed the builder sarcastically. "Funny that, is it not? No sooner have I agreed to one thing than there's another."

"This, I assure you, is the last thing."

"Then what is it?"

"It's the cave," said Eoghan.

"The cave?"

"The Cave of Gold."

"What about it?"

Eoghan looked at his sore hands. He could see he'd stretched the builder's patience to its limit.

"At some point we're going to inter Colm's clarsach. We need to build a wall to secure it for all time."

"I'll easy build a wall, Irishman. But whether it lasts for all time I doubt."

Ythan turned away from the geo. He'd had enough of stones for the time being. He looked out to the mouth of the bay and to the northern horizon. His blood ran cold and an old fear gripped him.

"Let's go back up now. Quickly now, Eoghan, let's go." He grabbed the old warrior's arm in his vice-like mason's grip and dragged him up the geo. When they reached the cliff top Eoghan pulled his arm free, outraged and struggling for breath.

"What's the matter with you?" he gasped.

Ythan said nothing, but moved back to the cliff's edge and pointed out to sea. On the horizon Eoghan could see six square sails heading west. Some were red, some orange and some had stripes of both. The two men looked at the ships for a moment.

"Who are they?"

"Norse." Smoke from a beacon on the headland directly west of them rose up on the air and drifted towards the mountains beyond. Ythan turned and looked to the north of Dunnet Head. Smoke from the beacon by the fort likewise rose up in warning, and drifted west on the prevailing wind. To the east it was a similar story on Duncansby Head.

They watched the six ships' slow, steady progress west.

"I have never seen ships like those before."

"Aye, nor do you want to again," said Ythan.

"Will they come here?" asked Eoghan, conscious of the relief as well as the fear in his voice.

"Eventually, yes," answered Ythan. "But they can see we are ready for them now. There will come a time when we won't be."

"So where are they going?" Even to himself Eoghan sounded like a child.

"To the long islands in the west. But I think these ones are for settling. The raiders usually have just one or two ships and they tend to be longer. Faster. Less heavy in the water. No, these are refugees. Poor bastards. There's a war on in their country. A long and bloody affair from all accounts. They will be trying to escape. To find a life elsewhere. Somewhere."

"Then God have mercy on them," said Eoghan, tears welling in his eyes. "For they are like ourselves."

Ythan laughed. "Like you wandering Irish hermits? Mebbe. But you lot set off for the four corners of the world for no reason, other than you have a fire in your head. No, these Norse folk are sailing to find a future far, far from everything they have ever known. Not because some god has whispered to them in the night but because they have no choice. It's the great edge of the world or death for them."

Eoghan watched the colourful sails grow slowly smaller. The afternoon was losing its lustre. Summer, too, was going over the edge of its time. Soon September would come with her legions of rain and her deep, low Atlantic advances of storms and depressions which would blow all too easily over this headland, the long undulating plateau, this Province of the Cat.

"So those are the Norse," said Eoghan, processing what he had just seen "... and I am Irish, as you keep reminding me. But you, Ythan, where do you come from?"

"Me? Just over the hill," answered Ythan, laughing softly.

"No, no," insisted Eoghan. "I mean, where do you *really* come from? You Picts – the Cattach – the Cruithne, as you call yourselves."

"Why, it's well known, isn't it? We come out of the ground." Ythan turned from the cliff, heading towards the chapel.

"What does that mean?" said Eoghan, following the mason. "How can I know who you are from an answer like that?"

Ythan stopped walking. For once he looked annoyed. The flicker of humour had deserted his eyes.

"Oh, I know who you are alright, you Irish – all three of you: I want, I want, I want! That's your names".

Eoghan stopped beside him. This sort of conversation made his new friend uncomfortable but he felt compelled to pursue it, to reach something inside this strange, resilient creature.

"If we must have a name," he said, "I think it would be Need. We have undergone a great journey, a long emotional and vocational ordeal which I thought I was too old and hardened to undertake, never mind to withstand. Grillaan, it's true, exasperates me. But he also inspires me, as I think he does all the people who come across him. We seek no Utopia here, no Garden of Eden or Tir Nan Og either, just a place where we can fulfil Christ's commandment to us: to love one another."

"It's a powerful instruction and no mistake," agreed Ythan.

The two stood, silent for a moment. The percussion of their words surrounded them, and they were happy just to listen, their echo mingling with the sound of the sea. Sharp-eyed Ythan saw a wren alight the western gable of the chapel.

"Well. You have one convert at least."

"Do you have a family, Ythan?" Eoghan, whose old eyes were not so quick, thought that the mason was referring to himself.

"I have a wife and four daughters."

"Ah," sighed Eoghan, "I envy you that. All my life I've wanted a family, but I put it out of my mind. That is until I came here, to this strange land where I can taste home."

"The Point of Cats has an unkan effect on people, I'll give you that," agreed Ythan.

"Yet this need makes me feel so empty, like a cup at the end of the night."

"Come, let's get out of the wind," urged Ythan as Eoghan grew sad. They walked to the chapel and sat down beneath a wall. The wren snuggled into a space between two stones.

"You're not empty, friend," said Ythan, hugging his toolbag. "Ambition is empty without humility. Landscape is empty without people. You're just alone, that's all. Your pals may be devoted to this Christ of yours, but you are devoted to loneliness."

Eoghan looked out over the cliff tops and down to the surf breaking on Dunnet Beach.

"It's the sea that makes us lonely," he said, "not Our Saviour."

"The sea is only the sea," said Ythan, opening his toolbag.

"It's because it moves so constantly," said Eoghan, "that I feel I have to move with it."

"Nothing moves," said Ythan, pulling a hammer out of his bag. He held it up, admired it. "Everything is one."

"Is that a Pictish thing?" Eoghan was smiling once again.

Ythan put the hammer back in his toolbag. "Look at this sandstone," he said and slapped the wall behind them. "What you see is Time saying *'no, not yet.'*"

"For a stonemason you're uncommonly obsessed by time," laughed Eoghan.

"Stone is time." Ythan got to his feet. He slung his toolbag over his shoulder and walked away towards the loch, to follow the path over the hill. Eoghan watched him go, his stride careful and full of purpose, yet unhurried. Soon he was gone. Eoghan looked up to the sky, to its cathedral vastness. The wren flew like a bullet from its refuge amongst the stones.

Caornan and Nessan came over the brow of the hill and looked down on Loch Bushta. Three beehive huts and the roofless chapel sat tidily at the top of the geo beside their newly planted fields. The young scribe felt proud as he looked at them, the barley catching the waving wind. He could see Eoghan sitting alone on a bench beside the chapel wall. To the east he glimpsed Ythan's back as it disappeared over the top of the hill on Dwarick Head.

"Maybe I should go home now," said Nessan. "Look, the mason's on his way. My mother'll be getting worried."

"You've only just got here. You've to report to His Holiness the Prior. And that, in case you've forgotten, is your mother's instructions. I'm to make sure that you do it," said Caornan.

When Grillaan had told Caornan there was to be a labourer to help them, and that he must go to collect the worker from the Tower and escort them to the chapel, Grillaan had *not* said the labourer would be female. Especially not this awkward, cheeky and reluctant young girl who was even now idly lying back and chewing on a piece of grass, enjoying the late afternoon Sun.

"My brothers used to catch trout in that loch," said Nessan, "but they can't now the chief has given it over to you lot."

"We're planning to build a well and bless it so that it will be holy. Isn't that more important?"

"No."

"Come on with you." Caornan tried to sound authoritative. "His Holiness will be expecting us."

"It pays to be frightened of druids, doesn't it?" said Nessan, getting to her feet.

"His Holiness the Prior, brother Grillaan, is not a 'druid'. He is one of God's chosen representatives on Earth, thank you very much!"

Nessan did not seem impressed.

"Aye, mebbe. But he'll probably put the hex on you just the same. I have a Groatie Buckie in my pocket, so I'm safe."

Caornan made his way down the hill.

"I have no idea what you're talking about. Hurry up now, it's getting late!"

So Nessan, the girl labourer, and Caornan, the young novice priest and scribe, moved down towards the chapel and the settlement. When they reached it Eoghan was gone. Caornan assumed he had gone into his hut to meditate. It would soon be time for evening prayers. Nervously he ushered Nessan toward the entrance of Grillaan's hut. A sheepskin hung across the entrance in lieu of a door. He cleared his throat.

"Holy Father," he began. "I'm sorry to disturb you but I have the labourer sent from Dungal of the Tower. I'm afraid it's a girl. Perhaps you would be kind enough to instruct her in her duties."

After a moment the sheepskin was pulled back and the grey head of Grillaan, the Prior, caught the afternoon light.

"A girl, Caornan? Are you sure?" Grillaan was smiling.

"Oh yes, Your Holiness. Here she is – Nessan's her name, from what I can gather," said the young scribe.

Grillaan looked at Nessan. Dressed in colourful woollen layers, her long curly black hair falling in a tangle over her eyes and her shoulders, Nessan looked back at Grillaan, taking in his undyed woollen habit, his white waistcoat, the in-stitched cross indicating his status.

"So, Nessan, you have come to work with us?"

Nessan said nothing, though her eyes never left the Prior's.

"Do you not understand my words, child?" Grillaan enquired in good humour. Still Nessan said nothing. Caornan spoke up.

"She understands fine, Your Holiness. Most of them understand Gaelic well enough, but this one's a bit of a minx. She's here as a penance."

"Then she can speak for herself. Can't you, Nessan?" said Grillaan and he offered her his hand. Nessan stared. Caornan pulled her forward. "Be polite, Nessan," he whispered. Clearly uncomfortable, Nessan took Grillaan's hand.

"Is there something wrong, child?" asked Grillaan. "Do I upset you in any way?"

"No, no," said Nessan, half laughing. "It's just... I was expecting a funny hat, or something."

"Indeed? Well, I'm sorry to disappoint you." Grillaan smiled.

"Och, no. It's just that our druids, well, they're big for their hats. And I thought, you know..."

"Nessan!" said Caornan loudly. "Show some respect. You will refer to the Prior as His Holiness and speak only when spoken to!"

Nessan looked at her feet.

"Be gentle, brother Caornan. Nessan is new to our ways, as we are to hers."

Nessan looked up.

"Now, I believe you have been kindly sent to us? Is that right?"

"Aye." Caornan prodded Nessan with his finger. "Aye, Your Holiness."

"For some... misunderstanding, was it?"

"Ach, I swear I thought the hen was one of ours. How was I to know it was one of the Fracher's clockers?" Caornan prodded her again. "... Your Holiness."

"Well," said Grillaan, smiling to himself, "we haven't got any hens here as yet, but I'm sure with your good efforts we will have. That can be your task: the procurement of hens." The Prior winked at Nessan.

"Oh aye, nothing simpler, eh... Your Holiness." Nessan was warming to this foreigner. "There's hens aplenty."

"Your Holiness, she's here to labour for us," Caornan reminded his superior.

"We are all here to labour for the Lord our God, Caornan, none more so than myself. In half an hour we shall have evening prayers. Do you like singing, Nessan?"

"Oh aye," replied Nessan, happier now. "They say I have a powerful voice."

"Good. Then you can join us. You may not understand the language but the tunes should interest you."

"I've got a wee pipe. Mebbe I could join in?"

"Nessan," hissed Caornan, "do not be so impudent!"

"I see no reason why not," agreed Grillaan. "Till then. Caornan will advise you what is required of you. God bless you." And Grillaan turned back into his stone beehive, pulling the sheepskin across the entrance.

"Well," said Caornan, "well, I never."

"He's not such a bad ould sprout," said Nessan.

"His Holiness is a Prior in the Church of Ireland. Not a 'sprout', old or otherwise."

Nessan snorted. "You said you wanted to see the cave," she said, laughing at Caornan's stiffness. "Come on and I'll show you!" and she set off at a run towards the geo.

The lanky Irish boy had no choice but to follow, his cheeks filling rhubarb red with the excitement of the moment. Hair flowing like black heather behind her, the Pictish girl with eyes the dusky colour of hazlenuts raced from the Prior's beehive. The late August afternoon lay lightly on the headland and Summer poured itself over the cliff in an endless, laughing waterfall, so keen to lose itself in Dunnet Bay. Both their lives were like the waterfall: no matter their difference in belief or culture, it was their youth, their energy, which flowed then. Around them Time did not matter. The loch, the burn, the waterfall, the yellow crescented bay – these places drank time and released it back for them both to enjoy. It was all the same to them – Irish, Pict, Norse. Whoever fills the silver loop. We are just the temporary light on the dancing water. The burn and the waterfall, so dramatic and various, exist whether they are seen by a human eye or not. The bards say that whenever the Queen of Time holds her moth-like court, she adds to our existence. We make no difference to her.

Nessan knew this instinctively. It was also her culture and her religion, it was what the Druids taught them. She knew the loch, the burn and the waterfall were alive, that they had voices, music she could listen to; and that is why she loved them. She also knew the story of the cave. She wanted to tell it to Caornan, when and only if she felt he was ready. A part of her, the hazelnut part, thought that he would be ready, eventually and that he was worth the telling. The other part – more waterfall than solid earth or flesh – wondered whether the cave might just make him unhappy, so far was it from what he understood.

# 19

Morning light was just beginning to bleed across the flat lands from the low furnace emerging from the distant north Sea. The night-shift had not yet finished, and the day-shift was still rising from their Atomicer beds in the Monopoly estate-houses. No matter the fifty or so years they had sat on the meadows and link-lands of Ormlie, and no matter the tidy gardens and maturing trees which surrounded them, these houses still looked to Colin like a temporary camp. Soon these sleepy nuclear wardens would also be on the road he was driving, heading west to their diurnal ritual of... something or other. Who knows really? Work? The displacement of time? He could imagine their bleary conversations with their half-asleep wives and partners as they ate (or did not eat) their breakfasts. He could hear their sedated, semi-verbal exchanges on shift buses ploughing through the weather of this morning, and every morning for the last half century. He had heard them since he was sixteen years old, from his first day sitting there on the bus, young, proud, feart, numb and excited all at the same time. That very day, he reflected now, he had begun his long campaign of simultaneously escaping and staying put.

Colin turned off the road at Forss, where broad-leafed trees seduce you into thinking you're entering another country. He drove up the narrow farm-road to the old steading of Skaill. This had been his great-great grandfather's farm once, until the nineteenth turned into the twentieth century. They had moved onto better things. "Better things" had been cattle dealing during the First World War when his great-grandfather had made what the family always referred to as "a fortune". Where this fortune had gone Colin was not sure. Certainly by the end of his father's life there was no money left, if there ever had been any to start with. Now, a hundred and more years later, here he was in his not-so-shiny but very expensive black car, driving slowly past the old flagstone hearth-home. The house, the steading, the byre, the barn and the threshing shed all looked handsome still, but naked somehow, stripped bare by the absence of a working human hand. The farm buildings had become "property". It looked to Colin as if someone had recently bought the place. Soon Skaill would be destroyed. Some prison-building architect would turn the old farm into a "project" for someone just like him with decommissioning money to spend, no common sense or taste, and absolutely no idea about preserving vernacular architecture.

He stopped his car. For at least a couple of years he had harboured the notion to come up here, but had never had the psychic space to translate fantasy into reality. There was something deep inside him that baulked at the very idea of 'going back'. Despite doing well for himself there was always an insistent echo on the back of the wind reminding him he came from a defeated, expropriated people, and that material dreams were illusion, obscene and undeserved. For him, for Skaill, it looked as if it was too late anyway. What was "too late" for him? Whatever it was it did not have the same significance as it did for the farm. His cloudy schemes of familial continuity meant little against the thousand years or so that Skaill had borne its Norse name. Before that the Picts would have called it something else, and before that the Iron Age farmers would have known it by a different name again. He started the car and drove on.

He parked the BMW in a space beside a planting of lodgepole pine trees and got out. He negotiated a rickety style over the fence and made his way up the short incline until he reached the top. As he climbed he could hear the collective whoosh-whaup-whoosh of twenty wind turbines which stood like giant angry air conditioning behind him on Baillie Brae. The long rays of the morning Sun flickered through the blades and were cut as if they were paper into the strange white signalling of some impenetrable code. The rowan tree he had passed at the foot of the hill, its branches full of berries red as rutting stags' eyes set violently against the shining green fingers of its leaves, seemed to vibrate as if it were surrendering to the perpetual strobe of the wind turbines. This was *Cnoc nam Freiceadain* – the hill of the watchers.

He stood on top of the hill looking out to the Atlantic beyond. The light was steady, yellow, endless. An oil tanker was heading east to discharge its crude on Flotta in Scapa Flow. Tonight the orange flare-off boom would burn a little brighter. Below him the light blue dome of the Dounreay Fast Reactor [DFR] dominated the coastline. It sat like a huge egg in a chaotic nest of large, brutal support buildings. To the west the small harbour at Sandside, where clusters of radioactive particles had closed the beach to the public; and there was the village of Reay, its white Norse kirk lending human construction a human face. Staring back at him as he looked down was the PFR [Prototype Fast Reactor], its reactor housed in a square green and black building, all steel and menace. Beside that, similarly clad in angular steel and concrete, was HMS Vulcan – or 'Vulcan Naval Reactor Test Establishment' as he had to remember to call it now. This was where the Royal Navy housed their own pair of reactors and had their nuclear submarine engines "serviced" by Rolls Royce. This was the tight, highly secret MoD zone within the already highly secret area of the Dounreay site: this was where the worlds of civil and military nuclear programmes exchanged body fluids. This was where no inquiring light shone in or out.

A mile to the east of this classic nuclear vista was the old US Navy base at Forss, where the Yanks used to listen to the comings and goings of Soviet submarines in the north Atlantic. The abandoned camp with its imported kit-built buildings was now reincarnated as an "enterprise park" – recently gone bust – with half a dozen tall wind turbines of their own bowling armfuls of nothing over the short sedimentary cliffs. Still further east, over the hill and still asleep, was Atomic City itself, its dull orange street lights a small star cluster of subservience and doubt.

From all of this the farmland rolled back south and east until it reached to beneath his feet, firmly planted on the north end of a long burial cairn, some five and a half thousand years old. Two more sat next to it like upturned earth-boats. As far as Colin could see, to the edge of every landed horizon, beneath the vast acres of peat and below the surface of the enlightenment fields, was the hidden story of everything he was. He looked down on the farm at Skaill. He loved the patterns the morning light played out over the flagstone buildings of the steading, turning it almost luminescent. He could imagine his great-grandfather and his father before him coming and going with horses and implements, their lives ahead of them, their lives behind them, their present his history, their future his present. More ancient human memory sprouted from the burial cairns beneath his feet, the energy of past lives like brambles coiling around him, the thorns yet to catch.

Memories, lived or passed down, were piled inside him and inside his people, like hay bales on a trailer. There was a pattern to it all, he supposed. He could see it out there before him, like waves in the firth. Was it this morning he'd spoken to Kylie about Nagelstein? No, she'd been sound asleep when he left, full of white wine and dreams. Yesterday morning. It was after the conversation about Nagelstein that one of the waves broke.

"Ah'm so bloody houngry, an there's nuthin in the hoose. Thur's no even a bloody biscad!"

That he could go out to the Co-op and get shopping himself never crossed Colin's mind. That the current contents of the fridge and the freezer could have fed them both for a week would have surprised him. He was sprawled on the bed in his suit. Also fully dressed, Kylie sat lightly on the edge of the bed beside him. *Like a pigeon,* he thought.

"This is the only time we see each other these days," she said.

"Aye, busy times." It was as if he were speaking to his feet. She realised he was waiting for something. Coffee? Well, he could wait. She stood up.

"Where ye goin?"

"Where d'ye think?" she snapped. "Work, same as e."

"I'm no goin til work," yawned Colin, "I'm goin til Dounreay."

"Well I'm sure they'll appreciate it if you put it in an appearance. I have to go. See you tonight?" Bag, jacket, quick last look in the mirror.

"I've got til see aat daft fuckan Yank." He'd been watching her dress, keeping his tone light to mask the tension in his gut. Kylie wasn't easy to wake up with these days.

"What Yank?" Her impatience went up a gear. Colin feigned interest in his tie.

"Och, Darcy Dagelstone or whatever his stupid fuckan name is."

"You know fine what his name is. What about?" Still annoyed, but interested.

"Och, iss chob."

"What job?" Almost through the doorway, Kylie stopped and turned right round to face him, her frown gone. Colin's heart lifted. *Bingo! That got through to her.*

"Ah dunno, exactly. Neither dis he. Aat's wan thing ye've got to mind aboot Dounreay, Kylie – nobody knows anything."

The frown came back. The clock won.

"Tell me about it tonight. I have to fly." No goodbye kiss. Out the door, revving her car, gone. Into the bright August morning.

Thinking about her now from this vantage point above his ancient heartland, Colin knew Kylie's state of mind was unhealthy, had been for some time. There was such anger in her, such impatience. Her thoughts and moods seemed to swirl like the weather over the barley fields below him. *But look who's talking!* Did *he* really have such a grip on how things really are? Free of the site and the flat, maybe he did. Standing here on Cnoc nam Freiceadain, he could actually *think*. About everything and nothing, the shades of the ancient dead beneath his feet. She would always be among them: his thoughts, ghosts, memories – whatever everything and nothing was. He was a space she must fill. Empty space. Full space. In she would come.

Did they make love that morning? No. Had they had sex all week? He couldn't remember. When they lay down together it used to feel like crossing a field or sailing amongst the northern isles. Now it was either like two hungry animals trying to eat one another, or two exhausted swimmers making for the shore. Either way it was as if they were trying to save their lives or to lose them. Back down the brae he got into his car and started the engine. Automatically checking the rear-view mirror he saw a black four-by-four slowing behind him. He knew immediately who this was. The Mercedes-Benz pulled up behind him and two Ministry of Defence police got out. One approached his car, the other stayed just in front of their vehicle. Colin buzzed down his window. Immediately the officer took his photo with a small camera.

"Have you any business here, sir?" A Yorkshire accent cut through the Caithness morning like a scythe. Colin said nothing, just took out his site pass.

"Oh, I see." The tone changed. "Very good, sir. Sorry I didn't recognise you. Can't be too careful."

He handed Colin back his pass. Colin buzzed shut his window, pulled out past the MoD vehicle, and drove off down the road to Shebster. The black Mercedes Benz followed him at a distance. Colin noticed that they were not displaying number plates. He had also noticed that the two goons were armed, each wearing a pistol. No doubt they had automatic weapons in the four-by-four. It was forbidden for the Authority Police – what locals called "e Atomic bobbies" – to take their weapons off-site. But these were not Authority police. These creatures were from the MoD. They could do what they liked.

He remembered the other night when he could not sleep. He had got up, poured himself a whisky and turned on the TV. The History Channel was screening a programme about the fall of France in 1940. He'd been struck by the footage of long columns of trucks following the panzers, all of them with Mercedes Benz insignia on their bonnets next to the swastika. Now it was as if one of those trucks was following him. There he was in his own BMW. The little panzer of his life.

He pushed all of that from his mind. As he drove on to Dounreay he tried to remember the singing of the skylarks and the whooping whistle of the shochads which had filled the air as he stood on Cnoc nam Freiceadain. He drove through the main gate and parked his car in his allotted space. He entered the big square green building where his office was, spoke briefly to Donna, his PA and a couple of other colleagues. He sat down at this desk and looked at the computer. Columns of Wehrmacht trucks moved from one side of the screen to the other.

Time passed. Then he was in an office with Darcy Nagelstein, the White Ape. Darcy Nagelstein was head of Gabfan Nuclear (UK), a man with a mission: to come in under budget and before the contract deadline. Neither of these things looked remotely possible. The old nuclear juggernaut of Dounreay turned just too slowly for all the hurry-hurry-time-is-money Americana Colin heard every day from junior Gabfan managers. '*You can't hurry the half-life of uranium*' was the common old-school reply. '*Mebbe so, but we as sure as hell can move it right off this site!*' was the retort of the Nuevo Atomicana. Moving it right off the site was one thing but there was far more auxiliary nuclear waste than Gabfan had bargained for, never mind that the entire site – every nut and radioactive bolt – was nuclear waste, and things were not going well. A few weeks ago Gabfan had offered Colin a job. He had looked into it and turned it down. No-one, it seems, did that to the Yanks. Colin suspected that Nagelstein was here with a writ from the NDA to sack him. What a relief that would be. Unfortunately for the White Ape it was not within his competence to sack Colin Harper even though, as he looked at him now, he could have quite easily killed him.

So there they sat, the company man from California and the site manager from Caithness. It would be possible to record here all that they said, or to note the contrasting looks on their faces, their cultural differences. Or how their body language betrayed them as the conversation progressed, or to chart the experience of the elder man over the inexperience of the younger, and how those attributes were of benefit to both, or how they reversed. Or how about describing the changing light as it poured in through the window off the sea as time passed, or the fact that those others in the room who were present at the start of the conversation were absent come the end? But that would only detract from the hard steel of the dialogue which, in truth, had neither beginning nor end, no settled subject or purpose other than the fact that it had to take place, like a tide washing up on a beach, again and again, forever. As it is, like the marks on the walls of the *Uamh an Oir*, the Cave of Gold, these are stray scratches of a greater narrative, notes and phrases from the lost pibrochd of communication.

– What I'm saying, son, is that things are not going at the speed we want. And things that we don't want keep happening, keep slowing us down.

– This place is a junk pile. What do you expect? – We have a business plan. A strategy. A timescale. I expect that to be adhered to.

– I'm not a miracle worker.

– You manage the site, boy. Who else am I gonna chew out?

– I have no authority over the sub contractors. All I can say is "do better". I oversee this. I overlook that. What do you expect?

– Look, we inherited you from the NDA. That's part of your government's letting go of control but not letting go at the same time. Listen... Colin... we can easily write you a contract, I've said as much before. We can easily bring you in.

– I'm already "in", aren't I? Here in this office, your office, which was the NDA office before you and before that it was the UKAEA when they ruled the roost. There's *sixty years'* worth of nuclear scrap metal on this site, Darcy, not just five minutes. Sixty years!

– We've cleaned up bigger shit in shorter time.

– Aye, but no here! You set a date. But what does that mean? It's arbitrary. A line in the sand, as you Yanks like to say. The tide comes in and washes it away, Darcy, that's what happens here.

– Don't we just love your quaint lil' ol' ways.

– Just look at what's happened this week alone. A leak in the waste shaft, again. How many times is that this year? And now there's this train!

– The flasks are lined with a titanium alloy encased in cast steel.

– Aye, an they're lying in a field just ootside Halkirk.

– They were empty.

– Mebbe, but the papers are full of it.

– You have a PR man don't you?

– We have Daimler.

– So why haven't you fired the asshole?

– Why don't I just fire everybody?

– We could arrange that if it guaranteed the contract met the price, if it brought us the bonus.

– That's all this bloody well means to you – price, contract, bonus. Contract, price, bonus. It's human beings I deal with. Men with families. Women and children, Darcy, you've heard of them?

– They don't concern me. They are all outside the wire.

– Gabfan will only be happy when the entire plant, every bit of dome and fittings, is cut up into the size of a postcard and buried in a hole in the ground at Buldoo.

– We can't afford to get involved in the social dimension of the decommission, Colin. Beyond these fences my interest stops.

– Why, then, is the MOD letting its police roam all across the north coast checking out every vehicle on the road? Even during the Cold War we never had that.

– That's an issue for your government, not for Gabfan Nuclear.

– No commercial pressure on ministers then?

– They are running a war on terror. All we concern ourselves with is productivity.

– There's radiation leaking into the sea but as far as the world is concerned, it isn't. The line south to Inverness will be shut for a week but that's ok because of our strict safety regime. How, exactly, does this affect productivity?

– You're going to have come up with a new narrative, son. Tidy up the site and get that asshole Daimler to set his smoke-signals right.

– Daimler is half way insane already.

– Then send him round the bend completely. Ten years from now – That's the endgame. Just make sure you're around to enjoy it.

– Is that a threat?

– Nope. It's a deadline.

– We're talking about the year 2025 and decreasing.

– We're talking about five and a half billion dollars and increasing.

– Darcy, I will never work for you.

– You all do, boy; you just don't know or won't admit it, that's all.

Now we can see a beam of light pouring in through the window of Nagelstein's office, and how Colin lets his eye climb that little column of the northern afternoon and follow it out to the Atlantic. Out there on that vast ocean there is nothing of the earth, the flagstone or the nuclear site. Out there on those briny acres Colin could be a boy again. He stood up. Darcy Nagelstein also stood up. Colin often wondered whether the White Ape knew his on-site nickname, typically cruel, and inspired by the white down of his body hair. He knew Nagelstein was more savage than any ape, that he would never climb a tree and look for honey beneath the bark or pick the fleas off his brother. *No*, thought Colin, barging along the corridor which ran like a spine through the office block, *this man will gladly bury us all at Buldoo*.

Back in his office, he sat at his desk and stared at the computer screen. People came in and out, put papers down on his desk, picked papers up: he saw none of them. Phones rang and people spoke to each other. Printers clicked and whirred; human footfall snare-drummed across the hard floor, or waltzed over the soft carpet. He heard nothing.

The road to his life at Dounreay, up to this second, had been a long and unlikely one. He was not yet thirty – a quick rise by conventional career standards – mercurial even – but the direction of travel had been circumnavigational. He started out as an apprentice fitter-turner, and there was a future for him on the site, a kind of family to belong to. Now there was only the White Ape, and all the humanity had been contracted out. The world of youth had gone. There were no fitter turners anymore. The family had left home.

His PA, a bonnie, capable Thurso girl came in to discuss his schedule. Her fresh face and open manner always cheered him, and for a split second he was tempted to draw her into his nightmare: *I am a finished man amongst my enemies. I am the wasting son of a wasted age.*

"Donna," he said instead, "I'm sorry, but can we just hold it over until tomorrow? Type the rest of that stuff up and leave it on my desk. Or email it to me and I'll read it the night."

"Ok, Mister Harper, will do." Donna put down her pencil "E alright?" She looked at him sorrowfully. A voice, his own voice, whispered to him. *Eurydice consigned forever to the labyrinth*. He left the office.

He walked around the site, or at least to the areas he was cleared to enter. Everything looked lifeless. He looked at the faces of the workers he met. He looked at the buildings and the machines they contained. *How can I believe in the shadows of the clouds on the sea and the honesty and decency of ordinary people, and still believe in all of this?*

Westminster wanted the plant closed, decommissioned. Holyrood wanted the nuclear industry buried, forgotten. Too much government, too many wants. Whatever the second thoughts of the British or Scottish politicians, they could not stop what they had started. Politics, fate and destiny were the holy trinity at work here. Money, of course, was like the head of John the Baptist: it predicated and topped everything. It was all the White Ape was interested in. The leaking waste shaft, the derailed train, all they represented was an amount of time lost, of money not earned by Gabfan and, as a result, less bonus for Darcy.

The waste shaft and the train – two incidents in one week. There was bound to be a third, there always was. Colin spent the rest of the day speaking to departmental and section managers, to security and union safety reps: everything was fine. He returned to his office late in the afternoon. Donna was on the phone. Everybody else was busy. The third thing, the third thing, the third thing: he had to put it out of his mind. He looked out of the small window at the sea, how it disappeared into the endless north. Just above the surface of the water, about twenty yards from the cliff, a great skua – a bonxie – was harassing a gannet to regurgitate its catch of fish.

He drove home later that evening past barley fields ripened to a bright, translucent yellow on either side of the road. The soft west wind rippled the crop; teams of swallows swooped in productive figures of eight, collecting insects above the grain. The calming pale blue dome of the sky brought into mind the similarly coloured dome of Dounreay, which was anything but calming. Natural and unnatural, both spheres reminded Colin forcefully that there must be many unknown worlds and possibilities in the universe.

Kylie was not in. He poured a whisky and drank it down. He poured another, and listened to the news on the radio as he ate leftovers from the fridge, cold. Food, for Colin, was only fuel. Kylie's fads for this or that usually stacked up, unattended, in the back of the freezer or in cupboards. None of it was what he considered "food". After eating he checked the reports he had asked Donna to prepare for him. Kylie was nowhere to be found. Her phone was either switched off or submerged in a gin and tonic somewhere. The TV flickered like a campfire in the corner. He went to bed.

Colin was not normally a good sleeper. He either had difficulty getting to sleep or woke up early as he had done this morning. Maybe it was because of his nervous and premature start to the day that he drifted off almost at once. He was not much of a dreamer, but when he *did* remember his dreams, they were usually variations on the same dream: he was travelling somewhere, on a plane or a train, or walking; he was alone, half-dressed or naked, and had lost (or was about to lose) his luggage.

As he slept his dream started off in a sunny, happy place, like the barley fields he'd admired as he drove home earlier. Then he was flying, or swimming – he wasn't sure. The light faded from the sky and he was running through the plant, naked, from the PFR to the DFR. He had something urgent to tell somebody important but he didn't know who, or at least he couldn't find the person. Faces heaved up and fell away all around him. His PA, Donna, threw her arms up in the air as he flew past her, as if she was falling backward into the sea. Screeds of A4 paper rose up in a blizzard as she fell, her arms held out stiffly. Then he was running along Victoria Walk – he had acquired some clothes by now – where the cliffs are joined by stone steps to the town. The sea was a mass of white-capped waves. Surf was crashing onto the beach with a deafening noise. Donna's pale face and stiff, outstretched arms seemed to rise up out of the wet sand as a ferocious north easterly gale blew in from the sea, lashing spray and foam over the Salvation Army Mission. Then it wasn't Donna any more but a tall figure with abstract, extended arms. Or were they arms? They morphed into two large grey shapes, like sails or scaffolding sheets. From the lee of the Salvation Army Mission a tall, heavily-built man in a hat and green suit approached him.

"*Fear not.*" The voice was soft, but perfectly audible. Colin thought this absurd: how could he hear a softly-spoken man over a howling gale and roaring sea? "*Go now to the angel. You are the finished man among your enemies.*"

Colin shouted above the wind. "*What's happening? Are we in a cartoon?*"

The cartoon man had a white beard and long grey hair which seemed unaffected by the wind. He wore – of all things – a monocle.

"*Arise now and go,*" said the tall grey man "*You know well what is happening.*"

"*No! I don't!*" Colin shouted, but the Yeatsian figure was moving slowly backwards along the beach towards the town, his sail-like arms outstretched. At the same time another form, a woman, emerged from the sea. Long, long hair streaming out behind her in the wind, ribbons of sea-colour flashing in the storm. The night was dark now, but with dream-sight he could see a long flowing gown, coloured, like her hair. Her mouth, though beautiful, gaped open – a silent scream. The swirling paper dropped earlier by Donna now turned into urban debris: shopping trolleys, pieces of furniture, televisions and computers, cars, an articulated Scrabster fish lorry. The terrible cloud swirled in the air and piled up the smashed mass at the feet of the slowly receding figure.

"*Fear not,*" the tall man kept repeating, "*You know well what you see.*"

"*I don't! I don't understand any of this!*" Colin was shouting, holding desperately onto a railing by the Salvation Army mission house to stop himself being plucked away by the wind. He watched, hypnotized, as the pile of debris grew bigger. So did the retreating female figure, whose arms had become wings. Slowly, slowly she moved backwards, her mouth still wide, a look of terror on her face.

"*What you see is a chain of events.*" The tall grey man spoke firmly, his voice and Irish accent distantly familiar to Colin. "*What you see as many things she sees as a single continuum: the catastrophe of human existence. You are watching the Angel of History.*"

Paralysed, Colin could only look on. The winged figure was still moving backwards towards the town, still with that look of terror on her beautiful face. The darkness of the storm cast into relief her vivid colour-scheme: yellows, browns and shades of russet flowed though her hair and clothes, which flashed like electricity through seaweed. Colin found that he was weeping, knew that he loved this ferocious woman, this angel, the most beautiful creature he had ever seen.

"*Why doesn't she turn back?*" Tears ran down his cheeks; pity and loss overwhelming him.

"*Alas, she cannot. Had she the power, she would set right in one moment all this destruction. She would like to waken the dead but sadly she cannot.*"

"*Why not?*" screamed Colin. The angel was looking at him, imploring him to save her.

"*Because the wind that blows so fiercely is the storm from Paradise.*" The relentless calmness of the tall grey man was terrifying. "*It has caught her wings so she cannot close them. She stares back at you because you are in the past. The wind that blows, it blows her into the future.*"

"*But her back is turned to it. She can't see!*"

"*Ah yes. The storm that rages now is Progress.*" With compassion in his voice at last, the man held Colin's gaze briefly before removing his monocle and slipping it into a pocket of his green suit. Then he tipped his hat, and disappeared up the steps to the cliffs.

Colin let go of the railing. He rushed past the mission building towards the angel, now well beyond the pile of debris, which kept on growing. But he could not get close to her. A chaos of dangerous objects was flying through the air, many of them crashing to the ground in metallic agony. The ruin was following in her wake, slow, relentless, irresistible; driven on by the wind she faded back, into the town and into the darkness.

He woke, tears choking him. Pure grief was like a physical blow to the chest, as he gathered his thoughts and remembered. The ache of one vivid image was overwhelming: his helpless dream-self reaching out for his dream-love, blown backwards into catastrophe. Kylie lay beside him sound asleep, fully clothed in hardly anything at all, her hair spread across the pillow like windblown straw. Despite the make-up still caked to her face, a dribble of saliva running down the side of her mouth, and the stink of stale booze and tobacco smoke, she still managed to look beautiful. He took a tissue from the box by the bed and wiped the dribble from her mouth which, with a snort, closed. He gathered her up in his arms and pushed his face deep into her hair. Kylie moaned softly as if she too was dreaming. Then she opened her eyes as the light of the morning poured in through the window and into her eyes like acid. She groaned.

"Where the hell did you get to last night?"

Despite the harsh words, Colin's whisper was gentle. She stirred, pushed herself away from him a little and lay on her back. She covered her eyes with the back of her right arm.

"Hen night," she croaked.

Losing the bright green and yellow dress she was almost wearing she made her way unsteadily to the bathroom. Relieved not to have his raw emotion exposed, Colin lay still for a minute, then pulled open the heavy curtains. The Sun threw its welcome light across Atomic City. Everything looked normal. Cars and buses moved freely in the street below. No sign of destruction. He rubbed his eyes. The embers of his dream cooled to ashes and he willed himself to sweep it from his day. Right on cue the radio-alarm went off. '*Good Morning Scotland. You're listening to the seven o'clock news with Gary Robertson and Hayley Millar.*' From the bathroom he could hear the sound of serious vomiting.

# 20

Fracher's creel boat chugged from the stone lobster claw of Scrabster harbour. It was a bright morning and the tide was on the turn. The Moon was bending the deep waters of the Atlantic Ocean back onto the flagstone cliffs of the north coast of Caithness. To the north east, as The Searcher cut across the bay, the sea was a rising and falling of foam.

"The Men o Mey are stirran," said Fracher. Mags sat just behind Fracher, outside the wheelhouse on the starboard side; Cushie, Fracher's dog rested his head on her lap.

"We'll get a good look at ay cave, right enough," said Fracher when they got a little further out. "But we'll no manage to get ashore, I'm thinkan."

"But, Fracher, that's the whole point of this trip." Alarmed, Mags got to her feet. Cushie looked up at her.

"Mebbe so. But there's a heave in ay sea I dinna lek. Even here in Thursa Bay thur's a swell. Mind e, id's never been ay same in iss part oh ay watter since they dumped all aat tons oh hardcore they dredged til deepen ay harbour for aat stupid bloody pier."

Mags had learned a lot about this strange, wise man over the past few weeks, and had got used to his frequent, short-lived tirades. She had also tuned her London ears to his Caithness tongue and had learned to love the way he spoke even though, quite often, she had no idea what he was talking about. His accent had sounded to her like an out-of-tune cello, but now she had grown accustomed to its music. She knew nothing of local politics but she was learning, and Fracher – alert to spot the quick and the curious – admired that in the girl.

Before them, immense against the northern sky, loomed Dunnet Head. Sunlight caught the sandstone and lit up the ancient redness of the stone. The geos which cut the rock and retreated back into the cliffs darkened in the shadows like entrances into the centre of the Earth. The Searcher proceeded steadily across the bay. Hoy was a long brown whale-back off the port bow. Fracher sucked contentedly on a roll-up. His weathered bonnet sat on his head at its usual contrary angle. He could feel the reassuring thrust of the old Kelvin engine beneath his feet. It was strange for him to have a female aboard. His wife Kirstag had hated the sea with a passion and would never come out with him, even if he had wanted her to, which he never had. She came from a fishing family and there had been an unspoken accord between them about the place of women, men, the sea and the land. The sea was masculine. The land feminine. Every time he set foot on the shore after a trip at sea the loss of his Kirstag flushed his mind and body in slow hot pain.

As they got closer to the headland they could see colonies of seabirds swarming against the cliffs like clouds of white pepper. Puffins, guillemots, kittiwakes and razor-bills swam around them and dived beneath the sea to surface triumphantly with a few sand eels clenched expertly in their beaks. Skuas and black back gulls soared here and there searching out their victims. Despite the fact that the Sun was well up in the sky Mags felt it cold. The raw ozone of the sea was a rough menthol at the back of her nose and on her tongue. Her eyes watered. She glanced West: a vast expanse of nothing stretched out hypnotically, blending sea into sky. A long red tanker was steaming out into the West, to feed, it seemed to Mags, its endless need.

Midway across Dunnet Bay The Searcher rode on the slow watery shoulders and into the depression of what was the beginnings of an Atlantic roller, which would crash as a wall of surf on the curving beach beyond. Mags could hear the soft grinding thunder of the waves which was the signature of the bay. As the west side of the headland grew taller she could make out the unmistakable open black mouth of the cave, some fifty yards from the opening of the Chapel Geo. The cave gulped like an oracle, an omphalos that led to a dark secretive, sea-weedy place.

"Ay swell's gettan pretty beeg," said Fracher, slipping the boat out of gear. "Ah really dinna thinks id's wise til put e ashore."

"But I have to get a look inside the cave!" said Mags. "It's inaccessible from land."

"Aat's as mebbe. Boot if a wave gets ahad oh e, e'll bay lost."

"Please try," she pleaded, determined now they were here.

Fracher said nothing. He looked at the sea and watched a couple of rollers pass beneath them. *Weel,* he thought, *at least they're no gettan any beeger.* He put The Searcher back into gear, opened the throttle and moved slowly towards Chapel Geo and the mouth of the cave. The tide was rising which made it easier to feel his way along the flat ledges at the foot of the cliffs which towered some three hundred feet above them. He had never noticed it before but there was what looked like an old drystone wall about a quarter of the way up the Chapel Geo. Fracher reasoned there must have been a landing place here at one time. To the cave side of the geo mouth he saw a rock formation which thrust out about six feet to form a natural pier, while the west side of the geo provided shelter from the worst of the ocean's movement. Fracher pointed.

"Ah could put e ashore on aat ledge. See!"

Mags followed his finger and saw where he meant. Cushie, sensing there was something afoot, pricked up his ears.

"I'll take her in chentle," said Fracher, "an when ay deck's level wae ay rock – chump, an dinna dilly dally aboot id, e hear?"

Mags nodded. She got to her feet and shouldered the small red rucksack with her torch, camera and notebook.

"Ten meenads. Aat's aal. No more. D'ye understand?"

"Ten minutes," she nodded again. Skilfully, Fracher edged his beloved creeler alongside the rock ledge. She rose and fell gently on the heave of the water. Mags was alert to the movement of the boat. Then the deck rose up and the barnacled ledge was in front of her. She sprang and was ashore. Cushie was at her heel.

"Damn e, doug, Ah didna say e could go an aal!" shouted Fracher, but for once the collie wasn't listening.

Mags waved to him that she was alright and then clambered carefully over the seaweed-wet stones that lay in a storm assembled chaos at the foot of the cliff. Fulmars soared and swooped above them, and the cliff ledges were full of them. Inching The Searcher back offshore for safety, a long dark brown shape speeding beneath the water caught the Fracher's eye. *Some size oh seals aroond here*, he said to himself, looking nervously towards the foot of the cliff where the girl and the dog picked their way gradually towards the mouth of *Uamh an Oir*, The Cave of Gold.

Each time Mags looked up at the cliffs and the long verticals and horizontals of Dunnet Head she felt its sheer bulk and Earth-force press down on her. After a few minutes she could not look up any more and concentrated instead on keeping her feet on the velvet slippery rocks. Cushie, on the other hand, trotted over them with ease, sniffing at this and that salty unusualness which took his fancy and barking at any seabird that came to close. There were several smaller caves with jagged entrances, invisible from the boat, their fissures running in ever-narrowing wetness to some hidden sandstone impossibility. Tempting as they were Mags ignored them.

The entrance to *Uamh an Oir*, when she reached it, was smaller than she had imagined. She realised this was because behind it the rock formation opened out into a small church-like space. Cushie stood before it panting, and crouched down on the flat red sandstone which acted as a set of steps leading to the entrance, his tail flat out behind him. Mags patted him reassuringly, slid off her rucksack and took out her small torch. She slung the rucksack casually back over one shoulder and moved towards the cave mouth.

"Come on, boy."

Cushie followed nervously. A panic of pigeons flew out above their heads like winged torpedoes into the light. Cushie yelped, and Mags laughed at her own small panic. The sun had disappeared behind a cloud, darkening the sky.

The cave was roomy. When her eyes adjusted to the dim natural light Mags estimated the ceiling at twelve feet high, twenty feet from side to side. It reminded her not so much of a cave but an ancient house, the smallness of the entrance disguising the unusually open interior. There was a thick carpet of kelp and long wands of tangle on the floor which glistened in a mass like wet belts or seething snakes. Water seeped from hidden sources along the upper walls and from the roof. Because of the hard acoustic of the cave, this sounded like the plucking of strange watery violin strings or a weird liquid glockenspiel. Mags listened intently for a moment. Cushie cocked his head to one side. Other than tangle, driftwood, the odd lost creel-buoy, and this off-key watery music, the cave was empty.

Mags sat down on a large stone and opened her rucksack, feeling for her head-torch, camera and tape measure. Swiftly checking her estimate of the cave's dimensions, she shoved the tape measure back in the ruck sack in case she left it behind. Suddenly sunlight flooded in through the cave entrance, as if a huge searchlight had been switched on outside. Now the chamber filled with a tide of yellow light, flickering shadows and beams bouncing off the red sandstone, right to the back wall. Covered in slimy green moss, this wall was strangely flush for at least six feet from the bottom. The flash from her camera filled the back of the cave with silver lightening, amplifying the natural light from outside. It was as if the very stone absorbed light. The back wall seemed distinct from the rest of the cave. She stepped closer, careful not to slip on the tangle, and pressed her hand on the wet green surface of the wall. The moss was not cold as she had expected. Moving her palm she could feel the roundness of a stone about the size of a melon. She hung her camera around her neck. Using both hands she felt other rounded stones, then more and more, reaching right down to the cave floor. Each time she pressed her palms over the contours of a slime covered stone she felt unusual warmth on her hand.

She stepped back. Were her hands so cold that the stones felt warm? She touched one hand to her cheek. She took another photograph. Again the flash filled the chamber with white electric light and again the stones seemed to consume it. She touched stone after stone and again and again she felt the same warmth. She sat back down on the big stone by her rucksack and pulled out her notebook, scribbling down the dimensions she'd calculated. Then, "*There is a wall in the cave and the stones are warm*". Underlining the last word, she looked at Cushie who was sitting at her feet and added a sentence that thrilled her. "*The wall is of human construction*".

Mags put her notebook back into her rucksack and stared at the wall. Perhaps it was a trick of the sunlight pouring through the entrance, or perhaps it was the emerald greenness of the mossy slime covering the stones, but the back wall of the cave was glowing. Cushie began to whimper. Mags remembered Fracher: "*Ten meenads.*"

"Ok, Cushie, let's go." She stood up, and the dog ran out into the daylight. Mags followed, shading her eyes with her hand. Gradually the outside world came back into focus. Every surface and edge seemed surreally sharp and defined. She could see The Searcher about twenty yards off the mouth of the Chapel Geo and could make out Fracher's figure in the wheelhouse. Mags waved. She could hear the engine as her skipper put it into gear and opened the throttle. Carefully she followed Cushie back to the landing place. She noticed that the water had dropped considerably in the short time she had been ashore. A coven of shags had convened on the exposed rocks, drying their black raggedy wings in the breeze.

Fracher moved the creel boat cannily to the rock ledge. There was now a heavy swell and he cursed himself for having agreed to this mad scheme in the first place. Concern, relief and anger fought for the foremost place in his mind. *Ten meenads, aat's whut Ah sayed til her, an whut hed she done? Steyed off for an hoor or more! City fowk, they hevna got a clue.* As he steered into the mouth of the geo he looked at the panting dog and the happy girl standing on the rock. Relief triumphed.

"Where ay hell hev e been?" he shouted from the wheelhouse window. "Thur's slack water an a Westerly kickan in!"

Mags didn't understand. Fracher edged the boat closer to the ledge, trying to judge the swell and the proximity of the rock. The water level had dropped a good four feet from when he had put her ashore earlier.

"Bay careful when e step doon. Ay weed'll make ay rock slidey!" he shouted to her.

As she was manoeuvring down to the lower ledge she saw a dark head emerge just off the port bow of the boat. *A seal*, she thought. Cushie darted in front of her to bark at the intruder, and caught Mags's right foot, knocking her off balance and backwards into the sea.

The deep ocean cold numbed Mags so that she felt nothing. She saw, quite clearly, the hull of The Searcher above her, and the green of the water, the bubbles beneath the waves as they crashed onto the rocks. Back on the surface again. Blue sky. Sunlight glinting on the water was blinding her, but she heard Fracher shouting. He had a long gaffing pole in his hand. Automatically she reached for it, but a powerful surge of sea pulled her away and down once more into the blue green cold. This time panic flooded her senses. The wave had dragged her beneath a rock ledge. She had banged her head and the waving kelp was wrapping itself around her arms and legs. Panic faded. *If I'm to die now, drown here, how beautiful it is, so green and yellow.* Then two bright blue eyes blinked at her among the green and yellow. A woman's face, and it was smiling. A voice was speaking to her: "*This is not your place or time, my friend. Come.*"

Mags felt herself being pulled to the surface. Sweet air filled her lungs. Fracher's gaffe caught the strap of her rucksack. She was hauled aboard and laid her on her side. Cushie licked her right hand which she had raised to her face.

Fracher kicked The Searcher into reverse gear. When they were beyond the swell he put her in neutral, got the blanket he always kept in the locker in the wheelhouse. Gently he eased off her rucksack and wrapped Mags in the blanket. She was shivering. He held her in his arms and wept.

The Maighdeann Mhara watched the boat move away across the bay. She swam back to the cave.

# 21

Bragi Boddason, the skald, decided to follow the wave. He had been asleep in an ante-chamber of the great hall at Bilskirnir in Thor's realm of Thrudvangar. He was exhausted after two days and two nights on his feet giving the people his poem about Loki, Idunn and the apples of eternal youth. The shadowless Sun was lurking low in the east on the morning of the third day as he reached into his pocket and pulled out a white handkerchief, which he then unfolded. This was Skidbladnir, given to Bragi by Freyia for his services to the art of love, (for it is well known that poetry is the wave upon which rests the ship of love). When fully unfolded, Skidbladnir is a very large ship indeed: white as ice, with three tall masts. When the sails are unfurled they fill with wind and will sail in any direction Bragi commands. Skidbladnir was designed by the trickster-god Loki himself; built by the black-haired, red-faced dwarf-sons of Ivaldi as a gift to Freyia, the goddess of love.

So great was the fame of the coupling of Jörð and Storegga, and so wild the wave of their resulting passion, that Bragi had to witness it for himself. For, as Bragi has told us, everything in the world is ***Skaldsparmal***, "the language of poetry". Bragi's art, his compulsion, is ***Bragarbot***, "a poem's improvement". So it was he sailed after the wave. The great white ship, Skidbladnir, with a crew of a thousand black-haired, red faced trolls, sped across the northern Ocean, a swift berg of sail.

# 22

It was early in the evening when Manson crossed the beach. He had spent all afternoon in the Castletown pub with Gilbert Henderson, editor of the local newspaper, *The Groat*. They had met at lunchtime and just stayed there. Manson had, to Gilbert's astonishment, paid him back his four hundred pounds.

"Fuck sakes, Manson, you gone into the fairy hill?"

"Something like that."

Gilbert snorted as he stared at the notes, then whistled through his teeth.

"That's a pity," he said, sliding the cash into his inside jacket pocket. "I was planning to blackmail you."

"Aren't you even going to count it?" Manson asked.

"What for? To find it's fairy money? I'm only going to spend it on this pixie juice anyway." Gilbert raised his lager to the sunlight struggling through the dirty bar window.

"What do you mean, blackmail me?" Manson could feel the gas of the lager bubbling in his stomach.

"I want you to be my secret Santa," said Gilbert, "but I don't suppose you'll be interested, now that you've come into some money. You obviously managed to con my respectable crook in Auld Reekie into buying that stupid fucking ring."

"Tell me what the hell you're talking about," said Manson, ignoring the jibe about the crook.

"As an ex-journalist you should know how dangerous it is to have people know what you're talking about," warned Gilbert.

"Anyway, when I think about it, there's no such thing as an ex-journalist. Once a hack, always a hack. Or are you going to tell me different? Are you going to tell me you're a painter now, eh? Weaselling away in that big fucking house of yours, slapping paint onto canvas with your dick, or whatever it is you artists are supposed to do. If I had a dick, that's what I would do – if I was an artist."

"Look Gilbert, just tell me what's on your mind." Manson got up and ordered another round, this time whisky – the lager was making him ill.

He came back to the table and set a pint in front of Gilbert. "I dunno how you can drink so much of that stuff," he said, "only people like Richard Nixon drink lager."

"Ah well now," said Gilbert gleefully, "that's a very good point. I always thought there was a bit of the Bernstein about you. A bit too alluvial to be a Woodward."

"Mister President, I have a very important appointment with oblivion. Will you just get to the point?" Manson drank his whisky. The light in the room became yellow and beautiful.

"I have something I want you to find out for me, to see if it's true."

"Isn't that *your* job? To find out if things are true?"

"Hell no!" said Gilbert, almost spitting out a mouthful of lager. "My job is to find out what's *going on*, not whether it's true or not. I'm a journalist, not a fucking magician."

Gilbert's words swam in Manson's head as he remembered them now, much as the seals were swimming in the bay just beyond the surf on Dunnet beach. *They'll be after the sea bass at the mouth of the burn now the tide's coming in*, he thought, approaching the Burniman as it flowed through the dunes. Up on the high marram grass a group of rooks was gathering. Manson thought back to the conversation he'd just had with his mad if not bad friend. The waves faded. He was back in the bar. The Maighdeann Mhara was watching his every move.

"I want you to speak to Daimler," Gilbert had said.

"Daimler! Why would I want to talk to him?" Manson asked.

"Because something's brewing out on the fun farm, and I want to know what it is. I'm the last person on the planet he'll talk to."

"But Daimler's a lizard," said Manson, swilling back some whisky.

"Aye, he is," agreed Gilbert. "He's also insane."

"Och, you're just saying that because he's a poacher turned gamekeeper," laughed Manson.

"He's a bag of parsley turned into a death's head mushroom, that's what he is! But he's the PR for the whole jing bang and he's the weak link in the chain." Gilbert was getting agitated.

"He's just a two-faced swine, that's all."

"No, that isn't all. I'm telling you, he's mad. I've heard he ponces around in women's clothes in certain clubs when he goes to Aberdeen. But then they're all fucking mad out there."

Gilbert paused, as if this were the saddest thing he had ever thought of.

"Look, you don't know the steps to the Dounreay dance. You live in a fucking bubble, Manson." Gilbert looked around the bar as if he was looking across a desert.

"The thing about being out there, in that place, is that you get detached from the real world."

"Like me?"

"No, not like you!" Gilbert blurted. "Fuck sakes, Manson, you're so self-obsessed! Maybe you dress up as a girlie too – I don't know and I don't fucking care, but as far as a recruit for Dounreay, baby they wouldn't let you over the gate. You have to be sane to get in there, but once you *are* in and you stay there long enough – that's when it starts to happen."

"What? What happens?" Manson could hardly believe it: Gilbert seemed on the brink of tears.

"The world changes. Reality changes. It slides from one end of the spectrum to the other. The more stuff happens on site, the more crazy that stuff gets, the more indefensible it is, the more the real world outside the gates slowly disappears. Oh, you walk about in it after you get off the shift bus. You go into pubs, shops. You walk the streets of Atomic City. You go home and fuck your wife, a melon, your cat, whatever. But you're not there, not really. You're back out on-site, where everybody's like you. Because to them us lot out here, *we're* all fucking insane, zombies, the uninitiated; once you're one of them you learn to hate us because you must love what you do, whatever it is, however dangerous or stupid or mad. But eventually the electrics start to overheat. Sparks appear. Certainties begin to melt, to fuse and burn. That's what's happened to Daimler. That's what happens to them all."

Gilbert had stopped talking then. But Manson could hear him still as he walked along the sand. Down in Edinburgh the Festival will be on, he thought, watching the surf crash onto the beach. Every street will be full, every close and corner of the old city packed with hopefuls wanting something, not even sure what, except they want it so badly they would kill for it. Rafts of eider ducks rose and fell with the surging sea. Manson did not see the Maighdeann Mhara or feel her eyes following him. The congregation of rooks had grown larger now. They seemed to pour from the trees around the Castletown planting. Their Gothic wings and rasping cries filled the air as if they were rounding up ghosts. Manson was dog-tired. A terrible boozy weariness filled his bones as the memory of the bar filled his head. He went to the foot of the dunes and sat down.

"You're drunk," he'd said to Gilbert.

"Of course I'm drunk. You'd have to be fucking mad not to be drunk. *You're* drunk."

It was true. He'd been well on before started drinking with Gilbert. Before he'd walked over the beach to Castletown he'd gone into the Dunnet pub. Bang on eleven. Freedom. To put your hand in your pocket and find *cash*. Manson only truly came alive when he was handing a twenty-pound note to a barmaid. Life without cash was unthinkable. So he chose not to think about it. He was in the Castletown bar with Gilbert and that was all there was space for.

"So Daimler's insane. What of it?" Manson asked.

"Nothing much, but it helps our case," said Gilbert, warming to his project.

"I wasn't aware we had a case," said Manson.

"Which is why you're perfect." Gilbert's tone changed suddenly. "Look, I want you to take him out."

"What? You want me to kill him?!"

"Fuck no," snorted Gilbert. "He'll do that of his own accord eventually."

He reached into his pocket and brought out the wad of money Manson had just given him. He counted out a hundred and handed the notes to Manson.

"Accidentally arrange to meet him," said Gilbert. "Take him for a drink. He likes to drink. And he's lonely. Everybody hates him, including all the fuckwits out on the site. Especially them. I hate him so I can't speak to him. He hates me. He won't tell me anything anyway."

Manson looked at the money. "Look, I'm not sure..."

"Of course you're not fucking sure, who is? All I'm asking is that you *talk* to the wanker."

"But why?"

"Why fucking not?!" exploded Gilbert. "Like I said, something's happening but I dunno what it is. All I know is Gabfan is up to something. There's a rumour running around Atomic City about a take-over but it's all fucking ming and mince at the moment. Does Gabfan want to be taken over, or don't they? I can't work it out. But sources tell me they're trying to stir up trouble with the union."

"Surely that's the last thing they want?"

"Well, you would think so," agreed Gilbert. "But, Manson, remember it's loony tunes out there. What's up to us is down to them. Look, there was a by-election just past. Some stupid young councillor was fucking around with expenses so he got the boot. One of the shop stewards from Dounreay was organizing for the Labour candidate and Gabfan have sacked him because they said he was doing it in company time at his work."

"Is that true?" Manson feigned interest.

"Who fucking knows? And quite frankly I don't fucking care!" Gilbert slammed his empty pint glass down on the table. "If everybody was to get sacked for doing things in company time there would be nobody left on the bloody site. What I do know is that the union has formed a Nuclear Liaison Committee with community groups, to give the impression of impartiality, and they're accusing the company of victimization."

"So what?" said Manson. "Everybody knows they run a black list. Everybody knows about the Official Secrets Act. The union's up to its neck in all of that."

"*Exactly*, amigo, but I want to know what Gabfan is up to? Are they gonna sell up or are they gonna fight off whoever it is that's after them? Or maybe nobody's after them?" Gilbert smiled. "Maybe it's a hall of mirrors?"

Manson stood up to go to the bar. "Do you think they'll sell up?"

"Dunno. It's mega-bucks out there," said Gilbert dreamily. "Billions."

"Gabfan's not likely to let that go. Are they?"

"No," agreed Gilbert. "Unless they've discovered they've got more of a fucking mess than they bargained for. Dounreay is poison, I know that. Getting the dumbos in the union to strike might be a manoeuvre to either attract a buyer or repel a boarder. Or screw more cash out of the government. All I know is, *something's up*."

As Gilbert had finished speaking two postmen came into the bar. They were drunk but still in uniform. They greeted Manson as he waited for his drinks.

"Howz id goin?" slurred one of the postmen, a short man with a Royal Mail baseball cap.

"Christmas bonus in August, is it, gentlemen?" asked Manson.

"Nah," said the taller postie, "wae wur on e pickad line. Boot aat fuckan Weekers come in aboot so wae pissed off here."

"You left a picket line? What the fuck is wrong with you?" roared Gilbert, who had been listening intently.

"Aye, why no?" slurred the little postie, pulling his Royal Mail baseball cap tighter onto his head, as if he were expecting rain.

"Fuckan Weeker's id piss anybody off," said the taller postie, trying to be reasonable.

"But you're supposed to be on fucking strike!" Gilbert roared again, getting to his feet. Manson got their drinks and moved over to the table only to see Gilbert lurch across to the two postmen at the bar. He sat down nervously.

"Wur no on strike," said the taller postman, his moustache twitching a little.

"What d'ye mean you're not on strike? You're in the fucking union are you not?" Gilbert was now between the two men, taking it in turn to stare into their faces, but having a little difficulty with the shorter of the two, as he had to bend down to growl at him.

"Wur no in e union," said the little postie, as if the statement might make him taller.

Gilbert did not react well to this information. "You're no in the union? No in the union?" He kept repeating the phrase as both question and accusation. "No in the union! No in the union! The Weeker's'll be in the union though, eh?"

"Aye," said the taller postie. "Id's them cunts aat's got us on strike. Wae only came oot fur e crack."

"The crack!" roared Gilbert, "The crack! You're supposed to be on strike to save the Royal Mail from being privatized, am I right?"

"Too fuckan late fur aat," the tall postman reasoned.

"You miserable fucking cretins!" exploded Gilbert. "If you were all in the union they couldn't touch you, but the Tories depend on useless fuckheads like you so they can implement their age-old policy of divide and rule. Yer digging your own graves, you pathetic wankers!"

"Here, min," said the little postie, pulling himself up to his full height. "Ah've choost aboot hed enough oh yer abuse."

This only riled Gilbert further. His chest swelled and he seemed to grow several inches beyond his six feet.

"Oh aye," he raged, "an what are you going to do when you're paid off in a week, a month, a year's time?"

"Id'll no come til aat," declared the taller postman, wiping Guinness from his moustache.

"Oh, aye? Won't it? I suppose you took the shares bribe and made yourself five hundred miserable quid, eh?" Gilbert leered at both of them.

"Weel, they wur offeran id til us," reasoned the postman again.

"Aye, like a one-way ticket to fucking Nowhereseville, and you pair of sleazers took it." Gilbert's face was now an inch from the two posties who stood closer together at the bar for protection. Gilbert continued to roar at them. "Just like you took every pay rise, improvements in conditions, holidays and pension and the like those Weekers in the union got for you. You make me sick! You're fucking parasites!"

That final insult was too much for the shorter of the two postmen. In an instant he and Gilbert were rolling around the bar room floor like two epileptic seals, slapping and gouging at each other to no observable effect. The taller postman and Manson remained motionless as if in unspoken secret pact.

It all seemed to have happened years ago. Manson lay back on a tussock of marram grass at the foot of a dune. Several rooks were now on the sand, hopping and cawing some twenty feet away from him. He paid them no heed. He looked up at the blue vastness of the sky. He remembered a report on the radio news as he struggled out of bed that morning, about yet another planet they had found some 25 million light years away. Only slightly larger than the Earth and with a similar metal core. Postmen, Gilbert, waves, sand dunes, rooks – were the whole lot of them on this other planet, wondered Manson? He shut his eyes. The Maighdeann Mhara swam beneath the breakers.

Eventually the barman had jumped across the bar and pulled the little postman off Gilbert, who lay on the floor laughing, blood pouring from his nose. "You're fucking doomed!" he shouted at the postmen who both skedaddled out of the door.

"An e'll bay barred, Gibbie, if ye keep iss up," said the barman as he pulled Gilbert to his feet. "What the hell's wrong wae e, man?"

"A surfeit of history, Charlie, a surfeit of history."

"Mah erse. Id's aat continental lager more lek," said the barman. "Stick til Tenants, Gibbie, an e willna fight wae ah cheil."

"You not going to throw him out?" asked Manson as Gilbert collapsed down beside him.

"Whit? An loose mah best customer? E mad?" asked the barman and disappeared behind the bar. "Kerry, get a buckad. Thur's bleed on ay floor ben ay hoose."

A tall girl in too-tight denims duly came and mopped up the damage. In no time it was as if nothing had happened.

"Aah, an angel," crooned Gilbert. The girl said nothing. Once her task was done she too disappeared behind the bar.

"Like I was saying... Daimler –"

"All right," interrupted Manson, tight-lipped. "I'll see what I can do."

"Just find out what you can. That's all I ask."

"You don't half take advantage, Gilbert, you know that?"

"Of course do," declared Gilbert triumphantly. "I mean, if you can't use and abuse your friends then who can you use and abuse, eh?" He smiled. "My god, Manson, a good bevy, sordid hokery pokery, and a fight. I mean, it doesn't get any better than this now, does it?"

Two pints later Gilbert started to tell Manson about his novel – again. Manson didn't mind. He was drunk enough to listen to anything. They both knew Gilbert wasn't writing a novel. The exchanges became more heated, the plot and the characters kept changing, until Gilbert couldn't remember what he was talking about. It reminded Manson of all the paintings he hadn't painted these past few years. At least it made them both forget the wayward industrial relations with the two drunken postmen.

"It's a post-postmodern novel, you understand," said Gilbert, as he swigged from his pint of lager, "about a time in our species development when humans have no faces, they just have a swipe facility for recognition."

"What, no eyes?" yelped Manson drunkenly. He stared blankly at the dried blood under Gilbert's nose.

"I have a publisher interested, and that's no word of a lie." They both knew it was a total lie. It was enough for them both that it *could* be true. That there might be life on a distant planet, or that the Royal Mail sell-off wasn't going to be a disaster, or that Daimler had once been a decent man – all these things were both true and untrue at the same time. All these possibilities Gilbert seemed to eat up like a hungry lion. He stood up.

"Where the fuck did I put my car?" he roared.

The barman's head appeared round the public bar as he poured a pint in the lounge bar.

"Yur no goan anywhere in any car. Thur's a taxi coman for e, so sit on yur erse."

Dutifully Gilbert obeyed. He leaned back and took a deep breath. "You're a good man, Charlie." Then, after a pause: "And so are you, Manson, beneath all that shite." And then he fell asleep.

Manson had got up and left the hotel to start back home across the beach. What was it to be liked the way people liked Gilbert? Gilbert was natural. It was easy to like Gilbert. Love him, even. As he drifted off to sleep at the foot of the dune he wondered what it was like to love someone. He thought he knew once, but now... Now it was different... Now it was difficult....

"You've been neglecting me," said the Maighdeann Mhara.

Manson looked at the ground.

"Do I make you unhappy?" she asked. He said nothing. He had no voice. He could feel her huge blue eyes burn the air around him. She waited patiently for him to answer.

At last he spoke, but in the voice of a bird, a rook.

"No. It's just that you're so difficult to find."

"But I'm always here," she said, kindly.

"No. Not here. Inside my head." The words a series of aawks and caawks.

"Ah," she said. "I understand."

At once Manson's heart lightened because he knew she did. Relief flooded his body like a high tide. He felt himself rise up as if caught on a huge wave, as if he was surfing towards the blackness of human destiny, beyond the sand-white shore of hope. For the first time in Manson's life he actually dared to believe. The sheer energy-release of this lifted him up, high up above the surf, the beach and into the thin blue air. He felt as if his heart would burst with pure joy and he wanted to cry out. But he was no longer physical, or human. He had dissolved into a breath of air, a flurry of breeze blowing the waterfall back up the clifftop on the headland, a tiny tornado twisting the sand into grainy tendrils on the top of the sand dunes. The grains became stars and large gas-boiling planets. They surrounded and illuminated him or the space he had become, the time which fished for him in the sea of itself.

Suddenly he couldn't breathe. Now the sand was real. It was being flicked all over his face. Instead of the beautiful sea-soaked endlessness of the Maighdeann Mhara's deep blue eyes, two small yellow-irised points of meanness looked carnivorously at him over the long grey knobbly hook of a beak. All the beauty of love and trust which is the universe drained itself of its vastness in a second and hid like a refugee behind the rock of Manson's heart.

He sat up and the rook hopped backwards. Manson cursed it because he knew it was his brother. The rook beat its wings upwards with an ancient and knowing reciprocal squawk. The air filled with the feathered night of a thousand rooks, who had gathered around Manson like a dark halo as he lay dreaming, their countless wing-beats and pitiless crying whipping the August afternoon into a black Sun-less confusion. They rose up in their lightless multitude and clutched the moment of Manson's joy in their many talons. Then, like some spectral arrow, they flew back, a ruinous and leaderless legion, into the Castletown planting, where their bickering swallowed the Summer, and Manson's glimpses of heaven tore apart like carrion on the road.

# 23

The Maighdeann Mhara sat beneath her waterfall. It was her music. Loki had been her lover in the days when the ice had gone north and the land was new and bare. So the story went. They had created a child, some said, which was lost in the tragedy of the flood after the first great wave came across the sea. Since that day, ten thousand years ago, the Maighdeann Mhara looked deep into the eyes of every individual she met, searching for her child, Eros, her son with Loki. That was one of the legends. But, as we know, people will say anything.

The sea is the place for her, Loki had thought, for the wave will come again. Some say that Muirgen, the otter, is Loki. Some say the Maighdeann Mhara lives on Idunn's apples, and that Loki, in the form of a sea eagle, takes the apples from Asgard to the headland. Others say that it is Bragi Boddason himself, the world poet, who brings the Maighdeann Mhara the apples of eternal youth and that she is his lover also. But Idunn is Bragi's wife and people love gossip. They also say that the Maighdeann Mhara plays the clarsach at certain tides and that from *Uamh an Oir*, the cave of gold, at Samhain say, or maybe Beltane, you can hear beautiful music pouring out like water flowing over rocks. Others argue the sound is more like the wind through the trees, but then their tongues have usually been made fluid from beer. There are many legends. Some say there is no son at all. Yet all agree, if they know anything at all, that through all her days, to herself at least, the heart of the Maighdeann Mhara remained pure – even through the loss of her son, which brought much pain. So far back in the flood of years was her black deed that it had faded from the cave wall of human story, from its tongue-runes. But the Maighdeann Mhara's weakness, her black crime, was – jealousy. In Manson's time it was a breath of wind over loch Bushta, a remnant in the whoop of a swan.

In Manson the Maighdeann Mhara saw a trace of her son, Eros. The salt in the apples he brought her from his mother's tree tasted of her child's tears. Remembering helped her forget. She had no son. She was a sea of regret. She thought on all of this with Muirgen asleep beside her on some seaweed, her bag, full of Time, at her feet. Then a figure appeared over the brow of Dwarick Head.

As usual Manson did not see the Maighdeann Mhara. He crossed the small beach to the rock from where his mother used to swim. He set the plastic bag of apples down beside him and stared out to sea. After a time he saw the otter. He turned around and there she was, as beautiful and colourful and as strange as ever. The blackness of the rooks faded from him immediately. The otter slid from the water and sniffed around the shopping bag.

"Muirgen tells me these apples are from your mother's trees," said the Maighdeann Mhara.

Manson nodded. Muirgen got the Co-op plastic in his teeth and pulled the bag over to her. She picked out an apple and inspected it.

"They are quite beautiful."

"First crop of eaters this year," he said. "The last ones I gave you were cookers."

"They were delicious, but they did not come from your mother's garden." She put the Co-op bag into her own bag.

Manson stared at the water, embarrassed

"You have a problem with telling the truth," said the Maighdeann Mhara softly. "It seems that what actually happens is never enough for you."

He tried to speak but the rooks had taken his tongue. She smiled.

"It's why you paint. You have to add to the general stock of reality. You are unhappy because at the moment you don't paint. I know life has been hard for you and that you come here because you loved your mother very much. Manson, I too know what pain and loss can do, what it is like to feel too much. Love can kill. Every time I look at you I see an echo of an old lost song, but one that will be restored to me, I am convinced. It as if you have risen up out of a darkness."

Manson was about to speak. *What does she mean?*

"Yes, the rooks," she said. "It is always the rooks with you. You have forgotten how to love. You have abandoned loyalty. No one can trust you. The ring I gave you as a token of my heart, my friendship – You sold it, did you not?"

Again Manson tried to speak but the Maighdeann Mhara released him from the burden of another lie.

"There is no need to resist the truth. You sold it in Edinburgh."

"How do you know?" he asked, somehow freed from the rookery.

"The American girl, Pearl. You remember her?"

"What about her...? You... you were Pearl?"

Muirgen emerged from the water with a mackerel. He lay on a nearby rock and proceeded to chew the head off the fish.

"It's just because I've had no money for so long. It ground me down. Reduced me, somehow. I was weak, I know. I..." Manson ran out of self-pity. He had nothing worthwhile to say.

The Maighdeann Mhara leaned over and touched his head. A sublime, kindly warmth travelled from his skull to his feet.

"If you need money all you have to do is to ask," said the Maighdeann Mhara, "I will give you everything you desire."

She looked at this strange man-child, this distant trace of her son, of her love that had been lost to her, of her weakness, her regret, her guilt. She saw the awkward pride and grief in his face.

"But that is not your way, is it?" she said. "You will never ask for anything. Because no-one trusts you, you cannot trust anyone. That tragedy has to end. Otherwise who, other than me, will mourn you? Who will sit here and stare at the sea for you?"

"Everything I touch turns to water," he said.

"No. There are better things to think. Light will shine on you. You must believe that. You do not know your heart's desire. No one does. Everyone makes terrible mistakes. You have money now. The second thing is that the least expected thing will happen to you."

The Maighdeann Mhara took her hand from his head.

"There will be a third thing. Something you want so much, too much. It is something you don't know yet. But you must resist it, Manson, or you will pay heavily."

He tried to understand what she was talking about but it was beyond him.

"When you go home this afternoon there will be a message for you," she said. "Things will change. I am your image now."

Having dispatched the mackerel and finished the elaborate ceremony of cleaning his whiskers and paws, Muirgen slipped back into the sea. He swam like a small brown torpedo for a distance and then disappeared beneath the surface.

"I envy your otter," said Manson after a few moments. There was no answer. When he looked around she was gone. A terrible, deep-rooted, rook-black loneliness filled him and he slumped in panic and despair. At last he got up. He left the empty beauty of the Peedie Sannie, the waterfall pouring over the small cave, the waves gently washing the silver shore. Slowly he climbed the rocky path up to the cliff top and walked back the way he had come, over Dwarick Head and down to Dunnet.

Manson sat in the pub a long time that night. The bar was not busy, which suited him. Who could he have talked to about the Maighdeann Mhara? Not to Gilbert, and certainly not to any of the other human shadows who seemed to him to have no purpose to their lives or reason to walk the earth.

Next morning he woke late. There was a message on his mobile phone from Beith at the art centre. *Their stupid exhibition must be over*, he thought, *she'll be wanting me to take my pictures back*. He threw the phone onto his ramshackle kitchen table. *Well, she can wait.* Then the phone rang. It was Beith.

Far from wanting him to take back the six paintings he'd entered for the annual Summer exhibition, she had money for him. All six paintings had sold! The buyer, she said owned the Lawnmarket Gallery in Edinburgh and wanted to mount an exhibition of his work this Autumn.

"Why can't he speak to me himself?" asked Manson.

"It's a she, actually, ye prick." Beith's Dublin manner was nothing if not forthright. "I don't want you to frighten her off. Christ, Manson, you know what you're like. It's like trying to help the Minotaur."

Lunchtime and he was in the pub again. Sitting across the table was Beith O'Donoghue, the director of the Caithness Arts Centre. With her long red hair and tailored green coat, she turned heads.

"Nine hundred quid," she said, sipping her white wine, "Don't worry, I've already snipped off the commission."

Manson looked at the cheque. "Coutt's Bank? Who are they?" he asked.

"Very posh. London. It appears you have an admirer."

"Who is she?"

"Dunno. She's posh. Scottish – which is unusual. Seems to have inherited a fortune of some kind and has opened a gallery. Big one. It's an ex-University Settlement building. She offered cash, I believe. She wants twenty-four large canvasses. She said there will be a letter in the post once we have had this conversation."

"Are we having this conversation?" he asked.

"Well I am. Feck knows what you're on. Anyway, I thought you were broke?"

"I dunno about anything anymore."

"Oh dear. Poor Manson." Beith looked at her watch. Manson took a long swig from his pint and looked at Beith's friendly face. Now she was checking her mobile phone.

"Look, yer good, yer just feckin useless, that's all." She put her mobile down. "Look, Manson, this is a great opportunity. Don't be frightened. But don't screw up. I'll arrange for the materials and stuff if you're short and I'll help with the framing.

undercover from the Drug Squad. "To experience another identity is to possess another soul." Daimler drank thirstily from his long green drink.

"What the hell's in that? Plutonium?"

"Radiation's all around us," replied Daimler. "I'm having the adolescence I missed. It's just that I'm having it as a woman."

"A Thai hoor," said Manson.

"Och, Manson, you disappoint me." Daimler laughed again. "I thought you, of all people, would know that the artist must keep the child inside himself alive."

"Nobody here is alive." Manson drank his whisky down.

"Maybe," agreed Daimler. "Let's just say I'm extending my nature."

"Yes, let's," said Manson, fed up of this game. "So, Daimler, what's going on with the union?"

"Just as Gilbert suspects," said Daimler. "Gabfan is going to pick a fight. Provoke a strike. Sack the entire man jack of them and put the entire operation up for sale. Or at least appear to."

Daimler's voice snaked round Manson's ears and hissed into his head. He could believe *what* he was hearing he couldn't believe *how* he was hearing it. This was a parallel universe, surely.

"Why?"

"*Why!* Because they have to. They've fucked up," said Daimler. "They're being pursued in the High Court by Samdoo, a South Korean outfit who claim they bought the Gabfan Nuclear name ten years ago. They say Gabfan's infringing their copyright."

"And are they?"

"Oh fuck aye. They'll have to change the name of the company, whatever happens." Daimler adjusted his wig slightly. "It's worth billions. I've even heard that they plan to sell the contract to themselves, or at least another part of the greater empire."

"How can they do that?" asked Manson, genuinely intrigued.

"Fuck knows. Look, this much is certain: Gabfan wants to take the heat off. If there is a strike it'll give them the chance to get in a new workforce and start again. Or they can genuinely put the

Oh don't worry, I'm not wanting anything. Except it reflects well on us at the centre. You understand that, at least?"

"Aye, Beith, I do."

He appreciated her honesty. They talked some more while he had another pint before Beith left to drive back to the Caithness Arts Centre. The Centre which was in a beautiful location in the middle of the county. Manson had never so much as set a foot across the door. Beith's perfume lingered for a long time after she left.

He stayed in the pub a long time. The next day passed in a blur. The following day a letter arrived. Just as Beith said. Twelve landscapes. Large. Twelve other pictures. Small. He tried to make sense out of the dimensions stated on the letter but the numbers kept going out of focus. There was an Edinburgh High Street address, a phone number, an email address and a website. The letter was signed by the Director's Personal Assistant. The Director did not seem to have a name.

He phoned the number. A female English voice answered. Manson asked questions. She answered. Yes, twelve large canvases and twelve smaller. The dimensions specified were just guidelines. He could price the work himself but usually work in their featured exhibitions, for a first-time artist, sold for around £3,000. Oh, he was not a first-time artist. Was Miss O'Donoghue his agent? She would send the contract to her then. The 1st of October would be the deadline. Too soon? But surely there was a backlog of work, was there not? Oh, there was not. Well, he would meet the Director presently. They could discuss it. She was greatly impressed with his work. She would contact him so there was no need to worry. Was that all for now? Then we will speak soon, Mr...eh...Manson. The conversation ended. The line went dead.

Then he was sitting at his kitchen table again. A bowl of apples in front of him. He stretched out to pick one. His hand was shaking.

# 24

The roof was on the chapel. Ythan's hand-carved slates graced the Naver oak beams and protected the priests from the rains of Autumn. The chapel was a wonder to behold. *It's like a great ship*, the people said to one another, as they listened without understanding to the blend of Latin chanting and Gaelic with which the three Irish missionary-priests celebrated their house of God and made it sacred to His Holy purpose. Grillaan was on his aged knees, his head bare, his arms stretched upwards, his eyes closed. Words poured from him, a music strange to the people of the Cat. They listened respectfully as Grillaan chanted:

*The peace of God, the peace of men,*
*The peace of Colm Cille kindly,*
*The peace of Mary mild, the loving,*
*The peace of Christ, King of tenderness,*
*The peace of Christ, King of tenderness,*
*Be upon each window, upon each door,*
*Upon each hole that lets in light,*
*Upon the four corners of this, your house*
*And upon all the souls that came from on high*
*Of these your children that are of the earth,*
*Bless, O Christ, this house, these people*
*For an hour, for ever, for eternity*
*Amen.*

Caornan and Nessan helped the old man to his feet. The girl saw that his eyes were full of tears.

People spoke kindly of the Prior, and agreed it had been a good day when the priests had come to this headland in the Province of The Cat. Dungal, Chief of the Cattach came forward and shook Grillaan's hand. Eoghan and Ythan drank barley bree from a clay pot. Clarsach and pipe music drifted through the air adding to the joy. The chapel was greatly admired. Except by the Druids who were nowhere to be seen. Some, who were closer to the old ways, said the chapel was like a muckle stone hen house, and it was true that Nessan had more than fulfilled her pledge in providing the priests with hens. They moved unfettered all over the place: red, black, white and brown. Like the coloured letters on Caornan the scribe's vellum. Or so Nessan thought one morning as she looked admiringly at the young priest's work. She liked the movement in the curls and flourishes of the letters. It was as if they were dancing, and Nessan loved to dance.

"They're like the marks the hens' feet make on the midden after they've had a good mash," she said, delighted.

Carefully Caornan rolled up the psalter. "This is the Gospel of Saint Matthew, first book of The New Testament of our Lord and Saviour Jesus Christ – not the footprints of your hens, Nessan." He smiled to himself.

But Nessan did not see him smiling. *Aye*, she thought, *you werna so lippan my lad when I took you down into the cave and told you about An Slanaigher and the Shee.*

When they had reached the bottom of the geo that afternoon, some weeks past, the light was beginning to fade and the great western cliff behind them obscured what sunlight there was. The rocks were wet and treacherous and some of the boulders were huge, and the cracks in the flagstone formation at the foot of the cliff almost impossible to cross. But Nessan knew a secret way. Soon they were standing in front of the great black open mouth of the *Uamh an Oir*.

"So this is it?" exclaimed Caornan.

"Aye. This is it, the Cave of Gold." Nessan swept her mane of black curls back from her eyes. "But why you want to stick the boy's clarsach in there beats me."

"It is the holy relic of Saint Colm, our order's founder and the brother of His Holiness Grillaan, the Prior," replied Caornan generously. It seemed to him he had told this annoying Pictish girl the same story about a hundred times. "It was blessed Colm's request that we inter his beloved harp in a far corner of the world where the word of God is new to the people."

"It would be better used at a ceilidh, I'm thinking," she said. "Anyway, shall we go in? Watch out for the pigeons." She edged into the open darkness of the cave. "There's a power of them that live in here. Big hooran bats an all."

"There's no need for language like that, Nessan," reproached Caornan, carefully putting one nervous foot in front of the other.

"I have no idea what language you use half the time, and that's the dog's truth. Oh, and watch for that now. I think it's a dead seal."

"Holy Mother Mary, what a smell!" Caornan screwed up his face.

"Aye, well, you'd smell the same if you'd been lying here as long. Now just hang on a second and our eyes'll adjust to the light."

Slowly the rounded openness of the cave revealed itself: a tapered space, nave-like, sloping down to the back. In a swoosh of beating wings, a frenzy of pigeons flew out through the entrance into the daylight, as Nessan had predicted.

"Do people ever come here?" Caornan asked.

"What do *you* think?" sneered Nessan. Caornan did not know what to think. Nessan relented. "Hardly anybody comes here. They're too feared."

"Why's that?"

"Och, An Slanaigher scares them away," said Nessan, letting the water which ran down the walls flow over her fingers.

"An Slanaigher? Who's that?"

Nessan was facing the cave wall, her hair so dark that Caornan could be sure of her presence only from the sound of her voice. He realised how much he liked that voice.

"A *what*, not a *who*. An Slanaigher comes out of the ground. She swims in the sea. She's a goddess. She lives in this cave. And she has her army of retainers – the Shee. They will do whatever she bids them and she keeps them in a huge pot and when she summons them out it's like the end of days." Nessan stopped, as if to listen herself to what she had just said. "So they say."

"Who? Who says?"

"The folk. But folk say a lot of things. They say she eats people."

"*Eats* people?" repeated the young scribe, incredulous but nervous.

"Och, others say that she's a kelpie, you know – a water horse?"

"*An uisge eachan?*"

"If you like," said Nessan, running wet fingers through her hair, which hung over her face like seaweed. "Nobody knows anything about An Slanaigher. She's like a storm-force from the sea, or like the wind from the top of the headland. The Shee are her children. She is the dark wonder of the world."

"Why is she a she?"

"Everything is. Isn't it?" Nessan moved her head from side to side, flicking water so that it landed on Caornan, patterning his face with its tiny coldnesses and sitting on his tongue like salty flecks of stone.

"Have you seen her?" he asked. Nessan stopped shaking her head and looked towards the back of the cave.

"No, but I've felt her."

"How do you mean?"

"I came here once with my brother. We were looking in rock pools for wilks, for bait. Just as we got to the mouth of this cave, a wild gust of wind blew out of it."

"Really?" Caornan felt cold. "Were you frightened? I mean, didn't you run away?"

"My brother did. But I just stood still. The gust passed and everything was back to normal."

"I think we should go out now," said Caornan.

"Once Cheemag the shepherd came down here looking for a lost ewe. His collie ran into the cave here afore him. As Cheemag followed the dog ran back out – hairless. As bald as a fish!"

"It'll be getting dark soon," said Caornan, trying to be matter-of-fact. "Come on, we should go." He grabbed Nessan by the shoulders and steered her to the light pouring in through the entrance. The warmth of the late afternoon reassured him.

"Is it so strange for you, Caornan?" asked Nessan seriously, disentangling herself from his nervous arms.

"What?"

"*Uamh an Oir*, An Slanaigher, the Shee, the stories."

"No," he lied, "I have faith in Christ our Saviour."

"To me, your writing is stranger," she said. "Those marks. They draw the stories down from the sky. They have a dark magic, I think. As if they have danced in from the great edge of everything."

As Caornan looked across the bay at the blueness of the water, a smile returned to his lips. The distant rumbling of the surf breaking on Dunnet Beach calmed him.

"Writing is a bit like you described," he said, "you know, the wind rushing out of the cave."

"All those things inside your head. Who put them there?" asked Nessan, pulling him over a red barnacle-pocked boulder.

"They are the blessings of God. That is what His Holiness the Prior instructs me. Ow!" Caornan rubbed a grazed knee.

"The Druids get their poems from the trees and the burns," said Nessan, showing no sympathy. "Man, but you're clumsy." She guided him across a flat piece of rock covered in green slime.

"Your Druids do not know God," he said, trying to keep his feet.

"They tell us they are the instruments of the gods and spirits. With their mad hats and wild rolling eyes who couldn't believe them? They say their staffs are frozen adders and that they can bring them alive if they want to punish you." Nessan jumped over a wide rock pool. "Would you look at the peedie partans in that?" she exclaimed happily. She put her hand into the pool and picked one out. "They look like they're made of black gold!"

Caornan knelt down beside her. He too was delighted by the bluey-black beauty of the little crabs. "Ink has the same kind of crab-sparkle," he said.

"That testament you showed me. Did you make it up? I mean, if it didn't come from the trees and the burns where did it come from?" Suddenly she was serious, all mischief gone.

"It is the divine word of God," said Caornan solemnly. "I just copy it. That's my trade – I'm a scribe... I do write wee poems in the margins sometimes, though."

"I knew it!" said Nessan triumphantly. "You *are* a bard!" She put the partan back into the pool and stood up. "Your little stone huts are like crab shells. They're like your peedie poems, only they're made out of stones, a clachan of songs."

Then she was off again, climbing up a stone ledge. Caornan clambered after her.

"And our new chapel, our wee cathedral, what do you think of that? Is it a poem?"

Nessan stretched out her hand and pulled the young priest up beside her. "It's more like an island."

"Not a stone ship?" he asked.

"Well, folk are saying that, aren't they?" She laughed. "Well if it is a stone ship, the three of you will sail it off into the sky." She darted off again.

"Maybe we will," said Caornan thoughtfully, but she was not there to hear him.

Soon they were back at the foot of the Chapel Geo, with the tide coming in. They stopped briefly to admire Ythan's wall. Eoghan's boat sat safely behind it, out of the salty reaches of the ocean. Nessan looked at it for a moment.

"Did you sail in here from the sky?" she asked.

"No," laughed Caornan, "We sailed in from Lough Swilly."

"Och, much better if you came from the sky, especially if you're a bard." She was gone again. Caornan watched her bounding up the steep incline of the geo like a roe deer, her hindquarters catching the fading light of the Sun. When Caornan reached the top of the geo Nessan was waiting for him.

"What kept you?" she laughed, and ran off towards the chapel.

Ythan was still working on the roof, putting finishing touches to a row of slates. The blessing of the building was still some days away. Nessan watched him intently. Caornan looked around to see if the Prior was on the go as it would soon be time for evening prayers.

"So what are your poems about?" asked Nessan, still watching Ythan.

"They are vanities," replied Caornan, shyly. "Not proper work."

"Fah!" snorted Nessan. "It's all work, proper or no! Gey stuffy god you've got." Then casually, "Do you write about me?"

"No," said Caornan sharply.

Nessan had been teasing, but disappointment now gave an extra edge to her voice.

"Well, bardie boy," she laughed, "what do you make them up about then, if not about me?"

"I saw a wren the other day," began Caornan after a pause, "and I thought how marvellous it was – so small when the world is so big."

"Ower big for yer peedie poems, I'm thinking."

"It's amazing what you can cram into a margin," said Caornan.

Nessan thought about this for a moment. "Why don't you make a poem about the people here. About Ythan there, working away? About the people out in the fields or at the fishing?"

Caornan was about to answer with something he had half learned from Grillaan when from up over the cliff top flew four white swans, some twenty feet above their heads. Ythan on the chapel roof raised his head to look at them passing so low and white and beautiful. The soft beating of their wings disguised the strength of their purpose. Nessan's eyes darkened and widened like hill lochs after rain as she gazed at them in wonder.

"Guiliog ee! Guiliog oh! Guiliog ee! Guiliog oh!" she sang to them as they passed. "Guiliog ee! Guiliog oh!"

As if it recognised the sound she made the lead swan answered: *Guilee! Guilee!*

"Guiliog ee! Guiliog oh!" sang out Nessan in return, and as the fourth swan flew over the little clachan of stone songs it honked out *Guiliog ee! Guiliog oh! Guiliog ee! Guiliog oh!* Then they disappeared over the ridge of the hill and settled on the loch.

Caornan stood watching the swans. Beside him Nessan sat down heavily on a stone, her hair a river of peat flowing over her shoulders, her lips parted, still gently reciting the call of the swans. Tears swelled in her wide eyes. Caornan turned to look at her. He felt as if he might melt into the earth. *I have never met a human being like you*, was what he wanted to say to her. He hadn't the nerve.

"Friends of yours?"

"They are the Children of Leir," she said softly. Caornan had to squat down beside her to hear the rest. "Long ago Becan of Atholl in the South of Alba became the Mormear of all the Cruithne. As a token of peace, and to prevent hostility from the Cattachs, Becan gave his daughter, Smert, as wife to Leir of the Cattachs. As the gods willed they loved each other and had four children. But Smert died and Leir was heartbroken. Becan sent his other daughter Nair to save Leir's life, but Nair was jealous of the love the four children had for each other and she planned to kill them. When the time came she could not do it. Instead she turned them into swans."

"The four which just flew overhead?" Caornan's voice had softened, for he could see that Nessan was far away, her tender years possessed by an ancient shadow as she repeated the story.

"When Leir found out what Nair had done to his beautiful children he turned her into a sea creature and that is where she remains. As for the children of Leir they have spent three hundred years on Loch Calder, three hundred years on the Durran Loch and another three hundred years here on Loch Bushta."

"What happens when their time here is up?" whispered Caornan. "Will they have to find another loch?"

"Ah priest," said the voice from inside Nessan, "perhaps this is the purpose of your coming here. The seanachie say that a strange druid, a foreign priest can end their spell. That the Children of Leir can be released by the sound of a bell."

"We don't have a..."

"Do not say anything more," said the voice, "All I hear is the voice of the swan:

"Guiliog ee! Guiliog oh! Guiliog ee! Guiliog oh!
Voice of the swan, and she in the mist,
Voice of the swan, and she in sorrow,
Voice of the swan in the early day,
Voice of the swan upon the loch
Voice of the swan, and she in the ocean
Voice of the swan, and it is so cold,
Voice of the swan, and it so keen
Voice of the swan, and she in the ocean."

Nessan stood up and moved away from Caornan. She ran a few steps in the direction of the ridge behind which lay Loch Bushta. She began to stamp her feet on the heather.

My one foot black,
My one foot black,
My one foot black,
I must fly!
My one foot black

At the mouth of the burn,
My other splashing
*Wounded.*

Then she fell. Caornan ran to her and gathered her up in his arms. She felt so small; yet so strong. *Like a swan*, he thought, *a black swan*. Gently he brushed the insistence of liquorice tangled hair from her face which was wet with tears. She smiled at him.

"Bardie boy," she said, "you had better get yourself a bell."

# 25

The Nuclear Archive was proving hard to sell to the people of Caithness. The establishment had bought it easily enough: the government, the Highland Council, the community councils. Politicians of every hue and at all levels would spout any old twaddle if they thought it made them sound important or be seen to be doing something. The much-vaunted community benefit from the Nuclear Archive was met by the community with complete indifference. Neither did the official line as to how "lucky" Caithness was to have such a sought-after facility sited in the Far north meet with any success. The Gallachs, thought Kylie, have given up the nuclear ghost. The Atomicers, on the other hand, were all for it. But the Nuclear Archive was going to be built in Wick, not in Atomic City, and even the selling of Dounreay to the natives, way back in the early nineteen-fifties, had been met in Wick with less than the hosannas of rapture which rose up from Atomic City at the proposal. Here was the post-war dichotomy, the social fault-line which had cracked open in Caithness. Until the beginning of the nineteenth century Wick had been a nothing sort of place. Just a smear of thatched buildings north of the river, it had boomed into a bustling herring port and still, come the nineteen-fifties, had a strong white fish industry. Thurso, on the other hand, had declined gradually since World War One from its position as market capital, trading port and principal county town to become an abandoned, sleep-induced hamlet, where emigration was the route to the future. Thurso, come 1956, was losing itself while Wick had become a real place with a strong civic identity. Now, in the post-nuclear age, it was Wick who had suffered the most, ironically, from the decommissioning of Dounreay. Its distance from the economic generator was graphically telling.

Kylie tried to tell them all this. The more she said to explain the history of the place the more Daimler and Nagelstein loathed her. Kylie persisted – they needed to understand where they were.

"It's not that they don't *know about* the archive. It's just that they don't give a damn about it."

Darcy Nagelstein was a large albino-like American – The White Ape they called him. With no neck and a bald head, his body was covered everywhere else in a thin down of white hair. When he spoke, his lips didn't move. Daimler was a Scot of a vague Lowland extraction, also bald, whose head came to a point, and who seemed to glow with some hidden inner fridge light. He was small, so skeletally thin his clothes conspired to drown him. Both stared at her across the desk with increasing contempt.

"You're not selling it right!" said Daimler impatiently, his voice unnaturally high, as if he had been breathing helium. "You've got a degree in English fucking literature, have you not? You're supposed to be able to write a fucking story!"

"I've advanced every angle you have proposed on every front you have suggested. They just won't bite. Look, if we built the thing in Thurso, no problem. But you want it in Wick. I would have more interest if I was selling bubonic plague."

"Not even the educational aspect?" pressed Daimler. "I thought we had a project good for go there?"

"We did," said Kylie, "Unfortunately circumstances changed."

"Didn't you offer them money?" Nagelstein asked.

"This particular 'circumstance' is beyond the reach of money. She died suddenly. Leukaemia."

"Your aunt, wasn't it?" said Daimler, approaching pity.

"It was. She was well-liked," said Kylie.

"Goddammit, they all want money!" Nagelstein announced, impatiently.

"It's not a question of money," reasoned Kylie. "I've offered every school in the county a brand new building, for god's sake. They're just not interested. End of story. It's as if they are trying to forget about nuclear. No Nuclear Archive is going to change that."

"Well, it makes no goddamn difference anyhow," said Nagelstein, "Cos it ain't ever gonna be built."

"I'm sorry... ?" asked Kylie.

"The fact that it is not going to be built is what makes it economically viable," said Daimler reassuringly.

"Maybe she should go to Albuquerque?" Nagelstein spoke directly to Daimler. "See how it's done over there?" Daimler said nothing. Nagelstein turned to face Kylie. "Whaddaya think of that? Ya could take a look at old Atomic Annie!"

Kylie had no idea what he was talking about.

"We *could* send her to Albuquerque, I suppose..." mused Daimler, his inner fridge light glowing more brightly.

"All that dry, sunny desert air. I haven't been there for years." Nagelstein pushed back his chair and hauled himself up to his full height.

"Yes... we could... But maybe it won't come to that."

Nagelstein ignored Daimler and moved to the office door.

"Yes sir! I sure would love to go back to New Mexico." He stared blankly, as if he had forgotten something, his shiny grey suit hanging from him like wet canvas. "Yes indeed. The Albuquerque Isotopes are a fine baseball team." He opened the door and disappeared.

"What is this with Albuquerque?" Kylie had reached the end of her tether.

"It's a state of mind," said Daimler, sharpening a pencil.

"Could you please tell me what you're talking about?"

"It's a nuclear theme park in New Mexico." Daimler concentrated on his pencil sharpener. "The home of Atomic Annie, the nuclear cannon. That's what he was talking about – I think." There was a pause as he looked at his pencil. "But don't worry, you won't be going there any time soon."

Kylie sat still as Daimler picked up another pencil.

"Caithness isn't a theme park," she said softly. Patreen's death had been hard.

"Isn't it?"

"Look, I really don't know what you want me to do?"

Daimler set down his half-sharpened pencil. His colour seemed to change slightly, like an alarmed squid.

"You haven't been here long," he began. "You earn good money. And when things get difficult you nail your balls to the floor."

"For your information – I do not have balls."

"Well your fanny then. You Oxbridge lot are all the same. I met tons like you when I was freelancing. You want everything done for you. Expectation is not the same as achievement. The NDA are still the overseers. Gabfan is here but who knows, they may be gone tomorrow..."

Kylie interrupted him, curiosity one step ahead of anger and grief.

"Are you saying Gabfan Nuclear might be selling out?"

"What I'm saying is that you are fucking useless. Now get out before I sack you."

The full enormity of what Daimler had implied did not hit Kylie until she was back at her own desk. The wave of history had just washed over her. Trembling, she picked up her bag, left the office and drove out of the plant, heading for Atomic City. She switched on the radio. The eleven o'clock news bulletin. "*Today nuclear authorities at the stricken Fukushima power plant in Japan have begun the process of freezing the ground beneath the damaged reactors. The full extent of the radiation leak caused by the March tsunami is not yet known...*"

Kylie almost drove the car off the road. A shift bus coming in the other direction flashed its headlights at her. The wave, she thought, it's the wave. But this was not her wave. Her wave was coming. The sky clouded and it started to rain. As she drove down Scrabster Brae the curve of a rainbow straddled Hoy, a fading brown strip on the north side of the Firth. By the time she turned into the Co-op car park the rainbow was, if anything, more intense. She remembered an argument she'd had at Oxford with a science student who said that she, as a Humanities student, looked down on him because she thought that scientists knew nothing of beauty. "*It was your own James Clerk Maxwell, a bloody Jockanese just like you*," he had taunted her drunkenly, "who created the most beautiful formula in history." She had expressed no interest in his opinion. But it was different now. Poetry had moved out into the material world. James Clerk Maxwell had used mathematics to describe how electrical and magnetic forces interacted to produce light. To be able to quantify and express something, she thought, that must be the measure of beauty.

As she walked across the car park towards the Co-op entrance she saw her auntie Patreen come out.

"Yer mither's askan fur e," she said. Then she disappeared.

Kyle went into the supermarket and bought a bottle of vodka.

# 26

Colin was forever teasing Kylie about her dreams. Lying beside him sound asleep, she was breathing softly. He was lying on his back, sweating and wide awake. He slid out of bed quietly. In the living room he opened the blinds and looked out of the window. Four in the morning but already it was getting light. As the roofs of Atomic City melded into the mirk he tried, as best he could, to recall his dream. He had been walking through some dunes, or across a beach. He saw a man with a huge tongue. Seven men were chained by their ears to the man's tongue. When Colin asked the man why this was, he man replied "*Ith becauth they are in awe of my eloquenth.*"

At school there had been a terrible bully called Black Robbie who always hung around the school gates on a Monday morning, demanding money from first-year boys he knew would have their week's pocket money on them. If you refused or struggled he would grab you by the collar, pull you up to his face and – because he had a lisp – his threat was "Geeths yer shullinths, bouy, orrull burtht yer nothe!" Once you wriggled free and the terror had subsided you could always laugh. Some poor Atomicers fresh from Pennyland Primary would wet themselves, a dark damp patch in the shape of Africa developing around their gowls. At least the local loons never did that, thought Colin. Absent-mindedly he ran his tongue across his teeth. What the hell did it all mean? What's the point of it all? He turned on his heel and opened the door into the spare room. His milling machine. *Ideas need* ***things*** *– and vice versa*, he thought. That was what engineering was.

Quietly Colin padded into the kitchen and made coffee. He returned to the front room, shut the door and put on the TV. These days he only watched Al Jazeera. His reasoning was that if the Yanks hate it, it must be good. Mainly, though, it was because it wasn't the BBC. He loathed the BBC for the shape of their maps, their ignorant metro-parochial smugness, but mainly for the fact that they couldn't even speak their own language. There was no such thing as an "r" in the BBC lexicon. The dollies who presented the weather would wave their little hands towards the tapered head of the map and witter on about somewhere called "*Scutlin*", where there would be rain and high winds in the "*fah noth*". At least with Al Jazeera you knew they were just two camels and a Toyota truck away from the gun-runners.

He settled down, sipping his coffee. Fukushima, Fukushima, Fukushima. Everything was about Fukushima. Around 160,000 people within a twelve miles radius of the plant would never be allowed home. Too much radiation for humans to withstand. If Fukushima was Dounreay that exclusion zone would be well west beyond Strathy and east almost half way to Wick, north across the Pentland Firth to Hoy in Orkney, and south to Loch Dhu in the boglands of the interior.

When the news from Japan broke on-site the reaction was a mixture of laughter at the "*stupid feckless Nips*" and a sharp intake of breath from those who knew what potentially, probably, most definitely was happening. There were three reactors at Dounreay and two at Vulcan, but not the slightest possibility of a similar incident happening here: absolutely nothing to worry about. That was the unwritten official line of the Authority. In Japan, there was plenty to be worried about. Colin watched as they re-ran pictures of the wave breaking, then the explosion. No amount of superiority from the NDA or racism from the sooth-mooth physicists made him feel any more secure. The Yanks had just ignored Fukushima. He'd heard Gabfan managers tell their workers to "*shut the fuck up*" about it. "*You don't need to worry your sweet ass about those babies,*" he'd overheard one of them croon in the canteen. The news-wave of Fukushima, they hoped, would just wash over Dounreay. Everything else did, including the truth and history. Colin knew, from an engineering point of view and purely instinctively, that Fukushima was all our "babies" now. He switched off the TV. The nuclear industry would deal with this latest disaster to its credibility the way it always did: by ignoring it.

He decided to go into work early. He never did this unless there was a specific job on, but he was uneasy. Nagelstein, the White Ape, had asked to see him and that was never good. It was to do with the unions. Ever since Gabfan and their two fellow American sub-contractors had come on site their relationship with the unions had been adversarial. It was only to be expected from Americans. This had taken the unions by surprise. Exactly why, Colin had never understood. But then the unions on-site had always been part of the establishment, and had always been kept sweet. The last thing the British government wanted – especially right now – was a strike at a nuclear plant. All the workers had signed the Official Secrets Act so they were all in it up to their necks anyway. They had made their Faustian pact. Everybody understood the lazy game. But nobody had told Gabfan Nuclear, or if they had the company had not understood a word. State security was not equivocal with profit. In a matter of months, after drastic changes to working practices, the union – for now there was only one – had joined with others to form The Nuclear Industrial Liaison Committee. *It's about protection from management intimidation*, they had said – *a united front to protect the future*. Fair play, Colin thought, but it won't work. For one thing, the union had been ploughing its own furrow for too long, protecting its members at the expense of everybody else, and in competition with other unions off-site. Times were changing and the needs of one trade were now the needs of everybody. Demarcation and protectionism meant nothing any more.

"What you need is one big union," he'd said to Jimmy Greenan, an engineer and shop steward.

"What? Like the Wobblies in America?"

"Mock if you want, Chimmy, but it's Yanks you're dealing with."

"They'll learn."

The problem was that was nobody was learning anything. Old ways. New ways. It was one or the other and there was only going to be one winner. Colin knew it wasn't going to be The Nuclear Industrial Liaison Committee.

Things had come to a head just before the Highland Council by-election for the West ward of the county. Young Dopey Donnie had been caught fiddling his expenses to such an extent that the police had been brought in and he had been forced to resign as a councillor. Rumour had it that he had been fiddling with his flies as well, especially when it came to single mothers who needed a house. Dopey Donnie's political ticket was as an Independent – independent of sense, politics and brains as far as Colin could see. He remembered when his father, Ould Dopey, used to be the Wheecher-In at the High School, letching at the fifth and sixth-year lassies from his white van. Young Dopey was only carrying on the family tradition of corruption. Now, however, his dodgy ways had come back to haunt him. Suddenly, like a Catholic at the Masonic Lodge, he had no friends. Labour saw this as an opportunity to fight back against the "nationalists" as they called the SNP. The problem for Labour was that the SNP was popular and well organised locally with lots of activists and members. Labour, on the other hand – other than on-site – was nowhere organisationally. This is where and when The Nuclear Industrial Liaison Committee stepped in. They sponsored a Labour candidate to contest the seat: a young trade unionist who would do exactly as he was told. The lack of party members was a weakness but the Committee got around this little difficulty by getting all their own members to join the local Labour Branch. Suddenly there were hundreds of new party members who arranged their reps onto the selection panel. Among the hordes of names that appeared on the membership list were many who no longer worked at Dounreay, or who had even left Caithness. Five of them were actually dead. The young lad was adopted. This salient fact had awoken the interest of Gilbert Henderson of The Groat. Colin knew him to be a rumbustious, sometimes drunken heap of a man who liked a good argument and who was always annoying the hell out of Daimler. He also happened to be secretary of the local chapel of the National Union of Journalists, so was very close to the Labour Party. Henderson had no problem putting his political loyalties aside in the pursuit of a good story. Fake membership of the north branch of the Labour party in the run-up to the council by-election made a peach of a story and he knew it. To add to the mix Gabfan had been trying to hound Jimmy Greenan for working for the Labour Party during company time. In the past this had been acceptable as union business but Gabfan Nuclear weren't interested in the past. Colin had said it was a storm in a teacup and that it would all blow over in time. Another wave washing over the dome of Dounreay. Gabfan, as he was to find out, had other ideas.

It was well after eight o'clock before the administration team started to come into the big open-plan office suite next to his. Colin had already been at his desk for an hour and a half, manifests and safety reports stacked up before him. By eight thirty the place was a human ant heap of activity. At nine o'clock he went down the corridor for his appointment with Darcy Nagelstein, head of Gabfan Nuclear UK. He pushed open the door which wasn't shut. It never was. The White Ape liked to see and be seen. Colin knocked just the same. No answer. He went in. The White Ape in a grey suit sat behind his big polished desk. There was a pad and a pen in front of him but no other papers. There never was.

"Harper," he said without looking at Colin or moving his lips, "we have a situation."

"Oh?" Colin sat down without waiting to be asked. He sensed Nagelstein was in a hurry to tell him something – but then, the White Ape was always in a hurry about something.

Nagelstein raised his head from the note-pad. "That goddamn waste shaft is impossible!" he snarled.

"But you knew that. I wrote a report."

"Yeah, yeah. I know." Nagelstein replied in a slow growl.

"Then you must admit it's not impossible," reasoned Colin.

"We could clean it up," the White Ape agreed. "But man, it'll take time."

"Everything takes time in the nuclear industry, Darcy," said Colin, brightly.

"Don't sass me, son. This ain't no industry. It don't make nothin'." He paused. "Except money and mess – and that's what I want to talk to you about."

"Money and mess. I see." Colin leaned back in his chair, playing for time. The White Ape stared at him, his narrow eyes almost disappearing into the end of his neck which constituted his head.

"That union mother. I want his ass run off this rig."

"Who? Chimmy Greenan, the shop steward?" asked Colin.

"That's the guy. We've got him conductin' union business when he should be workin for the company. In my book that's nothin short of a crime." Nagelstein lifted the pen from the desk. It looked like a toothpick in his big down-covered hand.

"We've been over this before. With the greatest respect, Darcy, it's not a crime to be in a union here."

"Well, I'm goddamn makin' it one!" declared Nagelstein, throwing the pen back onto the desk. "You're the top hand on the site," he continued, words sliding over his motionless lips like logs over a waterfall. "You gotta show leadership. Get rid of the son of a bitch."

Colin felt heat rise from the small of his back until it sat behind his eyes. "I cannot sack a man for participating in union business while at his place of work. He is a shop steward."

"He's a radical. A political. He was workin for the socialists. We won't tolerate that. Not here. Not now. Not ever!" Nagelstein banged his fist on the desk. Colin could stand it no longer.

"Look, just what the fuck is wrong with you people? Chimmy's an engineer. Do you have any idea how difficult it would be to replace a man with his experience? Fucking impossible, that's how!"

"He's a commie son of a bitch!"

"He's a fitter-turner son of a bitch!"

Colin got up from the chair. He walked towards the door, but stopped and turned. "If you have him sacked – and I'm not doing it, I can assure you – you'll have every man-jack on site on strike within twenty-four hours. You know that. They can organise a ballot at the drop of a hat. We cannot afford a walk out!" Colin realised he was shouting.

"If so much as a mother's son goes on strike they are all out of a job!" Nagelstein shouted back.

"Look," Colin tried to reason. "If Gabfan wants to enquire into collusion between the union and the Labour Party then you either take it up with them or you go to the police. They're already looking into a councillor's expenses. But in my opinion, you'll be wasting your time, whatever."

"Seems to me, son," the White Ape reflected, "that wasting time is what you guys have spent the last fifty years doin around here."

"I know what you think of us, Darcy," said Colin, trying to calm down, "and you may have a point. But, hell's teeth, we have dangerous radioactive chemicals stored all over the place. There's literally tons of toxic metal to process. We have shipments to make. We have at least twenty-five contractors on site. We have the shaft to secure. If that process is stopped – well, Christ – it's beyond dangerous."

"We are well aware of all that," said Nagelstein, leaning back in his chair. Colin moved back towards the big American.

"So why pick a fight with the union, with the Nuclear Liaison Committee now, at this time? I just don't get it."

"Because it's the best time."

"The best time? The best time for what exactly?"

"You don't have to worry your sweet ass about that, Harper."

"Don't I? I'm the site manager. I should know everything that's going on."

"You work for Gabfan now, son. We decide what you should and shouldn't know." Nagelstein's voice reminded Colin of sand being poured from the back of an artic.

"Is that a fact?" challenged Colin. "I don't work for Gabfan. I'm only *attached to* your poxy company." He paused and changed tack. "Look, Darcy, I can't do my job if I don't know what the fuck is going on!"

Nagelstein smiled. His lips moved across his face as if they were being pulled by wires. "I look after the interests of the company, Harper. That's why I get the film-star salary. You, what do you get?"

"Nothing much," said Colin. "But look, this is not about you or me and it certainly isna about Chimmy fucking Greenan, is it?"

"Waaal... not a lot." Nagelstein grin expanded into something resembling a Halloween smile.

"If the processes are interrupted, or stopped for any reason, this entire piece of Caithness could be radioactively corrupted for ever."

"And you give a damn about that?" Nagelstein asked.

"Well, aye. Don't you?"

Nagelstein stopped smiling. He leaned forward in his chair. "That's the trouble with you Scats. You think you own yer country, eh? I tell you, son, we make sure we own every country we come into. We like it that way."

Colin didn't know how to respond. He could walk out. He could say something profound. He wondered what they would make of the White Ape on Al Jazeera.

"Have I gotta whisper it to you, Harper? We got the power."

Colin looked at Nagelstein for a moment. Morning sunlight which poured in from the east-facing office window was now lighting up the entire room, and the fine down which covered the White Ape caught the light so that the hands, neck and face – especially the eyebrows – of the big American turned the colour of honey. Then it came to him.

"You want out of here, don't you?" Nagelstein said nothing. "Too much mess and not enough money. You've got a buyer for the contract, haven't you? Who is it, Darcy? Is it the French? Na, it widna be them, cos you hate them even more than you hate us. Another Yankee outfit, is it? Don't tell me? Ith the Japanese!" The White Ape stared at him with loathing. "Are you frightened of another Fukushima, Darcy? D'ye think the big wave's gonna get ye?"

"I want Greenan outta here. Is that understood?"

"Oh aye, Darcy," said Colin, "that much at least is understood." He turned and walked out of Nagelstein's office.

The corridor back to his own office and the administration centre was an endless green tunnel of silent noise. He reached his desk. Donna came in and put some papers in front of him. Her hair seemed to radiate in the light. Her perfume lingered after her like the fresh smell of Summer seaweed on the beach after the tide has gone out. Colin rested his elbows on his desk and cupped his head in his hands. Fukushima, Fukushima, Fukushima. Ith gonna burtht ma nothe! It's all our babies now. Like it or not, we are the daddies.

# 27

Mags sat staring at the flames in the salmon bothy fireplace. Outside a Westerly gale blew the water in the bay to a fervent foam and surf crashed onto the beach in continuous thunder. From time to time the wind caught the chimney, and smoke from the driftwood she was burning blew back out into the bothy. She didn't mind. It made the yellow flames in the grate dance like flowers in a meadow. She added some peats from the trailer-load Minker had sent her. Sanders the ghillie had dumped them in a heap at the back of the bothy.

"Ye'll mebbe hev til beeld thum a bittie til protect thum from ay haar," he had said. "Nuhain worse than weet peits."

He showed her how to do it. Now the smell of peat smoke was her new favourite thing. On a big wooden table sat her laptop, her camera and her papers. A mug and a half-empty bottle of red wine, some cheese and oatcakes were spread out around her place of work in a shambles of careful abandon. There was no internet connection and what mobile reception she could get if she stood on the cliff top to the East of the bothy had disappeared. She had just downloaded the photos she had taken of the bronze-alloy hand bell she had found up by the well near the loch and was enjoying the sense of achievement and remoteness, even though the village and the hotel pub were just fifteen minutes walk away. The bell was the only artefact she had found so far. It also sat on the table in an open shoe box.

The bothy was two rooms and a tiny bathroom with a toilet and an enamel-free bath. Mags had spent two whole days airing an old iron bed in the room on the east side, scrubbing it clean of mice droppings, dead moths, bluebottles and spiders. She had quickly painted all the walls a light blue, hung some cheap yellow curtains bought in a Thurso charity shop, and with an even cheaper downie, pillow and sheets from Tesco's she had a bedroom. The front room was spartan. The few bits of furniture were wooden and solid enough, especially the dresser. In a corner there was a sink and a rudimentary cooker which ran off a gas bottle. There were a few pots and pans, plates and cutlery – all a bit battered and sad looking. There was a curtain on a rail you could pull to pretend that it was a kitchen. But she loved the place and it loved her right back.

On fine evenings she would sit outside on an old bench made from fishboxes and two scaffolding planks, writing up her notes or reading, sipping tea or wine. She would watch the Sun sink down into the endless Atlantic when the sky was clear. As August wore on the sunsets got more spectacular and longer lasting. Nature continually astounded her. Once a pod of at least twenty dolphins came into the bay in pursuit of herring and she watched them for hours. Mags was never sure what nature was up to. She had to translate what she saw into what she understood. Everything was new, and it took time for her to adjust her mind to it all so that each beautiful thing became normal and, as a result, more beautiful. Mags took nature very personally. She loved watching the gannets dive for fish and the fulmars gliding above the cliffs. There were seals on the go all the time. They were more interested in what she was doing than she was in them. Some nights she could hear them barking and singing to each other from the rocks down on the shoreline. Occasionally she would see a pair of otters fishing down where the salmon fishermen used to tie up their cobble. As the weeks passed and the Summer wore on she could feel herself tighten physically and loosen mentally. She had become much fitter. Every day she walked from the bothy to the chapel site and then back again – six miles in total – and the cliff top path was quite a challenge until she got used to it. Then there was the digging at the chapel site. The turf was a struggle to remove until Sanders had shown her how to work a tusker, the spade the crofters used to use to cut their peat. "*The hill here'll tame lions,*" he said. "*Boot if e hev ay richt tools e can make a chob oh id.*"

At first there were blisters on her hands but they had toughened up after a few days. "*Choost leave ay spade here when yer feenished,*" Sanders had said, "*and rub yer hans in veenager when e get hom.*" She laughed to herself at how alike he and Fracher were. He used the absolute minimum of words to convey the maximum amount of information. The "veenager" worked.

Since she had started her dig she was always hungry. Fracher had shown her how to fish for mackerel and had loaned her a small rod. She loved the Kerr's Pinks potatoes and the large green cabbages she got from Mrs Mackenzie at the top of the track which joined the road down to the village. She was convinced she could eat her entire body weight in mackerel if she had to. When she was in Thurso she would stock up at the Co-op. She guarded the brown bags of Golspie pinhead oatmeal from the persistent mice as if her life depended upon it. With honey and raisins it was the fuel of the gods. So it was she constructed her routine. So it was she felt change seed and grow in her.

Ever since the scare when she fell into the sea it was as if her optical perspective had changed. Light seemed more powerful than before so she had taken to wearing sunglasses even when the Sun was obscured by thick Caithness clouds. Also her sense of touch and smell had heightened. Some things, like wool caught in the heather, she could not bear to touch, and she could smell animals on the wind. Even the peat smell of the headland had intensified lately. Yes, she told herself, I almost drowned and, yes, I was clumsy and impatient but what, actually, is happening to me? She could even smell the bumble bees. And the smell of the sea was overpowering. She had never experienced cold like that in her life before. The sea-water was so intensely cold it was unimaginable, unbelievable. Did she imagine that face she saw? Was it the cold making her hallucinate? Was it just a fantasy? No, that face –

a beautiful, smiling kind woman's face – it was a real memory, of that she was convinced. You cannot remember something you cannot imagine, she reasoned. The woman was real and that is all there was to it, just as her falling into the sea was real. She asked Fracher, the next day when she had calmed down, if he had seen her. "*A wumman?*" he'd scoffed, "*Now what wid a wumman bay doan under ay waater?*"

It was a fair question. She had hurt her head, that was true. She couldn't explain it and that was true as well. She couldn't explain the cave wall or the heat she had felt from the stone. The other, less physical changes in her were easier to explain. She remembered Fracher those weeks ago in the Comm Bar telling her about the Faroese fishermen and how they referred to Caithness as being "*doon*". It was hard for her to imagine a place this far north being south of anywhere. But she knew now that Caithness wasn't some exotic fantasy but a real place. Archaeology – as well as almost drowning – had helped her understand this. *How can such extremes meet?* she wondered, watching the dancing yellow flames in the fireplace. Oh, but they do. The day, last week, when she found the handbell, that was the day archaeology had stopped being an academic exercise and had became human. That was when her perspective changed, just as it had when she felt that icy undertow dragging her down. London faded to the periphery of reality and meaning. All that mattered to her was here on this huge northern headland in the far north of Scotland even if she did not know, as yet, what that was. But she knew, she felt, she was convinced that it would be revealed to her somehow. She was being challenged, tested by something that she had no name for. Destiny? Fate? The Future? Such unscientific terminology was unsatisfactory, but she did know that there on the cliff tops, on the great edge of Dunnet Head, was the rest of her life.

It was as if the real, the native people of Caithness, not the tourists, the incomers or the Atomicers, existed in dreams. Even in the short time she had been in the far north she could see that. The sandstone rocks on which she stood reached nine miles down into the Earth and were three hundred and seventy million years old. With such stuff to walk on what else was there to do but dream? Caithness was not flat as she first thought. It was raised up by the Earth in offering to the Sky and from time to time the Sky leant down to kiss the gift.

There was a loud knock at the door. Mags sat up in the chair, loosened from her thought dancing. She looked out of the small south-facing window. The sky had darkened and a flicker of yellow lightening tickled the underbelly of the black clouds over Olrig Hill on the other side of the bay. When she opened the door the wind had dropped and it was pouring with rain. There was a loud clap of thunder. Standing before her was a small man in a long raincoat, water pouring from his very large grey trilby hat. He spoke, but at first she could not make out a word he was saying. All she saw was a straggly grey beard belonging, she thought, to an old man.

"Mah doug's run off in ay thunner storm," he said again.

"Oh dear," said Mags, still only half understanding. The rain was running off his hat in small torrents. "Well, you had better come in out of this." She stood to one side to let him in.

"Thanks." He stepped over the door and stood dripping in the small lobby.

*Perhaps he was standing in a hole*, she thought. As he stood beside her now in front of the bathroom door he was much taller than he'd seemed at first sight. Six feet, she reckoned.

"D'ye mind if ah tak mah coat off? Id's sokkan."

"No. Please do," said Mags. "I'll hang it up here." She pointed to the hooks on the wall where her own waxed jacket hung.

He took off his coat and hat and handed them to Mags who turned from him and hung them on the hooks. When she turned back he was not there. She went into the front room and there he was, crouched over the fire warming his hands. He sensed her behind him and stood up. He was thin, dressed in a striking dark green suit.

"Awfully attractive fire you have here," he said in a very upper-class English accent. Where were the Caithness accent and the grey beard? His hair was straight and ginger and a well-manicured ginger moustache twitched on his top lip. He held out his hand. Mags stared. She noticed he had a crooked little finger on his right hand. There was flicker of lightening outside the window.

"Lopti Lofferson," he said eagerly. "Damned decent of you to give me shelter from the storm. Thought I was going to drown out there." He laughed as Mags shook his hand uncertainly. There was a clap of thunder. He sat down in the chair she had been sitting in.

"I'm Mags." She didn't know what else to say. The firelight caught his highly pronounced cheekbones, turning his hair a deep red colour. He sported extremely well-polished black leather brogues. They were bone dry.

"Charming old bothy." He looked around. "I see you've been giving it a bit of tender loving care." His eyes were huge and deeply blue. They focused on her like two lasers.

"Would you like a cup of tea?" she asked.

"Tea?" It might have been the strangest request he had ever heard.

"You must be cold after wandering around in that rain?" she persisted nervously.

"I suppose I am. You're very kind. But not tea, I think. I see you have a serviceable bottle of Cabernet Sauvignon on the table there. A sensation of that, perhaps?"

"Well, it's been open all night," said Mags, "and I'm afraid I haven't got a glass or anything. Would a mug be alright?"

"Splendid!" He smiled broadly revealing a perfect set of the whitest teeth Mags had ever seen.

She went to the table and picked up the wine bottle. It was full. She stared at it. *But I drank half of this last night*, she thought. There was another flicker of lightening. She put the bottle down.

"Isn't this quite marvellous!" he declared. There was very loud clap of thunder right overhead.

Disconcerted, Mags went to the sink, washed out a mug and took it back to the table. She poured some wine and handed the mug to him. He thanked her and drank it down in a gulp.

"That's much better," he said, wiping his moustache. Rain battered at the window. Mags took in the tall, well-dressed man sitting in her chair. *I could have sworn his suit was green.* Now it was most definitely blue, with a thin white stripe. His shoes were bright yellow.

"Your dog can't have gone very far." Mags felt out-of-control, and afraid. She kept her tone light, fighting back panic.

"My dog?" he asked, surprised. "What dog would this be now?" And he laughed.

"I thought you said..." Mags trailed off.

"Any chance of a refill?" He smiled and handed her the mug.

Mags went back to the table and poured him another slug of wine. She touched her cheek nervously. The bottle was full again. She handed the mug to Lopti Lofferson. This time he sipped the wine delicately.

"You have a strange name for an Englishman." She determined to come to terms with this person.

He laughed. "Goodness! I'm no Englishman. I'm Icelandic. Couldn't you tell?" He laughed again. "I don't have a dog either. Jolly comic, don't you think?"

Mags didn't know what to think.

"No, it's my wife I'm looking for. Sigyn is around here somewhere. You're right about that. She's forever wandering off. Very tiresome. But I don't think she would appreciate being called a *dog*. Oh dear me, no, no."

"But you said... I thought your dog had... oh, never mind." Mags sat down on the only other chair which was by the table.

Lopti Lofferson licked his lips. "This wine is going down rather well."

"Would you like another?" asked Mags. He handed her the mug. A clap of thunder, more distant this time. She poured more wine. Again the bottle was full. She turned to hand him the mug. His suit was a dark mustard. His shoes green.

"How come you drink the wine and I get drunk?" She gave up trying to understand. He seemed harmless. Lopti Lofferson laughed and drank his wine. His eyes shone out. *So darkly brown*, thought Mags, *not blue. Like two wet stones set in silver.* His hair was black. Mags stood up. The light from the fire increased in lustre. His suit was now white.

"Who are you?" Unequivocally afraid now, she felt her head spin.

"Why, Miss Mags, I be a happy chappie," he replied in a cod West Country accent.

"No, you're not!" she cried out. Lopti Lofferson knelt in front of the fireplace. Horrified, Mags watched him slowly stretch his hand into the flames. When he withdrew his hand and stood up he held a flame in his palm. He swallowed it as if it were an oyster.

"I do like some fire in my food, don't you?" He smiled broadly.

Mags fell back onto her chair, knocking over the wine bottle. Like blood, Cabernet Sauvignon poured out over the wooden floor.

"Ah sure now is it not a crime to be spillin' the mercies?" Now the accent was Irish. The bottle righted itself, and the split wine flowed back inside, a small red water-spout. Mags' archaeology notes flew up from the table, pages fluttering around the room like so many paper butterflies.

"Ah would ye look now, the immortals are with us." Still Irish. Then he was at the window, looking up at the sky and declaiming tragically, as if he were Hamlet. "I am sad. My wife is lost in the thunder of time." Before Mags knew any different she was beside him at the window. He grabbed her hand. "But you have seen my lover, have you not?" The colours of the Maighdeann Mhara filled her mind.

"See how the rain hess stopped." Lopti Lofferson's voice at last had a trace of Iceland. "This window, like your heart, is made of creestal glass. Now, maybe, I can find my ship."

"Your ship? What ship?" Mags was confused beyond endurance, beyond even fear. "I thought you were looking for your wife?"

"Oh, but I am." Gently he stroked her hair. His touch felt at once both hot and very cold. "But I am also looking for Skidbladnir. Shall we go outside?" He held her hand.

Then they were standing on the top of the cliff path outside the salmon bothy. The dark thunder clouds had passed and it had stopped raining. The soft crescendo of surf crashing onto the beach was the only sound. Lopti pointed to the sky in the west. Somehow his long coat, which she'd hung on the bothy door pegs, was hanging over his arm, his trilby in his hand. The clouds were light grey, indistinct.

"My ship is coming."

Blankly Mags looked up to where he pointed but she could see nothing. Then slowly a patch of cloud began to lengthen and darken, then lighten until it was quite white. Very gradually it dropped in elevation from the main cloud formation until it hung beneath it. As Mags continued to watch it took on the shape of the hull of a boat – a very large boat, perhaps half a mile long.

"My wife is a goddess of ships. Give a gift to the wrong goddess and what does she do? She gives it to a drunken megalomaniac skald. I ask you!"

The cloud-ship moved slowly across the sky over the bay. The air was still and breathless.

"Well, I had better away. Thank you for your generous hospitality."

He kissed her full on the mouth. She could taste fire and wine and felt his moustache inflame her face. Her will had abandoned her, yet a new strength began to form in her. Her eyes opened wide. She looked deep into the eyes of Lopti Lofferson. It was like looking down to the bottom of the sea. She knew with certainty that, in that instant, she was looking at and witnessing everything that had ever happened in the world. Then he released her. She had no idea whether she was solid or liquid. She saw him put on his coat and hat. She heard a small old man's voice: *Ay Comm door's blawn shut. Ah can hear ay combers sauchan on ay san. Ah'd better awey til ay creels.*

Mags watched him shuffle off round the eastern gable of the bothy. Then he disappeared. A bright beam of low sunlight poured from beneath the clouds lying along the horizon of the western ocean, dazzling her. When she opened her eyes the clouds changed colour and darkened once more. The cloud ship had vanished. Mags summoned herself back into her body and ran to the gable of the bothy. She looked up the track through the fields to the road to the village. She looked along the cliff top path. She looked down each way along the shoreline. No sign of anyone.

Back in the bothy the fire was still gently welcoming in the fireplace, her papers were just as she had left them on the table beside the laptop and camera. The wine bottle sat innocently half empty. Mags collapsed into the chair beside the fire and stared into the flames.

# 28

When the director of the art gallery finally phoned him Manson was none the wiser. The voice on the other end sounded just like the assistant he had spoken to the previous week, except this one was older, slightly posher, but with the husk of too many fags.

"The less you know about me the better it is for you, dahling," the voice had said. Manson insisted, surprising himself, that he needed to know something. "But, dahling, you have a deadline and there is a substantial cheque in the post to you. There is a contract to follow. You can get Beith to look it over for you if you like, but I can assure you, dahling, that it is very generous. What else do you need to know?"

The name of the gallery, for example?" Manson asked.

"Dahling, it doesn't have a name as yet. It's down in the Lawnmarket. Bex has already told you that. Don't worry your pretty Pictish head. It will have a name by the time the exhibition opens. Now I must run. Be a good boy. Just paint."

"Look what's your name? I need to know." He was getting angry.

"Well, if you insist. My name is Sigyn, but that will mean nothing to you. I am your good fortune, dahling, that is who I am. That is all you need to know."

That was it. Sigyn or whoever she was had hung up. Manson phoned Beith.

"Just go for it, ye great galoot," was Beith's advice. "Once the dosh and the papers arrive giz a call and I'll come over and have a shuftie. Look, it's not a dream, if that's what you're worried about. The whole thing's legit, believe me. Relax. She seems to have got yer measure and she's right – All you have to do is paint. I mean, the whole feckin thing, it's so old-fashioned! Soo nineteenth century!"

Beith was right. It was old-fashioned. He liked that. He didn't care what century she came from. All he had to do was paint. Twelve canvases six by twelve foot and twelve half that size, that's what she had said. Must be the available wall space, he thought. Then he stopped thinking.

Out in the garage where his mother used to keep the family car there were two rolls of sail canvas his father had been given by Wullie Piper, the old salmon fisherman, in exchange for installing an engine in his cobble. He half expected it to be rotten, but when he got them down from the shelf beneath the garage roof, and rolled them both out on the green at the back of his house, they were both almost as good as new. Dappled sunlight from the sycamore trees which enclosed the garden danced across the canvas. Browns and yellows, greens and reds throbbed into his eyes. The smell of the late August leaves burned into his nose. He lay down on the canvas. The rough feel of the material and the heat of the sunlight felt as if they were being tattooed onto his skin. When he got to his knees his hands felt swollen and hot.

He left the canvas unrolled on the grass and went back into the house. Cooler at the kitchen table he phoned Angie Geddes the joiner to order wood.

"E beeldan anither hen hoose?" asked Angie.

"Frames for twenty-four paintings, Angie," said Manson. "The wood has to be strong enough to take the tension of a nailed canvas."

"Ah'll bay ower ay morn at ay back oh ten. I'll take e oot til ay yerd. Wae'll sort id oot then. No be cheap mind."

That was how it progressed. Not so difficult, really. All you need is the necessary dose of insanity and a patron with a name that makes no sense in a gallery that has no name. With new positivity returned thoughts of the Maighdeann Mhara. Then a huge, empty longing opened out within Manson, that no amount of whisky or landscape could fill. Who was she? He had no idea. Every time he saw her his life became simpler and more concentrated at the same time. The less he had to try the more he had to work to stay within himself. The more he desired her the more his lust turned to softer feelings he had no experience of or use for. From the destructive act of his mother's death something was emerging at last. He didn't know what. Like the woman from the art gallery in Edinburgh he could put no meaning or face to it. Just a voice telling him something. He tried to concentrate, to reach inside his incomprehension and resolve it, but it seemed his mind both burned and froze, like ice on the handrail of a boat. He had no words for what he felt, just colours and shapes.

After he had been to the pub Manson caught a taxi into Atomic City. The artist had to buy his own materials, no matter what Beith thought. The Sun was out. The whole afternoon was blue – the sea, the sky, and the taxi driver's conversation. By the time the cab passed through Murkle and had come down Clairdan into the open river mouth of the River Thurso the sky had darkened. As Manson watched the taxi disappear up Princes Street it had started to rain. *Thurso is shit*, he reminded himself. Just one shop where he could get the oils, acrylic and pastels he needed. He knew what he wanted. The paintings on the wall of the shop made him nauseous, so he made his transactions swiftly. It had been years since he had bought paint in this quantity.

He left the shop carrying four plastic bags. Rain condensing with dust on the hot flagstone pavement gave off an unpleasant smell. At the newsagent, he bought a cheap pair of sunglasses. Even though it was raining the light hurt his eyes. Perhaps I'm developing a migraine, he thought, even though he had never had one before. As they passed him people's voices whispered and rasped into his ears like blunt saws. The noise of the traffic on the street – especially the buses and artic's with their hissing brakes – impacted him, painfully.

He sought shelter in The Comm. It was quiet, thankfully. Just an old man on a bar stool with a collie at his feet. Manson sat down on the stool beside him and ordered a drink from the skinny barmaid with more metal than teeth. He took off his sunglasses and rubbed his eyes.

"D'ye catch a welder's flash, min?" Fracher asked.

"It certainly feels like it," answered Manson grimly,

There he stayed for an hour or so. His eyes began to stop hurting. Whisky dulled his ears to the whispering he could hear from beneath tables and which slid in under the door. The bar had begun to fill up as shift buses from Dounreay deposited their human cargo, remnants of the Hi-Viz yellow snake, onto Olrig Street. Manson picked up his bags and left. He had no idea where he was going. Fortunately, the streets were quiet now that the twenty-minute nuclear rush had passed.

Doupie Dan sat on a public bench on the corner of Olrig and Traill Street, a giant among his rags. Behind him on a notice board a poster declared ***"Dounreay.com. Gone by 2025!"*** *Public relations and the Official Secrets Act are still strangers*, thought Manson. Doupie Dan was a tall well-built man. His long coat looked more like a jacket, as much because of his bulk as the fact that bits of material were missing and other bits hung off in strips. His feet sported one black sandshoe and one white. On his shaggy head was a battered bonnet. Manson had known this hulk ever since he had been at the High School. He would see Dan when they escaped down the street at lunchtime. "*E ken iss, bouys*," Doupie Dan had once announced to the group of pals he was with that, "*Ay universe is a vast ocean an wur aal pert oh a great beeg fish!*" His pals had laughed and taken the piss, but Manson had been fascinated by this shaggy giant, whose words came back to him now. They'd seemed to come from Moses himself.

"Weel, bouy, yur in a gran hurry til bay goan nowhere an nowhere's a gran place, maaan!" Moses removed the cigarette-doup-stuffed pipe from his mouth and spat spectacularly onto the street.

"Aye, Dan, yersel," said Manson.

"Ay world's goan til bay lichted up wae ay poer oh fower thoosan Suns," said Dan, matter-of-factly. Everything he said had an incantatory quality. "Fower thoosan Suns, maaan!"

Manson stopped. The ragged giant's words swam around inside his head, a shoal of sound. Doupie Dan looked at him closely. He fished into one of his labyrinthine pockets and pulled out a crumpled piece of paper. He signalled to Manson and offered the paper to him. Manson took it without a word. He knew better than to ask anything. Doupie Dan winked. "Fower thoosan Suns, maaan. Fower thoosan Suns."

Manson bowed his head briefly, an instinctive gesture of reverence for the ragged mystic. As he walked slowly away the phrase reverberated in his jangled head: *Fower thoosan Suns*. He crawled up Traill Street until he came to a new bar attached to a refurbished hotel. ***The Hot Green Chilli*** said the sign, in big green letters. Manson stood looking at the steep set of steps up to the bar door. Doupie Dan's crumpled up bit of paper was still in his hand. He was about to throw it away but noticed some writing. He set down his bags and straightened out the paper. Perfect copper-plate handwriting. *Welcome to Donald MacCrimmon's Magic Parlour. Miracles welcome but not expected.* Manson stuffed the paper into his jacket pocket and climbed the steps, opened the heavy glass door and went into The Hot Green Chilli.

The place was dark, for which his eyes sang welcome. He took off his sunglasses. The bar was long but the room was narrow. There was a small stage and PA at the far end, a kids' bouncy green elephant just left of the door. He went up to the bar and ordered a drink. There were only a few couples conspiring in the booth-like seats which ran along the wall opposite the bar. They were young and surprisingly well-dressed for Atomic City. In the middle of the large bouncy green elephant were four Faroese fishermen, one in each corner, asleep with their bags of vodka and chocolate at their feet, an empty Co-op trolley tipped on its side amid them. Fancy that now, he thought cynically, an art installation in Atomic City. He found a corner in one of the booths and cherished his drink.

Slowly the place filled up with more well-dressed young people, handsome boys and pretty girls. Despite the relief to his eyes, the rest of his senses were on full-alert to the point of pain. The whisky tasted of the earth the barley had grown in.

His tongue welcomed peat, honey and fire. Everything he touched projected its essence through his fingers, like soft electricity. But it was people's voices which alarmed him more than anything else. He seemed to hear everything everyone said all at once. When the bar was full and he thought he could bear no more of the multi-channelled babel, a slender young woman with shoulder-length blonde hair and a guitar too big for her got up onto the stage and started to sing. Manson's fevered eyes were drawn to the striking gold chain she wore around her delicate neck. The cacophony of voices faded and the singer's thin soft voice replaced it with the clarity of an acoustic torpedo. Every word and phrase exploded in his skull.

*One night when the moon was halved*
*and all the sky was green*
*I took my love to a distant shore*
*to a place he had never been*
*I cried 'Blow you Summer winds blow*
*and let your piper play*
*and when your song is over*
*we'll marry on that day.'*

There was a tune but it did not seem to go with the words. All Manson could see was the girl's mouth, opening and closing as each word escaped and as each phrase was formed.

*We waited for an answer there*
*my own true love and I*
*hoping for a blessing to fall down*
*from that bottled sky*
*but not a single word we heard*
*not a sound nor any sign*
*except for our anxieties*
*which were jangling in a line*

*My love he cried 'I'm cold now*
*my hands are thin and blue*
*all I hear is the laughing sea*
*and my love it laughs at you*
*oh take me to a secret place*
*we can call it Babylon*
*and let the light hide you from my face*
*my fool of Albion.'*

Manson now heard nothing, saw nothing, beyond this young woman with the big guitar, her soft huge voice which was threatening to drown the entire bar. She stopped singing. Manson let out a groan. Two girls next to him froze mid-sentence and stared at him. The singer began again. Manson felt once more the blackness of the thousands of rooks rise up around him.

*And with nothing more than a whisper then*
*into a bird he turned*
*and flew through the green dark sky*
*into the Moon which burned*
*all trace of him into its missing half*
*like the furnace of the Sun*
*and I returned to the morning*
*as dull as I had begun.*

The diva stopped playing her guitar and leaned forward, staring into Manson's eyes. Each word she sang nailed him – as if he were so much canvas – onto the frame of his own insignificance.

*Oh where is hope now*
*where is hope and all that I desire?*
*Lost in the Moon and the sea and the Sun*
*and the smoke and the mist and the fire!*

The last word she did not so much sing as whisper. Manson was transfixed. The singer put down her guitar and bowed her head. A few people clapped. Then she was gone, light from her necklace flaring softly behind her like a golden aurora. Manson was dumbstruck. He was fighting back tears as an older woman in a shiny red dress slid into the seat beside him, shattering the moment. Her hair had badly-dyed streaks of strawberry red, and in a large hand she clutched a long green drink. It was Daimler.

"I knew you'd be here."

Manson watched the rouged lips move up and down. The harsh bar light revealed five o'clock shadow beneath the make-up, and Daimler's perfume was augmented by the stale smell of cigarillos and gin.

"Oh, don't tell me you weren't on the lookout for me." Daimler tugged down the hem of his dress. "I know exactly how the gears grind in what Henderson has left to call a brain."

"I thought you'd run a mile," said Manson, his head still swirling from the girl's song.

"Everybody knows," said Daimler and he swigged, unladylike, from his gin cocktail. The well-dressed young people milling around ignored them.

"About what?" asked Manson. Right now he couldn't care less about anything Gilbert wanted to know, or already knew and wanted confirmed, or what Daimler was going to tell him or not tell him. He should have just left him to his fate on the floor of the Castletown pub. Never do anybody a favour.

"Look, I don't care one way or the other. Why would I tell you anything? That's what you're thinking." Daimler touched his strawberry curls. "I know you, Manson, remember? You were a shite reporter."

"What I'm thinking," said Manson, "is why're you dressed up like an old Thai hoor?"

Daimler laughed. Manson imagined watching a weasel be sick.

"To be outrageous is to be ignored. No-one here bats an eyelid." It was true. The new sophisticates of Atomic City were far too self-obsessed and busy getting drunk to bother with an old woman on the game, somebody they probably thought was

operation out for offer knowing that nobody will want to take it on. At the same time they can blackmail more money out of the government to ensure that they don't walk off the job. They can do any or one or none of that."

Manson's mind was being ground and milled like shards of metal. "Will they go ahead with it?"

"What?" Daimler was clearly irritated by the interruption.

"Will they get rid of the workforce?"

"They might." Daimler reflected. "Things are going well wrong on site. Decommissioning Dounreay is a nightmare from which there is no awakening. A strike would give them an excuse to back off and to get the London government to carry the can. Gabfan's out of its depth. The Yanks are out of control. Eventually they are going to put the knife in. What more can I say?"

Manson had no idea. They sat in silence for a few moments. Daimler sipped his drink. Manson stared at his empty glass.

"Can I get you another?" Daimler asked. Manson nodded. Daimler rose and minced on high heels up to the crowded bar. *He makes quite a good Thai hoor*, thought Manson. Across the partition he caught sight of the young singer chatting to some of her pals. Daimler returned with the drinks and sat down again, carefully adjusting his dress.

"You can tell Gilbert he can print what he likes and I'll deny it, even though everybody will know I'm the 'informed source'. Gilbert knows as well as I do that, as far as Dounreay is concerned, secrets always overtake reality."

Manson looked at Daimler as if he were seeing a nun on a fishing boat. Daimler grinned. His lipsticked mouth gaped like an open wound. "Anyway, I'm breaking the law with you just like a bad girl should."

"What d'you mean?" Manson would not have been surprised now had blood rather than language gushed from Daimler's mouth.

"I've been sacked!" announced Daimler. "As of five o'clock this evening I am no longer Head of Communications or whatever the fuck I was supposed to be for Gabfan Nuclear. I am at Her

Majesty's leisure." He laughed his weasel-boaking laugh and knocked back half of his mysterious green drink.

"I can see by the look on your face, Manson, that you don't believe me. Well, I didn't resign or anything else it will say in the press-release some young fuckhead will write tomorrow. Sacked. Because of cocaine they planted in my car." In spite of himself Manson was interested now. Daimler's lips had a red writhing reality of their own. "You don't think they do these sorts of things? No, you probably don't, being such a perfect narcissist. The Security Services will do anything, believe me. There's probably somebody from MI5 in here tonight watching me. The good thing about you, Manson, is that they have no idea who you are. Yet. Just don't do anything stupid, and don't see Gilbert for a while. Contact him, aye, but from a public phone or by smoke signals or..." Daimler put his hand flirtatiously and ironically to his temple. "...use your head."

Manson was speechless. This whole day had shredded reality. He reached back into the chasm of himself.

"What are you going to do?" he asked, eventually. Daimler's lips snaked together and bled into a smile.

"I'm going on the run," he said. "See where it gets me. Anywhere away from here." His eyes darted around. *He's terrified*, thought Manson. *Who could blame the poor fucker?* "The Cold War didn't end. It's just crumbling away, that's all. You think I'm a traitor – disloyal, but there's nothing to give loyalty *to* anymore. The world's changed. Dounreay's changed. I've changed. The truth is I'm nostalgic for the Cold War. You knew where you were. What's better than Armageddon to end any fairy story, eh?"

"You do look like you've dropped off the top of a Krizmuzz tree." Manson was beginning to slur. *Will I remember any of this tomorrow,* he asked himself.

"But you can't go back." Daimler seemed to be talking to himself now. "We can't take up the old positions anymore. These days everything's about material resources. Everything else is a game, including so-called democracy and the Scottish fucking Parliament. We're left outside now, dancing on the dark street. If they catch me alone, Manson, and if the story breaks, I could be rubbed out."

Two mauve-painted shutters blinked shut over Daimler's eyes and he stopped smiling. Manson had a fleeting image of Daimler's eyelids as the shadows of death. Something other than his own free will turned Manson's head and he looked out into the mass of young noisy bodies, some of them dancing. *Which one's from MI5*, he wondered? He saw the singer dancing. He could hear her voice although he couldn't make out what she was saying.

"The other thing to remember, Manson," said Daimler, "is that they hate you. They despise your history, culture, everything about you. Never forget that."

Manson had an urge to comfort Daimler, but his arms didn't move. He had no comfort to give anyone.

Daimler looked straight at him, grimly serious, all camp humour gone. "Never forget, Manson, the cause of death is life." He finished his drink. "I've got to go. Gabfan's new name is Tycho Nuclear, after the Danish astronomer, Tycho Brahe. They'll cook up some company bullshit, create a non-existent history. That's the gist of it." Manson couldn't find any words.

"I'm just a hoor," said Daimler. He stood up, pulling the crumpled red dress down over his stockinged legs. "Did you know that Tycho Brahe had a pet elk that got drunk and killed itself falling down a set of stairs?"

Manson watched Daimler's red-streaked wig weave in and out between the young people dancing on the bar-room floor. Then it disappeared. The four Faroese fishermen, now wide-awake and escorted by two bouncers, were being pushed out of the bar and down the steps, their vodka-and-chocolate-laden Co-op shopping trolley after them. Manson sat back and closed his eyes. Blackness throbbed like a beating plastic sheet inside his head. Was it the drink or the migraine he never got? When he opened his eyes the singer was sitting opposite. Her golden necklace shone out under the coloured lights of the bar.

"Hi," she said, "my name is Fand. I hear you're a painter."

# 29

Bragi Boddason, the skald, sailed west in search of the wave. The passion of Jörð and Storegga had created a wall of water two hundred feet high travelling south, north and west at a hundred miles per hour. But the great white ship Skidbladnir was also swift across the sea and soon, north-east of Shetland, her crew saw the back of the mighty water arc. Bragi's thirst for Bragarmál, (poetic speech), was as great as his thirst for ale; but the poem's improvement, (Bragarbot), meant that he must fill his poem with actions if it was to increase his fame. So Bragi commanded Skidbladnir to sail now in the sea of the air. The great white ship rose up into the clouds. Skidbladnir ran ahead of the wave and over the northern lands of Scotland, known to Bragi as The Province of the Cat. Many were the legends of the people who lived there: how they danced in the shadows of fires they burned in the mouth of caves. For it was well known that in all of Midgard, (the human world), these cliffs and dales have produced great exponents of poetry, music and art. For the gods (the Æsir of Asgard), the achievements of the people of Midgard, as you might expect, were of no real importance. But as Bragi was only a self-proclaimed god, merely tolerated by the Æsir, and because Skaldskaparmal – the language of poetry – was his major concern, Bragi had a special interest in this Scottish land and the people who lived there.

From the sea of salt and water to the sea of the air the great white ship Skidbladnir navigated with ease to the vast sea of Time.

There Bragi could look out and see the people of the Province of the Cat below him, free in Space but trapped in Time, and locked into their history. Occasionally, spirits who were free of these manacles would walk through Midgard and through Time, leaving their imaginations' manifestations behind as markers of their passing: paintings on a wall, or the pentatonic scale of music, or a poem which lives on the tongue, or even a girl's footprint preserved in the sand on the floor of a cave where she dances in the torchlight with the spirit of a wolf or a wildcat; whatever the imaginative outcome, Bragi saw and felt them all. His tongue may be a slave to Bragarmál, his ambition too often counted in barrels of beer, but Bragi was no fool: he knew from hard work and experience that all is fluidity and transformation, that in the world of art and memory – as in all of Ginnungagap (the Mighty Gap) – permeability is everything. There are no barriers between the moment and the age. Self-proclaimed god or not, Bragi knew that spirits live in walls and stones, and that the dead can speak. To look back in Time is to look into the future. The sea of salt and water is no different to that of the air and the sea of Time. Bragi knew also that to drift in any sea is fatal. So he instructed one of the dwarf-sons of Ivaldi to drop anchor. As he watched the great iron hook disappear beneath the hull, Bragi thought regretfully how all the great works of imagination which swim through Time are rendered, by their very journeying, anonymous.

Three great white sails were lowered from Skidbladnir's three tall masts, and the anchor held. Bragi looked down on The Province of the Cat. It was one broad land with a division of mountains which ran through the middle from the eastern seaboard to the northern coast. To the far south a great river which ran into an open firth formed its furthest border. To the far west huge mountains, petrified as mythical creatures, guarded the Sunset. The land running east from the great turning point of a cape in the distance was a pleasant land of wooded hills, fertile straths and wide mouthed sandy fjords. The north-eastern portion was a high plateau of open ground, bookended by two mighty headlands which reached out like two arms to the Islands of Orc in the north which lay like stone whales across a stormy firth running between two vast oceans.

From his vantage point on the ship Bragi could see that the people of Cat looked east to be born and west to die. To this end they built many stone temples and burial mounds. He could also see that on the north coast where the eastern and western halves of the province met, they had built metal chambers where they had placed vessels of sleeping fire which for the people of Cat represented both life and death. Bragi was intrigued by these new metal cairns. He could see that Loki had been here. Only Loki would have shown them the hidden ways of the ancient smithery of Surt. Only Loki could bring the secrets of Muspell to mortal men. Bragi knew that this would make a difficult poem to tell to the audience in Val-hall. For this was the art of the Midgard serpent, which wrapped itself around the world. One of Loki's three fiendish children, the result of his union with the giantess Angrboda, the Midgard Serpent had the red death-light of Ragnarok in its eyes. Bragi wondered sadly why the people of The Province of the Cat, when they lived in such a fine, rich and handsome land, had allowed Loki to enchant them into creating this elaborate and dangerous ceremony. If they could free themselves of the Great Trickster, they would see that this ceremony will bring them death sooner than enlightenment. But Loki was full of great cunning with countless hidden powers and the gods, the Æsir of Asgard, had many problems with him.

From the high deck of Skidbladnir Bragi could see in the story of the rocks that The Province of the Cat had experienced an earlier wave, the passion of which lay like blood between the formations. For we must understand that from out of Ginnungagap, The Mighty Gap, the actions of gods and giants are but themselves sweeping waves, each caught in the cycle of pulse and echo, so that the love-eruptions of Jörð and Storegga are at once and many times over a force which passes through Time. The destruction it guarantees for those caught up in its passing is for others only a filigree of colour on a sandstone cliff. This is the memory of the wave. For Ginnungagap (The Mighty Gap) is not empty, but a series of stoor-wormholes. If you enter you disappear and become the darkness of matter we cannot see, and are added to black energy we cannot comprehend.

Bragi decided to move his great white ship. He gave the command but Skidbladnir did not move. The anchor was fast. Bragi ordered the roughest-looking of the Ivaldisons who crewed the fabulous ship to climb down the cable and free the anchor. This the red faced, black-haired troll did without question. He went down into the sea of the air.

# 30

Three men in white radiation suits and helmets climbed out of the hatch and closed it after them. One by one they took off their helmets and sat down on metal benches. Beside them was a large metal door and beside that another ladder which led to yet another hatch which opened onto the roof of the cement plant, or DCP as it was known. It was a quarter to seven in the morning and the night shift was about to knock off.

"Weel, Charlie, e've done a great chob here," said Colin. "Yer entire crew can feel prood. Everyhin done safely an aheid oh schedule."

"Oh aye," replied Charlie Miller, the waste manager. "Wae are prood tae hev developed an innovative use oh nitric acids which dissolves all iss shite, includan us if wae fell intilt. International quality standards, e unnerstan."

"Yer grasp oh ay technical detail is truly inspiran," said Colin.

"It's sumhain Ah pride mahsel on," said Charlie. "An thur's anither twa reactors more oh iss raffinate hoo-hah til go. Plus all ay ither stuff. Id's never endan."

Colin smiled. "Hoo-hah" would be another one of Charlie's technical details. All three men were covered in sweat. "Enough til see e through til yer retirement, eh min?" said Colin.

"Real process workers dinna retire," said Morris Mowat, feeling left out, "they choost irradiate awey."

"I didna think e wis real, Morris!" teased Colin.

"Cheezus," snorted Charlie, "hae's yer ownkle, is hae noh?"

"Hae's Kylie's ownkle, noh mine."

"Wae process iss, wae process aat. Then wae bury id in a hol in ay grun," said Morris philosophically.

"Aye," laughed Charlie, "even if aat hol in ay grun is above ay grun."

"Are wae noh ay cunnin bastards' oot here?" Colin agreed.

"Ah ken iss hes passed ablow ay collective radar," said Morris, "boot iss is ay twentieth anniversary oh ay DCP here."

"Weel... *technically*, id's only been workan fur seventeen year," said Charlie.

"Since they started beeldan id, Ah mean," said Morris. "Christ Ah mind aat day fine. An now, what hev wae got? Five thoosan five litre drums."

"Thirteen thoosan fuel elements from ay peedie test reactor hidsel," added Charlie, sharing in Morris's reminiscence.

"Then thur wis aal aat ither shite from abroad wur noh sposed til talk aboot," said Morris.

"Lek Ah say, bouys," interrupted Colin, "Id's ay grasp oh technical detail aat Ah find so reassuran."

"Then yer a beeger fool that Ah thocht e wis," said Morris reassuringly.

"Ahm sorry, Morris, boot Ah canna get aal dewy-eyed and nostalgic aboot a cement plant," replied Colin.

"Everyhin's neutralised. Aat's ay point," said Charlie, almost to himself.

"Ah feel richt neutralised, an noh mistake," agreed Morris.

Colin was about to say something about the Scottish Government's Highly Active Waste policy of '*on-surface or near-surface storage*' when there was an almighty clatter of metal on the roof above their heads.

"Whaat ay fuck wus aat?" Charlie Miller stood up.

"E dinna hev any cranes operatan here choost now, hev e Morris?" asked Colin.

"Noh. Ah hevna signed any permits that Ah mind on," answered Morris, clearly shaken. He got up and moved to the metal ladder which led up to the hatch above their heads. "Boot see if aat clowns oh contractors are fuckan aboot thur'll bay bleed on ay immobilized raffinate yet!" And he started up the metal ladder.

"Come doon oot oh aat," shouted Colin. "Id's noh yer chob."

"Nohbody kens whut thur fuckan chob *is* – at's ay problem wae iss choint," answered Morris, opening the hatch and pushing himself through. Colin and Charlie watched his radiation protection safety boots disappear above them.

"Hae's noh been richt ever since Patreen went," whispered Charlie, sympathetically.

Morris Mowat had worked at Dounreay for forty-four years. He thought he had seen it all – construction, reaction, explosion and decommission – but nothing had prepared him for what he was seeing this morning. A huge cast-iron anchor – at least he thought it was an anchor – had attached itself to high-pressure stainless steel piping which ran along the roof. A thick, rope-like cable was attached to the anchor and disappeared up into very low white cloud above the cement plant.

"Whaat in ay name oh goad is iss?" He didn't know what to think. *Could it be the Army?* The site had been used in SAS manoeuvres before. Suddenly, from the cloud and down the cable slid a squat figure. He wasn't military, Morris could see that. *Must be a fireman*, he thought. *Aye, that'll be hid.* But as the figure got down onto the roof and stood before him Morris could see he was no fireman. Twice as broad as anyone Morris had ever seen, this chiel had strong thick arms, long black curly hair which fell down his back in a mane, and a broad pug-nosed red face. The figure pointed to the anchor and began to wrestle it free. Morris could see he was holding his breath almost as if he was under water. Instinctively Morris went to give the man a hand. The anchor was cast-iron and well beyond human lifting. He was about to say so, and add the fact that they were bloody lucky there was no-high pressure steam going through these pipes, when the strange looking individual heaved the anchor free. Morris was stunned into silence. Without a word, the man grabbed the cable and shimmied back up it until his leather boots disappeared into the cloud, followed by the anchor itself, and the entire cloud formation moved off out to sea. It was as if nothing had happened! Morris gaped up at the sky. *A boat? How the hell could id be a boat?*

Charlie Miller poked his head out of the hatch. "E aal richt, Morris? Thur wis a hell oh a clatteran and bangan goin on up here."

Still searching the sky, Morris spoke slowly: "None oh ay contractors employ Filipinos, Charlie, do they?"

"Filipinos? What ay hell e on aboot, min?" said Charlie. "Come doon oot oh ayr an wae'll go an sign off. Wae can get a moarnin pint at ay Beak's." He disappeared back down the hatch.

Morris couldn't take his eyes off the sky. *Aat boy wis more Apache than Filipino*, he thought. Out at the sea it was another fine morning in late August. The Sun was already well up and the western horizon looked blue and endless. Morris could see the curvature of the Earth, a thing he loved. Usually. Now it terrified him. Of the white cloud he could see no trace. The boat shape had dissolved. But the vision of the thick-set man with the black hair and the red face shimmying down and then back up the cable would stay with him forever. Morris looked down at his boots then up at the sky again. *A Comanche – mebbe a descendent fae wan o ay reservations, workan fur the Yanks. Mebbe that wis it?* He climbed back down the hatch.

"Yer awful pale lookan, Morris," said Colin, "E better get hom an get some kip."

Morris said nothing. He wanted to speak but language had abandoned him. He and Charlie left the cement plant and signed off, got changed and caught the shift bus back into Atomic City. Colin went through the procedure of being de-nuked, signed out and went back up to his office. Only half-past seven but already it had been a long day. *Just another eight hours to go*, he thought, *and I'll be free. Or drunk. Or asleep. Or all three.* He was just trying to decide which would be the most delicious when Jimmy

Greenan came in unannounced and sat down. He looked nervous, and although he had just come on shift he had a day's growth on his chin which was unlike him.

"Youz know, don't youz?" Jimmy's Lanarkshire accent grated slightly.

"Know what, Chimmy?" asked Colin.

"They want to re-employ the men on individual contracts."

"But yer no on strike yet?" Colin reassured him.

"No. But we will be." Jimmy was curt as ever.

"Chimmy, yer leading yer men up ay garden path. Whatever sordid scheme Gabfan hev up their sleeve this is choost ay wrong thing til be doin at ay wrong time." Colin got up and went over to the door to see who was in the main office. Just the usual crowd, everyone slowly getting to grips with their forthcoming day.

"They're using the local election as an excuse. They're gonnae offer us a pay freeze an rip up the pension plan. Redundancies. An no negotiation." Jimmy hadn't turned, and spoke to the empty chair, but Colin heard every word. He knew the scenario inside out.

"Then dinna go on strike. Id's industrial suicide." He strode back to his desk and sat on the end. Jimmy looked uncertain.

"Look, Harper, they're no gonnae shut the plant. They cannae. This isna a shipyard or an oil refinery. There's nuclear fuckin reactors here." He might have been speaking to himself, or to a child, or to some white light shining out of a dark place.

"I hev noticed, Chimmy" said Colin.

"We had a good thing goin here. Fuckin Yanks ur destroyin everythin!" Jimmy looked on the point of tears.

"They're up til something an no mistake," agreed Colin. "Choost whut I'm no sure."

"You're the site manager, Harper, if youz dinnae ken, who diz?" Jimmy's eyes seemed to be trying to escape from his face. His distress was whipping him.

"Look, ay Yanks hev bought ay ferm. They treat us like ay livestock. Oor own government sold us off. Buldoo's goin til be a big repository, Chimmy. They're goin til bury sixty years oh bad dreams doon there." Colin looked at his computer screen.

"They're decomissionin a nuclear plant, Harper, no an entire population." Jimmy was trying to convince himself.

"Wur part oh ay fixtures an fittans, Chimmy, we go doon intil ay dump too." Colin looked at Greenan. "Why e hev til go marchin intil id at ay heid oh ay band beats me."

Jimmy looked at Colin. "Can they... I mean... can they sell the entire plant?" The magnitude of it horrified him.

"Here's ay thing, Chimmy," said Colin slowly. "They can do exactly what they want."

"But why?"

"Money." His phone rang. Colin answered. Nagelstein's voice crackled and smoked into his head like a fusing circuit board. He let the savage acoustic snarl and burst for a few moments. Just when he could stand it no more Nagelstein finished and hung up. Colin put the phone down and looked at the small dishevelled man sitting across from him. Jimmy looked like he had just gone three rounds with a prize fighter.

"This is all wrong," said Colin.

"Yer telling me," Jimmy agreed.

"No, no you an yer stupid fuckin union!" snapped Colin. "Chimmy, e canna see further than ay nose on yer own face."

"I always kent youz wur wan oh them." Jimmy tensed.

"Id's no aat, ya pathetic Weegie hoor!" Colin stood up again. "Id's aal oh iss!" He pointed wildly at the open-plan space beyond the window partition.

"Whit? Ye mean this office?" asked Jimmy confused.

"No, no, no! Id's iss entire place, iss plant, iss nuclear fuckin reactor. Look at me, Chimmy, what d'ye see?" Jimmy stared at Colin, now well out of his comfort-zone. "I'll tell ye... look at me! I'm a Thursa loon. Look at me! I came here when I wis sixteen. Drafted in, if e lek. From ay High School. So whut dis aat make me?"

"Well, I come here fur a joab. Tae work," said Jimmy reasonably.

"Aye. An aat at least at makes e honest. Aat dome oot ayr's oulder than me, Chimmy, boot wur goin til end up in ay same place. D'ye know where that is, eh?" Colin now had his face close to Jimmy Greenan's face. Jimmy said nothing, his mouth twitching.

"In ay fuckan grun, Chimmy, aat's where!" Colin had been pacing during his rant. Now he stopped short, took a deep breath and threw himself down in his chair. "So Ah ask e wan more time: whut dis aat make me?"

Jimmy was almost weeping by this point. "I dunno," he said, holding in a sob.

"Well, Ah'll tell e, Chimmy!" said Colin as if in a revelation, "It makes me a hypocrite!"

# 31

Sometimes the sound of the sea terrified her. She would sit and listen to it thundering onto the shore. It had beauty, yes, she understood that; but it had no mercy. Mags sat at the south end of the Salmon Bothy watching the Sun sink into the deep western Atlantic. Everything here was beautiful – that was part of her new problem. Her old problem had been that she had not really understood beauty. Not in nature anyway. Holiday beauty, as she remembered it from her childhood and student days, was not like the beauty of Caithness. Here everything had a purpose and a function. On this peninsula nature was not a pet to be stroked and indulged; it was not for sitting and admiring as she was doing now. People here did not waste their time on such unproductive activity. In the far north of Scotland nature fed or consumed you; it either sustained or destroyed you. It gave you everything, and then asked for it back. It loved humanity to the point of extinction. As far as it went, that was the extent of her new problem.

The sound of the sea was a constant reality from her vantage point on the cliff. A perpetual crescendo, it was unrelenting and inescapable. Whenever she looked down to the beach, a perfect parabolic curve of sand dunes stretching for three miles north to South with an endless arc of froth-salted combers crashing onto the shore, it broke her heart.

Part of her longed for the mechanical cacophony of the city. That part was bleeding into the sunset. It did not die easily. Mags sipped her wine and leaned back, resting her head against the sandstone wall of the salmon bothy. She admired the smooth belly shape of Dwarick Head, its purple heather gown and its broad brown shoulders. She knew, as if a dark voice from the headland had whispered it to her as a sacred truth, that she would never go back. If she were to die now, she thought, she would be burned on the beach and have her ashes scattered on top of Dwarick Head.

The wind rose, hurling itself across the sea from the north-west. Soon the bay was a boiling mass of white. The gale blew in across the barley fields and the link lands beyond. She watched it, her eyes seeking the back of the wind. It was easy to look at the land, it flooded east. It rippled. The square patches of yellow grain seemed to drag the wind down. *Like Fracher's fish on a line,* she thought, *drawn to his line cast on the wind, their fatal allure.* She saw it all so clearly. *The wind is blue.* She could taste the blueness of it on her lips. All these names she had learned, that Fracher had told her: Thurdistoft, Greenland, Inkster, Bourifa, Sinegeo. They also became a taste. Blue. They swam behind her eyes, like the sea. Cattle stood in the corners of the fields. Black congregations. Solid against the wind in their collective bovine beefery. To Mags they looked like they had just landed from heaven, blown in, fat and daft.

She knew nothing about this place. How could she? She was so young and it was so old. She stood up and walked back into the bothy. She looked at the bell sitting in its shoe-box, rusting. She looked at it closely. She even got out the daft glasses she had bought in Lidl's, the kind that fold up into nothing like the pair Lady Minker wore. She stuck them on her nose. There it was! But it was *sound*, not sight that had her attention. She could hear the sound of the sea. As if for the first time. A voice, like Fracher's but different: *Nothing is as it seems.*

She looked at her laptop. She was trying to write about the dig: the chapel, the headland; how even the little work she had done had revealed to her the immensity of it. Not so much the human remains – they were simple enough; they just lay beneath the peat, subterranean products of Time, of Life. How does it make sense? How could she make all this sensible to the academics back in the university, those who were going to judge her, give her the doctorate her parents so badly wanted her to have. None of it made sense even to her right now, standing by a wrecked old table in a dilapidated salmon bothy with an ancient strange thing in a bloody shoe-box! A human hand had made that bell, perhaps over a thousand years ago. It wasn't Irish and it wasn't Norse, so it had to be Pictish. But she knew very little about the Picts. Professor Benison in London denied they even existed: "*They were Roman mercenaries from Scythia.*" She had no idea whether he was right, and *he* had no idea if he was right either. It seemed to her then that the business of denying the Picts their right to historical space was more important than the actual truth, if any, of what he was saying. The "actual" truth, she realised now, is that he doesn't give a damn whether the Picts existed or not. This morning in the Co-op she'd had a revelation: not only did the Picts exist in history, *they were still here!* They drove tractors and ploughed the big square fields. They hauled creels out of the Pentland Firth. They worked at Dounreay. They asked you "E waantan ingan saace way aat?" when you ordered from twenty different versions of pie and chips on a pub menu. They drove buses and swept the streets of Atomic City. *That* is what history is – that's what the Picts are: the continuity of human existence. To deny them is to say you hate people. Every time she knelt and stuck her hand in the peat she was touching another person, another time. That's all it was – as personal and impersonal as that. The Irish priests who had set up their chapel in the ninth century must have met the same people she was meeting in the twenty first. Names and faces might be different but they were essentially the same people. They had to be. The landscape, the weather, the constant motion of the air and the continual beating of the sea – all of that hammers out shapes in people. And it was those shapes she was learning to recognise. The more she spoke to local people the more she understood what it was she was digging up. It was them. The people. They came out of the ground.

She saw the dog before she saw the man. Fracher came in and sat down. He was wet. He never bothered with unnecessary communication like "Hello", or "Can I come in?" Cushie came up and licked her hands.

"Ah wis haulan creels off ay Sneuk an ay wind kicked in – ay squalls come oot oh nowhere at iss time oh year. Ah thocht Ah'll dodge in here where ay Pipers hed thur cobble. Good placie. Id's oot ay wind an ay tide's on ay turn, so mah boatie'll noh bay chowed til matches choost yit." He pulled out a half-bottle of rum and set it on the table. "Ee know iss, Ah hevna been in iss place for ower thirty year."

She smiled. She was pleased to see him. Fracher looked approvingly at the fire. Cushie lay down if front of it to dry his coat.

"Ah suppose id's noh a bad wee nest." He looked around, appreciating the warmth. Mags said nothing. She hadn't the heart to tell him she didn't understand what he'd just said about matches. Fracher nodded at the rum. "Weel, get a gless – unless e want may til sook id oot ay neck!"

Mags had bought some cheap tumblers when she had bought her incredible folding glasses. She took the looking-glasses off her nose put the drinking-glasses on the table in front of him.

"Bile ay kettle an wae'll hev a toddy," said Fracher. "Thur's a chill til id ay day. Always ay same come ay hairst."

When the kettle had boiled and they sat sipping hot rum, Fracher pointed at the bell sitting in its box.

"Amazan lookan thing," he said.

"It's the bell I told you about," said Mags, proudly.

"Hid's ould, Ah ken at," said Fracher, standing up to look more closely.

"Over a thousand years, but I can't be sure. I'm going to have to crate it up and send it back to the university. They'll carbon date it and clean it up." Hot rum flowed comfortingly through her veins.

"Thur'll no doot bay some ingravans on id," said Fracher, casually. He sat back down.

She wanted to tell him about Lopti Lofferson, her strange visitor. She wanted to explain to him how her senses had become heightened to the point of insanity after that encounter with the woman in the sea. But she couldn't.

Fracher sat back in his chair, drank his rum and enjoyed the heat of the fire.

"Weel," he said after a moment. "Here *e* are on *yer* heidland, and thur's *mahsel* across ay bay on *mine*." He laughed to himself. Outside the westerly wind sighed against the windows. The fire in the grate pulsed and smoked, as draughts of its power blew down the chimney. Cushie raised his head half-heartedly, then returned to his dwam.

"I've often wondered, Fracher, how it is you survive?" Mags asked after a time.

"Ah've often windered ay same thing mahsel," he mocked.

Mags realised Fracher's face reflected his personality: divided. His dark brown eyes were shaded, deep and questioning; yet his mouth was friendly, sociable and kind.

"Ah hev mah pension and then thur's what Ah get for ay lobsters. Ah play mah fiddle. Ah miss mah wife. Boot whut can e do? Ah survived ay fiery apocalypse oh Piper Alpha. Oil an ay nuclear hev burned may bad. Ah left ay wan an ay ither took mah Kirstag. Ah've been on mah own fur twunty-five year, boot Ah've got a hoose, a boat an a doug. Many men hev less."

"The Piper Alpha... That accident was in the '80's, wasn't it?" Mags was hesitant.

"Id wis murder. Boot id wis a wan off. Leukaemia, on ay ither hand, is on-goan. Nobody can see id, boot id's murder none ay less." Fracher drank his rum. Mags watched the collie, stretched out asleep in front of the fire. "Beeg industrial institushans murder peedie fowk – aat's hardly news. Id's ay way oh ay world. Occidental, ay Nuclear Authority, fahever id is. Wae get burnt, irradiated, buried in ay grun. Here. There. Everywhere. Nohbody takes responsibeelity. Nohbody goes til chail."

Mags didn't know what to say. Fracher's eyes were watering.

*He's thinking of his wife*, she thought. *Change the subject.* "I'm hoping to excavate in the Cave of Gold."

Fracher turned his head. "Weel, e'd better do id sooner rether'n later. Ay neap tides'll bay on ay run afore ay month's oot. Yer cave is susceptible til high waater."

"I want to see what's behind that back wall."

"Whit wall?" he asked. "Hid's aal solid rock."

"There's a wall – and not a natural one," she said firmly. "It's covered in seaweed so nobody will have seen. Not unless... well, unless they know it's there."

"So hoo did e ken aboot hid?" He looked at her inquisitively.

"I just... I don't really... Fracher, it was *hot*."

"Ay wall?" He snorted, spilling his rum.

"I know it sounds crazy, but it's true!" she insisted. "Cushie knew it as well."

"Weel, hay can do many things, aat doug, boot takan's noh wan oh thum."

"You don't believe me?" Mags felt exposed and hurt. She'd said more than she intended, but she'd expected more of him. Sensing he'd given offence, Fracher caught Mags' arm as she made to stand up, and looked her in the eye.

"Ah've noh reason til disbelieve e, lassie. E choost decide when e want til go back an Ah'll take e. Wind an tide dependan, ahcoorse."

They sat companionably for a while, drinking hot rum and enjoying the fire. Eventually the wind died down and Fracher got up. He stuck the rest of the rum back in his pocket, and went back out to where he'd tied the boat. Mags went to the door after him. Beyond the rocks she saw Cushie, his nose over the side and into the wind as The Searcher pushed through the Atlantic swell and out into the bay. It is true what Fracher said, she thought, the sea is alive. She thought of this man who had taught her so much in such a short time, and of all the hurt he had experienced. Is there any justice in history? She thought not, but she was too young yet to know. But she would know, one day. She was beginning to see that archaeology was about looking into the ground, where she found the people. But she could see also that she was staring out over this great cliff at the edge of her understanding. Things were happening to her, had happened to her, since she had come here that she had no name for. She had listened to Fracher's story about a piper going into The Cave of Gold and wishing for three hands: two for the pipes and one for the sword. She was fascinated by the story's Time dimension, where five minutes in the cave is a hundred years in the outside world. The disturbing image of the piper's dog running hairless from the cave stuck in her mind. Fracher had told her about Donald Mor MacCrimmon, the great piper to the clan MacLeod, who had been forced to leave his native Skye in the early sixteen hundreds and seek refuge in Sutherland with the Mackays – Fracher's wife's own people. MacCrimmon had invented the piobrochd, the ancient form of music which has no earthly home but darts and lives in the shadows in the cave.

"Boot Ah dinna ken muckle aboot id mahsel," Fracher had admitted, modestly.

Mags knew that Fracher's music was part of his defiance against the world. The sea, for him, was also more than just waves dashing off a rock and lobsters out of a creel. Although she was young, as if she had just been newly born, still she understood that he found his courage in the sea, just as she must find her destiny in the cave. They were two of a kind, she realised, as she watched his creel boat disappear around the back of Dwarick Head. They were both striving for something: he an old man and she a young woman; experience and ignorance; strength and weakness. Oh why, like the piper, was she compelled to enter The Cave of Gold? She went back into the bothy, shut the door and sat down by the fire.

# 32

The year after the chapel roof was complete the health of Grillaan, the Prior, began to fail. He rarely ventured outside his stone beehive hut, where the girl Nessan would bring him his food, and where he would contemplate his life and resign himself to his maker. One of his last journeys was to go down to the village along with Caornan to visit Ogun, the smith. Grillaan had decided it was time to inter the holy clarsach of his brother Colm, the soon to be saint, in the Cave of Gold. To do this properly and with due ceremony and reverence he had also decided the chapel needed a bell. The building was a simple structure with no steeple, so the previous Autumn Grillaan had spoken to Ogun about a handbell. Now the bell was ready. Grillaan insisted he would go and collect it.

Ogun's place of work was a long low smiddy where the burn from the loch beyond the village met the sea. Ogun was a tall slim man with extremely powerful arms. His clothes were made from blackened leather and his complexion was black also, from smoke and soot, so that his teeth and the whites of his eyes shone out with an increased intensity. He wore a red scarf around his neck along with a bronze band, and he had bronze bracelets around both his wrists, at the end of which his two great hands danced gracefully with tongs and hammer. *He's more like a devil than a smith*, thought Caornan, as Ogun greeted the Prior.

Outside Ogun's smiddy and beside the burn there was a boor tree with a rough wooden bench beneath it. Grillaan and Ogun sat here together, looking out across the beach.

"You have come far, Christian, and achieved much," said Ogun.

"We have been here four years now, but our work is only just beginning," replied Grillaan. "My part in it is almost over."

"It seems strange to me the work you do. I can see no temper in it," said Ogun, the practical smith. "The Cattach are happy in their own ways. If you bend them from that metal it will be disastrous for them. They will become weak."

"You talk like a druid, Ogun," said Grillaan, smiling as always. "Be at peace. You have nothing to fear from us."

"That is what all our enemies say," said Ogun softly, with a touch of malicious mischief.

The Prior flinched. "We are just deliverers, be it of the word of God or of the holy relic of my brother's clarsach. The instrument was handed down to him from our father and his father before him, stretching back some five hundred years. It was Colm's expressed wish that we deposit it in a sacred place in the north of Pictland and build a chapel there. He sailed here once himself, and it made a great impression on him."

"So you put the clarsach in *Uamh an Oir*, the Cave of Gold. You leave your chattels in some-one else's dream-house."

"I consulted your chief Dungal and he has given us his blessing. You, Ogun, are the first to express opposition to the plan."

"I am not in opposition," said Ogun, "and unlike the Druids who hate you, I do not hide in the hazel groves. I like you, Grillaan, but you are a Christian."

"And you are an alchemist," laughed Grillaan.

"I change things, yes," agreed Ogun. "The people fear me for it. But from my anvil the sparks dance into their feet. From my forge comes the power to cut the Earth. My smiddy is a place of life."

"From what I can see you are a cult of one." Grillaan did not want to insult this strange, intense character. He needed him. Everybody needed Ogun, the smith. And he was grateful to him. He chose his words carefully.

"For the Cattach I am necessary. I may be a cult, but I am not a myth." Ogun smiled at the Prior. "Your Christ, on the other hand, is a myth."

"He is the truth and the light," said Grillaan.

"Perhaps," said Ogun, glad to have the Prior to talk to and genuinely enjoying the conversation, "but all myths are both true and untrue. Christianity is dangerous because it insists upon being the only truth. The Druids at least understand that if one myth is 'true' then all myths are true. I don't have to tell you how preposterous it all is. Everything anyone says about truth is a lie. Faith kills because it inevitably leads to war, and since the Romans left Alba that is a condition unknown to us. Now the Norse are coming. Who knows what they really want or believe in?"

"I imagine they are farmers at heart," said Grillaan.

"Aye," laughed Ogun, "farmers with swords and war ships."

"Christ is the dove of compassion and peace," said Grillaan, "the lamb of God."

Ogun stood up and stretched himself to his full six feet. "Aye, it's some menagerie you have, right enough. Come and I'll show you your bell."

Caornan, who had been listening to the conversation intently, helped the Prior to his feet, and the three of them walked back to Ogun's smiddy.

From beneath a wooden trestle covered in tools Ogun produced a parcel of rough cloth. Dramatically he cleared a space on the trestle and unfolded the material. Caornan gasped; the ageing prior's trembling hand was reaching out to touch one of the most beautiful things Caornan had ever seen. So bright was the metal work and so fluid the engraving. Who would have expected this?

"So you like it, eh boy?" teased Ogun.

"It's ... exquisite." Awestruck, Caornan could think of no other word.

Ogun picked up the bell and handed it to Grillaan. "It could stand a bit more buffing but I think it'll do you for what you want."

Grillaan held the bell as tenderly as if it were a child. "I see you have inscribed a cross on it, Ogun. God bless you for that."

"It is your sign. But there's also an adder eating its tail, which represents eternity. I thought you would appreciate that."

Grillaan held the bell up so that the morning sunlight caught the polished bronze.

"What does the butterfly represent?" asked Caornan.

"It is the soul of man," said Grillaan.

"Well, immortality, at least," said Ogun modestly.

"Caornan is right. It truly is exquisite," said Grillaan. "Ogun, as God is my witness, you have made us something remarkable and in his name, I thank you."

"Come then," said Ogun, "let's step outside and you can hear the song in her." Gently he took the bell from Grillaan and the three men went out into the light. Ogun turned to Caornan.

"I take it you'll be doing the ringing. Hold the handle loose in yer palm... like this. Then swing it in a good arc... like this." Ogun swung the bell back and forth and the sound which came from it, so sweet and doleful, drifted over the bay, up into the air, and across the headland. A part of Caornan, like a butterfly, followed it, never to be returned to his body.

Up by the chapel on the headland Nessan stopped milking the black cow. The sound of a bell, soft and distant. Four swans flew over her head towards the Loch of Bushta. As if in recognition of the bell they cried out before they landed on the water – "Guilee! Guilee!" Nessan caught her breath and almost spilled the wooden bucket.

"Where did you learn to make such a bell, Ogun?" Grillaan asked as the smith handed it to Caornan.

"The nails which hammered your druid to the boor tree were made by a smith," said Ogun. "The bell itself is only two plates of wrought iron with a bronze finish. Precious enough, I admit, but my hands are the sum of a thousand years of working."

Caornan took the bell carefully from Ogun and was surprised by its weight. The face of the smith was as black as wet peat and his eyes seemed to grow ever whiter as they looked into Caornan's.

"With my naked eye," said Ogun, "I can see beyond the stars." He smiled, his teeth a row of rough pearls set on a black beach. "But you, young scribe, you have the true power of the occult. You imprison the dance of the word-smith on your calf skin. Your code, your writing – ah, sweet child – it terrifies our Druids because they, alone, know its true power. They fear, I think rightly, that you are the true bringer of death."

He turned in a black fold from Caornan and walked back to his smiddy.

"Ogun!" Grillaan cried out and the smith stopped and turned. "What payment will you take for the bell?"

Ogun smiled again. "Dungal, the Chief of the Cattach, pays me well enough. It is his fortune to possess the wealth to furnish the metal. Your bell was made under his sanction, and for that you are welcome. Take it, please, and go."

"But you must want something?" Grillaan insisted.

Ogun stood before the dark doorway of his work place. Smoke poured from a rough chimney above his head. Surf crashed onto the beach below them.

"To you, Christian, I stand on the edge of the world. What could you give me that I would want? Be still. The wave will wash over all of us eventually." He turned and disappeared into the smiddy.

The Prior and the scribe stood looking at the empty doorway for a moment, its blackness an hypnotic glue. Then Caornan tied the bell into a bundle and slung it over his shoulder. Grillaan made the sign of the cross and Caornan took him gently by the arm.

"Come now, Your Holiness, we must return to the chapel." Caornan led the old man slowly back along the path up to the cliff tops, stopping every now and again so that the Prior could get his breath and admire the view. Sometimes he would pray, as if he were on a pilgrimage. Please God, thought Caornan, be kind to our old brother.

It was late into the afternoon before they got back to the chapel. Nessan saw them appear over the brow of the hill as she fed the hens. From the other direction, from Dungal's fort, came Ythan the mason, his tool bag slung over his shoulder as usual. Eoghan, who was delving in one of the small fields, waved to his friend. He put down his spade and went to meet him.

"I have come to see what bools the Spring tides have washed up down at the foot of the geo," said Ythan. "You said you'll be wanting a wall built before Beltane."

"In the cave? Aye," said Eoghan. "Grillaan is of a mind to inter his brother's relic, but whether it's this year or next we'll have to wait and see. The Prior's not fit for much this weather and I fear he won't see another Summer."

As they walked a silence fell on them. When they reached the top of the geo, Ythan spoke.

"Do you know that the old folk call this the 'Geo of the Dead'?"

"That's fitting," conceded Eoghan.

"Aye, for you Christians," said Ythan. "You're obsessed by death."

"That's why Christianity will never catch on, not in the long term."

Ythan burst out laughing. "I thought you were an ordained Christian priest, Eoghan! Are you not supposed to convert us all?"

"Och, not me," said Eoghan, sitting down at their usual spot so they could admire their boat and pier-wall. "I'm an old soldier. I've killed people. Admittedly most of them were trying to kill me at the time... but no, Ythan, I suppose I'm just not good enough for Grillaan's church."

"Maybe nobody is."

"Maybe," agreed Eoghan. Ythan changed the subject.

"You getting much cod off The Sneuk?"

"Some."

Another silence. They weathered it contentedly enough.

"It'll be a worry what to do for the best when he does go. If we're to keep a presence here we'll need new blood from Ireland." Eoghan spoke as if thinking aloud.

"More missionaries, eh?" teased Ythan.

"Someone who could plough with a beast would be welcome." Eoghan scratched the back of his head. "But no doubt we'll get diplomats and politicians."

"Och, the Druids'll turn them into birds, don't worry." Ythan got up and slung his bag over his shoulder. "I'll away down and see what's what. You'll maybe get a wall out of it yet."

"Will you need a hand?" Eoghan asked.

"No with the stones," smiled Ythan, "but I've got a wee jug of whisky you could help me out with later on."

Eoghan warmed inside at the thought. "You're a terrible sinner for one man," he said.

"It's true," agreed Ythan. He set off down the geo and soon disappeared from sight behind some large red sandstone boulders.

Eoghan got up and walked back to the field. He was disturbed at his work a second time by the arrival of Grillaan and Caornan. By the time he got to the Prior's hut Grillaan had lain down on his simple trestle bed and had fallen asleep. Caornan was sitting on a turf seat just beside the entrance. Eoghan ducked down and looked in. His old friend was breathing regularly. He stepped back and stood up.

"That stravaig's done him in," he said to Caornan. "I said I would easily go with you, but oh no, he had to go for the infernal thing himself." He looked at the bundle lying at Caornan's feet. "Is that it?"

"Aye," said Caornan, half asleep himself.

"I'll have a look at it later," said Eoghan, looking out at the sea. "I'd only be tempted to ring it and I don't want to wake the ould fellah up."

"He's the same age as yourself, Eoghan," scolded Caornan, tired and annoyed.

"Nonsense! He's hundreds of years older than me!" Eoghan heartily enjoyed his own joke, but then saw the young cleric was weeping. He knelt down beside him. "Och, forgive me, son. I've a rough old mouth on me." He put his arm around the young man's shoulders. "He's seen a lot in his life has Grillaan. He is my true brother and the only holy man I have ever met. I would follow him anywhere. You're the same, brother Caornan. Why, haven't we followed him here to the edge of everything known to man? I'd follow him further if he asked me."

"What's to become of us?" Caornan's voice was thin and fearful.

"No man can know what is on the road ahead of him. We just have to get on, day by day." Eoghan suddenly felt awkward and inadequate.

"God knows, doesn't he?" Caornan's voice was full of doubt and fear.

"We have to believe so, Caornan," Eoghan replied. "Our Holiness the Prior believes it to be so."

"But you don't?"

Eoghan could feel his mouth go dry. He thought of Ythan's whisky. "Grillaan has enough faith for all of us. He's my Chief. I believe in him."

He stood up. He knew his words were not what the boy wanted to hear. He looked around the headland – up to the loch and over to the hill beyond. Dunnet Head had stripped every unnecessary thing away from him. He was grateful for that. That perhaps the priesthood had gone the way of money and women, well that fact would be of no help to Caornan at this precise moment. He knelt down and picked up the bell.

"I'll put this in the nave for safe-keeping until His Holiness is fit to bless it. Go get yourself something to eat, my darling boy, we have evening prayers in half an hour or so."

Eoghan walked towards the chapel and Caornan watched him disappear inside.

"Here, bardie boy," said a friendly heathery voice, "You'll be needing this." It was Nessan. She handed him a bannock with a thick wedge of white cheese. "You look like you've climbed all the hills in the Naver. You're as white as a swan."

Gratefully, Caornan accepted the food. He was starving.

When he got to the foot of the geo Ythan also had an appetite – for stone. The cave mouth seemed hungry too, its jaws black and open. It always looked as if it was about to swallow something, as if it could chew up the whole headland, drink the entire sea. He put down his tool bag and did some reconnaissance. Just as he had expected there was a fair scattering of stones, and there had even been a small rock fall just east of the geo-mouth where the strata were weak and exposed, so there was plenty of flat stone to work with. For building a wall it could not be better. His wall was all around him, bits and pieces of nature, and he would make them whole again, turn it into something new and beautiful. His wall was already building itself in his mind. *Nature used time to build this cliff*, he thought, *but I will use my hands*. He picked up a piece of sandstone and smelt it. The sea flooded his senses, and the ghost of a desert, the embedded memory of equatorial sunlight and the trace of heavy, crushing ice. The story of the world was in the stone he held in his hand. Ythan was in his element down at the foot of the cliffs, amongst the rocks on the stone ledges, at the mouth of the cave: he was in the world of stone.

He went into the cave to remind himself of the dimensions he would be working with. The usual squadron of nervous rock pigeons flew out above his head in a pumping of fright and feathers. Aye, he thought to himself as he looked at the back cavity, to block that up as the old Druid wants will take a wheen of stones. He was so deep in thought that he did not hear the woman come in. He did not see her either, as she sat down on a rock just behind the one he was sitting on.

"Your wall will be a grand thing, Ythan."

Ythan just about passed out from fright. The rush of anger he felt at being disturbed fell away when he saw her. She stood up. Light pouring in the cave entrance lit up her long auburn and yellow hair which flowed into a long multi-coloured cloak. She was beautiful, but unlike any woman he had ever seen. She was young but with the poise of a much older woman. He was about to speak, but her words came first: "Don't be alarmed. I mean you no harm."

"What harm can you do me?" asked Ythan.

"We all do harm without trying or even knowing," she answered. "That is our shared tragedy."

She came closer. She was dripping wet.

"You're wet," said Ythan. "Have you been in the sea?"

"You are cold," she said. "Have you been out on the ice?"

Ythan looked at her sharply. The material and cut of her clothes, even their colours, was foreign to him.

"You will build your wall, Ythan," she said, "and it will last two thousand years."

"Who are you?" he asked.

"No-one knows who they are" she laughed. "Ythan, what does it matter who I am? You will build your wall, that is all that matters."

"Why does that matter to you?"

"Because I need a home," she replied at once.

"A home? Here!" Ythan looked at the dripping wet surface of the cave. "The Irish Druids want to put their relic in here. No one can live here. It will be blocked up."

"I know about their clarsach. I know what they want," she said calmly. "It suits me."

Ythan scratched the back of his head as he always did when presented with a practical problem. But this woman, what she was talking about, was not practical. "Can you not just tell me your name?" he asked, exasperated. "That would be something."

"My name is Nair," said the Maighdeann Mhara.

Nair. The name swam around in Ythan's mind like a Spring cod off The Sneuk. Nair.

"An unusual name." Ythan tried to concentrate. "An old name. Not even from our language."

"Time keeps everything and changes everything," said the Maighdeann Mhara. "You, of all people should know that."

"Nair is a myth," he said flatly. "She's not a person." He'd remembered.

"Am I not here before you?" she asked.

"I don't know," he answered.

"I am the one who has suffered for her actions. Because I was jealous, Leir turned me into what I am, a creature of the sea. And do you know what I was jealous of, Ythan?"

The Maighdeann Mhara had moved her face close to Ythan's. Her skin was smooth and translucent, like seaweed in a rock pool.

"I was jealous of the great love my husband's children had for one another and for the love they had for their father. I was jealous that they were not my children, that they were my sister's, and I wanted to kill them! I wanted to destroy them! I was out of my mind!"

The Maighdeann Mhara moved to the back wall and pressed her hands against the stone. She sobbed, her body heaving. Leaning against the cave wall she turned to face Ythan. He saw seawater from the dripping stone run over her shoulders, yet her shoulders remained dry.

"I ordered one of my servants to kill them," her voice cracked with emotion, "but she refused. I was Queen of the Cattach, if there was to be any killing then I had to do it myself. So I took the four children – the daughter Fionnuala, the son Aodh, and the twins Fiachra and Conn – to Loch Calder where I planned to drown them. When we got there I could not do it. I could not kill them. A feach had given me a rod of enchantment so instead of drowning them I turned the four children into swans. When Leir found out what I had done to his beautiful children he flew into a rage and his power was such that he condemned me to the ocean for all eternity."

The Maighdeann Mhara let out a deep, terrible moan. Her pain filled the cave, and echoed thunderously into the innermost recesses of the headland.

"All because I was jealous of love. A love that was there to sustain me. Now I search for love. A love that I will never find. I have destroyed myself."

Ythan stood transfixed by this outpouring of grief. He did not know what to make of this beautiful tortured creature. Was she some wandering mad person? How could her story be true? 'The Children of Leir' was a yarn his grandmother had told him, it was a myth, a legend, a wonder story. Wasn't it? The Maighdeann Mhara had slumped to a multi-coloured heap at the back of the cave. *Whatever else she is,* he thought determinedly, *one way or the other, she's a woman in pain.*

"Good lady," he spoke softly, stepping towards her. "Why don't you come out into the sunlight?" He offered her his hand.

The Maighdeann Mhara raised her head. Her eyes were blue opals set in mother of pearl. "Thank you for helping me," she said.

"I have done nothing," said Ythan.

"You have listened. Now you must build."

"It is what I do."

The Maighdeann Mhara grasped his outstretched hand. "I know."

Ythan pulled her to her feet. She weighed nothing at all.

"I will go out into the sunlight," she said. "but you must stay here a moment. Do not follow me immediately."

In an arc of colour she moved swiftly to the cave entrance and was gone. Ythan stood where he was. He couldn't have moved even if he'd wanted to. He'd only come into the cave to measure the wall. His right hand began to tingle a little. As he rubbed it the hand felt warm, as though it had been dipped in hot water. He put it to his cheek. The heat from his fingers pulsed into his jaw. He snatched his hand away. The tingling was not unpleasant, but the heat – in this cold cave – made no sense. Clenching and unclenching his fist, he went outside. Sunlight dazzled until his eyes adjusted. He looked across to the geo, then east towards Dwarick Head. No-one to be seen. A lazy audience of seals bobbed and sniffed the air a few yards offshore. Ythan picked up his tool bag and slung it over his shoulder. He clenched and unclenched his right fist again and again. Then he walked back to the Geo of the Dead.

# 33

Harvest rain poured down near midnight as the taxi pulled up outside the old hospital, shuddering to a heavy halt on the sodden shingle drive. The back door opened and two red high heels poked out. Two black-stockinged legs followed. Daimler stood up unsteadily. As he adjusted his rumpled dress, one of the heels snapped, sending him staggering back against the cab.

"Hey min, watch ay car!" barked the taxi driver.

Daimler bent down, took off the useless shoe, and threw it into nearby bushes. Grabbing his coat and bag from the back seat, he slammed the door. Fumbling in the handbag for money he paid the driver and hopped drunkenly along the wet flagstone path. The taxi disappeared down the driveway in angry swish of yellow light and carbon monoxide. The rain washed make-up down his cheeks and over his stubble. His blonde wig grew heavy with water, its red highlights soaking into the bodice of his dress. He tried to focus on the Yale key in his hand. A couple of short jabs missed the lock. He concentrated hard, and was about to take a third shot at it.

"Daimler, ya fuckin queen! I want a word wae youz!"

Daimler turned around. Willie the Pimp was standing right behind him.

"Well, I've nuthin to say to *youz!*" Daimler routinely mirrored mannerisms or imitated speech patterns of the last person he spoke to. He was never aware that he was doing it, and the parroting was usually discreet. Tonight, however, he was drunk and uninhibited; and Willie the Pimp, even more psychotic than usual, was not amused.

"Smart cunt, eh?" he sneered, punching Daimler in the face. The knuckle-duster on his black leather glove split open the rouged skin below Daimler's eye.

Daimler fell sideways against the door and slid to his knees.

"Where's mah fuckin money?"

Daimler put his hand to his right cheek and felt blood warm under his fingers. "I don't have any money," he said weakly.

"Aye youz do!" snarled Willie the Pimp. "Ye owe me for they last twa sessions. Twa boys, twa hoors a piece. That's four hunner bar! So where is it, missus?"

"I've told you. I don't have any..." A boot knocked the wind out of his midriff. Daimler collapsed onto his side.

"Youz've got lots oh fuckin cash, ya cunt!" Willie the Pimp kicked him again and picked up the house key that Daimler had dropped. Nodding towards the bushes, he stepped over Daimler, opened the door and went in. Two figures in black emerged from the bushes, and began to kick Daimler savagely. After a minute Willie the Pimp reappeared in the doorway carrying a laptop bag. One of the other thugs bent down to pick up Daimler's handbag, and all three men disappeared.

Daimler lay on his side, his hands cupped over his face. His mouth, bruised and torn, was open but his scream was silent. Soaked by blood and rain, his dress clung to his thighs, exposing his ripped stockings and bony knees. Scarlet under the stair light a small burn of blood flowed from his head, a vibrant tributary pouring into the dissipating sea of rain water on the paving. His eyes, wide open and terrified, stared out over the taxi tyre-tracks chevroned into mud on the drive.

Kylie swung the car aggressively into the drive of the old hospital, nowadays a block of bijoux flats. She had been calling Daimler's mobile all evening, but it was switched off. Daimler never switched off his phone. *Typical*, she'd thought bitterly, *Just when I really need him he goes AWOL*. She didn't see him until she got out of the car. *What the hell…?* Her stomach lurched as she approached the door. The woman was bleeding. *Attacked? Here?* She knelt down, unsure what to do. Disbelief numbed her for seconds as her stressed brain struggled to compute what she was seeing. Daimler? She felt for a pulse but found none. Frantically she reached into her bag for her mobile and jabbed the screen. "Ambulance, please!" Daimler's blonde wig lay like a sodden dead polecat, three feet from his shining bald head, a red blood stain disfiguring its glamour. The red burn of blood flowed from Daimler and out into the sea of the rain.

# 34

Mags had never seen the Moon so bright or so full or so big or so orange; it had a purple halo, like a cosmic collar. The Harvest Moon, Fracher could have told her. The stars literally burned out of the sky, a jade cloth punctured by a million diamond holes. Venus, to the west of the Moon, was a small explosion of light. The Plough hung like a phosphorescent scythe on the silver-black wall of the northern night. Orion belted the endless plaid of the eastern sky with a waistline of stars. As she stood on the clifftop outside the salmon bothy everything magnified and radiated as if her eyes had become telescopes, her ears two radio receivers. The sound of the sea became all the music she had ever imagined. She lay on her back on the grass. The wine she had drunk relaxed her brain, opening her to sensation. Her dinner lay untouched on the bothy table so there was nothing in her system to stem stimulation. She looked up into the shimmering tapioca swirl of the Milky Way. It seemed to her the entire shining universe was revealing itself to her. Overwhelmed, she began to tremble, and closed her eyes. She sensed someone or something around her but she felt no threat. The earth beneath her assured her that everything was alright, no matter what. She laughed out loud. *Boy, have I changed.* When she opened her eyes Lopti Lofferson was looking down at her.

"I never did find my dog," he said, and laughed. She laughed too, and then he kissed her. She felt intense heat. He touched her hair. She saw a halo of fire. His hands moved over her. Her clothes burned, her jumper and her jeans vanished in the heat she felt she had become. Lopti was speaking. She could not understand, and yet she was replying! White heat was flowing through her. She grabbed him, pulling him closer then pushing him away. All the while the heat grew until the sky seemed to melt. The stars and the entire night were being poured like milk from a jug; poured into her. Lopti Lofferson was pouring, heaving, spinning, flying, wrapped all around her both within and without, while light and heat boiled everywhere. At last it grew still.

They were no longer on the cliff top by the salmon bothy. They had reached a place where sleep was born, where everything was stretched, where heat and light had reached the edge of their purpose because there was no physical matter to maintain them. Here, where Lopti Lofferson had taken her, at the edge of everything, there was no heat, no cold; she was neither anxious nor complacent. She was the essence of herself. She could go no further.

*Is this love?* Her question drifted unspoken and unanswered in the calm.

"We must go back," said Lopti Lofferson. Everything swirled into reverse. Heat and light became music and colour. Her memory became her imagination.

She lay asleep on the cliff top beneath the Harvest Moon as the surf broke gently on Dunnet Beach. Lopti Lofferson lay beside her for a moment. He made sure she was comfortable. She was fine. He went into the bothy and pulled the duvet from her bed. Back outside he wrapped it gently around her so that she was not exposed to the night or the cold ground.

"You will need the sea for company," he whispered into her ear. "Remember: the Moon is Lopti's lamp. From tonight onwards each time the Moon is full you too will shine."

Then he was gone.

# 35

*It will be Skaldskaparmal, the language of poetry, they will try to kill off first, those who survive the wave,* said Bragi Boddason. *The fruit of the passion of Jörð and Storegga will change everything.*

Bragi Boddason was not given to sentiment. He was, after all, a god – the god of poetry – even though he said so himself.

*After the wave they will wallow in abstraction, in a world where language has neither subject nor object, where Bragarmál (poetic speech) will be impossible. The people will be terrified of themselves because they will not know why they are alive. Bragarbot (the poem's improvement) – the ultimate aim of the Skald – will be impossible. I tell you this,* said Bragi Boddason, *because it is my purpose.*

He had steered the great white ship Skidbladnir directly to the east of Orkney. He could see the mighty wave coming. He could see to the south-west the arrowhead of Duncansby Head, the great plateau of the Province of the Cat stretching beyond that. He manoeuvred Skidbladnir directly into the curve of the wave, and rode its surf towards the blood-red cliffs.

# 36

The thin yellow snake of the night-shift was winding its way out through the plant gates as Colin arrived with the rather thicker yellow snake of the day-shift. Except they didn't go in. They gathered in a fluorescent crowd either side of the security kiosks. On the passenger seat of his BMW lay that day's copy of the John O'Groat Journal: "***GABFAN NUCLEAR TO SACK ENTIRE WORKFORCE! Union ballot backs strike call!***" shouted the banner headline.

He parked in one of the disused bus spaces outside the gates. Normally he would have gone to his reserved space on-site. Not today. He got out and threaded his way through hundreds of men in yellow day-glo jackets. Many of them held banners: "*Workers to Save Plant!*", "*SAFETY Before Profit*!" As he flashed his pass at a bemused security guard he saw two TV crews arriving. Behind them was Gilbert Henderson from The Groat. He avoided him. The night-shift met the day-shift in a confluence of excitement and anger. A lot of the older men who had treated their union more as a necessary burden and a social club were quiet and pensive. The younger ones were the source of most of the noise. Colin got the sense that no-one really knew what was going on. Why were these people gathering like this on this particular morning? Why was the company pursuing this policy of confrontation? What was to be gained? The men knew that the very industrial processes they were engaged in made an indefinite strike impossible. The plutonium, uranium and other elements they were handling were subject to the physical laws of nature, not those of industrial relations. Radiation, like discontent, had to be contained.

Colin noticed Gilbert Henderson talking to union officials. The TV crews were already filming interviews with supposedly random individuals. How will this be seen, he wondered, by the rest of the world? Will they care? Will these hundreds of men remember today as something significant, a special day in their lives? What was it that determined these events, these actions? If the company thought it had power over this workforce, days like these only proved how dependent upon them it was. *Could this*, thought Colin as he looked around him, *be what they call history*? From out of the crowd Jimmy Greenan grabbed his arm. "Ah telt youz, Harper. I telt youz, but youz widnae fuckin listen!"

"Nobody's fuckin listenan til anybody, Chimmy." Colin ran through the main gates, down the long driveway and across the wide car park to his office block. Inside, the hub administration office was empty. For a moment he marvelled at the vacated desks and unlit computer screens before turning into his own office. No sooner had he sat down and switched on his computer than his office phone rang. The White Ape had a strict code concerning mobiles: never to be used on site; rarely off-site; and never, ever when it was company business. The White Ape knew too much about security surveillance to trust mobile networks. Nagelstein's voice drawled and cracked like pepper in his ear. He put down the phone and walked down the corridor to Nagelstein's office.

At the end of the long desk sat The White Ape, Kylie perched on a chair to one side of him; across from him an even larger man than Nagelstein, whom Colin had never seen before. Jet black moustache and jet black hair – dyed Colin guessed – and an expensive grey silk suit. His large flat face held a frown. There was only one other chair so Colin sat on it. No-one said a word for a moment; then Kylie spoke.

"This is Mac Barker, Colin. Mac's the CEO for Gabfan Europe."

"Pleased to meet you." Colin leaned across the desk to shake the man's hand. Barker responded half-heartedly. His hand was huge, somewhere between a ham and a spade. *What the hell are you doing here?* Colin flashed this thought at Kylie. Last night as they ate, in bed, over coffee this morning – She'd mentioned nothing about this. They had talked about the strike and what might happen. Nothing about this big Yank.

"Never been on a demolition job like this in my life," shouted Mac Barker in the loud twang which was his normal speaking voice. "Was here all last night and an hour this mornin. Not so much as a bang or a crash. What's goin on, son?"

Colin realised the question was directed at him. He felt his mobile vibrate in his jacket pocket. "We have a situation," he said.

"Damn right you have a situation!" shouted the Big Yank. "But I don't think it's one you're aware of."

"The company should stop giving the union ultimatums," said Colin. "If I could just speak to the shop stewards we could resolve this today."

"From today the union has no place on this site." Nagelstein was firm. Colin slipped the mobile from his pocket.

"The union – in one form or another – has been here since the first brick was laid. There have never been any problems. None that haven't been resolved by negotiation." He looked at the two men. They were up to something. He glanced at his phone. A text from Kylie – *Daimler's been murdered.*

Nagelstein leaned forward. "You're the site manager, Harper, so there's something you should know. Gabfan Nuclear has sold the operation here."

"Sold... sold what? To who?" Colin's mouth went dry.

"As of the first of next month Tycho Nuclear will be the lead contractor at Dounreay," announced Mac Barker.

"Who the fu..." Colin didn't know what to say. He looked at Kylie. She was staring hard at the desk. "Just who or what are Tycho Nuclear?"

"That don't concern you, son!" shouted Mac Barker. "The only thing you need to know is that you ain't part of the operation any longer."

"I'm not?"

"Nope!"

"I've worked here all my life." Colin's eyes narrowed as they focused. So this was where things were going. "With respect, you guys know nothing about Dounreay, nothing about its history and less about site culture."

"I know one thing, son!" twanged Mac Barker, the Big Yank. "Doodly squat gets done here ninety-nine percent of the time. The truth is we have a considerable bonus at stake here. This 'situation' as you call it, well, we can't tolerate it any longer, no sir."

"Again," Colin spoke slowly, "and with the greatest respect – just who are you exactly?"

"Who *am* I?" bellowed Mac Barker. "Why, I'm the guy who's *firing* you! That's who I am!"

"I've never seen you before in my fucking life!" Colin shouted back. The gloves – at last – were off.

"Tycho is a leading component of our parent company, Harper, that's all you need to know," said Nagelstein. "Like Mac says, it don't concern you anymore."

"Ya see, son," the Big Yank confided, calmer suddenly, "we're over every nuclear and military contract like vampire ants, both here in Yoorp and in the States. We do what we have to do, take what we have to take, and move on. Job done. Everybody's happy."

Colin felt his phone vibrate again. "As you must have noticed, not everybody's happy," he said. "They're on strike out there. It's all over the news even as we're speaking!" He glanced down at his mobile. *Stay calm.*

"We're gonna take 'em back on individual contracts. The hot-heads and the trouble-makers can stay in town." Nagelstein was a man in his element.

"You can't do that!" Colin said.

"We can shut the whole rig down," said The White Ape, the blonde hairs on his neck holding the sunlight. "We can easy get more swingin dicks."

"Guys that'll actually goddamn *work*!" agreed Mac Barker.

Colin felt his skin grow cold. "At this exact moment there are men in the DFR removing fuel rods from the reactor core. You can't just stop that procedure. We could have a major incident. You really have no idea what decommissioning entails, do you?"

"You think your monkeys are the only boo-boo's who know about this shit?" snarled the Big Yank. "Hell, the world's full of hungry nuclear hands. In the former Soviet Union there're literally thousands. They'd be over here quicker than jack-shit, and at half the pay cheque!"

"What about loyalty?" asked Colin. "Does everybody have to be in it for their own gain?"

"That's why everybody's here, fellah!" Mac Barker's eyes had widened in disbelief at this greenhorn's naivety. "And let me tell ya somethin else, son – I have never, in my long legged life, seen such a 'procedure' as ya call it in operation as I have seen in this place!" The Big Yank turned to The White Ape. "Goddamn, Darcy, are they all like this chickenshit?"

"We want you off this site as of now, Harper," snarled Nagelstein. "Clear your desk but leave your computer alone."

"And what is your role in all of this... Miss Swanson?" Colin practically hissed her name.

Kylie said nothing. Nagelstein spoke for her.

"Kylie's gonna act locally for Tycho."

"Well, well." Colin laughed but there was no humour in it, just a hollow bark. "What a surprise."

"Just sign the resignation letter and the confidentiality agreement we've drafted for you," Nagelstein continued. "You sign them, you walk away, and you get a pretty package. Set you up for life. Start to blabber and make trouble? Break the Official Secrets Act an all? You'll never work again, and the honey won't flow. It's up to you."

"Do anything stupid, son, and hell – you may end up in Guantanamo!" laughed Mac Barker.

Colin's phone vibrated. *We need to talk*. He stood up. "You people really are something, aren't you? Fortunately for you I'm easily fixed. But you have a strike on, and shit-loads of highly radioactive material in a far from stable state. You can't ignore that. You can pay off all the men if you like, but the social stink from that will choke you. Especially if there's spilt uranium on the shop floor. Think about it: the political repercussions will be seismic."

"Don't make me laugh," Nagelstein leaned back in his chair. "Your MP will say anythin we tell him to. Your MSP says nothin at all. The local councillors don't know what to say. The result is the same."

"Same all over the world, boy!" agreed Mac Barker. "Same all over the world! Do ya think that if ya get your own lil country it's gonna be any different? You'll have the same power-push as Burkina goddam Faso!"

Colin got up and walked out. The Big Yank's words buzzed and twanged after him like an out-of-tune banjo. As he strode back along the corridor he could hear Mac Barker's big fat hand playing it, plucking it, killing it. In his own office he sat down. *Gone by 2025,* he thought to himself. *We should get T-shirts made. Thousands of them.* His brain was sharpening, like a crofter in the spring time ploughing the beach to clean the blades of his implement. Green light from his computer screen caught the freckles on his arm. The banjo noise faded to a pipe tune. The big fat hand became slender fingers. A single note, pure, like a fulmar on the cliff-edge, hung over the reactor dome as he glanced out at it from his window. *All the birds flying to freedom. Gone by 2025.*

Colin drove through the main gates of the plant for the last time. The crowd was long gone. Half a dozen men formed a picket-line beside one of the security kiosks. *These are the remnants*, he thought, *the bits and pieces left behind once meaning has moved on.* His life lay behind him like so much redundant paper, or the steel filings he remembered in the swarf bucket on his lathe when he was an apprentice. It was a long sail, this, from blue dungarees to the end of the world. What *was* his world? He no longer knew. He felt cold. As he drove into Atomic City two combine harvesters edged nervously into a field.

*A single note hung over the dome like a fulmar.* The image stuck, played out in his mind. *All the birds*, she said, *are flying to freedom*. Was that Kylie speaking? Was that her voice in his head? *Everything that wasn't tied down was soon to be blown away.* He read that somewhere. The gates of the plant were flapping. Did he dream that? His eyes were heavy now, but at least he was home. In the flat he sat down, leaned back on the couch, and almost immediately fell asleep. Dreams piled up like scaffolding poles in a corner of the atomic site that was the inside of his head. Voices turned to birds, and birds back into music.

When Kylie came home she found him fast asleep, curled up like a child. She tried not to wake him but her physical presence disturbed something vital to Colin's peace. He woke up and looked at her. She stood, still in her coat, in front of the TV, in the twenty-first century the most powerful place in any room.

"There was nothing I could do." She might have been talking about the death of an old pet collie, or a flood in some far off land.

"I know." He rolled onto his back. He lay there for a moment, then sat up.

"Daimler's been murdered. Kicked to death. They dinna know who did it." Kylie sat down beside him.

"I know," he repeated, even though he didn't. Daimler's death had been the atmosphere around him as he had driven back into town. Like the nauseating stink of stale tobacco smoke. The information had lodged in his head like a vague childhood memory or a football score; noted, remembered; meaningless.

"They didna ask me. They told me. They... he... Barker..." Kylie's voice trailed off. "Yer no angry?"

"No."

"Why no?"

"Because, Kylie, life is now simple."

"Aye. Mebbe for you."

Colin stood up and moved to the window. A car passed along the street. A woman carried her shopping eagerly to somewhere.

"Weel," he said, "it seems til me e hev a choice til make.

Stay or go. If e stay, yer on mega bucks. If e go, they'll choost get somebody else."

"But I've betrayed you!" She slumped down onto the couch.

"Och." He sighed as he turned to look at her. She was beautiful in her guilt. "Ay whole thing oot ayr's a betrayal, wan way or anither."

Colin moved to sit down beside her, and put his arms around her. She was just a peedie lassie again who had stolen something from the shop, or her mother's purse, or had cheated in class, or had her frock ripped off her by an iron spike. *We all learn the hard way*, he told her silently. He buried his face in her hair and thought about his milling machine.

"I have a future," he whispered into her ear.

# 37

Now Manson could go nowhere outside the house without wearing dark glasses. Light, the very quality he relished and worshipped, now imprisoned him in the shadows behind shining bars of solid heaven. When the red fingers of the dawn crossed the cheek of the eastern sky they filled Manson's eyes with white hot coals. When the Sun poured its arc of scarlet into the sea, the August evening became a forest fire boiling into the Atlantic and deep into Manson's head. In Caithness, with its flat landscape and vast sky, escape was impossible.

All day, and every day for two weeks, he painted. The light that fried his eyes poured through his fingers onto the canvas. Landscapes, headlands, seascapes – all studies of Dunnet Head – huge explosions of colour, form and movement, all worked onto the canvas like tattoos. He worked tirelessly and without much sleep or food, until he either fell over or slumped into the huge armchair which sat in the corner beside the fireplace of the upstairs room he used as a studio. Days mixed into each other like the colours on his palette: blue, yellow, red, green, orange, black. His eyes were free of pain, and his right arm moved as if it was the source of the light itself, which danced through the leaves and branches of the sycamore trees in the garden outside his house.

One by one the canvases filled up with this fresh vision and passion, this new born compulsion to suspend the world from the edges of his eyes. He had never felt so alive, so excited yet so comfortable. Each brush-stroke surprised him and reassured him.

The studio filled with representation after representation of the natural world, layer upon layer of light and colour. The Spring peats cut and stacked on the headland turned into stars; harvest bales in the fields around the village were transformed into comets, bursting and reforming on the square before him. Manson, back firmly in his native place, was reborn. It was as if the future was moving through him into the figures and shapes he created.

When he looked in the mirror, when he went down to the bathroom to wash the sweat from his face, he would run trembling fingers over the mirror's surface, tracing the reflected contours of his face as if he couldn't quite trust who he was seeing before him, afraid he might disappear. When he went up to the shop for more whisky or bread, Nan the Shop would laugh in her good-natured way, remarking on his metamorphosis:

"Oh boot my, Manson, are ye no lookan younger every day? Whut's yer seekrad?"

Little did she know or Manson realise that he *was* getting younger. For those who consort with the creatures of the fabulous dimensions – the Shee – the world of sensation becomes intense, and the direction of the life-force is changed. Unbeknown to Manson, he was on a journey back into himself. Like a river which flowed from the sea to the mountains, the more Manson moved forwards in time the more he became the boy he had never been. The more he worked the more energy he mustered. The deeper he looked inside himself, and the more he hated what he saw, the more beautiful and vibrant became his paintings, especially those of Dunnet Head. No-one had painted the Caithness landscape like this before. So the critics were to say. Maybe, more truthfully, they could have said: no-one since the last artist they did not understand (and therefore resented).

Manson did not know it, but the cost of this art to himself, the price he was paying, was rising. He did not realise either, that from now on his personal life was dead. His emotional life up to this point, had lain mostly dormant and underdeveloped. Now, as his painting progressed, it had sprung to life like a hungry animal, aching to be released and fed. Once up and out, *feeling* began to consume him. Manson could no longer interpret things. He was a creature in love with sensation. But the sensation was moving. He was turning from sensation to intense feeling, as if his skin was exploding: he felt he was *becoming* pure colour.

Manson had no idea what was happening to him. He just picked up his brushes and painted. He knew nothing at all. It was as if he had abandoned knowledge, or knowledge had deserted him. He had no need for knowledge any more. To care for someone or something is to possess knowledge of each or all of them. But Manson, shed of knowledge, was freed from caring about anything. He was done with empathy. He'd had plenty of that once, before his mother's suicide. But like the wild geese, it had flown. His mother's desperate and tragic act had driven him to sociopathic behaviour which he had come to accept as normal. Now he was free of it. Emptied of everything, he was becoming a person who never existed. If you do not exist, you are entirely free: it is impossible be late for your dinner or your own funeral.

August bled into September, and Manson's studio, the front upstairs bedroom in the large rambling house in Dunnet, was full of paintings; twenty-four in total, as requested. It was a Monday morning at a quarter to eleven, the Sun was shining and a combine harvester was cutting barley in the field across the road from the house. He rose and closed the curtains. The whisky bottle beside his chair was empty. Downstairs, the kitchen looked even worse than usual. He could find nothing to eat or drink beyond water from the tap. His phone still held some charge. "I'm done," he told Beith. He thought she would know what he meant. She did. Two hours later they were sitting in the hotel bar. Manson hid behind his dark glasses. Beith on her phone to the gallery.

"They're everything you could have wished or hoped for," he heard her say. Then there was a discussion about time and money. Manson felt empty. He stared at the glass on the table before him. Eventually Beith hung up.

"Well, that's that," she said. "I'll arrange transportation tomorrow. The Arts Centre will package them. There'll be a charge, of course, but nothing criminal." Beith was happy. In fact she was amazed. This was as close to a miracle as she had ever sat. "I know none of this stuff interests you, Manson, but you could at least say something."

Manson said nothing.

"The paintings are wonderful. You know that." Beith was trying to be sympathetic. "The landscapes, I mean. The headlands are... well, fantastic. But, Manson, the two portraits of the girl... who is that?"

"The girl?"

"Come off it, Manson!" laughed Beith. "The nude one with the golden necklace. In one of them she's playing clarsach, surrounded by apples."

"Oh, aye, her." Manson remembered. "She's a singer."

"Hmmmn," mused Beith, half smiling. "Some singer." They sat in silence for a bit. "Look, I've got to go. Get some rest, Manson, you're done in."

Again he said nothing.

"Promise?" she insisted.

"Aye." Beith kissed him on the cheek and left.

Manson didn't go home. He sat on the same chair at the same table most of the day. The Sun was high in the sky. He could hear a combine roar and grunt as the driver changed gear when a tractor and trailer came into the field to take away the grain. The corner of the bar where he lurked was dark. Most people who came in to order food or to buy drinks went outside to eat and drink at tables and benches beside the wall below the gates of the kirk next door. Another week or so and the tourist season would be over: the Hymer mobile home owners from the campsite by the beach would all be gone.

The first thing he noticed about the girl was her dark glasses. When she came in and sat down with the older man she did not take them off. This interested Manson, even though, as Beith had pointed out, he was "done in". There was something chilling about her. He sat and watched her sip her lager and eat her soup and sandwiches while the old man sipped his rum. Necessity being an empty glass, he went up to the bar. As the barmaid served him the old man raised his head from his drink.

"Weel, Manson, wae dinna see much oh e in ay Comm iss weather."

It took Manson a moment or two to disentangle the swarm of vowels and consonants. Mags and Fracher were watching him expectantly.

"No," he said eventually. "Been away. Been busy."

"Wur ay last oh ay Mohicans," Fracher said to Mags. "Manson's wan oh ay few true local fowk left in Dinnad. Is aat no right, Manson?"

"Aye, spose so."

"Iss lassie's a local now an aal, efter a fashan," Fracher was enjoying his ethnological thread.

Manson said nothing, but looked at the "lassie". Small and slim, tanned, long hair streaked lighter by the Sun. *It's because I haven't slept*, he thought, *she's not **really** glowing*. The light in the bar was poor, forcing Manson to take off his dark glasses. At that precise moment Mags did the same thing, and their eyes locked. Both froze within themselves. Both saw the Maighdeann Mhara looking back.

"Mags is stayan up at ay Piper's salmon bothy," Fracher was saying. "How's aat for hardy?"

Fracher could tell something strange had passed between the couple. He didn't mind; they were young and he was due out at the creels in an hour. Mags' car had broken down and he was giving her a lift home. She was hungry and he was thirsty, so here they were. He liked Manson. He knew and liked his parents, and he knew that, like himself, Manson was singed by tragedy. *Each one of us faces our apocalypse*, thought Fracher as he looked at the pair of them looking at each other.

"Mags is an archaeologist," said Fracher. "Shay's workan up at ay ould chapel." Manson said nothing to this information. Having the Maighdeann Mhara close silenced him. "Manson here's a bit oh an artist, eh bouy?" Fracher goaded good naturedly. "If e dinna watch oot hay'll paint yer peecture."

Mags too found speaking difficult. She had only glimpsed the Maighdeann Mhara once before under terrifying circumstances; now she was confused, excited and frightened at the same time. It was Manson's eyes. They were the eyes she had seen beneath the water in the geo. This was not what she needed. It had been a fortnight since the incident with Lopti Lofferson, and her system had begun to calm down. Now this.

"Do you know anyone called Lopti?" She tried to sound casual.

"No." She believed him and was relieved. Fracher stood up.

"Weel, lassagee, Ah can easy gee e a run up til ay bothy."

"Thanks, Fracher, but I'll walk. I need the exercise. I'll see you tomorrow. I can get the bus back in to collect the car."

"Aye. No doot. Bay seean e, Manson." Fracher smiled and left them to it.

"He's looking after me," said Mags, unprompted.

"I can see that," said Manson. It was true. Looking at her, he could see quite easily. Being able to see normally without being blinded lifted his mood, and the pair became increasingly relaxed. Two hours later the Sun had moved far enough across the sky to make them both think about going out.

"Fracher said you live here," said Mags.

"Just across the wall. Want to see?" teased Manson.

"Is it an old house?" she asked hopefully.

"Aye. Wan oh the ouldest in the village."

Manson bought some whisky. They put on their dark glasses and left the pub, crossing the car park to the house. As Manson led her round to the back door, the only entrance he used, Mags admired the apple trees against the high garden wall. He apologised for the mess, but Mags was oblivious. What she saw was a beautiful old house: a big kitchen at the west end, a long corridor with several rooms off it, a large front room with two huge windows facing south and east, and a bedroom at the back. Upstairs she delighted at the two rooms, especially the front one which overlooked the beach and which Manson had made his studio. Through the east window she saw a combine leave a newly-cut barley field, and from the south-facing one she watched surf arc out across Dunnet Bay.

"This is the most beautiful house I have ever seen." As she stood at the window watching the sea, he moved close behind her and put his arms around her waist. She leaned back against him briefly, then slid from his grasp and moved to an old arm chair beside the fire place.

"You painted these?" Taking off her dark glasses she paused before each canvas in the order Beith had left them. She picked up then set down each one as if the frame was delicate crystal. Manson heard her gasps and sighs, like wavelets breaking over small stones.

"The headland... You paint the headland..." He tried to caress her but each time she eluded him, like a fish. He gave up and sat in the chair. There was a crumpled sheet of A3 on the floor. Snatching up a battered scrap of cardboard under some peats near the fireplace, Manson smoothed the paper on top of it and reached for one of the broken pastel crayons scattered in the hearth. Without a word he began to sketch her. But she would not stay still. She went through to the other upstairs room – Manson's bedroom when he was a boy. Without thinking she began tracing her fingers over the surface of a dressing table, the carved wooden door of a wardrobe. Warmth bled from them into her fingers. She withdrew her hands. The drawers of the dressing table slid out, the door of the wardrobe swung gently open. The curtains on the two windows blew in towards her even though the windows were shut. None of this alarmed her. She laughed out loud. She ran downstairs, and in every room the same thing happened: drawers slid out and in, as though in recognition, in welcome; cupboard doors opened out and swayed gently as she passed. Towels, table cloths, jackets and coats hung on pegs all danced as she drew close to them. Old windows which had been firmly shut for years slid gently up to let the September air nourish the house with fresh salt air.

She ran out of the back door and into the garden. A fortress-like wall separated the house from the manse and the kirk next door. As she ran across the overgrown lawn, flocks of sparrows and starlings joined thrushes, blackbirds, blue tits and finches in the branches of the apple and sycamore trees and in the ivy on the walls in such a chorus of chirping, tweeting and warbling that Mags could hardly hear herself think. She danced along the path beside the strawberry patch Manson's mother had planted some twenty five years ago. She spied bunches of tiny strawberries, which exploded with the distilled salt sweetness of the ocean and the Sun. She had tasted nothing like them. The flavour was so intense that she almost wept. She ran through the blizzard of birdsong and back into the house. Upstairs she found him still in the chair. He handed her the paper.

"It's you," he said. An angel stared back at her. A strange-looking angel: a smiling but startled face; auburn and ochre hair flowing out like liquid fire; her hands open wide in a gesture of acceptance; wings blown backwards, as if by a powerful wind.

"This is not me," said Mags. "This is the woman I saw beneath the waves."

Manson smiled.

"No," he said, "it's you."

# 38

Kylie's life changed forever the night she found Daimler bleeding to death. Up to that point her existence had been a predictable, sometimes bumpy, but pleasant enough melody. In the pouring rain, with a man's life blood flowing away in front of her, that melody became a fugue.

The first part of her new life, after the change, was consumed by the understanding that everything about her existence was wrong. A new voice spoke out loud and clear: "*This is what happens when no-one cares about anything.*" It was a strong and compelling voice. Then a contrapuntal, reassuring voice form the old predictable life would assert itself. She would capitulate to the pleasant, if sometimes bumpy, melody of life before the rain and the blood. The narrative of her life was like a line which she would dip below and then rise above, again and again, in an exhausting pattern: a series of objective and subjective episodes of chaotic music, none of them ever complete.

She would try to escape from this pattern by pretending to be someone else. When Nagelstein offered her Daimler's job, instead of telling him "no" and resigning, she convinced herself that she did not know who Daimler was and that she had never worked for Gabfan before. So being new – newly invented by herself – this was a great opportunity for her, whoever she was. Once in post she went on trips she would never before have considered. In one month alone she went to conferences and trade fairs in Edinburgh, London and Paris. These jaunts she justified to herself and to her office. When she returned she could barely recall the substance of the trip, where or why she had gone, or what she had done while she was there. Nagelstein was amazed when she proposed going to Japan, to Fukushima, to offer solidarity and to connect with "the situation" there.

"The French are muscling in on the action, Mr Nagelstein," she told him forcibly. "There's a lot of money to be made there if we're careful."

"Your job is to deal with the press here," he told her.

"It starts with a story here but ends in a contract there," she'd replied tantalisingly. The White Ape did not care if there was a story. He was, however, interested in a contract. So was Mac Barker, the Big Yank. "Then get her blonde ass out there, Darcy! Can't do any harm. She's gettin on my goddamn nerves here for sure. Every time she opens her goddamn mouth it sounds like fuckin Japanese to me anyways."

So Kylie flew to Japan. For two weeks she was extremely busy in Tokyo meeting with representatives of the Department of Energy and Tepco, the Japanese state nuclear company which produced the electricity. She drank cocktails and ate sushi with ex-Dounreay safety engineers now working through EDF, the French state nuclear energy company, for the Japanese government. She watched videos of the tsunami destroying coastal communities, and footage of the great wave washing over the nuclear reactors at Fukushima, the resulting explosions and the smoke cloud rising up into the sky. She respected aloud the brave but doomed workers who did their best to make good a bad situation. She spoke to representatives of community groups and medical experts, who expressed great concern at the actual and potential rise in diseases such as thyroid cancer in children, referencing data complied after Chernobyl.

"Something for you to look forward to in Kit Niss?" as a doctor said to her one night after too much saki.

She built up a comprehensive picture of post-tsunami Fukushima, and projected how a similar incident could be managed if it occurred on the north Coast of Scotland. This was her stated pretext in going to Japan in the first place. As to Fukushima itself she never got within a hundred miles of the disaster site.

Everyone Kyle met was convinced she was genuine in her concern for the environment and the future safety of the nuclear industry throughout the world. Most were impressed by and agreed with her arguments for open access to information and sharing expertise. For a while she even convinced herself. In her role as global ambassador for Dounreay and Tycho Nuclear – as Gabfan had become – Kylie was, by chance or genius, brilliant. Nagelstein and Barker would have been delighted if they had learned of the success of her trip. Their company name was now well-known around the world, whereas before Kylie went to Japan no-one had heard of them. As it turned out the two Americans never knew because they never asked and Kylie did not tell them. Once she was back in Atomic City she simply blanked everything. Her PA Sara, who had accompanied her everywhere she went in Tokyo and even put her to bed when she got too drunk, kept a record of every person she met and everything she did and said. Officially. She even filmed and recorded a lot of it, secretly, on her smart phone. It didn't, in the end, matter a damn who knew what about anything. By the time Kylie came back the strike had been broken and Tycho Nuclear had the workforce where they wanted them – up against the wall and by the throat.

The change of the company name and the abandonment of traditional industrial relations did not, as it turned out, have the desired effect. Not to begin with. The money wasn't coming in quickly enough. In their eagerness to maximize profits Gabfan – now Tycho Nuclear – ensured they made a loss. The British government, although no friend of organised labour, balked at the company's methods in dealing with the union and withheld bonuses. The company threatened to shut down the entire decommissioning operation unless bonuses were met and other significant investments made. (They never elaborated on what these investments were.) The Scottish Government tried to act as peacemaker in the industrial-financial stand-off, but as it had no money Tycho Nuclear paid no attention. By ignoring Edinburgh Tycho achieved part of their strategy, which was to be free of social responsibility to the local economy. London saw this as a good financial move and relented a little on the bonus payment. In response Tycho Nuclear softened its anti-union language. Seeing this Edinburgh stepped up its efforts to negotiate even though no party, including the trade union (whose officials all hated devolution to their British roots), set any store in anything the Scottish government said or did. Eager to mollify the company, local politicians and development agencies abandoned social plans and economic strategies designed to protect and stimulate the local population and economy. As a result the people of the north of Scotland were left with no plan for the future. *Gone by 2025* was beginning to have distinctly ominous overtones.

The workforce returned to work under individual contracts, a two-year pay freeze and increased pension contributions. For Tycho the gravy train was flowing again. Secretly they stepped up their plans to sell off the entire operation. Both governments convinced themselves that they had extended their power. The British government claimed that the power of trades unions in the nuclear industry was broken, that sensitive areas of prime national interest were no place for organised labour, and that private enterprise was more cost-effective than state subsidy (even though Westminster was paying more for less).

Westminster calculated that injustice was preferable to disorder. The Scottish government made much in the press and media of its role in "bringing together both sides of the dispute" even though at best they were on the margins of "the situation". The trade union was not actually in dispute with anyone. It was only trying to protect its members' interests – which was the reason they existed in the first place. The union congratulated itself on being pragmatic, on demonstrating loudly that it had the long-term interest of the industry in mind (even though that industry in Caithness – and in Scotland in general – had no long-term anything except the nuclear repository at Buldoo). The White Ape and the Big Yank felt like kings. The people of Caithness, as usual, got nothing. This was their general experience of history. Those who thought about it saw themselves as slaves of a system which did not consult them on any point at any time.

As the days after the strike turned into weeks and as Kylie came back from Japan, it was little consolation to the people of Caithness that history was to prove, as it always does, that masters ultimately depend upon their slaves; and that over time the relationship between power and the individual changes, along with concept of what is "good". What humanity arrogantly insists on proposing, history has a habit of disposing.

Such thoughts drifted in Colin's mind like a fog bank around the Pentland Skerries on a Summer's night. He spent a lot of time in the two-storey apartment sprawled on the sofa, flicking from channel to channel on the TV, unable or unwilling to concentrate on anything. Since Kylie had come back from Japan she had been sexually demanding, which Colin found extremely difficult: he had no desire for her at all. Their usual patterns had been reversed. Neither of them recognised the other.

Having undergone a metamorphosis, Kylie looked to sex for reassurance. Unconsciously she sought love at every opportunity, wandering in the desert of her fugue, searching for the fabulous, and ill-equipped to recognise it if and when she found it. The gods who might bring her fire could no more see her than she could see them. There was no hero to save her; nothing to prevent her from rising above the melody line of her life, only to sink again into chaos. Kylie needed psychological help and chemical medication. Unfortunately, no-one was looking at her closely, and everyone except Colin thought she was marvellous. For Kylie – and for Caithness – the tragedy was that the will of the gods and the actions of the heroes of history always fail under observation. She was sealed inside her own shell, her inner life like nuclear activity inside the metal jacket of the Dounreay dome, boiling invisibly beyond human reach. Kylie's strength was curiosity. In time that, combined with experience, would translate into wisdom. There were always drugs to ease mental disease; solutions for irradiated metal that could not be decommissioned. Life would force her, despite herself, to employ her intelligence for her own preservation. Within Kylie, although she was not conscious of it, was the future of her own people. Within her was the watermark of history. One morning a test confirmed she was pregnant. In that discovery life began and, tragically, it started to end. She did not tell Colin she was pregnant. She decided that it was not her who was expecting, but someone else.

Colin's sensed there was something different about her, quite apart from her increasingly mad behaviour. His response to all of this was to plan and build a model of Dounreay. He had his milling machine, but to construct the dome from a lump of steel he needed a lathe. One night on his fifth pint in The Comm a drunken farmer was boasting about the smiddy in his grandfather's steading.

"It's a bonny wee lathe," he shouted above the football, "as good as ay day id wis made."

"A lathe e say." Colin set his pint on the bar. "What kind oh lathe?"

"Id's Cherman," said the worthy. "Off ay Kaiser's yatt."

"Whit?"

"As shure as am standan here. Mah grandfaither got id efter ay first war. Dinna ask may how."

"Can I see id?" asked Colin.

"Ah dinna see any reason why no," reasoned the man.

"Tomorrow?"

"Aye. If yer able!"

"What's yer ferm called?"

"Lokistoft," said the farmer proudly. Colin knew exactly where that was. He bought the man a dram, got his phone number and left the pub happier than he had been in years.

Next day he drove out past Castletown to Lokistoft, bouncing up the long pot-holed track. The farmer was nowhere to be seen, but a young man twice his size jumped down off a tractor to meet the car, and Colin explained why he was there.

"Och, faither'll be sleepan id off," laughed the son.

The smiddy was under the roof of a new building. "Och, wae hedna ay hert till flatten id. Id's fill oh history an chounk."

It was love at first sight. The lathe was four foot long, with a pedal so that it could be driven by foot power. He ran his hands over it the way he once had Kylie, lying on the beach so fresh and beautiful on their first holiday to Crete. Stamped on the back of the lathe was a metal plate: ***Hamburg 1908***.

"How much d'ye want for id?" asked Colin. The young man said nothing. "Twa hunner?"

The farmer's son still said nothing and walked off. He came back with a variety of spanners and a bar, and within half-an-hour the lathe was unbolted, unwired and in the back of Colin's car.

As he installed the Kaiser's lathe next to his beloved milling machine and began to work on his model of Dounreay life began to make sense to Colin. This was his votive offering to himself. This was his cave painting. This was his bison and mammoth. This was his hand print on the rock.

Nothing that had happened in the past mattered any more. He realised he had been pedalling furiously in the wrong bicycle race and now he'd fallen out, been excreted out of the peloton of Dounreay. Constructing his model gave physical shape to his freedom. Strangely, as he worked, the room grew cold. No matter how he cranked up the heating the place was always freezing. His breath formed around him in small Arctic-blue clouds. *Maybe*, he thought to himself as he blew on his frozen fingers, *this is the colour of death*? It was the colour of Daimler's eyes as the light left them for the last time and the boots cracked into his skull.

# 39

Aboard Skidbladnir Bragi Boddason was having trouble with the crew; the thousand black haired, red faced dwarf-sons of Ivaldi. They were used to constant physical labour (on land or under it) and were growing discontented following the love wave of Storegga and Jörð across the sea. Bragi was sympathetic to their complaint.

*You dwarfs*, he told them, *have been generated from the soil by the gods in Asgard. You were given life and sent down into the earth to live as maggots in the flesh of Ymir. But through the power of the gods you became conscious and intelligent, and were given the shape of men though you lived in the earth and in rocks. The gods made you build Bifrost, the rainbow bridge which connects heaven to earth. So it is fitting that you, the true children of Ymir the earth giant, you who are created from his surf-blood and his bones, that it is you who join me now to collect the booty from the wave of love which runs before us across the silver sea. Everything good is in the future. Soon, my children, you will hunt for gold in these drowned Pictlands. Maggots you will be no more.*

The thousand red faced dwarf-sons of Ivaldi gave a collective cheer and forgot their complaints, for their love of gold was greater than anything else.

So as Bragi anchored Skidbladnir off Dunnet Head, the magic of Skaldskaparmal – the language of poetry – coupled with the persuasion of Bragarmál – poetical speech – did its work once more.

# 40

Mags needed help. If she was to excavate the back wall of the cave she required willing people who were interested in the past and capable of physical labour. Fracher was beyond value in so many ways but this was one thing he couldn't help her with. He had, however, made a good suggestion: "Why d'ye no go an see aat fowk aat ay Caithness history placie in ay toon?"

Mags had little enthusiasm for this suggestion. Her first and only visit to Caithness Time was, she remembered, less than fruitful. She could not understand why her project had met with such hostility. None the less, because her heart was full of optimism and she felt empowered by her recent experiences, she decided to approach the museum once more. Time was hammering on and no other option had presented itself. Soon the season would be over. The battering seas enraged by the Westerlies would make her work impossible.

Two women stood behind the reception desk at Caithness Time staring intently at a computer screen. Mags stood for a moment waiting for one of them to speak to her. Neither did, nor showed any sign that they had noticed her presence. She coughed softly. Neither woman raised her eyes from the computer. "Excuse me."

A narrow faced woman with a badge which read "Kili" looked up. Mags recognised the curator she had met before. Kili, it was plain, did not remember her. The other woman, who had the look of a person made of pastry, looked up momentarily from the computer screen. Mags saw from her badge that she was called "Fili".

"We met maybe a month ago," said Mags. "I'm Mags Beaton from the London School of Economics." Kili and Fili stared at her. "I came to see yourself," Mags continued, directing her conversation towards Kili. "I'm a post-graduate student. An archaeologist. I'm conducting a dig up at the old chapel on Dunnet Head, remember?" Still no response from either woman. Mags persevered. "I'm at a crucial part of the work and I need some volunteers to help me with the last physical bit. I have to remove some stones from an old wall and I can't manage it on my own. I was wondering if there are people attached to your museum, people who are interested in the archaeology of Caithness, you know, who might have a couple of hours to spare maybe for a couple of days, over a weekend say. Anyone really. Just one person would be a real help."

Kili's eyes narrowed into her already narrow face. "Find anything?" she snapped. Mags was taken aback by the aggression of the question.

"Yes," she said, "as a matter of fact I have."

"Well?" demanded Kili.

"A priest's handbell, I think." She stopped. Anger replaced uncertainty. "What I've found is not the issue here. All I'm asking is if you know of anybody who could..."

"Nobody's interested in any of that stuff." Fili still hadn't looked up from the screen.

"It's local history. It's important stuff," insisted Mags. "I've heard there's an archaeological society I could contact. I looked on your website but I couldn't see a link."

"That's because there isn't one," said Kili.

"I see. D'you not think there should... be..." Mags looked closely at the pointy face. Finding it hard to speak she glanced at the tartan-clad marmalade jars and other assorted knick-knacks on the shelves of the shop just across from the reception. Down the corridor was a large sign proclaiming a display about Dounreay. Kili was staring at her. Fili was still ignoring her.

"Look," said Mags, "I write to you, Kili... to the curator... a letter explaining what I..."

"We got no letter," interrupted Kili.

"The postal service up here is notoriously bad." Fili chipped in for the first time, again without looking up.

"The dig could prove to be significant. All I..."

"Nobody up here is interested in that kind of thing."

"You seem to be keen on the history of the atomic plant," said Mags calmly. "I see from the local paper that you're both recently back from Albuquerque. Productive trip, was it?"

"What are you implying?" Mags would never be coming back to Caithness Time. If that was the mission of these two gorgons then they had succeeded.

"I read that you plan to extend the nuclear section of the museum," she said, "even though that goes directly against the stated intention of the institution when it was proposed to the local people. Are you going to exhibit fuel rods in your art gallery?" Mags could feel her face flush.

Fili, the manager according to her badge, got up from her seat and leaned over the counter slightly. "Maybe you're not aware, but Dounreay is the major employer here," she said.

"By 2025 that will represent seventy years of Caithness history. There's seven thousand years of history waiting to be discovered out there under the peat."

"So you've found an old bell." Kili could hardly contain herself. "Relative to the history of organic life on Earth, the miserable fifty millennia of homo sapiens represents something like the last two seconds of a twenty four hour day. The entire history of civilized humanity takes up only one fifth of the last second of the last hour!"

"Life is beautiful and precious," said Mags. "Do you ever consider that?"

"Please! Don't patronise us."

"For godssake, Celtic monks are important! Your museum should tell their story!"

"I'll be the judge of that!" snapped Kili.

"We're trying to tell a different story at Caithness Time," said Fili.

"This isn't a museum," said Mags as she headed for the exit. "It's a bordello of history!"

Then she was out on the street. The morning had dulled and it started to rain. Even so Mags put on her dark glasses.

"History is an apple wae time at ids core!"

She turned around to where the voice had come from. In an archway of the old Town Hall, in an explosion of rags stood Doupie Dan. Mags had never seen him before but was intrigued that he too sported dark glasses. His had white plastic frames. She opened her mouth but did not get as far as speech.

"Ay apple hes a precious seed! Ye canna taste time!" Doupie Dan hopped from white sandshoed foot to black sandshoed foot.

"W-what do you mean?" Mags stammered.

"Wur forbidden til look intil ay future." Doupie Dan was swaying slightly. "Boot time isna empty. Every second is a narrow cave mooth, an through id will come An Slanaighear!"

He hopped around the corner of a boarded up shop and was gone.

*What sort of place is this*? Mags felt she might explode. She turned and walked towards the traffic lights and the Co-op car park.

"Ah'll help e." Another voice! Mags turned again. This time it was a young girl sitting on a public bench outside the Highland Council service point. She had a tangled mass of curly black hair tied back with a green scarf.

"Sorry?"

"Ah sayed I'll help e," repeated the girl. "Ah wis in Caithness Time til get a furry gonk fur mah peedie sister's birthday an Ah heard e arguan wae aat English wifies."

Mags smiled. "I'm English too."

"Ur e?" The girl seemed surprised. "Ah lek standan stons an stuff an whut yer doan sounds really interestan. Til me, at any rods. Ah can shift stons."

"Can you? You're a bit young." Mags was getting used to the dialect.

"Yowng, is id?" The girl snorted and tossed her curly hair back. She stood up and lifted one end of the public bench three feet off the ground. "Ah do karate an aal!"

Mags laughed out loud. A couple of women leaving the fish shop across the street looked across disapprovingly.

"How old are you?" asked Mags.

"Sixteen an three quarters." The girl set the bench down gently.

"And what's your name, Wonder Woman?" laughed Mags as she raked in her bag to find her mobile.

"Nessan."

"Well... Nessan," said Mags finding her phone. "Are you free this weekend?"

"Aye," said Nessan, "Free as a swan."

# 41

It rained. Autumn, Winter and Spring. The harvest had been poor and now the sowing was threatened. Hunger moved through the land of the Cattach like a grey stone shadow of suffering. As the deluge continued into Summer the people began to despair. The Druids and the Fili, the high priests and poet-lawmakers, met in the sacred grove to plan destruction of the Irish priests on Dunnet Head.

Their reasoning was simple enough: ever since the foreigners had come to settle in the Province of the Cat the people had grown restless and discontented; less certain and respectful of the old ways. Their society depended upon a rhythm to function. That rhythm came from nature and a knowledge of the world; the individual's place within that, and the balance each person maintained with others in the clan. The success of Cattach culture was the laws and customs they created consensually from mutual need, and from human experience, were not handed down from on high by some "other divine" or deity: their laws and customs, like the people themselves, came out of the ground. The Druids and the Fili were united on this point: the influence of the Christians was undermining their society. The Irish priests bamboozled the people with some version of Tir Nan Og which promised them everything hereafter, so that they were less likely to actively engage with the here and now. Their job, as tradition instructed, was to protect the people from destruction. The discussion went like this:

– *The idea of there being only one god is infantile.*
– *Can these fools not see that the world is a complicated system of time and space?*
– *A belief in one all-seeing creator is childish irresponsibility. It is beyond reason and socially corrosive.*
– *We fought off the Romans and their barbarism by believing in ourselves and valuing what we have achieved.*
– *If there is nothing to hold us together we will be easy meat for the Norse if they come West in any number for our women and cattle.*
– *These Irish missionaries know nothing of our poetry or our world.*
– *They have betrayed Dungal's hospitality and kindness by infecting the people with the sayings of this Christ, their hero. They're becoming as passive as sheep.*
– *These rains – surely, they are a warning from the future?*
– *The great wheel has turned. We must act or embrace disaster. – Dungal will not kill these sorcerers. He has been beguiled into protecting them.*
– *Then we must send to the High King for soldiers so no dishonour stains our Chief.*
– *So be it. Let it be done.*

And it was done. Word was sent south to Breidi at Dun Phadraig by the great river, and a detachment of soldiers was duly deployed north.

All the while it rained. Summer was at its high mark and, despite the worries of Eoghan and Caornan, Grillaan was still alive. Frail certainly; not half the man he was, but alive.

"Och, he's from O'Neil stock," Eoghan said to Caornan, when the young scribe expressed his anxieties concerning the Prior. "He'll see the boots off many half his age."

One day towards the end of June Eoghan had helped his old friend back from a rare visit to the chapel for prayers, and Grillaan lay down to rest on his simple bed in his hut.

"God forgive me," said the old man. "I'm afraid I've led you and the boy on a wild goose chase."

"How's that now?" said Eoghan, trying to be cheerful. Grillaan's thin white face was drawn tight over sharp cheek bones, his bleached hair almost gone, his eyes pale and distant.

"This place," said Grillaan, his voice a loud whisper, "maybe this was the wrong place."

"But this is where Colm asked you to come." Eoghan tried to reassure the Prior. "He gave you the map."

"To inter his clarsach. To plant the seed so that the word of Christ may be known; to put the light in the dark place." Grillaan spoke as though he were in pain. "Yes, I know. I've justified our work here to myself and before God a thousand times."

"Doubt is natural, Grillaan. Does the Bible not give us Thomas as an example?" said Eoghan, surprising himself by citing scripture.

Grillaan laughed softly. "I know times are tough, when Eoghan the warrior uses the good book as a reassurance."

"Och, you're a terrible influence, right enough," smiled Eoghan.

"I've cheated death this Winter past but I won't swerve him come the next one. Eoghan, the time has come to put the clarsach of our holy brother Colm into the golden cave, bless it, seal it up and be on our way."

"On our way?" asked Eoghan, nervously.

"Aye, on our way," repeated Grillaan. "You take the boy back to Donegal. He will have a good life there and you must look after him. He is a good lad but he is a child of his passion so I fear he will make no priest. It is God's will." He lay back on his straw mattress and listened to the sea beating on the rocks at the foot of the cliff.

"What of you?" asked Eoghan after a moment. Grillaan closed his eyes.

"You will give me a good Christian burial inside the chapel, as is our tradition. I will return to the bosom of the Lord and into Christ's care."

"And the chapel?" quizzed Eoghan. "We have spent so much time and effort building it, are we really to abandon it now?"

"We are not abandoning it, Eoghan. We are giving it to the people."

"What if the people don't want it?"

"Then they will give it back to the headland." Grillaan opened his eyes, leaned over slightly, and took Eoghan's hand.

"Listen. Death is coming here, and in a form that not even you, brave fighter, can counter. It will come soon, I think, from Norway. Or from the rains. Or from the Cattach themselves." He paused a moment as if something had unsettled him. "Or from the sea." He released Eoghan's hand from his grip, lay back, and closed his eyes.

"Organise the clarsach, Eoghan, that's all I really ask of you – for Colm, for the love of God and the tenderness of Christ, and because we must love each other in this world." In silence Eoghan watched the Prior until he was sure he had fallen sound asleep. He pulled the rough woollen blanket over Grillaan's shoulders and left the hut. Outside, Eoghan stopped in amazement. It had stopped raining and the Sun was out!

Caornan was crossing Bushta Hill on his way back from an errand to the fort. What was written on the vellum Grillaan had asked him to give to Dungal the Chief, he had no idea. He had given his word to deliver it unwrapped and unread. *It must be part of his preparation for death*, he thought. As he reached the rim of the hill he sat on a long flat rock for a rest. It was a precious moment to dry out in the sunlight, so rare so far this sodden Summer. He looked to the north and caught his breath. A huge rainbow arched right over the headland. He knew from his studies that this was God's sign to Noah that the flood would not return. *After the flood*, thought Caornan, *what then? The fire of the great Revelation? A woman clothed in the Sun? A beast rising from the sea? Breastplates of fire, jacinth and brimstone?* He sucked on a piece of grass. *What did all that mean? What on earth was jacinth*? He had no real idea. "*The word of God, as it is given to us in the Holy Book, is a spirit guide for us to live our lives.*" He had listened to Grillaan say this many times. "*It is the great song of our blessing. Each day when we read it is as if we find it for the first time. It renews us as we learn. Its signs are for all time.*"

Caornan had no doubt that this was true, even if he wasn't sure what it meant. But lately, each day as he sat at his rough desk on his rough stool, copying the sections of scripture assigned to him, the feeling grew stronger that what the texts were saying had nothing to do with him, his life, his time. As each prayer passed his lips the certainty that the incantation had any meaning for who he was or where he was diminished. He remembered what Ogun the smith said that day when he and Grillaan had collected the bell: "*If one myth is true then all myths are true.*" The words beat out clearly in Caornan's mind like a hammer ringing off an anvil.

As faith in his vocation was falling away his attraction to and his feelings for Nessan were increasing. As he looked over the bay to the mist-topped mountains in the far west, Nessan's countless stories of the legends of the Cattachs had more potency and relevance than anything that he copied out from the gospels. He could believe in Nessan. She was real – flesh, blood and bone. She needed no abstract evocation to give her meaning. Every time she spoke she brought music to the moment. When she came into his company – any company – she lit up the air. She laughed easily. She sang beautifully, and she moved through Time as naturally as the waterfall fell from the clifftop to the sea.

He looked down from the hill to the loch and the chapel beyond. A thin plume of blue smoke drifted up into the air from the fire which was always burned in Grillaan's hut to try and keep the old man warm. The four small fields of damp green barley breather and the drills for kale and cabbage sat tapered as he had left them. Some of Nessan's hens dotted about, pecking at the ground like feathery machines.

Caornan resolved to talk to Grillaan about his predicament. The Prior, of all people, would understand. He would be able to guide him, reassure him – put him back on the right track or onto a new one.

As he lay back on the long flat stone to take in the blue patches in the sky and the white and grey clouds scudding by on the ocean wind, he saw an adder similarly sunning itself on a rock just three feet from his head. He knew enough to stay very still. This was the time when these small serpents came from their burrows to draw energy from the Sun, to mate and shed their skins. The adder was about nine inches long and must be, he thought, a female as they were generally bigger. *There you are viper,* Caornan said silently to himself, *lying here just like me to find some strength.* The adder's perfect dash of a body was a sumptuous wet leathery design: dark green flecked with yellow and black with spots of red, all sparking off the zig-zag pattern which ran from its head to its tail. Hot orange eyes seemed fixed on him. Had it been resting on an upturned piece of sandstone which was right beside his head Caornan would never have noticed it. As a boy back in Donegal, Caornan had been warned it was bad luck to meet an adder. *But how*, he thought, *can it be bad to meet something so beautiful?*

Ogun had engraved an adder just like this one on the bell, except the smith had it eating its tail. *Eternity*, he'd said. *What does that mean?* wondered Caornan, watching the adder's eyes flash open and shut, its black forked tongue flickering in and out as it breathed and tasted the air. Folk say an adder's bite can kill you. For certain there were many adders on Dunnet Head. When he'd shown Nessan the bell she'd remarked that it would take an adder the size of Buthag the milk cow to kill him. He remembered how she'd run her fingers over the engravings, a silent communion trying to feel the energy of the animals, as if she believed in the life portrayed on the bell. "*It has the feel of freedom,*" she had said, softly. She told him the Druids taught that the adder was a symbol of regeneration because they shed their skins. The Chief Druid of the Cattach wore an adder's egg, or adder's stone round his neck as a symbol of his power.

The adder on the stone stayed perfectly still. Slowly Caornan sat up. Yes, he would have to talk to Grillaan about all of this. Carefully he got to his feet, bade a silent farewell to the adder and set off down the rough path to the chapel. A yellow butterfly followed him for most of the way. He remembered Ogun had said that a butterfly represented immortality, Grillaan that it symbolised the soul of man. Nessan whispered to him, that morning in the chapel, that the butterfly was the sign of love, the badge of the heart as it fluttered through the air.

By the time Caornan got down to the chapel at the top of the geo it was raining again. He found Eoghan, Ythan and Nessan standing together outside Grillaan's hut.

"Where have you been?" Eoghan was unusually sharp

"Up at the fort with vellum for the Chief," said Caornan nervously. "His Holiness the Prior sent me." Eoghan paid no attention.

"We're going to inter the holy relic of Colm. The tide will be at its lowest in an hour. Come with me to the chapel and we'll lift the thing."

"Is His Holiness... well?" Caornan asked, hoping nothing was wrong.

Despite his bad humour, Eoghan recognised the boy's concern. It softened his mood. "Aye, lad. He's fine. Come now. It's time." He turned to Nessan. "We'll help the Prior."

Caornan stole a glance at Nessan, who stood silently by Grillaan's doorway, a green shawl over her heather curls. Beads of rain ran down her cheeks. Caornan envied that water.

An hour later a small procession made its way gingerly down the Geo of the Dead. Eoghan and Caornan carried a rough litter bearing an oak kist with Colm's clarsach; Ythan and Nessan carried the Prior on another. They passed Ythan's pier wall with the curragh tied up safely, negotiating a stretch of slippery rocks until they reached the gaping mouth of *Uamh an Oir*, the Cave of Gold. A large dog otter slid off a tangle of kelp into the sea. Two ravens sat on a ledge of the cliff above and watched the strange parade.

Eoghan and Caornan went into the cave with the oak kist, ducking for the pigeons which made their usual startling escape.

They placed the kist on a small plinth Ythan had built to the back recess. Stones for his wall were piled neatly on the opposite side of the cave. Nessan and the stone mason helped the Prior to his feet, and with the aid of two sticks Grillaan made his way into *Uamh an Oir*. Eoghan opened the kist and took out the clarsach, closed the lid and set the ancient instrument on top. Then he and Caornan gently helped their beloved Prior to get down onto his knees. There was silence, save the distant sound of the sea crashing over rocks at the tide's ebb. The four figures stood in reverence behind the old priest. Slowly Grillaan lifted his arms up and out before him in a gesture of supplication. His voice was low but strong, thin but full of passion, so that it filled the cave with its tenor.

*O Father of truth*
*O Son of mercy*
*Free us at this time*
*Free us at every time*
*From the weakness of our blood*

*You Son of God*
*Grant us forgiveness*
*In our false swearing*
*In our foolish deeds*
*In our empty talk*

He paused. The echo in the cave made the strings of the clarsach tremble. Light from the afternoon Sun filled the cave, highlighting Grillaan's face, and turning to silver the water which ran down the back wall of rock. Grillaan continued, as if inspired by the sunlight.

*I am bending my knee*
*In the eye of the Father who created me*
*In the eye of the Son who purchased me*

*In the eye of the Spirit who cleansed me*
*In friendship and affection*
*To place here my brother Colm's clarsach*
*For now and for all time*
*As music was in life's beginning*
*So be it here with you, O God, at time's ending*
*For the sake of my brother Colm*
*Whom you hold ready in thy bosom*
*So I can join him when my song is over*
*Through Your own Anointed One, O God*
*Bestow upon us this, the fullness in our need*

Grillaan lowered his arms and folded them across his breast. He gestured to the four behind him to come closer, and the five of them stood each with an arm around the other. Unseen, the Maighdeann Mhara, with her bag of Time, hovered in the shadows of the wall behind them. She was smiling. Grillaan's voice filled the cave once more,

*My children*
*The congregation of Uamh an Oir*
*This Cave of Gold*
*Know this*
*Before us is Colm's instrument*
*As we are all the instrument of God*
*Know also that*
*The Son of God will be shielding us from harm*
*The Son of God will be shielding us from ill*
*The Son of God will be shielding us from mishap*
*The Son of God will be shielding us this day and night*
*And forever*
*May the Father take you, clarsach of the sea*
*In his fragrant clasp of love*
*So that when you cross the flooding streams*

*And the black river of death*
*May Mary the Virgin's Son Himself*
*Be a generous lamp to guide you*
*Over the great and awful ocean of eternity*
*Amen*

Eoghan and Caornan echoed "Amen", made the sign of the cross, and carefully raised the prior onto his feet. Nessan handed him his sticks; then she and Caornan walked with Grillaan, tears streaming down his cheeks, to the mouth of the cave and out into the daylight and the now smooring rain. Back in the cave Ythan handed Eoghan a small clay flask from which the old warrior took a swig, then handed it back to the stonemason who did likewise. Eoghan lifted the clarsach off the kist, opened the lid and placed the instrument back in its box for the final time. He hesitated, then put the box on top of the small plinth. Then the two men began to build the wall. Eoghan passed stones to Ythan, the stonemason placing them carefully to match the wall in his mind's eye. His fingers brought heat to each stone.

Before Grillaan had stopped praying the Maighdeann Mhara had opened her bag of Time. The Shee danced all around the cave. Out on the rock ledges the seals barked and sighed. Muirgen, the dog otter, climbed out of the sea and returned to his couch of kelp. From their cliff shelf above the cave one of the ravens flew up into the grey blue sky, a black secret of feathers soaring over Dunnet Head.

# 42

The hotel was one of the new ones which had sprung up at the bottom of the Royal Mile since the Parliament building opened in Holyrood in 2004. It was stylish, clean, Scandinavian and soulless. Manson lay on the bed, staring at the puritan white ceiling. Two large windows which opened onto a tiny balcony were wide open and he listened to the city night grinding, roaring and whooping to itself, a noisiness both terrible and addictive. Acoustically, Edinburgh was at once empty and full, specific and universal.

He had caught the early morning train from Thurso and arrived at Waverly sometime after two o clock. He went straight to the gallery down on the Lawnmarket to meet Bex, the voice on the phone. There was no sign of the mysterious Sigyn, his benefactor. Bex was a tall woman, *well-bred*; *like a racehorse*, thought Manson. His heart sank as she spoke. So she was just another ectomorphic cupboard-dweller who had some sublimated and unwritten hegemonic hold on the arts: the type of creature Manson loathed. He decided to ignore his prejudices, for his selfishness knew no bounds: he was prepared to suppress himself for the benefit of himself. His greed constantly surprised him by its rapacious hunger. The gallery was a large well-lit space in a huge rambling building which had once housed the veterinary college. Manson laughed to himself. His brother had studied there for a year. This was his father's futile and short-lived attempt to turn his brother into a vet. In the far north it is every crofter's dream to have a vet in the family. As it turned out his brother became a highly-skilled pool player, grew his hair long, and acquired a very expensive cocaine habit. Luckily for him the North Sea oil industry swallowed him whole, subsequently catering for his every financial and chemical need.

By the time Manson reached the gallery all twenty-four paintings were up on the walls. Two young men atop a mechanical ladder were focusing lights. From behind his dark glasses Manson could hardly believe his eyes. What was all this stuff?

"The work looks magnificent, don't you think?"

Manson ignored Bex. In his present state, her voice brought to mind someone sawing logs, or doors opening and shutting. She handed him a copy of the exhibition catalogue. It looked good: his name against one of his studies of the headland. But "***The Great Edge***"? What did that mean?

"I don't remember agreeing to that." He jabbed at the paper.

"Well, you wouldn't return any of our calls, texts or emails. Beith O'Donoghue found those words written on the back of that painting." Bex waved at the programme cover. "Sigyn thought it wonderfully appropriate as a title for the exhibition. Don't you?"

"Oh... aye," said Manson cynically. "Wonderfully." He had no interest, and no energy left to suggest alternatives. He assumed that these people knew what they were doing.

At last Bex had taken him to his hotel. *Did he have everything he needed?* He needed nothing. He needed everything. After hours staring at the images flickering across the huge flat screen TV he got up, showered, and went out into the noise of the night. He walked up the High Street. It was pleasant enough. Not too many people. He was relatively sober. His eyes did not hurt so much now that it was dark, and the street noise was irritating but manageable, like mild tinnitus. The opening was tomorrow night. Maybe coming down here was a mistake. His vanity had over-ridden every other concern, including his greed – a real clash of Titans. His hard-headed selfishness made up the trinity of his qualities. To deny that, Manson reasoned, was pointless. *I can paint, it seems. Everything else will follow from that.*

It had been the singer Fand who had brought painting back to him, that night he'd met Daimler in The Hot Green Chilli. The pieces he had given to Beith for the Caithness Arts Centre Summer exhibition he had done years before, in the days he first imagined that he could be a painter. Those days passed soon enough. His mother's suicide. His father's fatal grief. Death had sucked the marrow from his bones. It seemed futile to put nature down on paper or canvas and he had stopped trying. His sketch book had remained closed for years.

Then he met the Maighdeann Mhara. Looking into her eyes had changed his life. In the deep blue eyes of Fand he'd seen again the eyes of the Maighdeann Mhara. She had gone home with him that night, and they had wound around each other on his unmade bed like two adders in the early Summer Sun. Next morning she'd explored his house and had come out of his shed with a bag full of apples. He found her in his studio arranging the apples in front of the fireplace. For reasons best known to singers she had brought her small clarsach with her. Content with her display of apples, she had sat down with the beautifully carved instrument and started to play. The same charge thrilled him that early morning as had shaken him the night he first heard her perform. The golden band sparkled again around her delicate throat as she began to sing. Morning light poured through the east-facing window, turning her blonde hair to gold as well. The whole room glowed, mellow and golden. Her voice and the clarsach brought the sea into the room. The light, the music, the sea – they flooded into Manson. Without thinking he began to draw her. Then he reached for paint and a brush and that flashed across the paper, then on canvas. Fand played on. Suddenly life was back within him. He was a boy running across the beach, the headland, the world. For a while he was back with himself. He existed. He was present. He was alive. Her name was Fand and he knew who she was. His "gift" had returned. This was his second instalment of good fortune. The voice on the Peedie Sannie: *Remember, my name is Fand.* He lived in a house of water.

One drawing led to another, this canvas to the next. Fand left him to it, leaving traces of her scent wherever she drifted throughout the house, like an otter. The paintings got done. One after the other, without let-up. Then he was done. He phoned Beith. They met in the pub. Then Mags came into the pub. So, he thought, this is what history looks like: just a series of bits and pieces which add up to resurrection. Each moment is like a proclamation which cites that today, potentially, is the day of the Last Judgement, and nothing is lost.

The crowded indifference of the city bars suited him. He did not have to pretend to be anyone. He was too exhausted for that. He felt like a container which had been emptied out. He could hear Beith in his head. "*Get some rest, Manson, you're done in.*" He would get some rest. Just as soon as this circus was over. He could hear Fand singing. He could hear Mags laughing. Absent-mindedly he drew a crumpled piece of paper from his jacket pocket and glanced at the spidery handwriting: "*Welcome to Donald MacCrimmon's Magic Parlour. Miracles welcome but not expected.*" Manson laughed out loud. Doupie Dan: the only man in the world who made sense.

That night he lay on his bed in the Lutheran hotel, the whisky by his bed hardly touched as he listened to the endless swish and drone of the traffic on the street below. He drifted in and out of consciousness like the tide on the beach. Incomprehensible dreams were crammed into bottles on the shore of his sleep. All that night as he had moved like a basking shark from bar to bar his mobile had kept ringing and beeping. He'd ignored it. Now, as the morning rose to meet the North Sea sky and poured its early September sunlight over the broken teeth of the Old Town, he picked the infernal thing up. Messages. In a phone, not a bottle. ***Press conference @3 2day***. A dinner in some Japanese restaurant later on. He grimaced. He'd rather be on Dunnet Beach. But this was the deal, and after today he'd be left alone. Tonight was just about making money, and everybody knew that. People could say what they liked about the art, but what the work on the walls meant was secondary to what it was worth. That was fine by him. Edinburgh was a twenty-four-hour city. He'd find a quiet, friendly bar and hole up until he was required. He recalled Andy Warhol's reply when he was asked how he knew a painting was finished: "When it is sold."

He found a bar just off The Meadows. Quiet. Dingy. Open at seven in the morning. He always thought the Southside was Auld Reekie at it's best, and he ended up there whenever he was in Edinburgh. Behind his dark glasses he looked out at the floating world. Everybody gives you wrong directions, he thought, especially when you're drunk. He had a daft game, which was as close as Manson ever came to a method. He would stop people on the street and ask them where a certain street was. Except the street didn't exist because he had just made it up. People, generally, tried to help, and did their best to point him in the right direction. Ultimately Manson had no direction whatsoever. The laws of probability would allow for the existence of the street and the directions being correct. This game had got him to this bar. It was an old game.

Gradually the game turned into something else, as is the nature of all games. On the flat plain of Manson's imagination there was a war going on. The city crushed his consciousness to silence and noise. Even his dreams, reluctant and filmy, suffered from this environmental attack. The last one he recalled was about three tall men dressed in long red outfits with square shields and spears; they were killing other men dressed in long brown outfits. It made no sense.

He could not shake off that dream. The nature of his conflict meant he believed he was in control of everything. It was laughable. He finished his drink and left. Manson moved through the mystery, the conceit of the city. It was still early. He could taste the salt wind from the Firth of Forth on his tongue. For hours he wandered happily, plunging back into the tourist swirl of the High Street. Each step along the ancient paving stones brought him closer to the gallery and reinforced what he knew about himself: that fear of his own success was choking him. He did not trust where the talent came from so why should he trust where it goes? But he had no option. He had signed up to the deal. Vanity drove him on. Wars have been won and lost over less. Manson's war was lost from the start.

Time passed. When he arrived at the gallery at three it was full of people. His terror intensified. His war went on. This was the press event arranged by Bex. He had no idea what was expected but went in, every second feeding his insecurity with the red meat of the future. It seemed to Manson that few of the media people assembled had looked at his paintings, or if they had they had made up their minds despite what they saw. It was a revelation to learn that he was a "naive painter" and that he had obviously been influenced by Turner and John Bellany. How did he feel about being so successful so suddenly? How did he feel about all the paintings having sold already? Did he worry it was all hype?

Seated at a table with Bex, Beith O'Donoghue and an older, slightly disdainful-looking woman, Manson couldn't help himself.

"Aye, of course it's all hype. But what d'ye expect? I paint what I see, no what's there. As for other painters, well... I love James Guthrie. The way he uses paint, how he draws with it, what he sees, what he shows. That's a painter. If I was as good as him I'd be happy."

All of which was true but nobody was happy with what he said. The three women beside him all began to talk at once. The press pack was disgruntled because he wasn't playing to format and few of them had heard of James Guthrie. Twenty-four hours ago they had never heard of Manson. From then on, the harpies piped up before he could think of anything to say.

In half an hour the ordeal was over. There was a crowd of people in the gallery where the exhibition was hung, but he headed for a long white-clothed table with charged wine glasses in an appealing row. He scooped up a glass of red, just as the snooty woman from the interview table swished up to him.

"I'm Sigyn."

*Of course. He should have twigged.* Tall, blonde, middle-aged and glamorous, groomed and confident. Manson felt out-of-his-depth. A small silver ship caught his eye as it swung expensively on its chain round her perfumed neck.

"I hope you'll forgive me for barging in during your interview," she continued. "I'm just so excited. Although I come from Sweden, my mother is Scottish, and I visit the north of Scotland quite regularly. On my last trip I bought this gallery. When I saw your work in the Caithness Arts Centre, I couldn't believe it. I knew you were what we were after."

"Really?" said Manson, "What's that, exactly?"

"Art!" she exclaimed. "This is our very first exhibition. Darling, we're all so tremendously happy with you." Well-dressed people pushed past him, glass in hand, to find a space to look interesting on the gallery floor. Nobody seemed to look at the walls.

"That's good," he shrugged.

"To have the entire set sold before an exhibition has opened is unheard of," said Sigyn rapturously, stroking her flute-glass of wine. Abruptly she turned away to speak to someone who caught her attention. Manson's head was reeling; he was just beginning to think he was on a ride at a funfair when Pearl emerged from the manicured crowd.

"Who would ever have taken you for a painter?" Her nasal American accent grated on his nerves, more accusation than question.

"What does that mean?"

Thinking that Manson's question was directed at her, Sigyn turned back to him.

"Seven hundred and twenty thousand pounds," she said, smiling broadly.

"How much of that do I get?" Stunned, but trying to hide it, Manson ignored Pearl, hoping that perhaps he'd been mistaken and she was someone else entirely.

"What we agreed in the contract." Sigyn's smile became cold.

"What if I want more?" asked Manson. He had seen no contract that he could remember.

"Keep talking," she smiled, "and you might get nothing." Manson held her gaze, but swallowed, his wine now metallic and sour. Sigyn's smile became friendly once more.

"Would you mind if I asked you something?"

"Fire on," said Manson.

"When I was in Caithness the scenery made a big impression on me. It is flat like Sweden, yes, but oh so different. When I saw your work I loved the way it suggested the place, but these... well, they are so very different. So much scenery."

Manson's hackles rose. "There's a big difference between scenery, which I despise," he said, "and landscape, which I paint. Scenery is unpeopled. Landscape is named."

"Yes," said Sigyn, "I suppose I can see that. But then why are there no people in your landscapes, other than the girl with the apples?"

"Because landscapes *are* people!" Manson's glass slopped wine in every direction. Sigyn moved back a little.

"Just relax, Manson. Enjoy your evening. We'll talk later." Sigyn slid into the crowd.

Manson could no more relax in this crowd than a roe deer. Those intense two weeks of creativity had been translated into three-quarters of a million pounds. *How had all of this happened*? Pearl was still there, looking at him. Very still, in a white dress and with her pale colouring, she might have been a figure sculpted in alabaster. When she spoke she shattered the illusion.

"Your paintings are violent – They beat people up."

Manson smiled. "Well, my subject's a coast of widows and wreckers, right enough," he said.

"In the time we spent together you never once spoke of art or poetry." Pearl looked forlornly around the gallery, then fixed her eyes on him once more. Those eyes of sea and caves and death. "You never looked up one painter or poet, yet Edinburgh is supposed to be full of them."

"Look, for years I'd given up painting." Manson was off-guard now, his voice shorn of irony. "This is an episode, that's all. Artists are driven by ambition and ego rather than blessed by talent or creativity. I tend to give them the swerve."

"There are lots of artists here tonight," said Pearl, a smile curling and softening her mouth.

"I know. I need to get out of here."

"Sandy Bell's?" Manson nodded.

Much later in the bar, full of fiddle music and whisky, one question birled in his head: was there a world out there he could be a part of? *Sandy Bell's is like a small cave*, he thought, scanning the familiar space, heaving with folk like himself, enjoying the music. *This could be the end of the world. A good place to be.* After midnight Pearl led him out into the street. "*Where to, painter man?*" she drawled. He woke up next morning in his hotel, Pearl asleep beside him. The dinner at the Japanese restaurant – he'd missed it altogether! With the usual breaking-strain of a Kit-Kat he'd succumbed to Pearl's desire, if that was what it had been. He nudged her awake.

"I have to go north."

"I know," she said, "it's what you do."

"Something's happening." Manson struggled with words. "It's important."

"Another exhibition." It wasn't a question.

"Aye. No. I just need to get there," he said.

"You'll never come back," said Pearl.

"Look," said Manson, sitting up and holding Pearl's shoulders, "I know who you are." Gently Pearl took his hand and placed it on her cheek. Outside Summer was coming to an end. In that instant Manson was happy. He fell asleep. In his dream the three tall men in red brandished their weapons.

Much later he woke. He felt immediately and intensely the absence of everything. No landscape of croft parks or dunes. No sound of surf. No sea. Outside was the city. Pearl was gone. Beside the whisky bottle on the table was an apple, one small white bite taken from its curving red blush.

# 43

Colin worked for weeks on his stainless steel model of the Dounreay Fast Reactor. His greatest difficulty was getting the dome right: it was a bit too big for the jaws of the Kaiser's peedie lathe, so he had to improvise. He rigged up his milling machine to finish the work. Getting the dome an exact sphere was tricky. He checked and rechecked his measurements, ultra-careful in setting his cutting tools. He loved the beautiful old German navy lathe, but it belonged to another age. *That's the thing with historical narratives,* he realised, *they all come to an end – that's if they're not exploded by events before then.* History, narrative or no narrative, has to blow up into revolution from time to time. He had read somewhere that during the French Revolution some of the more excitable of the insurgent citizenry had shot at the clocks in Paris, as if they wanted, literally, to free themselves of the time of Louis. Was that what he'd done with Tycho Nuclear? To The White Ape and The Big Yank? He should have known better. History is a continuum, and it pleased Colin to create a 3-D model of his recent past with the help of a tool from the First World War, from a ship which had been scuttled by its own crew. *This*, he thought, *is how we all must manufacture our freedom. From the age of mass slaughter in the trenches, to the potential mass slaughter of the Cold War, to now when the fruitless seeds of atomic Armageddon are being buried at Buldoo; this is the continuum of blood-time.* Recent events had exploded his own history, chilled his own blood, set his time to zero-hour. Someone had shot up his clocks. The new age he was about to enter had a circumference infinitely wider than the old lathe could cope with. How serene it made him feel, finally understanding this. It was like watching a time-lapse film. How satisfactory, to explore and realise the capacity of the modern milling machine to engineer his desire, to whittle the past into the shape of the future. The metal shavings shorn by the mill were like history's DNA collected tidily in his scurf box. Time had come to a standstill, but it had also moved on. *Now*, said Colin to himself, as he looked proudly at his finished model, *there is no 'once upon a time' anymore*. To the gods in the morning of history, those who scuttle the ship of war always smell the sweetest.

Colin set the model on the coffee table, opened a can of beer, and sat back on the sofa, levelling the remote at the flat-screen TV. He was watching American cartoons dubbed in Gaelic with English subtitles when Kylie came in at half-five, her coat wet with rain. Without a word she slumped into the chair opposite him.

"What the fuck is that?" she sneered.

Colin realised she was drunk. "My model oh ay DFR. Id's what Ah've been workan on iss past while."

"Waste oh fucking time," growled Kylie.

"On ay contrary," he countered, raising his beer can in mock salute. "Id's a study oh time."

"Pish!"

He was irked. "Look, Kylie, id's symbolic. You should..." She cut him dead.

"Kylie?" she asked. "Who's Kylie? There's nobody called Kylie here."

"Really." He smirked. "Then who are you, Madam?"

"My name is Reny," she answered brightly and at once.

"Reny who, my lady?" Colin fought to keep a straight face. He was enjoying the joke. Resisting the urge to laugh, he sat up and faced Kylie. Laughter sank back inside him. She was pale, trembling. He got up. "E ok, Kylie? E been in ay Comm? Who were e way?"

Staring, she stood up. "Who the hell are you?"

Colin's patience snapped. "Look, ever since e come back from Chapan, e've no been yer sel. Ah think e should see Doctor Burns. E need help."

"I don't need anything or anybody! You're like the rest of them out there: pathetic peedie men, crawling around on the bottom of the sea. Well, here's the thing: I have them all exactly where I want them."

She was still trembling. For a moment Colin just saw his lassagee again, the one he'd chosen to share his life with, and his heart went out to her. "E never get thum, Kylie," he said, shaking his head. "They get e."

"That's what you think!" She'd moved to the window and looked out, her arms holding shut her wet coat, as though she were cold. "You see nothing, but I can see everything!" Then her mood changed again. Quiet, nervous, sullen. Her accent switched to her work voice, the one she'd first invented at university. "I've seen him. Standing in the shadows, across from the Pentland. I've seen him. His clothes all rags and blood running over his face."

"Who? Who the hell are e talkan aboot?"

"He had his arms outstretched, like he was asking me something, but I couldn't hear a word. His hands were covered in blood." Kylie's face pressed against the window as if she wanted to move through it, out into the air of her vision. Her breath left a small map on the glass.

"E've seen Doupie Dan. Hae's banged his nut. Beeg deal!" Uneasy despite his words, two strides took Colin to her side. "Hae's always fallan ower. Id's a wunner hae's no deid."

He laughed, hoping to draw her back from wherever she was heading, but Kylie turned violently and pushed him with such unexpected force that he staggered back, almost falling over the coffee table.

"It wasn't Doupie Dan. And the person I saw *was* dead."

"Who? Kylie, you're ... who's deid?" Colin took her arm, trying to force her to look at him.

"Daimler!" She spoke the name as if the breath was being forced out of her. Jerking away she rushed to the sofa, scattering the cushions as though looking for something. "My name's no Kylie! It's Reny! And I have a future!" She started to laugh. Then, before Colin registered what she was doing, in one swift adrenalin-stoked action she heaved Colin's model of the DFR from the table and swung it at the TV. The screen splintered into a spider's web where the steel struck it. There was a flash as both model and TV bounced off the floor. Images of monkeys with hats and the chatter of the Gaelic language disappeared in a thin haze of acrid smoke.

There was a profound silence. Colin stared at his DFR dome and its associated buildings, upside-down beside the murdered television. Kylie/Reny's eyes were lit by an inner fire.

"I'm off to Dunnet. I must interview the monitors!" Before he could stop her, she was through the door and gone.

"For godssake, Kylie, yer pished!" Colin grabbed his jacket, felt for his car keys in the pocket and ran after her. To his relief, he found her on the street below staring at the pavement. "Ye still want til go til Dinnad?" She nodded. Gently he took her arm and led her to his car where he coaxed her in. She was compliant, as though she had forgotten what she was doing. He'd intended driving her straight to Burns's surgery down by the river, but he hesitated. *Maybe it would be better if she sobered up first? Take her to the doctor afterwards.* He strapped her in, his mind a blank as he drove across the bridge and took the Clairdan road to Castletown. He had no idea whether or not there would be a monitoring crew on the beach. Since his sacking he'd lost track of what was going on out on the site. He'd also stopped going out socially, so he didn't even get the site gossip. Kylie was staring at the windscreen. Passing Murkle she spoke suddenly.

"You don't believe me, but I saw him. I did see him!" She repeated the last words over and over again until they turned into the car park behind the sand-dunes at Dunnet beach.

The monitoring unit's two trucks and trailers were parked up. Half-a-dozen men in standard issue day-glo yellow jackets and coveralls were standing in a semi-circle around one of the two monitoring vehicles. He recognised Morris Mowat and his crew. As soon as he parked the car Kylie got out and made straight for the beach. *So much for her panic to get here then*, thought Colin. He realised now she'd had no interview lined up with the monitors. Flustered, and not wanting to ignore the men, he got out. Morris Mowat spotted him.

"Weel, choost look who id is? If id's no ay invisible man?" he said.

"Id's yer sel, Morris," replied Colin, shoving his hands in his pockets to stop their shaking. "Hevan a bit oh bother are way?"

Two men were on their knees looking under one of the monitoring machines.

"Id's iss new machine," said Morris, "Id's called a Spider, an id monitors til a high level. Id can pick up anyhain aats ayr."

"E dinna say," said Colin, winking.

"Aye, Ah do say," said Morris. "An Ah ken Ah shouldna, boot e ken all iss shite anyway."

"Is id a remote?" asked Colin.

"Aye," nodded Morris. "Boot id keeps tippan ower when wur testan id."

"Fuckan nightmare," said Willie Geddes, another of the crew.

"Niver mind," said Morris, "as e ken, Harper, thur's an engineeran solution til every problem."

"So they say," agreed Colin.

"Weel then," continued Morris, "Wur halfway through oor shift and Benny Calder ayr, hay says... weel, whut did e say, Benny?"

"Ah sayed 'Fuck Iss for a game a soldiers'," obliged Benny Calder, "an Ah went hom til mah hoose in Castletoon ayr, an took fower casters off an ould couch. Fitted thum on is pile oh shite an, hey presto! Engineeran solution!"

"Since then id hesna cowped wance!" Morris was clearly impressed.

"Aye," laughed Colin, "You monitoran boys are ay genius oh ay workforce."

"Ah've always sayed id," agreed Morris. "Anyway whut takes e oot here consideran Ah hevna seen sicht nor soond oh e since ay strike."

"Och, been busy," Colin lied. "E ken how id is."

"Ah ken id peys til mind on who yer freends are," said Morris, serious now.

"E'd better run efter aat tottie oh yurs, Harper," said one of the crew, nudging his colleague, "or she'll bay shaggan aat Norwegians aats been watchan us aal day."

"Norwegians?" asked Colin, glad of the distraction.

"Och, dinna listen til Rosser," said Morris, "hay thinks ay whole operation is a Chames Bond film."

Colin laughed. "Is id no?"

"More like a Benny Hill film," said Morris, grimly.

"Showan yer age noo, Morris. Anyway, like ye say, Ah'd better catch up wae Kylie." Turning to go, relieved Morris hadn't asked what Kylie was there for, Colin shook his friend's hand and waved at the monitoring crew, who heckled him until he was out of sight. Then they turned their attention back to their faulty machinery.

Colin headed down to the beach. The tide was out and the sand seemed to stretch for ever, north to Dunnet and south to Castletown. Kylie was a small figure in a long cream coat, talking to two other small figures. He zipped up his fleece and set off to join her. *The fresh air, this beautiful place*, he thought, *it'll do her good.*

The early September Sun was still high in the south-western sky. Colin walked into the wind over the shimmering wet sand. Out beyond the surf a pair of bonxies were harassing young gannets. The last of the easy gains for them. Sandpipers peeped and dodged at the tide's edge. Up on the dunes a colony of terns was squawking and squealing, raggedly cutting the air with their slender wings. In a matter of days most of the seabirds would be gone. They were fuelling up for the many months at sea ahead and the Winter to come.

The two figures with Kylie were tall, both wearing dark glasses and long raincoats. The woman's long and blonde hair was blowing like Kylie's in the wind. Colin tried not to appear anxious. He smiled at the two tall strangers and gently gripped Kylie's hand. She pulled her hand away and turned back to the couple.

"This person doesn't know who I am. This person thinks I am mad."

Colin groaned inside, but was thankful to see the man smile.

"Pleased to meet you," said the man, holding out his hand. "My name is Loki." Colin shook his hand.

"I'm Sigyn," said the woman, offering her hand. "We're from Sweden."

"I'm Colin," he said, "and this is Kylie."

"My name is *Reny*!" Kylie glared at him, then took off.

Frightened of making a bad situation worse, Colin didn't follow her.

"She's been under a lot oh stress, lately."

Loki and Sigyn smiled, but said nothing.

"Doesn't the Swedish government hev a ship called Sigyn, fur transportan nuclear waste?" Stressed and embarrassed, Colin had said the first thing that came into his head. *Christ! I'm obsessed by the industry, even though I've left it.*

"Is that so?" smiled Sigyn.

"Diggin fur spoots?" Anxious to change the subject, Colin had noticed that Loki was carrying a rubber boot which he held by a string. Sigyn was carrying a bucket.

"Spoots?" echoed Sigyn, quizzically.

"He means razor clams, darling," said Loki. "No. This is for you." He held out the rubber boot by its string, so that it swayed in the wind. Taken aback Colin stared at the boot as he automatically accepted it, vaguely troubled also by the colour of the two Swedes' raincoats: Loki's was yellow and Sigyn's green – He would have sworn it was the other way around.

"Wan boot...?"

"You used it once it to haul a sample of radioactive waste out of the effluent tank on the plant." Sigyn spoke as a mother would to discipline a favourite child.

Colin dropped the rubber boot. Loki bent down to pick it up, his ginger hair and tidy moustache pale against the dark glasses. Colin noticed that the little finger on his right hand was crooked.

"Better have it back," said Loki. Colin did not take the gift, and stepped back.

"Is iss some sort oh set-up? Ah can tell e Ahm no really in ay mood." Kylie was splashing about in the waves.

"No set-up, I assure you." Carefully, Loki set the rubber boot back down on the sand.

"Are e from SEPA?"

"We're from Asgard," said Sigyn.

"Never heard oh thum." Colin turned to walk off. He needed to get Kylie home.

"Do you deny the boot?" Loki smiled, his teeth flashing in the sunlight.

"That wis a long time ago." In spite of himself, Colin rose to the bait. His alert mind, exhausted by Dounreay and now full of anxiety for Kylie, needed resolution. These strangers were opening doors he'd shut many years ago, bringing ghosts alive. "Things wur different then. Ay machine wae usually used wis rusted up. Ay extension airm wis seized solid. E hed til improvise. Wae hed boffins breathan doon oor necks aal ay time."

"The problem is," said Loki, "because you did not switch on the activators in the tank you monitored only what was in the wellington boot, not what was in the tank. That radiation you flushed out into the sea."

"You might want this as well." Sigyn pulled a sandwich from her coat pocket (which had now returned to its original yellow) and offered it to Colin.

"It's the one you dropped into the reactor," supplied Loki. Before Colin could react, Sigyn withdrew the proffered sandwich and dropped it into her bucket beside the rubber boot. "They couldn't understand how the liquid sodium in the fast reactor cooling-system was oxidizing. Don't you remember?"

"Did they ever discover it was because you dropped your – how do you say it? – your *piece*?" asked Loki. "Yes, you dropped your lunch into it." He laughed. She laughed. The wind laughed.

"It wis an accident," said Colin. "They widna let us oot fur wur break. It could've happened til anybody on ay shift." He was angry now, fed up of being toyed with. "Look," he said flatly, "choost who d'ye work for?"

"Let's just say," said Loki, "that we are in constant opposition."

"To what?"

"The forces of order and reaction – the enemies of Loki." Loki's coat flashed both yellow and green, as if it were some warning sign.

"Loki? Ah know ay name. He's a character in a film?" Colin thought back to Morris Mowat and *Chames Bond*.

"Yes, tragic, is it not, that Hollywood has turned me into a cartoon anti-hero? At least it is a Scottish actor who plays me. Europe does have the reputation of building its civilization on reason. Unlike the Yanks. Wouldn't you agree?"

Whether or not Colin agreed with this prejudice, he never made his reply. Kylie had walked back up to them out of the sea. Sigyn set her bucket on the sand and gestured to Kylie. "Look in here, child."

To Colin's astonishment Kylie knelt down obediently beside Sigyn. As they both peered into the bucket their blonde hair twined, like adders dancing in the sunlight. Sigyn's words were for Kylie.

"This bucket is to catch all the venom from the fangs of the poisonous snake which has wound itself around you. A snake is wound tight around the world, just as there once was around the head of Loki, until I drew it off."

At first Kylie saw nothing, but gradually, as if she was seeing it from above, as if she were a camera on a space satellite, she could see the whole of the north, in miniature. She gasped.

"What?" urged Colin, "What is id e see?"

"You will see soon enough," said Loki.

As if she were a goddess, Kylie stared down on creation. Below her was Sutherland, Caithness, Orkney, Fair Isle, Shetland, Faroe, Wester Norway, Iceland and Greenland. *This is my dream. I recognise everything.* As she watched a wave washed over all of it, and everything clouded. Tears rolled down her cheeks, tears of relief and tears of terror. Watching the wave, she experienced absolute certainty that everything has been expected; that every second is a narrow door, through which might step the future or the iron hook of the past. She saw a beach with two people on it.

"Who are they?" Her hair and Sigyn's were still entwined, forcing her to keep looking into the bucket.

"Ask and Embla, the first two people in the world," replied Sigyn. "They were made from driftwood: the man from ash and the woman from elm. Ash the life-tree and elm the life-giving vine."

"They're beautiful," breathed Kylie.

"They were made by the three sons of the son of the man who was licked into being by the Frost Giants' cow." Loki's eyes twinkled as he licked his moustache.

"I'll take your word for it," said Colin.

"And why not?" reasoned Loki. "You accepted more fantastic but less interesting things for years out at Dounreay without so much as a whisper."

"The three sons of Bor gave Ask and Embla breath and life, consciousness and movement, their faces, speech and hearing, and sight." Sigyn whispered into Kylie's ear. "They gave them clothes and names." Kylie felt herself falling down. Sigyn put her arm gently around Kylie's shoulder. "From Ask and Embla are descended all who walk in Midgard – This world, where Kylie Swanson is your name."

Suddenly Kylie knew herself to be down on the beach with Ask and Embla. She reached out to Ask, the most stunning man she'd ever seen. She was overcome by desire for him. He stretched out his arms to her. Her body was filled by warmth, by a returning melody.

She looked up. Colin was looking down at her. They were both on their knees by the water's edge. No Swedes. No bucket, no rubber boot, no sandwich. The beach was empty. The Sun shone down and surf roared out in the bay. Colin got to his feet and pulled Kylie to hers. He put his arm around his peedie lassagee and walked her back to the car. The wind had risen, now blowing in from the south-west, warm but strong.

The dunes above Dunnet Beach formed a rough concave arc shouldered by a green swathe of marram grass. The grass held the dunes more or less in check, but the entire chain was a living, ever-moving serpent of sand some forty feet high and three miles long. As they crossed the sand to the car park, Colin looked up at the profile of the dunes against the light. Carved from the dunescape by the random artistry of the wind, he thought he saw the exact sandy likeness of The White Ape.

# 44

Bragi Boddason – the first poet in the world as he would tell it, if you would listen – stood on the deck of the great white ship Skidbladnir and looked out at the darkening headland. The wave was not far off now.

*The Earth-world forms*
*The clouds are ravens*
*Searching for perfection*
*They rest on ancient cliff-ledges*

*Sea-blood in the distance*
*Is the beginning of music*
*They fly free and high*
*These harp-ravens*

*Sorrow slides through fingers*
*Death hides behind the heart-hand*
*Secret to the end is the song of the great edge*
*In the praise-cave of gold*

When he'd finished the poem Bragi felt cold. He thought of his home in Asgard, his wife Idunn, and her golden apples of eternal youth. Come soon wave, he said to the sea.

# 45

Manson came back from Edinburgh a made man. Everything he had wished for with regard to money, or hoped for in relation to his art had come to pass. These were his episodes in history. Things had unravelled in a certain way and that was that. But they were over, they were history. With money in the bank, his art work critically acclaimed and popular, the gallery was producing a series of prints which Sigyn assured him would make him a wealthy man. Yet, as he sat in the Dunnet pub and the first September rain smoored across the stubble fields outside, Manson still fretted: *what is my heart's desire?* Parents, school – even Sunday school – everyone with influence had impressed on him that when you get what you want it will make you happy. Walking the streets of Atomic City picking up pennies from the flagstone, he'd dreamed constantly: *If I can just get what I want, then life will be sweet.* He had been convinced.

He knew now that was all guff. He would learn that it was also fatal. He was addicted to lies in the same way that his mother was addicted to truth, anti-depressants, pain-killers and sleeping pills. One thing he had learned, he told himself – and this was before money, success and events had confused him – was that it is the truth which kills most people, not lies. It had certainly killed his mother and by extension his father. Death comes from unlikely quarters.

He sipped his whisky. What had Edinburgh, Sigyn and the Lawnmarket Gallery shown him? That art has no relation to morality for one thing. That nothing of value was achieved without associated danger. That was another. He was certain of that now. They'd asked him for this and he'd given them that. They wanted more – Bex, Sigyn, even Beith – they always want more. *Of course, he would paint more; absolutely, it would be different; but no, not too different.* Right now, he had no intention of painting ever again. Quite how future historical episodes would unfold he had no idea. It's a double joy to deceive the deceivers. That was a third thing. Most definitely. It had been a productive trip, but Manson was under no illusions: if he didn't fulfil the contract he had signed they would sue. In the end, though, they would move on eventually, find someone else to hang on the wall. The beast had to be fed. Now that he'd tasted success it was a revelation that he felt no envy for that person.

Meanwhile the same old emptiness filled him. He longed for knowledge, of the world and of himself. He longed to *feel* part of history. What he wanted above all was to see the Maighdeann Mhara. Since he'd been back he had gone often to the Peedie Sannie but she hadn't appeared. Was he being punished? Did she not still control him? Did he not love her? Yes, she did and yes, he did. Why can't she just be a *woman*? His position was hopeless.

His mood was spiralling rapidly downwards when Mags breezed in wearing overalls and a waterproof jacket. She was soaking wet and covered in peat.

"Fetching ootfit," said Manson. The pub was too small to ignore her.

"I put it on especially," retorted Mags, the fresh goodness of outdoors wafting away the stagnant air in the pub.

"I love a woman in a mess," Manson said. "Dram?" Mags nodded and sat down. He got a whisky from the bar, and Mags sipped, savouring the brown barley heat on her lips and over her throat.

"Your exhibition's a big success," said Mags. "The Groat's full of it."

Manson snorted and changed the subject. "E look miserable."

"Uch," she sighed. "It's just the dig. I've recorded everything. Photographed each stage and object. Done everything by the book. It's just that I can't get the university to take what I'm doing seriously even though they're funding me. I thought my pal Helen could come up and give me a hand with the heavy stone work in the cave, but she's in Peru. The only person I've managed to get to help me is young girl from Thurso, and she's a bit strange."

"Well, she's female," sympathised Manson, thinking of Fand.

"You really are an arse, you know that?"

"So they say," said Manson truthfully.

"I don't suppose *you'd* give me a hand, would you?" Mags felt embarrassed even asking.

"I'll paint e a picture. I'll buy e drink. I'll talk til e all day... But I'm no guddlan aboot in ay clart lookan for ay glorious coprolites oh some ancient Irish hermit."

"That's that then! Ok… Tell me this, then. Tell me about the woman beneath the sea."

"What woman?" Now it was Manson who was uncomfortable. Playing for time, Mags got up to shake water from her jacket and glanced out of the window.

"You know what I mean, so don't deny it. I know you've seen her as well. I can tell from your eyes. The look on your face. All this energy that you have – I recognise it. I can't explain it. But you know more about it. You're closer to her somehow. I've only seen her once – just for a split second. But you have a direct connection. Intimate somehow..."

"What d'ye think I am? Some kind oh crazy person?"

Mags wasn't deflected. His eyes told her she was right. There was a frightened boy in there.

"You're a special person, Manson, I know that."

"Dinna flatter me. There's no need." His voice softened. "I'm choost... hungry... confused."

"What's happening to you is happening to me," she said. Manson bristled.

"What d'ye mean?"

"You know very well. The way light affects our eyes. Time..."

"Time?" Manson almost sobbed the word. "Every day I grow younger..."

"I'm an archaeologist. My business is Time. But I feel I am drowning in it."

"What can I do?"

"Take me to see her," said Mags firmly.

"I canna."

"You *can*. Just look at us, Manson, with our dark glasses. We should join a society for the blind!"

Mags laughed, the tightness in her voice gone. The dram had relaxed her, but it was more the relief of coming clean with Manson – someone else who'd glimpsed this weirdness.

"As far as the Maighdeann Mhara's concerned, wur all blin."

"Is that her name?"

Manson grimaced. "It's what ay locals cry her. In folk stories... fuck sake, what am I sayan?"

"You *must* take me, Manson." Mags was pleading now. "If you don't, god knows what will happen to us."

"All right, you two?" The barmaid leaning on the bar looked round at them, concerned enough at the raised voices which were distracting her from the TV.

"Aye, Cheannie, id's ok, choost a domestic." Manson winked and smiled. Cheannie laughed and turned back to the screen.

"Well?" Mags wasn't letting him off the hook.

"Ok, ok! I'll take e up til ay Peedie Sannie. Wae'll sit on ay rock I always sit on an wae'll wait. That's aal I can do." Manson scooped the remainder of his dram.

"When?"

"Once iss rain's off, an I..." He looked at his glass. "When I feel... better."

It took a few more drams for Manson to feel better. When at last they left the bar they crossed the carpark to his house and she helped him pick some apples off the trees in his garden. He handled each one gently and put them in a plastic bag. He bit into a red one. "Hev a bite," he said, offering it to Mags. Mags sank her teeth into its small hard roundness. Sugar and salt on her tongue.

"It tastes of the sea!"

"Northern apples," said Manson proudly. "There's nuthin lek thum."

At last Mags managed to bundle him into her car. They drove up to the House of the Northern Gate and parked at the bottom of the track. Thankfully there was no sign of Minker, his wife, or Sanders the ghillie. They walked slowly down the old peat track to the cliff top. The tide was at mid-point, the Sun due South, and the clear blue water highlighted the shell-white sand on the two little beaches. From behind his dark glasses Manson could make out three seals lolling in the water beyond the gentle surf. *That's a good sign*, he thought.

They climbed down. Manson led Mags to the rock from which he'd once dispatched his mother's tranquillisers. This was where he sat when he came to meet the Maighdeann Mhara. They sat in silence. Fulmars swooped and glided above their heads.

"Do you think she'll appear with me here?" Mags suddenly doubting the wisdom of her scheme.

"Dunno," shrugged Manson.

"It's a stunning place," said Mags after a while, looking out to the Head O'Man and deciding to relax and enjoy the peace. "Are those ravens up there?" She pointed at two dark pairs of wings, shining in the blue bright light.

"Aye," replied Manson, not looking.

"My god," whispered Mags, "an *otter!*" Manson had already spotted Muirgen, and his stomach lurched. The otter hauled a sellag out of the sea onto a rock opposite them and chewed off the fish's head. Manson felt the familiar wave of warmth well up inside him. He turned around and there was the Maighdeann Mhara. Beside her was her bag of Time. He pulled his own small plastic bag with his mother's northern apples from his pocket and offered them to her. Mags had also turned around. When she saw the Maighdeann Mhara she stood up. Muirgen raised his head from the sellag in alarm.

"*Bi ciùin, a Mhuirgen.*" The Maighdeann Mhara spoke gently. "Muirgen cannot settle when there are people around." She reached for Manson's bag and smiled as she looked into it. "He never forgets," she said to Mags. "If you sit down Muirgen will be happier."

The Maighdeann Mhara sat beside them on the rock, her hair shining like strands of wet seaweed across her shoulders, her long coat of shifting colours flowing over the curves of her body. A fulcrum of all available energy, she absorbed the late afternoon sunlight as it flooded the bay and bounced off the water and the red sandstone cliffs. The fulmars were attracted to her from the cliffs, hovering and swooping around her. To Manson, the Maighdeann Mhara had become pure colour, and without even realizing it he had pushed his dark glasses up onto his head. He glanced at Mags – she too had discarded her shades, all pain recently caused by bright light now forgotten.

The Maighdeann Mhara bit into an apple and smiled her delight. She opened her bag to deposit the rest of the apples. Time flooded out. Enveloped, Mags felt the Maighdeann Mhara reach out and take her hand. "Do you like the fulmars?"

"Yes. Fracher says they pair for life."

"They do. Like yourself they are recent visitors to our shores. A century ago they were not seen here. But what is Time, to them or to us? The fulmars are the opposite of sorrow." She reached out for Manson's hand so that the three of them were linked. Manson sought out Mags's other hand. Time cradled them.

"You are like brother and sister," said the Maighdeann Mhara. "You are both searchers. You seek the same thing. You seek it in colour and form, Manson, and in dreams – the only realm in which you can be truly happy. You, Mags, look for it in objects and buildings and in the traces of humanity locked up in the past. That is also a dream." As she spoke the Maighdeann Mhara drew them closer, until their heads rested on her shoulders. She stroked their hair. "Manson is dazzled by the beauty of his creations. You, Mags, are enchanted by the music of the past."

Manson and Mags felt disembodied. The only reality was the sea-harp of her voice and the hush of surf on the beach. The Maighdeann Mhara too felt freed of the pain in her existence. She knew Leir's children would be released soon and would be going home. *Here is my own son, at last, and a girl that he loves. What more could a mother ask? Jealousy is terrible. My crime was selfish, but I'm free now to enter my own domain.* She would open her arms to the coming storm. The Maighdeann Mhara unbuttoned her long coat and drew Manson and Mags like infants to her breast.

"You will find your hearts' desire."

Manson knew now what that was. Mags's face was close to his. With the Maighdeann Mhara embracing him Time poured over the cliffs like water, and he pushed himself into the place of love, to stay there forever. Who was it he made love to? Did it matter? Mags felt the hand of desire clasp her breast and she kissed it. She kissed Manson as Time took him away. She saw the face of the Maighdeann Mhara. Then she saw the darkness at the back of the cave. She saw the wave.

# 46

Grillaan died on a day of torrential rain.

Near mid-day Caornan went in to see whether the Prior needed anything. The old man smiled and shook his head. The young scribe bowed respectfully and left him. Since morning prayers Caornan had wrestled with his conscience, and had resolved to speak with Grillaan, but because of the old man's frailty he had wavered. Now something, a small confessional urgency, made him turn on his heel and go back into the hut. As he did so a wren flew out from the lintel of the low doorway. Caornan found the Prior as he had left him moments before, lying back on the bed, his eyes wide and staring heavenward, his mouth caught in a half smile. His arms were by his side, his fingers were clenched. Caornan knew at once he was dead.

Instinctively he straightened Grillaan's fingers and crossed his hands together. Without stopping even to pray he ran out of the stone hut to find Eoghan.

The old soldier priest was sharpening a sickle with a whetstone outside his hut. Caornan couldn't get a word out, but Eoghan understood at once. He dropped his tools and ran. His old friend was at peace. Respectfully he closed Grillaan's eyes, then knelt beside the rough bier and began to pray. Caornan stood in the doorway. Eoghan began to weep. Caornan's alarmed soared. He had never known the warrior to shed a single tear. But there he was, on his knees, his broad shoulders heaving, his sorrow fathomless and as boundless as the sea and the rain beyond Grillaan's cell.

Caornan left Eoghan with his loss. Automatically he walked over to the Geo of the Dead and looked down. The boat was still there by the harbour wall; the sea still washed over the rocks. *How can Grillaan be dead? He was old, yes, but surely death had no hold on him?* Terror, however, had a hold on Caornan. Ever since that day in distant Donegal when his father had taken him to St Martins in Ceann Casshlagh to see Grillaan, the Prior had been his rock, his centre, his security. His conversations with Grillaan had been his true education. Learning to write Irish, Greek and Latin was a secondary thing. Now, just when he so desperately needed to speak with his master he couldn't. What was he going to do?

It had been five years ago. After his father left the monastery Grillaan had sat him down and talked to him plainly. *They say you are a bright boy. That you have the makings of a scholar. Time will tell. Whether you will make a monk let alone a priest, well, that is a different proposition. The church is a vocation; you understand that, don't you?* "

*Yes, Holy Father.* He'd nodded uncertainly, like the child he'd still been.

*Fortunately we are free here in Ireland from the oppressions of Rome. You will be baptised, most certainly. You will wear the brown habit as we all do. You will keep your hair long as is the custom of the O'Neils. We see no need to mimic Christ's crown of thorns in a tonsure as the Romans do. In Ireland, sadly, it is the slave who has his head shaved. You will be taught the ritual of the mass and how to pray. You will confess if you so desire, but your conscience is your own, Caornan. In that God delights. We practice a flexible monasticism here at St Martins so that when you have some training and you wish to leave you can. If you wish to return, you can do that also.*

*Oh, I will never leave, Holy Father*, he had said, too eagerly. Grillaan had smiled, and it was that smile Caornan learned to love and to trust.

*Don't be so quick to commit*, he'd said. *In truth, our life is a form of penitence and we are all martyrs of one kind or another.*

*There is the white martyrdom of exile, and I will be asking you to undertake that as a novice once your initiation is complete. I will embark on the green martyrdom, and journey to a foreign land to spread Christ's holy word. I will never return. The final penitence is the red martyrdom of death, and only God knows when and where we will meet that. So, Caornan, do you think you are ready for such a journey?*

He had lied. The Prior had known his reply to be both untrue and honest. He had heard the same reply from many brave and clueless boys over the years. Now Grillaan was dead, and he was still not ready. He watched the waves crash over the sandstone ledges, then fall back in a chaos of sucking salt spray and broken rolling stones. What he had wanted to tell Grillaan, what he needed to confess, was that he had no desire to be a scholar, a priest, a monk or any kind of martyr. The whole jing-bang of meditation and rules seemed designed to make the natural world repugnant. He wanted to write poems about the colour of Nessan's hair and the curve of her thigh. He wanted to run with her naked into the loch. He wanted to shout out loud to the hugeness of the headland that he didn't believe in God, that God was just a complicity with the kings and the chiefs, and that the smell of Nessan's neck was all that mattered on this earth.

Soaking wet, Caornan walked back to the chapel to dry himself by the fire they always kept lit in a corner opposite the altar. Eoghan emerged from Grillaan's hut as he passed. They stood and looked at one another for a moment. Then Eoghan grabbed him and pulled him to his chest. Caornan thought he was going to pass out from the fierce embrace and the trauma of the afternoon.

"Our chief is gone," said Eoghan, releasing him. "We will bury the Prior tomorrow. There's no point waiting for this interminable rain to stop. We will lay him to rest in the chapel. The funeral will be simple. You will say a requiem. I will sit with him tonight."

Then Eoghan walked off, his head bowed, older somehow. He disappeared inside his hut.

The next morning it was raining still. Eoghan and Caornan conducted their morning prayers in silence. Then they rose from the altar and proceeded to raise three large flagstones from the beaten earth floor. With an iron pick he had borrowed from Ythan and a wooden spade Eoghan began to dig a grave. Last night he'd been too concerned that it would flood, so sodden was the headland. So be it if he was covered in mud for the burial. Earth is our truth, he thought. Caornan ferried the stone and soil to an alcove in the wall. When the grave was dug they went to Grillaan's cell. Gently they washed and prepared the body for burial, sewing two blankets together to form a shroud. By midday a small crowd had gathered self-consciously in the chapel. Nessan, Ythan, Ogun and a few other Cattach who knew nothing of this Christian ceremony. They were there because they knew that Grillaan had been a good man. No-one mentioned the absence of Dungal and his retinue from the fort.

Eoghan and Caornan placed Grillaan's body on planks of wood supported by two rough trestles. "Keep it simple and short," Eoghan whispered to Caornan as he knelt before the altar. "We're not looking for a mass, just sincerity."

The young scribe's mind went blank. His mouth dried and hot panic flashed through him. He thought of Grillaan, imagining his face before him, and he tried to remember the intensity of that time in Donegal. He crossed himself, got to his feet and turned to face the tiny soaking congregation.

*I am going home with you,*
*To your home, to your home*
*I am going home with you*
*To your home of Winter.*

Terror shrank and his voice grew in strength so that he was almost singing. His soft tenor bounced off the hard, stone acoustic of the walls, contained by the softer belly of the wooden ceiling.

*Death with oil*
*Death with joy*
*Death with light*
*Death with gladness*
*Death with penitence*

*Death without pain*
*Death without fear*
*Death without death*
*Death without horror*
*Death without grieving*

*I am going home with you*
*Child of my love*
*To your eternal bed*
*To your perpetual sleep*
*Amen.*

The row of faces looked at him kindly, but blankly. Eoghan stepped forward and together he and Caornan lowered Grillaan into the grave.

"Bayjayzus, boy," whispered Eoghan, "you managed not to mention God or Jesus once. What sort of requiem was that?" Caornan had no idea. The words just came. As they lowered the body, lightning flickered in the doorway, and the sky shook with thunder. But his terror had gone. Eoghan pulled up the heather ropes and bowed his head:

*Give us O God, the joy of repentance, as our brother Grillaan, our beloved Prior who we bury this day, repented.*

*Give us, O God, the joy of forgiveness as Grillaan gave us both joy and forgiveness, he who you have now in your own domain.*

*Dear God, wash from us the stain of corruption. Cleanse us now as we give you our brother. He has both finished and begun his mission, forever in the name of Jesus, your son who you gave to be our savour.*

*Amen.*

Eoghan reached for the precious handbell, and rang it three times. Sound pulsed through the chapel. He handed the bell to Caornan.

"Take this, lad, and lead these people twice sunwise round our chapel, ring it softly as you go."

The small group of mourners followed Caornan obediently, walking silently in the rain. The peel of the bell dappled in the downpour, pooling in the air like smoke on a still night. When the ceremony had finished the people disappeared into the mist. An occasional flicker of lightning and a disgruntlement of thunder provided a bigger music to ease their leaving.

Eoghan began shovelling the brown peaty earth back into the grave. When he had finished Ythan sombrely placed the three flagstones back into position and placed a small cross on the middle stone, whittled from an off-cut of oak from the rafters. In time Ythan could carve something permanent. Outside the rain fell in rods and the sky grew black. Nessan, her plaid pulled up over her head, stood outside the chapel sheltering as best she could in the doorway beside Caornan. Eoghan, with Ythan behind him, emerged from the chapel, his brown habit covered in wet peaty soil. He set the pick and shovel against the wall.

"Grillaan is now on his Immram." Caornan, still holding the handbell, looked at him blankly. "It's what the old folk call the journey to the other world. The bell gave him music to see him on his way."

"Just as I always suspected," said Ythan, producing a small stone jug, "When you scratch a Christian you find a Cruithne."

"I'll have you know," said Eoghan, pausing to take a swig from the offered jug, "that we are kin to the High Kings of Ulster."

"Aye," said Ythan, "aren't we all?"

Nessan grabbed Caornan's hand and pulled him away from the chapel. She set off up the brae to Loch Bushta, cradled by its hill. A group of swans swam just off the far bank. Nessan led him to a dent in a lip of rock beside the well on the south bank of the loch. A burn flowed from here down to the cliff before cascading into the sea. Tucked into this sandstone niche they held onto each other for warmth. Caornan was still clutching the bell.

"Why don't you ring it and see if the Children of Leir will dance for us?" said Nessan.

"Why would I do that?"

"Because of the legend," said Nessan, rubbing his hair with her plaid to dry it. "Because the sweet ould fellah is dead. Because you don't believe in all that jibber-jabber. Because now you'll be going away. Because you love me." She kissed him squarely on the lips.

"You shouldn't have done that," gasped Caornan.

"Come, ring your bell, bardie boy." Suddenly she sprang from their shelter and stood on the bank of the loch.

"Guiliog ee! Guiliog oh! Guiliog ee! Guiliog oh!" she sang out across the water. "Guiliog ee! Guiliog oh!"

Four swans raised their heads from their feeding. As Caornan joined her on the bank he heard a swan cry out, "Guilee! Guilee!"

Nessan could hardly contain her delight. "Ring your bell, oh ring your bell now!"

Caornan swung the handbell. Its solemn sweet music filled the heavy air above the loch, echoing around the hill and out over the headland. Four swans rose from the water in a majestic display, wing feathers splashing, then beating through the air, as if impelled by the bell.

"Guiliog ee! Guiliog oh!" Nessan called out.

"Guiliog ee! Guiliog oh! Guiliog ee! Guiliog oh!" replied the swans. They flew so low over the heads of Caornan and Nessan that both ducked and tumbled onto the heather. The bell was jolted from Caornan's hand and disappeared behind a clump of moss. The four swans settled on a small patch of grass just beyond the well. By the time Caornan and Nessan got to their feet again the swans were nowhere to be seen. In their places, sitting on the grass were a girl and a boy with two younger boys, twins, yawning and stretching as if they had just woken up. Before Caornan could speak, Nessan reached up and covered his mouth with her hand. Instinctively she pulled them down onto their knees so as not to be seen.

"Where did they come from?" whispered Caornan. Another feather of lightning flickered across the sky. Nessan whispered back.

"They're from the childhood of the world." A rumble of thunder broke open the northern sky.

The four children rubbed at their ankles, which looked raw and red, as if they'd been bound. Nessan sensed that Caornan was about to burst from curiosity, so she whispered directly into his ear: "*The tall blonde girl is Fionnuala of the fair shoulder. Her brother, Aodh, is god of the underworld. The twins are Fiachra, the Raven Hunter – he's the dark one. Conn, his brother, is Reason.*"

The children gathered themselves together and hugged each other. Conn looked around them, and then they all ran off along the path towards Dwarick Head. At the top of the waterfall behind Caornan and Nessan stood the Maighdeann Mhara, tears of relief rolling down her cheeks into the burn, her bag of Time open at her feet. Were you to look now into her bag you would see the face of Manson looking out. *They are gone,* she seemed to speak to the thunder as it lingered over the hill, *and nothing so good is come to take their place*. Muirgen the sea otter pushed his head against her ankle. *Nothing so good, my beloved one, will ever come again.* She bent to stroke the long back of her whiskered friend, then picked up her bag and closed it. *Now I am free to die*, she told the rain. Her golden coat glistened. She was free of her crime. The curse was lifted from her. The Maighdeann Mhara went down into the cave to wait for the wave.

Flickering and roaring as it moved, the storm cloud over Bourifa Hill drifted from the top of the headland low over the three beehive huts, the stone clachan of songs; over the stone ship of the chapel, with its wooden hull of a roof. Like a huge cat or the world serpent it spat at the chapel roof. There was a colossal crack, then a sucking of air, and a boom as if from a vast drum. Flames like orange tongues shot up from the chapel roof. Despite the rain, half the wooden structure was alight.

Caornan and Nessan saw and heard none of this. They had slid into the stone shelter by the well. The young scribe unwound the plaid from the Cattach girl while she pulled his brown habit over his head, and they lay down naked on the dry bracken, and loved each other until the rain stopped and the storm of progress had passed.

They did not see, either, six soldiers sent by Breidi, the High King from Dun Phadraig in the South. Tall, long hair tied behind their necks, red cloaks flowing over their horses' haunches, they rode over the hill carrying long spears and decorated angular shields, flat swords sheathed at their belts. Their strong white horses had red-painted manes and metal fittings shone on their bridles and saddles. As they approached the chapel – the roof by this time a charred smoking skeleton – they divided into two groups. Their chief and one soldier remained mounted while the four others dismounted and drew their swords. Two ran towards the chapel from the cliff side, the other two from the loch side. Eoghan was struck by a soldier when he appeared from his hut. He fell dead to the ground, and his blood soaked into the peat. With another stroke of his sword the soldier cut off the old warrior priest's head. Ythan tried to run for it, but the chief signalled to the mounted soldier who galloped after him and ran him through with his spear. The soldier dismounted, drew his sword and beheaded Ythan. Both heads were put in a sack which one of the soldiers handed to his chief, who hung it from his saddle. The rest of the soldiers searched the chapel and the two other huts but fond no-one. At a sign from the chief, all six re-mounted their white horses and rode back the way they had come. Two ravens circled above the smouldering chapel. Still it rained.

# 47

The railhead at Georgemas Junction was proof of the nuclear duplicity. Newly completed, at thirteen metres high and with a capacity to handle one hundred tonnes it was the largest railhead in Britain to service the nuclear industry. Colin hated it. He glared at his ***John O'Groat Journal.*** Georgemas was the front page story. Gilbert Henderson had included an unofficial grainy photo of workmen on the railhead platform in hard hats and orange day-glo jackets, checking a pair of locomotives hitched to carriages carrying nuclear flasks. *Christ!* thought Colin. *One of those men might have been me.* Not anymore. The photo was fuzzy, but he recognised one or two of them. He remembered the lively conversations about nuclear power he used to have with the other apprentices all those years ago, when he was young and green. After they'd been shown around the DFR, the processes of nuclear fission was explained to them: how the heat generated produced steam which powered turbines. The scientist who had led their tour assembled them at the end and asked if there were any questions. Googs Mackay had been quick as a flash: "*Thur must bay a better way til bile a kettle, eh?*" The mystique and the fear of the closed nuclear world they were being groomed to collude in collapsed as they all burst out laughing, much to the scientist's disgust. Innocence and intimidation were swatted into perspective as the entire apprentice cohort, some two dozen of them, creased up in idiot glee. It was a moment Colin never forgot, and the essence of his success at Dounreay. They could say what they liked but, secretly, everyone knew it was all ridiculous. That clarity was the only real power he had ever possessed.

Had Colin, like Kylie, studied literature or history, he might have recognised earlier the nature of tragedy. In ancient Athens, drama and the political system of democracy grew up together. This modern narrative had evolved over a shorter historical period, and in a place where the established system of representative government had fallen into disuse. It was the fate of modern Caithness (the ancient Province of the Cat) that the county's ability to survive nuclear occupation during the seventy years of Dounreay was hindered at almost every turn by the local civic authorities, who believed Caithness's economic future depended upon its prolonged existence. Despite official statements on social policy and press-release promises of economic development, via the United Kingdom Atomic Energy Authority (UKAEA) and the Nuclear Decommissioning Authority (NDA), the British government did everything it could to ensure that they did nothing at all to implement anything – except that which lay counter to what they promised.

Seventy years flew from the bag of Time, and no-one grasped what their passing meant. Arbitrary moments were important to individuals and agencies only as and when they themselves were historical players. So it was that successive local authorities and state government *approached* an honest solution to the problem of what to do with post-Dounreay Caithness, but none reached it. Political powers could work whole-heartedly to harness the energy released by splitting the atom in order to ensure destruction of imaginary enemies; it was less impelling to facilitate a future for those who were their political or administrative responsibility, but who lived at the great edge of their central radar. Local civic authorities, on the other hand, were ill-equipped to grasp the causes of events in their completeness. For them Caithness was a fixed entity, while Time flew around it like the planets and stars around the Earth – *Poor us!* they thought. *What a pity we have no influence.* For both the British state and the local authority these seventy years were too complex and multiple; too approximate, separate and singular to be seen as "History", part of a continuum of events with causes and outcomes.

Like everything else in the nuclear industry, the railhead at Georgemas Junction had been built on a lie, a ruse to slip the plan past the noses of alarmed local politicians before shifting the environmental goal-posts. Colin had overseen many shipments of waste by sea from Scrabster but now the pace and scale of the decommissioning project had increased. Two years ago he had also overseen the first ever shipment of waste from the railhead. He had been amazed by the size of the facility, and had pointed out to the NDA that what they had built was almost three times the size of what they needed. But he'd been an innocent, then. Gabfan, now Tycho Nuclear, wanted more, and they wanted it quicker. The plan on Colin's desk was to transport forty four tonnes of fast breeder nuclear material from Dounreay to Sellafield. Ninety trainloads. The Georgemas railhead was way over scale for that. Was there another plan? And if there was would someone kindly tell him? No-one did. Now he was reading in Gilbert's feature that even more of the nuclear stockpile was to be transported off-site.

As he read the news article, gulping black coffee and ignoring his toast, Colin knew exactly who and what was behind this. The White Ape's face and voice emerged from the sand-dune of his memory. "*We gotta get all this shit outta here!*" He could still hear The Big Yank scream across the conference table; the White Ape agreeing readily; the two-headed dog of Time and Money barking at his shoulder; the NDA altering a strategic military and political decision on the sly. As his old chargehand Bennie Manson used to say, "*Far's yer democracy noo, eh?*"

Colin knew there were many tonnes of uranium rods on site which had been irradiated inside the reactor to make plutonium. Technically, the Authority owned these uranium rods. Officially, the plutonium was for other power stations. But Colin knew – everybody knew – that the plutonium was for military use. That was why Dounreay operated as it did, and why Ministry of

Defence police were roaming the back roads west of Atomic City, harassing crofters' wives returning from Tesco and tourists with cameras who lingered too long to enjoy the view. Tycho Nuclear wanted "*all this shit outta here*" and ships were costly and slow. Transporting highly radioactive material, whether plutonium or uranium, the length and breadth of Scotland had never been the plan – at least not one the civilian authorities had been made aware of. The plan had changed. The lie grew bigger. Colin flung his copy of ***The Groat*** to the floor. *This shouldn't matter to me any more.*

Fabricating a stainless-steel model of the DFR had been Colin's way of revisiting the promises of the 1950's, his way of saying sorry, a votive offering of sorts. He kept it locked in the back room beside his lathe and milling machine, as the sight of them sent Kylie into a rage. There was little left to smash in the flat except the vodka bottle she'd come home with whenever she'd been out, which was less and less often. It was weeks since she'd ventured to the site, and nobody from Nagelstein's office even phoned to find out where she was or what she was up to. He could see no evidence that she was "working from home" as she claimed. What he could see, increasingly day by day, was that Kylie wasn't "working" at all.

Nights were the worst, unless she (or he) was in a drink-fuelled coma. Her dreams were hallucinogenic and violent, and she invariably woke up more exhausted than when she went to sleep. Slowly they were both becoming like zombies. Kylie had always been slim, but now she was like a stick. He couldn't get her to eat anything. She seemed to exist on air. He had always taken pride in his appearance but he, too, had abandoned all that, sprouting a beard and letting his hair grow over his collar. Everything he had been seemed useless. You either lived your life for yourself or you didn't; you used your freedom to reach your personal goals, or you lived a swarm-life, obeying laws and observing codes laid down for you. He knew the irony was that, even if you struggled free, you still belonged to history; retrospectively, action became the unconscious instrument of the general direction of humanity.

His problem was that he had no idea what that general direction, or its aim, was. He'd thought he knew, once. Atomic energy: free and immortal! That idealism had been destroyed, crunched down by the NDA, Tycho Nuclear, and Kylie's trauma.

If he didn't help her they would both be damaged, or dead. One night she had come home, vodka in bag, and had raged and ranted until she fell asleep on the floor. He'd gone to fetch Burns. It was Wednesday night so he knew where to find him. The Comm lounge had been packed, a group of local folk musicians the focus of attention. Amongst them was Burns, six feet two, head tilted back, thick glasses balanced on his nose, belting out a bothy ballad. After what seemed like twenty verses Colin's anxiety had soared. *How many times can e come in by Huntly toon?* he thought. At last the crowd applauded and Burns sat down. Colin pounced.

"Doctor, Ah need e til come an look at Kylie."

Dr Burns put down his pint and pushed his glasses back up his nose. "I'm in the middle oh a session, min," he said, not unreasonably.

"I know. Boot Ah hink shay might herm hersel." The doctor looked at him. "Ahm no choakan."

"Fuck sake," sighed Burns, "Yer lucky my bag's in the car."

Leaving his pint where it was, Dr Burns got up and followed Colin outside to collect his bag. The flat was a five-minute walk from The Comm. Kylie was still out cold on the floor. The doctor knelt to take her pulse.

"She's pished," he said.

"God, doctor – Even ah ken that much!"

"Give me a hand." They carried her through to the bedroom. "Is she on ony medication?"

"Only vodka," replied Colin sheepishly. He started to explain: Daimler's death, the job and the trip to Japan, the obsessive behaviour, the drinking – everything.

Burns grimaced. "The definition oh an alcoholic is somebody who drinks mair than their doctor. Havin said that, we need to get her tae New Craigs in Inverness as soon as possible. She needs treatment and medication I cannae give her."

"That bad?" Colin hadn't expected this.

"Bad?" scoffed Burns. "Yer lassie's fucked, Colin, min. She needs attention. First thing in the mornin I'll phone New Craigs. You just get her there by mid-day. Leave it wae me. If she goes willinly then I dinna need tae sign the forms. If no, I will."

"Thanks, Doctor." Burns moved to the front door.

"Och, I get a bit lek that mysel, at times," he said, trying to reassure Colin. "There's nae point givin her onythin, just sit by her and mak sure she disna choke on her own boak. Noo, I must awa back tae The Comm. I've got the *Barnyards O Delgaty* tae murder yet."

"More Huntly toon?" asked Colin, smiling at last.

"Na, na, Colin. It's the Turra coo this time. D'ye no ken onythin?" Then Burns was gone. Colin could hear the doctor's broad Buchan tenor as he set off to rejoin his pint:

*As I geed doon tae Turra merket,*
*Turra merket fur tae fee*
*I fell in wae a wealthy fermer,*
*the barnyards oh Delgaty!*

The chorus was lost as the doctor turned the corner and was gone.

The next morning was not good. Kylie had lost the plot, hysterical and hallucinating: Daimler was behind the curtains; he was under the bed; the house was going to fall down. He got her to drink some coffee. He explained they were going to Inverness, that Dr Burns had arranged it, and that she wasn't to worry, that it was all for her own good. Pale and thin, she just sat and looked at him. She wasn't dressed, so to prevent a scene he just wrapped her in her long cream raincoat. At least she would be warm and dry. It was well after nine before he got her into the BMW, threw an overnight bag onto the back seat, and set off. The morning was dull and by the time they crossed The Ord it was raining. Every one of Stevens' fish lorries seemed to be on the road. He pulled in at Golspie to call Burns's medical centre, relieved to be put straight through to the Burns himself. Colin told him she had put up no resistance so far.

"Everythin will be fine," said Burns. "Just turn up, tell them fah ye are, explain I sent ye, an the system will kick in."

Colin drove on. Kylie stared blankly out at the Moray Firth, the drilling rigs at Invergordon, the Cromarty Bridge. By the time they got to Inverness the rain was a monsoon. Despite missing a turn-off they reached New Craigs by mid-day. He parked and told to Kylie to wait a minute until he came back. She said nothing. He hesitated, but decided not to lock the door in case she panicked. The torrential rain was enough to deter any thought of bolting. Anyway, she had no money and where would she go? Colin ran into reception. Within five minutes two nurses were escorting Kylie down a corridor. *She's like an arrested spy in that long raincoat,* thought Colin uneasily. He sat in a waiting room, drinking terrible coffee from a machine. He paced inside the hospital entrance, watching an easterly gale blow the heavy rain sideways across the car park. At last a young doctor came to find him. His "wife" was suffering from mental and physical exhaustion; she was experiencing anxiety attacks, and they would be keeping her in for up to seventy-two hours for observation and assessment. After that they could decide what treatment, if any, was best. He gave Colin his card. Colin looked at the card. He looked at the doctor. He looked at the rain. *Could he see her*? The doctor said no, it might set her off and anyway they had given her a sedative. They had his contact details. Everything would be fine. Best go home.

Exhausted but relieved, Colin thanked the doctor, glad to get back out in the driving rain to the car. He was just turning out of the car park when he caught a glimpse in his rear-view mirror of a slight figure in a blue hospital gown running from the main entrance, two nurses in hot pursuit. He slammed his foot on the brake. The figure stopped running, holding its arms out as if trying to embrace the rain and the wind, which blasted the soaked gown like a sail out behind it. It was Kylie. She stood in this pose of supplication for what to Colin seemed an eternity. She looked so thin and helpless. Then the two nurses led her gently back to the building. Colin's mouth was dry. He watched until there was nothing to see. A car behind him tooted its horn. He put the BMW in gear and sped down the New Craigs driveway and out of Inverness.

He re-crossed the three bridges and was soon following the east coast of Sutherland. The Moray Firth was grey and sullen, flinging itself onto the long red-ochre strands between Brora and Helmsdale. He climbed The Ord. The rain relented slightly and the cloud began to thin. As he cleared Berriedale and looked north along the Grey Coast of Caithness he nearly drove off the road and had to stop the car. A wispy cloud formation beyond Lybster looked for all the world like a woman, her arms open wide, being blown backwards across the sky. *Kylie in the clouds?* he wondered: *the lost angel of decommissioning*?

He reached Atomic City by four o'clock. Back in the empty flat, he crashed onto the couch and fell asleep almost immediately. He dreamed of a train-load of nuclear waste leaving Georgemas Junction. Instead of disappearing up the railtrack and out into the vastness of the Caithness bog, it took off into the sky and disappeared into outer space. Nuclear ghost riders in the sky. The Atomic Valkyrie.

When he woke he tried the number on the New Craigs doctor's card. The duty nurse was friendly and reassuring. She was still sleeping. This was normal. She was dehydrated but on a drip. Could he call back in the morning? Still completely shattered, Colin went to bed. It was late now and the Thurso street-lights glowed sickly orange. The radio usually soothed him, but tonight it seemed as though the music and chatter was playing backwards.

The next day was much the same. A different nurse said Kylie was stable. In the afternoon Burns stuck his head around the door.

"Fit like, min?"

Colin was listening to Radio 3 – unheard of. Shostakovich's Fifth symphony sawed its way through the air in the kitchen.

"Muckle beeg banjo music aat, is it no?" The doctor turned down the volume. "Wur haen a bit oh a sesh the night in the

Comm. Some oh the Gaelic choir's comin in. Ye should come, loon. Better fur ye than sittin aboot here."

Colin nodded. Kylie was in the best place, getting the best treatment. What was he worried about? Burns left as suddenly as he'd arrived. *Checking up on me.* Resentment bubbled, subsided. *At least Burns gives a shit,* thought Colin, putting on the kettle. No coffee left and no milk. He sighed, but got his jacket.

It was lunch time and the street was full of High School pupils, like young Nazis in their black uniforms. Thank God there had been no dress code when he was there. You wore your own uniform, which meant he and his pals dressed like The Clash. He shook his head at boy-racers from the college revving their tarted-up cars around the circuit of Princes Street, Traill Street and Olrig Street. As he was about to cross the road a two-door red Vauxhaull pulled up beside him, stuck in the lunch-time traffic jam that happened every school-day. The boom-boom of bass and drum music thumped out of the car. Five boys were packed inside, all shouting at each other, pointing at school-girls walking past, and laughing. Before it roared off again the ruddy-faced driver lowered his window and shouted at Colin: "*Yer a fuckan paedo!*" Colin watched the car disappear around a corner in a grind of revving and gears. Cold anger boiled in his gut, tightening his chest and neck and swimming hotly across his brow. Exposed and hesitant, like a fledgling off a cliff, Colin stepped off the pavement. He reached the Co-op, bought his coffee and milk, and went home.

Sometime afterwards Colin phoned New Craigs. How was she? Should he come? No, she was awake but resting. Could he speak to her? No, but call back tomorrow. Same time? Yes, same time. That was the conversation. He mulled it around in his mind. He should go anyway. But what good would that do? They had his number. She was in the best place. Getting the best treatment. She was resting. This was good. Wasn't it? He should rest. He tried. At last he fell asleep on the couch.

He woke up about eight o'clock at night. Stiffly he stood at the wash-basin. Streaks of grey in his long hair. Beard. Thinner?

He should go out. He put on his shoes and jacket and headed for The Comm.

His face was wet with drizzle when he pushed open the lounge bar door. The place was already busy. About twenty people were squeezed into a corner singing a Gaelic song. Burns was one of them, glasses on the end of his nose, mouth wide open, his hearty voice bouncing off the walls and low ceiling. Colin went through to the public bar where it was quieter. He ordered a pint and was about to take a sip when a voice roared out, "Harper, you're nothing but a snivelling fuckin cretin!" Colin looked round. Gilbert Henderson, editor of the ***John O'Groat Journal***, sprawled in the corner beneath the TV with another tall, well-dressed man he didn't recognise. Henderson was the last person he wanted to see: loud, indiscreet and aggressively friendly – mostly just aggressive. Despite this Colin liked him. There was something unrelenting about "ay editor" (as folk called him) that he admired, and they had always enjoyed a good working relationship.

Colin sat down. Gilbert was drunk. This wasn't unusual – he'd shared the editor's ever-ready hip flask on many occasions. Tonight, however, there was something unhinged about Gilbert, and Colin feared the worst.

"Fuck sakes!" roared Gilbert, "What's with the beard? You turning into a hippy? A hippag? A hippagee?" He roared and laughed at his own Joycean joke. Colin said nothing and neither did Gilbert's tall companion.

"Harper used to be the site manager out at Dounreay until Psycho Tycho ran him off!" Gilbert's introduction reached the whole bar clientele, most of whom were used to Gilbert and more interested in the football match on the TV above their heads.

"Harper is living proof against local class apartheid – or he used to be. The token Gallach who proved that natives can climb the nuclear tree, eh, Harper?"

"Only til fall off," said Colin.

"This guy claims Orcadian heritage." Gilbert pointed at the man beside him. "He's from Australia."

The man leaned across Gilbert and proffered his hand. "Warren," he said. Colin noticed that he had a crooked little finger on his right hand.

"Warren Peace!"

"Interesting name," smiled Colin. Gilbert had probably used this joke several times already.

"Many people of Peace in Orkney, I'm glad to discover," said Warren Peace, good humouredly. "Lots of them in South Ronaldsay."

"If it's any consolation to you, Harper, I'm gettin the heave as well." Gilbert slapped Colin on the shoulder, almost knocking him off his stool.

"Shit!" Colin was stunned.

"Gilbert's exaggerating, as usual." Warren Peace had caught the genuine shock on Colin's face. "We're making him a managing editor, but he's not taking it very well."

"I'm being sent to fuckin Inverness. Fuck sakes!" announced Gilbert. "How would *you* feel?"

The question was directed at everybody in the bar. Then Gilbert leaned forward confidentially. "This cunt's an executive of the parent company of the paper – the Scottish Territorial fuckin Press," whispered Gilbert loudly. "More like the Scottish Tangential fuckin Press! Nothing makes sense. Everything's being centralized. No editors anymore. Gone."

"Secretly, he's flattered," said Warren Peace who had heard everything.

"Flattered am I?" said Gilbert. "Oh aye! Glad, maybe – to be out of the cess-pit of news and lies and all that other stuff we print in the paper. I'm bein punished!"

"Men should either be treated generously or destroyed," said Warren Peace. "Isn't that the theory?"

"Aye," agreed Gilbert, "because they'll take revenge for slight injuries, but for serious ones they're fucked, so you're safe."

"The truth is," sighed Warren Peace, "that there's nothing more difficult to take in hand, more perilous to conduct, or more uncertain in its success, than to take the lead in the introduction of a new order of things. Don't you agree?"

The question was directed at Colin.

"Difficult to know." He looked closely at Warren Peace. *His suit's changed colour*, thought Colin, *how can that be*? "Haven't I seen you somewhere before?"

"Where would that be now?"

"On Dunnet Beach," said Colin. Just then his phone beeped. His heart quickened. A text from Kylie.

"If you screw a man you better make sure you screw him so he's that fucked you don't have to worry about his revenge." Gilbert's waving glass sprayed beer over the table and Warren Peace.

"So – you no longer work in the nuclear industry, Mr Harper?"

Colin was still looking at his phone. ***Goodbye***.

"He got out before the whole things drops over a cliff." Gilbert was too drunk to notice Colin's expression.

"Really?" Warren seemed interested.

"Aye, They've lost all their rights but the bloody union still thinks they've won a good deal with Tycho and the NDA because there are no redundancies – the *now*." Gilbert was holding court. "But once Tycho Nuclear's done then everybody can go fuck themselves and it's over the great edge to nothin. That not right, Harper?"

"Looks lek id." Colin was still looking at his phone.

Warren Peace looked around the bar at the men staring up at the football on the TV above their heads. "The promise given before Dounreay was built was a necessity of the past, is that not the way, Gilbert?" he said. "That's what you think the Territorial Press is up to as well – the broken word is a necessity of the present."

"It's the entire atomic jing-bang," said Gilbert. "Harper would tell you if he wisna such a skelped cat. The Official Secrets Act runs through their bones like the message in Blackpool rock.

Look around yourself! Never mind decommissioning a bloody nuclear reactor or two, if you dismantle a people, you insult them, show them that you have no confidence in them; you show them you're a coward and a bully and that you trust nothing. In the end the people hate you, as they will come to hate Dounreay."

So the conversation went on, competing with the football commentary, singing from the lounge, and the general racket of the pub.

Colin's phone rang. A call this time – Inverness number. New Craigs? He barged outside, mobile in hand. – *Colin Harper? Yes, we're terribly sorry. Your wife's body. Just over an hour ago. Recovered from the River Ness.*

The pub door opened behind him. A wave of noise and the smell of humanity washed over him. He saw Kylie. She was standing on the Kessock bridge parapet, traffic flowing past. A few cars had stopped, drivers and passengers speaking to her, trying to stop her. Her arms were outstretched, her long blonde hair and her raincoat flowed out behind her in the wind. Then she stepped back. Gone. She dropped like a leaf into the fast-flowing river, and disappeared.

"Nothing too upsetting, I hope?" Warren Peace's thin ginger moustache curled in a smile as Colin re-joined them. Gilbert Henderson had got up from the table and had pinned Jimmy Greenan to the wall.

"Only three things of any significance happened in nineteen seventy-seven, Greenan, you prick. The Queen's Jubilee, the Sex Pistols LP, and the explosion in the Dounreay waste shaft!" Humiliated, the Dounreay fitter jerked free. He laughed nervously at Colin, then scuttled away through to the lounge bar, where Burns was leading the Gaelic choir. Gilbert slumped into his seat. Warren Peace smiled and put his arm around his new managing editor.

"You have a great sense of History, Gilbert."

"Fucking spineless little rat of a man." Gilbert was lapsing into melancholy. He drank his whisky.

Warren Peace laughed. "The wise man does at once what the fool does finally."

"You callin me a fool?" snarled Gilbert.

"A wiser man I have never met," Warren Peace put up his hands in mock surrender.

Gilbert lurched across the table towards Colin.

"There's a long train of nuclear waste leaving Georgemas tonight, in secret and contrary to all agreements signed by the NDA and Gabfan." Gilbert was shouting. "And that useless cunt Greenan says the union can do nothin about it. I've got a reporter and photographer out there, but no nationals are interested. Are *you* interested, Harper? Do you even exist, Harper?"

"You always get the story, Gilbert," beamed Warren Beatty. "That's why we want you in Inverness. There is redemption in everything."

"There sure as fuck is no redemption in nuclear waste," said Gilbert Henderson, now stony sober. "No salvation for the radiation roustabouts."

The bag of Time opened. A buzzing began inside Colin's head so that he couldn't hear what anyone was saying. ***Do I** really exist?* he wondered. Gilbert and Warren Peace were deep in conversation. The football match on the TV had long ended. Colin stood up. He pulled the doctor's card from his pocket and dropped it onto the pub floor where it was consumed by Time, trodden by the feet of radiation roustabouts. He pushed his way through to the crowded lounge bar. A sea of bodies. He'd wanted to find Burns, but changed his mind. Jimmy Greenan was standing on his own by the toilets. *He doesn't exist either*, thought Colin.

It was a nearly midnight when Colin exploded from The Comm in a silent white rage. A few late night taxis hissed by on the wet street. The buzzing in his ears eased. He walked down to Sir John's Square. At the traffic lights sat the red two-door Vauxhaull with the same cram of boy-racers. Lunchtime's cold anger met white rage. The driver's window was rolled down, the boom-boom base and drum music thumped out as loud as ever.

Colin stared at the driver, the same ruddy face that had flung insults earlier.

"What e lookan aat, ya cunt?" snarled the boy-racer. As hard as he could Colin punched the boy-racer full on the nose. Blood exploded onto the steering wheel. He grabbed the dark hair and banged the head beneath it off the inside of the door. The boys in the back seat were trapped and couldn't react, but the one in the passenger seat leaped out. Meanwhile Colin opened and quickly re-slammed the driver's door against an arm reaching out from the back, crushing the mouthy driver's shin in the process as he tried to get out. Both boys screamed. Colin ducked as the boy-racer who'd run round from the passenger side swung a bottle at his head. He felt it skim past his right temple. Swivelling, he caught the boy on the chin; the momentum sent him sprawling. Colin looked down at him, appalled, the wave of rage spent. He stood panting as the driver roared into gear and sped off on a red light, leaving his pal to scrabble to his feet and run off down Olrig Street. The lights had blinked through their cycle a couple of times during the fracas, but it was so late there was no other traffic, and no sign of the police. In a flurry of rags and dreams, only Doupie Dan rose up from his slumbers in a doorway and ran after the fleeing boy-racer, shouting his mantra about the sea and Time, his black sandshoed foot following his white.

Colin crossed the street. Not stopping to look behind him, he walked off quickly towards his flat. He still heard the boom-boom of the base and drum music in his head as he closed the door. It echoed with the violent pounding of his heart and the pain in his right hand. He snorted. He should have remembered what Clarkie Calder had told him when they were apprentices going through to the dances in Wick on Saturday nights: "*Always keep yer thumb ower ay outside oh yer fist when e punch some cunt. Itherwise e'll break id.*" Clarkie had enjoyed a fight. "*An always stey calm. E'll get a doin if e let ay bleed rush til yer heid.*"

He crashed onto the couch. Staying calm was impossible now. Almost immediately he got up again. Snatching his car keys from the coffee table he went out. The sky was beginning to clear. The moon was three-quarters full in the south-east, thin cloud like a dark halo around it; Venus was bright and low in the east; the Plough, his favourite constellation, was pinned high over the western horizon of the night. He drove out of Atomic City. He could see the lights of the Georgemas railhead as he approached the Halkirk turn-off. He drove on, turned right down the A9, South towards Spittal and the Cassiemire. At Mybster he turned off and followed the single track road to Westerdale, peeling off to the right at the junction. He drove on up to Harpsdale where he could see the village and the railhead below. He stopped the car, turned out the lights and switched off the engine.

On either side of him barley fields glistened from the rain in the moonlight. He was expecting the MoD police to appear at any moment. He waited. Nothing happened. The lights of the railhead were a neon island in a sea of blackness. There was the H-frame crane which had caused so much consternation and debate. "*We can hire cranes, you know. This isna a shipyard,*" he'd suggested at one meeting. The mandarins from the NDA had ignored him as usual. This was "*an issue outwith his competence.*" Well, they wouldn't ignore him now. He could clearly see two diesel shunting engines and seven carriages, their distinctive flasks full of toxic cargo. He watched the train move slowly from the rail head out of Georgemas.

His headlights still off, he drove down the brow of the brae towards Halkirk and the rail crossing. Five hundred yards from the crossing he stopped and switched off the engine once more. He waited for the MoD to appear. Still nothing. By the time the train reached the crossing it would still be travelling quite slowly. He watched the column of lights move along the railway track towards him. He started up the car engine, still checking for headlights, maybe even a helicopter. Nothing. Not so much as a fish lorry since he'd left the town. The train must be about five hundred yards from the crossing. He put his foot lightly on the pedal and the car picked up speed. The train got closer. A hundred yards from the track crossing Colin pressed hard on the accelerator. The BMW responded instantly, hitting eighty, then ninety miles an hour. He saw the twin diesels and a couple of carriages flash past before the flimsy barrier and his windscreen shattered. The bag of Time opened wide like the mouth of a cave, and swallowed Colin.

Up on his croft on Holborn Head Fracher was walking Cushie along the track by the neep park. It was a good night for the coanies and he already carried four for the pot in an old tattie sack. Cushie raised his head. With the sniff of a fifth rabbit in his nostrils the collie disappeared up a drill. As Fracher turned to look back up the track he saw a ball of flame shoot up from low on the eastern horizon somewhere near Halkirk. He stood perplexed for a moment. Then he heard the delayed dull percussion of an explosion. In his bag a coanie kicked its back leg, dead but still running to life.

# 48

Loki loved the Moon. His love, however, was so overwhelming that she split into four to escape him. As Loki stands now on top Dunnet Head, at the great edge of Scotland where the Province of the Cat falls into the sea, the light of all four Moons illuminates the sky. He watches the long love-wave of Storegga and Jörð strike out north-west to Iceland, wash over Faroe and Shetland and swamp the northern Isles of Orkney. He summons his love to melt the ice of the Arctic and the Antarctic, to take the salt out of the sea and for all the wild animals in the world to do his bidding, but his love will not do so. Loki has no creations, only corruptions. The four Moons hang unexploitable, indifferent; the result of true power, not love. He cannot possess them. Loki stands impotent and angry. He declares contrarily that history is eternal, yet also that it must end. In his childish temper, he calls the four Moons "*whores*", then turns on his heel and walks all the way to nowhere, always empty and always the same.

Bragi Boddason hauls anchor, and the great white ship sails north-west of Dunnet Head into deeper sea. He turns her mighty bow north-east to face the coming wall of water, two hundred feet high and travelling at one hundred miles an hour.

Aboard Skidbladnir Bragi guards a vat in which the spit of the Æsir is mixed with honey and blood. This rough mead is the drink of poets, and brings knowledge and wisdom to those who sup it. Bragi guards it with his life, just as back in Asgard his wife Idunn guards the golden apples of eternal youth.

Bragi had seen Loki on Dunnet Head. Now he sees the sea-wall-wave of Storegga as it roars over Hoy. He can feel Skidbladnir shudder as the sea is sucked from beneath her keel. He knows this is the most important moment in his life. His crew, the one thousand red-faced black-haired troll-sons of Ivaldi the dwarf, stare out in silent terror as the silver light of the four Moons shines steadily down.

# 49

Mags awoke on the beach naked. She found her clothes neatly folded beside her boots, the small bag with her notebook and mobile lay on a sandstone ledge above the tide-line, just a little distance from where she lay. Despite her nakedness she felt warm, calm, and relaxed. The late afternoon Sun shone down onto the Peedie Sannie. Manson was nowhere to be seen. Nor was there any sign of the Maighdeann Mhara or the otter. Not even a seal. Refusing to think, she gathered her belongings and clambered over the slippery boulders to where the burn fell as a waterfall over the cliff in front of the small cave. She shivered as the cool fresh hill-water showered over her body and through her hair.

She dried herself as best she could and dressed, but she couldn't find her dark glasses. It dawned on her she didn't seem to need them. The light no longer burned her eyes as she blinked round her: the Peedie Sannie with the finger of rock sticking out into the blue sea; and the two short shell-white beaches which curved to either side of it; cliffs towered east and west of her; wind and sea-carved sedimentary sandstone rippled in a wave behind her, leading to the paths up to the hill and Dwarick Head. Thousands of fulmars snowed the red cliffs, gliding in the thermals above the summits and out over the sea. Mags spun right round slowly taking all this in. The sheer beauty of the moment stopped all sensation. *My God! This is perfection...*

She stopped trying to understand. She felt purged of anxiety and of something else she could not quite give shape to, and a total sense of well-being possessed her. She felt resolved. She did not question what had happened. There was no need, she told herself: this is me now. Manson is... was... well, he was not there. This also did not disturb her. All she knew, with a conviction which surprised her in its matter-of-factness, was that he was where he wanted to be, where he needed to be. That could be back in the pub for all she knew, but somehow she knew he was not back in the pub. Mags gathered her bag and jacket and climbed the cliff-path back up to the hill-track and followed it by the loch to the road end by The House of The Northern Gate where she had left the car before she and Manson went in search of the Maighdeann Mhara. As she opened the car door she spotted Lady Barbara in the garden of the big house, a wide-rimmed white sun-hat on her head which made her look like a large daisy. Minker himself, gin glass in hand, was standing in the doorway looking down towards the village. Mags waved. Lady Barbara, gardening fork in hand, waved back. For a moment Mags thought of going to speak to them but changed her mind, got in the car, started the engine and drove down to the bothy.

She pushed open the thick blue bothy door. The place was exactly as she had left it. Her laptop, and all her books and notes spread across the table in abandoned organisation. She sat down to switch on her computer. She looked across the table to the small window and out over the bay and to the green open farm land which spread across the shoulders of Olrig and Clairdan Hills to the South. The openness of Caithness was what she had come to love more than anything else. *The sky is as vast here as the land is broad. Like an animal*, she thought simply, *it will swallow me*. This didn't bother her now. It did at first. Everything back then – oh so long ago – had intimidated her. Then she had felt the need to protect herself against the openness, the silence, the light. Now the land had opened her up. Now she could laugh at herself in the silence and see herself in the light. This, she discovered, was a place where no-one locked their doors and no conversation need have a beginning or an end. This was her ideal. This was the Caithness she constructed for herself. This was her necessary society in her perfect landscape. Here was the past she had been waiting for. In this ground she could begin herself. The sea, as she looked at it through the bothy window, went on forever out into the north and the west. She could imagine it pouring over the great edge of the world in a niagra of dreams and talking.

She looked at her notes. She looked at the handbell snug in its cardboard box. She looked at the labels she had made ready for the bell, for the three pieces of pottery she had found, for all the things she was convinced she would find. Mags imagined herself as the new Flinders Petrie, Caithness a new Egypt, an unknown land north of Troy, slowly revealing the narrative of a lost myth, putting the forgotten story back into real time. Like Flinders Petrie she was a stickler for keeping a clear time-line in her research, noting everything and comparing every small detail with every other small detail. Petrie was her hero. His methodology made archaeology possible. She laid her equipment out on the table: small folding shovel which could be used as a pick, hammer, chisel, trowel, brushes (various), earth-shaker and sifter, tape-measure, notebook, small box of chalk, pencils (pens are no use in the rain), camera, digi-recorder, batteries, ordinance survey map, water bottle. That's all I need, she said to the table. She could carry that lot on her back, easily. She thought of Professor Benison back in London. So far she had sent him only tentative reports of her progress on the dig. From him she had heard absolutely nothing, but that didn't matter. She had come to the far north to find herself, that had been her project, if she was truthful. Now everything had changed. Now the thing she was looking for was actually looking for her. Whatever that was, she knew it was waiting for her behind the wall in the Cave of Gold, in *Uamh an Oir*. Mags picked up the hammer. *I will do this*, she said.

The next morning she drove into Thurso to pick up Nessan at six. It was early because they had to catch the tide, but Nessan was there in front of St Peter's as arranged, in jeans and a waterproof jacket, her rucksack on her back and her long black hair blowing in the September wind. Nessan climbed in.

"You ok this morning?" asked Mags.

"Fit as a butcher's doug." Nessan's smile filled the car.

"Still sure you want to do this?" Mags pressed, as Nessan flung her rucksack in the back seat.

"Oh aye!" Nessan clicked in her seat-belt. "Ah've thocht oh nuhain else aal week. Id's excitan."

Mags drove through the sleeping town and down the Gills brae to Scrabster harbour. Fracher was at the inner pier beside the Fisherman's Mission where all the creel boats tied up. Cushie panted excitedly at his feet. High water made it an easy step down onto The Searcher.

"Weel, e've got a good day for id," said Fracher. "A peedie sky in ay Nor East, boot nuhain til worry aboot." He looked at Nessan. "E a sailor, Nessan?"

"Oh, Ah dunno aboot aat." Nessan seemed nervous now they were here.

"Och, thur'll bay a bittie oh a swell when wur oot past Holborn boot wance wur in open watter wae'll bay fine."

Nessan did her best to believe him. Mags sat down beside her and put her arm around her young helper.

"If we explorers stick together we'll be fine." Cushie nestled his white head in Mags's lap. Idly, Nessan stroked his ears as The Searcher pulled slowly out of the harbour. Once she was level with the lighthouse Fracher let out the throttle and the Kelvin engine coughed into life. The creeler put her nose into the sea and cut across the firth as she was designed to do.

The sea was just as Fracher had said. The water was turquoise, sparkling in the sunshine. The Atlantic heaved and rolled, but the wind was a gentle nor-easterly and the salt air felt good on Nessan's lips. She relaxed and began to enjoy herself as the beautiful bulk of Dunnet Head grew bigger and craggier the closer the creel boat got. Fracher took his bearing from The House of The Northern Gate and soon he could pick out the dark open mouth of *Uamh an Oir*, the dark cut of the Geo of The Dead a little to the West.

Fracher cut the throttle as he approached the old pier-wall, the cliffs towering above him. As the geo was in the lee of the wind and the tide was high, getting the two young women up onto the rock was not as difficult as he had feared.

"E noh coman wae us, Fracher?" asked Nessan.

"Noh, lassie. Ah hev til look efter ay boat," He passed up their rucksacks. "Boot ay doug'll go wae e."

Cushie needed no telling and sprang from the boat to the rock ledge like a small black panther.

"How long have we got, Fracher?" asked Mags.

"Aboot an hoor afore ay tide slackens."

"Can we come again tomorrow, if the work is more than I thought?"

"Och aye. Ay forecast's good an ay tide'll had aboot ay same." Fracher smiled. "Good luck wae id anyrod."

"Thanks, Fracher," Mags smiled back. "You're my best pal."

Cushie sped over the rocks as Mags and Nessan followed more gingerly. The Sun had risen higher in the eastern sky. The cave entrance opened up before them, a yawning black mouth.

"Id looks lek a beeg open gob aat's goan till eit us," joked Nessan.

Mags knew exactly what she meant. The two guardian ravens circled above their heads, night in their wings. Mags looked up at them for a moment, then back to the cave.

"Well, let's go and pick at some of its back teeth then," she laughed, and walked resolutely into the darkness. Nessan followed beneath a flurry of pigeon wings and tiny falling feathers, brave with Cushie at her heel. They put down their rucksacks and let their eyes adjust to the light. Beams of sunlight danced along the wet sparkling walls. Mags took out her camera and got to work. After measuring the wall with Nessan's help, she selected what she thought would be a safe place to knock out an entrance so as they could take advantage of a natural rock ledge to reach the top. Mags chalked numbers on all of the stones from the roof to the cave floor that she planned to remove. They were warm as she touched them. For all their apparent solidity and despite the slipperiness of the long centuries the first stone was quite easy to remove. As Mags loosened the first stone a waft of air blew out from behind it. She jerked back in confusion – *How could that be?* She said nothing to Nessan, just handed the stone down to her. After four stones had been removed, chalk-numbered and set to one side, Mags shone her torch into the new darkness. She could see nothing. Cushie started to make anxious collie noises.

"Shoosh now, dougie," Nessan's voice was comforting and Cushie's whimpering stopped.

Slowly and carefully Mags removed another four stones. Now she could look over the top.

"See anyhain?" asked Nessan impatiently as Mags shone her torch down into the undisturbed darkness behind the wall.

"No... I dunno... not yet." Mags could see a ruckle of stones and a couple of shapes on the rock floor but it wasn't possible to make out more. They worked on, removing more layers of stone until it was possible to step over the remaining wall. Nervously, torch in hand, she stepped into the resting place of Colm's clarsach, undisturbed for over twelve hundred years. The air smelled fresh and sweet. Nessan handed in her rucksack. She took out her camera to record every square foot of the cave. Working carefully with her small brush, she knelt down and brushed at the hard rock beneath her hands and knees, making sure she missed nothing.

"See anyhain at all?" Nessan was impatient, feeling vulnerable on her own.

"Just more stone. Hang on... These stones have been shaped and..." Mag's voice became muffled, then "My God! Nessan! There's some wood here – looks like a box!"

Mags felt sick. Without touching the rotting wood which was about the size of a shoebox, she brushed around it, uncovering a piece of metal. It was badly corroded but she could make out the shape of a lock. Her heart was pounding. She photographed the box and the lock. She measured them. She wrote the information in her notebook. She then pegged a pathway from where she was back to the entrance through the wall.

"Ok, Nessan, you can come in now, but stay on the path I've marked. And watch that dog."

No sooner had she uttered the words than Cushie bounded over the wall, sniffing at Mags's rucksack which she'd set beneath it. "Stay, Cushie!" yelled Mags, horrified, as Nessan followed him. The dog immediately lay down.

"Sorry," said Nessan, "Hay choost chumped ower afore Ah could get ahad oh um."

"Ach, not to worry," said Mags, calmer now she knew the dog was prepared to heed her. "He's doing no damage."

Nessan crawled over to Mags.

"Amazing, isn't it?" said Mags. "I have no idea what it is."

"Id's the sound-box frae a clarsach," said Nessan immediately.

"A what?" asked Mags.

"A clarsach. A *harp*." Nessan might have been talking to Cushie. She looked at the box more closely. "Ah play ay clarsach. Learned id at ay Feis."

"Are you sure?," asked Mags sceptically, scribbling in her notebook.

"Aye, Id's more or less ay same size as mah own een." She saw the lock. "They must've hed id in a case or sumhain. Wid ay case hev rotted awey an left iss? Ay sound box'll bay made oot oh oak Ah expect."

"I suppose it would make sense for Irish priests to have a harp," mused Mags. "Please don't touch it, Nessan."

"Looks pretty sturdy til me," said Nessan. "Oak's a hard wood."

"Well, it's been locked up in here, in the dark for over a thousand years." Mags ran the beam of her torch around the unseen space at the back of the cave. Nothing there but Time dripping off the walls. *Where did that draught of air come from?* She could see no passage, crack or fissure which could explain it. She stood up, then froze. It was if she was touched by many soft hands. Nessan crouched quite still. Cushie whimpered, his tail between his legs. He could see everything. Cushie could see The Shee dancing.

He could see Manson fixed to a rock by heavy chains. He could see a pile of wealth, the accumulated treasure of all the shipwrecks in the Pentland Firth, gleaming just beyond Manson's reach. He could hear clarsach music pour like water from the rock walls, echoing around the stone chamber before fading suddenly, replaced by pipe music, sounds rebounding past the opening Mags had so carefully excavated in the wall. He could see the Maighdeann Mhara rise up from the cave floor to face Manson. Cushie watched and growled deep in his throat as she threw back her head, her long hair flowing behind her, her arms outstretched as if pleading to Manson, who wrestled desperately with his chains, unable to break free. All the while the draught that had blown through the wall opening to greet Mags intensified, and a wind blew around the cave. The Maighdeann Mhara struggled against it but she was not strong enough to resist. Cushie's ears flattened tightly against his white head. He whimpered as the beautiful and colourful female vision Manson had known faded to a grey old woman, then to dust, which was swept up by the wind and spun out of the cave.

Cushie bolted over the broken wall. Mags reached out to stop the dog but as she did so she saw that the wall was no longer open, each stone was in place as if it had never been disturbed. The whole cave shuddered. Mags and Nessan clung to each other. The shuddering seemed to go on for ever. They could hear a roaring, the sound of a great in-rush of water crashing behind the wall.

"An Slanaighear." Nessan's whisper was lost amidst the chaos of the dead who danced around them.

Fracher had held the Searcher a short distance off the geo while he waited for Mags. The Atlantic swell, even on such a beautiful morning, was dangerous and the girl had no sense of time at all. Many creelers over the years had been sucked beneath sandstone ledges or into keel-shattering geos, tempted by the lobsters that lurked safely amid these dangers. He kept his engine throbbing in neutral, adjusting his position now and then as the tide demanded. He looked uneasily to the north-east. An unusual metallic grey which had hung in the sky all morning had intensified. There was something else. Where were all the fulmars? He looked up at the cliffs. Empty. He turned off the engine. The silence was profound and unsettling. The wind had dropped and the sea had fallen still. He could feel the boat being dragged backwards, away from the cave. Rattled, Fracher looked over the side. The water in the bay was flowing westwards along the headland like a river.

*Jeezus! Cushie?!* Cushie was running panic-stricken among the rocks, his shining black pelt now patchy, all but hairless. In shock, Fracher opened his mouth to shout to his dog but no sound came. When he reached the water, the frantic dog dived straight into the sea. Fracher held his breath, but the collie did not resurface. Stunned, Fracher now had to contend with the current. He put The Searcher into gear and literally went with the flow which was dragging the entire mass of seawater out of the bay and into the western approaches of the Pentland Firth. Fracher managed to turn The Searcher about so that he was making some controlled headway on this fantastic tide. His instinct was to go with it – he did not want to be aground when it came back in. When he was pushed north west of Dunnet Head he saw the wave.

He had no time to be terrified. The wave towered over South Ronaldsay and over the eastern districts of Hoy, then seemed to hang suspended for a moment before rolling over those islands and on, a huge curtain of water pulled by a giant hand across the Pentland Firth. Fracher tied his left hand to the wheel with a piece of softline, and opened up the throttle. He heard the Kelvin engine cough and roar as he turned The Searcher's bow to the wave and steamed right into it. Everything was water and noise, boat and man lifted up, then tipped down as if over the edge of a cliff. Fracher was thrown forward and banged his head off the wheelhouse window. Then he was thrown to the port side of the wheelhouse, and hung there, his left wrist fastened to the wheel. In his stunned state he could see the back of the great wave pour over the coastline between Duncansby Head and Dunnet Head. He had no clue where he was or even if he was still on the sea. He had no idea that he had literally surfed right over the giant wave-crest. As he pulled himself to his feet he felt blood run down his cheek from a cut on his head. From the window he recognised the west side of Stroma – well, at least he was still on the sea. He couldn't see the lighthouse. Could it really have been swept away by whatever it was that had happened? There was such a sea haze it was as if he were seeing everything through a distorting lens, even though the Sun was still shining brightly overhead.

The Storegga wave broke violently over Dunnet Head and along the north coast: an explosion of water and energy, swamping and ravaging the exposed townships along The Coast of Widows and the villages of Dunnet and Castletown at the southern base of the headland. The wave washed the dunes clean away from the top of the beach and flooded the farmland beyond for miles to the east. It powered over Thurso and crashed westwards into the nuclear plant at Dounreay. On the east coast of Caithness the wave was even stronger, destroying everything that could not withstand it, sweeping it away in its wake. So great was the force of Jörð and Storegga's passion that the pulse of it sent the wave as far west as Cape Wrath. From the flooding of Shetland and the swamping of Orkney in the north it swept across the Moray Firth, spending itself at last in a flurry of exhaustion, destruction, debris and froth on the shores of the Firth of Forth. Those who survived the apocalypse could not tell whether it had lasted a minute or an hour, a second or a day.

Fracher undid the softline, engaged the throttle and turned The Searcher back towards Dunnet Head. As he rounded the headland the wave-water started pouring back. He kept her nose firmly in the flow and prayed that he wouldn't be pushed back across the Firth onto the gigantic cliffs of St John's on Hoy.

When the shuddering stopped Nessan and Mags were on the floor of the cave where they had sunk in terror. Mags blessed the day she bought the strong torch, but as she shone it through the pitch black her heart sank. Solid stone.

"An Slanaighear."

"What the hell are you talking about?" Mags's cool finally snapped.

"An Slanaighear," repeated Nessan. "Mah Grannie used til tell may aboot ur."

"Nessan..." Mags felt as though she was losing her mind.

"Ay god aat lives in ay sea," said Nessan. Ignoring her, Mags shone her torch onto the wall again. *God or no god,* she thought, *if we don't get out of here we'll die.* She touched the stones. *Cold now. How could...* The coldness of the stone sent a small shock through Mags that pierced all reason and left her calm. They had passed beyond the futility of such a question, of any question. Her heart lightened in her breast, and she pushed one of the stones at the top of the wall which she knew she had already taken out. It fell back into the main body of the cave. Light poured in and caught Nessan's liquorice-black hair. The girl was staring at the sound box of the clarsach.

"Come on, Nessan, we have to get out of here." Mags pushed away another stone. Nessan lifted the sound box and stuffed it unceremoniously down the front of her waterproof jacket. She slipped the tarnished metal lock into her pocket and ran to help Mags with the wall. Within a few minutes they were free, and soon they were out in the daylight. From the bottom of the cliff they could not see what had happened, but the water in the bay was unrecognisably brown and agitated. Through the haze Nessan spotted The Searcher about a quarter of a mile off the coast. She waved and shouted as if she were warding off a tribe of devils. Mags was relieved to see Fracher and the boat, but respite was brief. The haze across the bay had cleared, and a colossal plume of smoke rose some two hundred feet into the windless air behind Atomic City – from the general direction of Dounreay. The

Searcher nudged into The Geo of The Dead and the two young women clambered aboard. Fracher opened the clutch and the luckiest creel boat in The Province of The Cat cut across the bay back to Scrabster.

No-one said a word. Mags and Nessan began to realise from their surroundings that their trauma inside the cave had been matched in the world outside. Mags stared speechless at Fracher, who just shook his head. Midway Fracher pointed: a huge white sailing ship was sitting off Dunnet Head. By the time The Searcher had reached the lee of Holborn Head the strange white ship had gone.

The countryside was sodden and destroyed, exploded by the huge wet bomb. Houses sat craggy and violated, windows and roofs gone. Animals by the score lay dead in the fields. A blue cargo ship with two huge cranes and the bridge up near the bow lay on its side like a toy between the old Bishop's Castle and the Eye Rock. It had sat off the Scrabster Roads for a week waiting to transport nuclear waste. Two steel hatch-covers lay like discarded open Bibles on the flagstone rock. The unnatural movement of the sea and the crashing insistence of the waves had easily overcome the toxic transporter, its open cargo-holds gaping cod-like towards the north, spewing dark silence and invisible industrial blood into the sea.

Scrabster harbour was washed clean. Not a boat left. Most modern buildings were matchwood, only a few stone-built ones remotely recognisable. A trawler lay embedded in the porch of the roofless hotel. The harbour fuel tanks had been obliterated and the air was thick with the smell of gas and diesel. There was not a person to be seen. There was no movement at all. The pier where the creel boats tied up beneath the Fisherman's Mission was empty. All the cars – including Mags's, and even the Mission itself were gone, spread like ripped coloured cloth beneath the Scrabster Brae. Fracher couldn't take The Searcher into the harbour – it didn't exist. The wave had washed up tons of silt and sand, blocking the entrance. A busy modern port was now nothing more than a polluted beach.

Fracher turned The Searcher about and headed for Thurso river-mouth. It was impossible to process thought. Everything he had known was either gone or damaged. As he looked from the wheelhouse to the shoreline his eye tried to adjust to what was not there, to what he expected to see but couldn't. He could not make out whether or not his house was still on Holborn Head. The bay was full of wreckage: the occasional roof, a shed, furniture. Several bodies floated past, lifeless. Fracher was relieved he didn't know any of them, or he'd have felt he needed to stop, pay his respects somehow rather than ignore them. They were beyond help.

By the time they got to the river mouth Fracher, Nessan and Mags were in a state of deep shock. Fracher's mind went back to that night on the Piper Alpha and the infernal horror that had burned into his memory. He had often reassured himself that he would never, in his lifetime, experience anything similar. Now his eyes scanned the townscape trying to interpret broken images fashioned by the wave from what was once Atomic City. Behind Holborn Avenue, up Castlegreen Road, throughout the Atomics the houses were flattened. After a while he stopped looking.

The Searcher sailed into the mouth of the River Thurso. Soon after the initial wave-surge the incessant force of the river-water had forced a channel through the sand pile deposited along Thurso East. Fracher edged his creel boat carefully through this channel, relieved to find space by a twisted ladder which led up to what was left of the old pier. He tied the boat up and the three of them climbed up onto what was once the riverside road, now a sandy shoreline. Ironically, only the ruin of Old St Peters remained, its twelfth century walls poking doggedly from the silt which covered the Fisherbiggins.

The fisherman, the archaeologist and the girl. Who would dare to tell, truly, the story of what they saw, had seen, and had experienced? Everything they had left so casually behind them to visit the Cave of Gold was transformed now, destroyed. The trio stood on a broken harbour wall in a limbo of powerlessness and non-comprehension. Amongst the wreckage that floated past them down the river was an NDA poster, drifting face-up on the surface of the water: "***Gone by 2025***". The Storegga wave had beat them to it; it had forwarded the clock, but in the same moment pushed back Time. Did they in their trauma recognise that the super-wave which had washed over Atomic City was no more destructive than the wave of power-nostalgia with which governments had already imprisoned and sterilised its future? A man-made toxic wave had obliterated the life of a community, controlling and crippling it with reactionary laws, then deleting its past in censorship? History would call this a tsunami, a natural phenomenon. Ironically, this wave brought fulfilment for those already dedicated to pessimism's power, and they were rewarded for their loyalty with destruction. The wave homogenised everything into a soup of democratic antagonism. Regardless of birth or status, creed or culture, when the wave struck everybody in this place enjoyed a joyless, pointless, floundering death by drowning, or by being struck by debris. In time, everything the wave brought would be quietly welcomed by another destructive confluence of economic powers, to which all submerging societies inevitably succumb. For these people, now, it was not so abstract. Their lives were destroyed.

If, however, like Bragi Boddason, you see history as splinters of Time shot through with incident, episodes which can, do, and will occur in any age or epoch, you might understand the wave as a portal, a passage both into and out of the dark cave of soothsayers, priests and politicians. For Atomic City it was too late. Pointless to warn of hubris when the tragic lessons of history have not been learned.

*So this is what I was trained to understand, but failed to see.* Mags staggered away alone, leaving her rucksack on the pier beside Fracher and Nessan. Dozens of expensive cars, upturned or crushed, littered the drenched banks of the River Thurso; dead bodies everywhere, many of whom she recognised. Silently she walked through what was left of the town. The wave had washed in and then washed out again. The Salvation Army building, which had lost its roof and its back wall, was identifiable, but along the rest of the promenade and the former beach were piled high the confused and random debris-heaps of destruction.

Fracher would not move from The Searcher. He sat down on the pier and stared at the river.

Nessan stuffed the clarsach sound box and the rusting lock into Mags's rucksack and ran. Clambering over who-knew-what, she followed the river channel until she could see Ormlie Hill. Parts of the school on the hill were still standing! Perhaps the higher ground had escaped the worst? Hopeful, Nessan ran on, desperate to find her family in the sink estate of High Ormlie. She found them safe, the housing scheme untouched by the wave. Forgotten and ignored alike by the wave, the state and social services, they were alive and dry. The people of High Ormlie had watched the wave plough up the river and flood the surrounding fields as far as they could see, leaving the town below them a mess of masonry, flowing water and shattered lives.

On-site at Dounreay the electricity had failed, and the back-up generators plus their supply tanks had been washed away. Water stopped flowing over the reactors, so the heat inside increased as the water boiled. As hydrogen mixed with the air there was an explosion. Another explosion damaged a suppression chamber below one of the reactors which helped condense steam, resulting in a massive discharge of radiation. Fires broke out. No one knew what to do. Everything had happened so quickly that all emergency procedures failed. Everything fails in the face of catastrophe: that is its emphatic quality. The north-west wind blew the grey-white plume of smoke and dust south and east, gently depositing a thin snowfall of radiation over the Province of The Cat.

The Storegga wave – however it was conceived – had washed over The Province of The Cat and had destroyed most of it. The damage to the five reactors at Dounreay and at HMS Vulcan was turning the far north of Scotland into a toxic zone where levels of radiation rendered life impossible. Those with cash-wealth in banks were systematically evacuated during the days immediately after the disaster, whether or not they were contaminated.

After decontamination, the poor with no financial resources lived blockaded in their housing estates in Atomic City, behind roadblocks manned by armed MoD personnel in radiation suits. Anyone who approached the roadblocks was to be shot. Some did.

Bragi Boddason says it is tiresome to talk continually of destruction. It does not lend itself to Bragarmál. In the days that followed, Nessan watched helicopters fly over Atomic City from her small house on High Ormlie. She read the pamphlets they dropped, telling people which areas to evacuate. Her family shut their door. They were not amongst the areas designated. Nessan played her clarsach. She played *Uamh an Oir* by Donald Mor MacCrimmon, and thought it a short sail, really, back to 1610. As the wind blew around the estate Nessan heard the same piobrochd she played on her clarsach; the same lamentation that blew through her dark hair; the same as the wind of Time, which blew through the branches of the tree of her family's lives, and the lives of those families immediately around them. Whatever happened, that music would survive. In their local authority houses high on the Hill of Ormlie Nessan and her clan hoarded the gold of history. Rain generated by the cynical cult of industrial war poured down onto them, sealing them forever in the repository of their innocence, as the waste was supposed to have been sealed up at Buldoo.

Mags was evacuated and ferried over The Ord with hundreds of other people in a convoy of buses, and treated along with everyone else from the toxic region in an un-named, secret and temporary decontamination centre somewhere outside Inverness. Eventually she went back to London with the sound box from Colm's clarsach and the lock from the cave-floor which Nessan had left in her rucksack. She did not show them to Professor Benison at the university. She didn't contact her university at all. She sat in her flat for weeks, shunning contact until her mother forcibly took her home. Mags wept for hours in her mother's arms.

Fracher came to his senses, still looking at the river. Atomic City was too dangerous. He climbed back onto The Searcher and headed across Thurso Bay. Under the lee of Holborn Head, between the lighthouse and the ferry pier, he tied up to an old cast-iron schooner mooring eye, leaving some slack on his line for the tide. Stiff and hungry, he scrambled up the rough path to the lighthouse road. Emergency lights flashed and flickered around the harbour below, sirens cutting through the air. Scores of people in white overalls and breathing apparatus ran here and there like energetic maggots. He turned his back on the harbour.

In fifteen minutes he reached the croft. *Still there!* It had been washed hard by the wave right enough but the bulk of Holborn Head had taken the destructive force of the onslaught. His hen house had gone, and there was no sign of animals in the surrounding fields, but the old Fergie still sat under the gable end. Inside the croft-house Fracher forced shut the damaged door. He took off his jacket and sea-boots, poured a large dram of rum into a broken cup, and dragged a chair to the fireplace. Astonishingly, there was still a glimmer in the grate. Fracher laughed aloud. *Weel, Kirstag, that bloody peat must be nuclear! Mackays are impossible til kill.* Carefully, he balanced three peats around the red ash and watched sparks fly up the chimney before orange flames took hold. Still on his knees, with a pang he remembered Cushie, whose favourite place was right here by the stove. He sipped his rum, and resigned himself to the fact that he would never see his old pal again. His fiddle was still hanging on the wall. *Och*, thought Fracher, gratefully, *ay morn Ah'll take ur doon an fund a tune in ur.* Then Kirstag came through the kitchen doorway. She was carrying a small basket of freshly-cut chives and thyme.

*Come til yer bed Fracher. Yer tired.*

*Aye*, he said, *Ah will.*

Two MoD operatives found him dead in his chair. Sometime later the bloated hairless corpse of a collie washed up on Dunnet Beach.

# 50

After the wave, after he had allowed his hungry crew to plunder the rich debris of disaster, Bragi Boddason turned Skidbladnir's bow North, away from The Province of the Cat. Back in Asgard he dispatched his crew, the thousand troll-sons of Ivaldi the dwarf, who went gladly back into the ground. The huge white ship with the three tall masts he folded up again carefully into the size of a handkerchief, and put it into his pocket. Taking a deep breath and pushing open its huge doors, Bragi stepped into the great hall of the Æsir and took his place. Then he began this story.

# ABOUT THE AUTHOR

George Gunn is a writer whose work is rooted in, though never limited by, his native Caithness in the Scottish Highlands. Born in 1956, he cannot remember a time when he did not write. Working offshore as a young man he lived in Edinburgh, serving his writing apprenticeship with encouragement from Scottish mentors like Hamish Henderson, Angus Calder, and David Morrison in Wick. Since then, he has produced nine published collections of poetry, and over 50 plays produced for stage or radio.

An active member of the Edinburgh Playwrights' Workshop throughout the 1980's, his vision of his art might be described as "by the people: for the people". This commitment was at the heart of The Grey Coast Theatre Company, which he founded in 1992. By its closure in 2010 the company had mounted 35 productions, produced in the spirit of Hamish Henderson's 'carrying stream' of folk culture, and including new plays by Highland writers as well as music commissions and education projects for big, site-specific community plays. A campaigner for a National Theatre of Scotland, he believes professional cultural activity must be grounded in the people and the places that generate its energy and ideas. Far from compromising quality or becoming parochial, this rootedness guarantees its integrity.

Mindful of his public responsibility as a writer in the bardic or skald traditions, he does not limit himself to 'creative' writing. He writes a regular topical column "From the Province of the Cat" for the online magazine Bella Caledonia. A prose book about Caithness, "The Province of the Cat" was published by The Islands Book Trust in 2015. Also in 2015 he collaborated with the Caithness fiddler/composer Gordon Gunn on the CD "A Musical Map of Caithness".

He has broadcast series on BBC Radio Scotland and Radio 4, and his work has been translated into Icelandic, French and Gaelic. He has been Writer in Residence for The Aberdeen Alternative Festival, Banff and Buchan District Council, Orkney Islands Council, The Strathnaver Museum, The Scottish Poetry Library, and The Ceilidh Place, Ullapool. Until recently writing tutor for North Highland College UHI, he currently runs the Ravenskald Writers' Workshop in Thurso, where he lives with his wife Christine.

In 2016 "The Great Edge" (then unpublished) was shortlisted for the Dundee International Book Prize.

*BY THE SAME AUTHOR*

*POETRY:*

**Sting, 1991**
**On the Rigs: Images of a Life Offshore, 1995**
**Whins, 1996**
**Winter Barley, 2005**
**The Atlantic Forest, 2008**
**Stroma, 2011**
**A Northerly Land, 2013**

*PLAYS:*

**Songs of the Grey Coast & The Gold of Kildonan, 1992**
**Atomic City: A Spoken Opera, 2010**
**Egil Son of the Night Wolf, 2010**

*PROSE:*

**The Province of the Cat: A Journey to the Radical Heart of the Far North, 2015**